Rachel Lee was hooke[...] and practised her craft [...] all over the United State[...] author now resides in [...] full-time.

Julie Miller is an award-winning *USA TODAY* bestselling author of breathtaking romantic suspense—with a National Readers' Choice Award and a Daphne du Maurier Award, among other prizes. She has also earned an *RT Book Reviews* Career Achievement Award. For a complete list of her books, monthly newsletter and more, go to juliemiller.org

Also by Rachel Lee

Conard County: The Next Generation
Cornered in Conard County
Missing in Conard County
Murdered in Conard County
Conard County Justice
Conard County: Hard Proof
Conard County: Traces of Murder
Conard County: Christmas Bodyguard
Conard County: Mistaken Identity
Conard County: Christmas Crime Spree

Also by Julie Miller

Kansas City Crime Lab
K-9 Patrol
Decoding the Truth

The Taylor Clan: Firehouse 13
Crime Scene Cover-Up
Dead Man District

The Precinct
Takedown
KCPD Protector
Crossfire Christmas
Military Grade Mistletoe
Kansas City Cop
Beauty and the Badge

Discover more at millsandboon.co.uk

CONARD COUNTY: CODE ADAM

RACHEL LEE

THE EVIDENCE NEXT DOOR

JULIE MILLER

MILLS & BOON

First Published in Great Britain 2023
by Mills & Boon, an imprint of HarperCollins*Publishers* Ltd
1 London Bridge Street, London, SE1 9GF

www.harpercollins.co.uk

HarperCollins*Publishers*
Macken House, 39/40 Mayor Street Upper,
Dublin 1, D01 C9W8, Ireland

Conard County: Code Adam © 2023 Susan Civil-Brown
The Evidence Next Door © 2023 Julie Miller

ISBN: 978-0-263-30729-0

0623

MIX
Paper | Supporting
responsible forestry
FSC™ C007454

This book is produced from independently certified FSC™ paper
to ensure responsible forest management.

For more information visit: www.harpercollins.co.uk/green

Printed and Bound in the UK using 100% Renewable Electricity at
CPI Group (UK) Ltd, Croydon, CR0 4YY

CONARD COUNTY: CODE ADAM

RACHEL LEE

Chapter One

"Lizzie's gone!"

From the moment Valerie Brighton had heard her sister May's sobbing voice on the telephone, Valerie had hit high gear. She'd quickly arranged for an indefinite leave from her job as a detective with the Gunnison, Colorado, police department, then hit the road for Wyoming with a couple of hastily packed suitcases.

Her two-year-old niece was missing. Vanished. May had said that search parties roamed Conard County looking for the child. There was no way Valerie could stay away. No way.

She passed through mountains with deep verdant valleys into the rolling range surrounding Conard City. Wide open, it was great ranch country, and it was vast. Except for those mountain ranges to the east and west, it seemed almost endless.

Keeping herself to just above the speed limit maddened her. She couldn't drive fast enough to suit herself. May needed her. Her niece needed her. Even though her badge would probably get her through any traffic stop, the stop would still cost her time—time she refused to spare.

What was that old problem she'd worked on in a long-ago

physics class? The one where they had calculated the time saved by traveling over a long distance at one speed and compared it to traveling at a much higher speed? The higher speed only saved a few minutes, much to her surprise.

Just a few minutes. She had to keep reminding herself of that as her foot tried to press more heavily on the accelerator.

God, May must be living through an indescribable hell.

Just about five miles before she reached Conard City, she caught sight of a small bundle on the shoulder of the road. Her heart nearly stopped as she jammed on the brakes and came to a skidding halt on gravel. Her niece?

"Oh, please, God," she whispered. "Please. Not my niece."

She jammed her black SUV into Park, then ran back along the road to the white heap.

Not her niece. No. She started breathing again. A dog. A medium-sized black-and-white dog, struck by a car and appearing dead. She would have turned to leave, but then the animal raised its head.

"Hell," she said to the empty spaces. "Hell." She couldn't leave that poor dog like this. A sliver of sorrow managed to pierce the huge sense of anguish that squeezed her heart.

Bending, heedless of her tailored black pantsuit, she carefully lifted the dog, hearing it whimper. Poor thing. Poor, poor doggie.

She placed the injured animal in the back of her SUV and hit the road again, this time driving faster. Now she needed those few minutes. Every one of them. As much as that dog needed a vet.

Just as she spied the town before her, she saw a sign.
Mike Windwalker, DVM.

Valerie swore again at the inescapable delay and turned

onto the rough gravel road leading to a large building labeled *Veterinary Hospital and Boarding.*

She braked on an unpaved parking lot and hurried inside. At the reception desk she said, "I found an injured dog on the roadside. He's in the back of my car."

There was no hesitation at the desk. A technician appeared immediately from the back and he hurried out to the car with her. With gentle hands, he checked the dog all over. Valerie waited impatiently.

"We'll get him inside," he told her. "You want to sign him over to us?"

"Sign?"

"Then we can take care of him, depending on what we can do. Or put him to sleep."

Valerie stomped down on her own impatience, allowing concern for the animal to creep in again. "No, I don't want to sign him over. I'll pay for his care, whatever it is."

Inside, the vet was waiting, and he regarded her with gentle dark eyes.

She signed several papers with an angry slash and left her cell phone number. "Any deposit?" she demanded. "Look, I've got to get to my sister. Her baby has disappeared."

The clinic grew suddenly silent, except for some dogs barking in the background.

"May Chamberlain," the vet said with a short nod of understanding. "Get on your way. We can worry about money later."

The dog disappeared into the back as fast as Valerie disappeared out the door.

May. She had to get to May. She had to help find her niece.

Chapter Two

May's house sat at the very edge of town, a large two-story brick structure with a front porch that was decorated with white pillars and white gingerbread. A few cars of various ages lined the street. Valerie pulled into the driveway behind her sister's blue Explorer.

Then she headed in the front door, unsurprised to see several women her sister's age surrounding May like broody hens. Probably keeping her company. Probably trying to steady her through this awful time.

The instant May saw Valerie, she rose from the black leather couch where she'd been seated and ran into her arms. May began sobbing, wrenching sobs that shook her entire body.

"Lizzie is gone," May wept, her voice almost smothered by worry and grief. "She's *gone!*"

Valerie held her tightly, wishing to God she could offer some comfort other than her presence. "You need to sit," she said quietly, feeling her sister's weakness, the way May clung to her as if for physical support.

"Come on," she prodded gently. "Please sit. It won't make the waiting and worrying any easier, but it'll keep you from collapsing."

Still shaking, May allowed herself to be guided back to the couch. "Val, I'm going out of my mind!"

Sitting beside her, Valerie took her sister's cold, trembling hands in hers. "I know you are, sweetie. I know you are."

May lifted her tear-stained face to look at her sister from reddened, swollen eyes. "She was gone when I woke this morning. Gone from her crib. They think she might have let herself out during the night. Oh my God, my poor Lizzie!"

The sobs renewed and Valerie wrapped her arms around her sister, holding her tight. Her own heart squeezed so hard that it hurt. "Where's Chet?" she asked eventually, referring to May's ex-husband.

"He's out with the search parties," one of the young women answered. "I'm Gina, by the way."

Valerie gave her a brief nod. "We went to school together, right?"

Gina nodded, her own eyes red-rimmed.

May demanded brokenly, "How could Lizzie have gotten out? How?"

"It happens," Valerie answered. "It happens." She knew it did. During her law enforcement career, she'd seen it happen a couple of times. Inquisitive or bored kids, knowing more about opening doors than their parents imagined. Always a terrifying situation.

"I can't bear to think of her out there all alone. It gets chilly at night and all she had on were her fuzzy pajamas."

May's sobs renewed but slowly they lessened. She'd spent all her energy crying. Eventually, she eased away from Valerie and grabbed a handful of tissues from a box on the glass-topped coffee table. The interior of the house, in contrast to the outside, was decorated in a modern style.

Wedgwood blue paint covered the walls, giving color to an otherwise colorless room of black, white and chrome.

Valerie glanced down at herself and saw her suit jacket was pretty much decorated with black and white dog fur. A match for this room, she thought humorlessly. She clenched her hands, struggling to remain calm even as fear rattled her heart.

One of the women, also vaguely remembered from school days, brought a plate of store-bought cookies from the kitchen and set it on the table. Her name was Jenna Blair, Valerie seemed to remember. "Eat something, May. You need the energy to get through this."

Her sister could probably also use a pill or a shot to help her calm down. Valerie shook her head slightly. May wouldn't accept it. The sisters were both stubborn, sometimes to a fault.

She glanced at her watch and saw that night was approaching. So many hours since she'd left Gunnison. So many hours since May had called her after making the terrifying discovery. No one could even be sure how long Lizzie had been gone.

Night. A small child toddling out there without protection, without much-needed warmth as the night's inevitable chill deepened. Her mouth went dry with all the possibilities she'd been refusing to consider: the cold, coyotes. Other dangers, places she could fall into and hurt herself. Drowning in some creek, unable to get out of it.

She yanked her thoughts away from those paths. She couldn't afford to think this way or she'd be useless to May.

But she couldn't forget the last time she'd held Lizzie, a sweet-smelling little bundle of giggles and grins. A bit devilish, too. Pulling the upholstery buttons off an overstuffed chair. Leaning through the stair railing, calling out with glee. The kid in the bucket swing who couldn't seem to fly high enough. A little daredevil. Lizzie loved her thrills.

"You know," she said to May, "Lizzie is probably out there having a great time. You know how she loves an adventure."

May nodded but her face didn't brighten at all.

Maybe that hadn't been the smartest thing to say, Valerie thought. Reminding May of her daughter's mischievous nature wouldn't help. Nothing could help, least of all when she felt like shattering herself.

But she couldn't do that. May needed her to be strong right now.

"Isn't any cop keeping in touch?" she asked the room at large. "A family liaison or something?"

May spoke almost angrily. "What good will that do? I don't need another person trying to tell me not to worry."

"I was thinking more along the lines of keeping you posted about what's going on." Right then she knew she was going to have a problem with this two-bit sheriff's department. At least if Lizzie wasn't found soon.

THE LIAISON SHOWED up less than an hour later. Her name was Kerri Canady and she was accompanied by a fluffy white service dog.

Valerie eyed her with curiosity, thinking that dog indicated what might be an interesting story. Apart from that, she was annoyed that the woman arrived wearing a dark green uniform windbreaker, an obvious reminder of what was happening to the temperature outside. God, didn't anyone think?

Kerri squatted in front of May, her voice gentle.

"Mrs. Chamberlain, we haven't found Lizzie yet. But we're going to keep on looking through the night and we'll expand the search area."

May regarded her from dry eyes, her face ashen. "I can't believe you haven't found her yet."

"Kids, even little ones like Lizzie, can sometimes walk a surprising distance. We're also going to recheck the search area we've already covered. If she's out there, we'll find her."

May's voice rose. "*If?* Where else would she be? Where? She'll die of the cold tonight! You know that, don't you? You know that!"

"Kids," Valerie interjected, needing to offer a thread of hope, "are surprisingly resourceful. She probably got tired and crawled into some safe place to sleep. A place that's warm. A place that's harder to find." But the deepening night outside seemed to be creeping into her own heart, and her own expression of hope sounded hollow in her ears.

May's desperate eyes pinned her. "Do you really believe that?"

"I do," Valerie answered firmly even though she didn't. "I've known of it happening. There was a four-year-old. Nights were cold. After three days everyone was about to give up when one of the searchers found the boy ten miles from the campsite he'd left. Other than scratches, he was fine. Hungry and cold but fine. Still, he'd traveled *ten* miles."

May nodded jerkily. "Okay. Okay." Then she sank back into the depths. "She's gone," she whispered. "Gone."

Valerie looked at Kerri. "How many searchers do you have?"

One corner of Kerri's mouth lifted. "Half the damn county, seems like. People have been coming from everywhere."

"And the search radius?"

"We're expanding to ten miles right now. With all these helping hands pouring in throughout the day, we've got plenty of people out there."

Valerie nodded. She no longer felt quite as annoyed with the sheriff's department, but the feeling hadn't fully subsided. "How come it took you so long to get here?"

Kerri frowned slightly. "You know, I was dealing with the victim of a different kind of problem. As for everyone else, they're either searching or maintaining necessary patrols. If you have questions about how we're handling this, I suggest you talk to Detective Redwing. He's got oversight."

"Not the sheriff?" Valerie knew she was being difficult but didn't care. She knew how a police department operated. They couldn't just drop all their work to focus on a single task, no matter how urgent. But sitting here like this, unable to do anything, was edging her concern for May and Lizzie with a trickle of anger.

"The sheriff," Kerri said, "has oversight of *everything*. As you know." Then she rose from her squat and sat in a nearby chair. The service dog stayed right beside her.

Valerie turned to May. "It'll be okay." She wished she believed it.

Chapter Three

The next morning brought a bright blue sky that struck Valerie as a betrayal. As if the weather cared.

But last night had been chilly enough to be of major concern to those who believed a small child was lost out there. Despite the story she had told May, she knew all too well that such stories rarely had a happy ending. Such endings were exceptions to a nearly hard and fast rule.

Just after midnight, May had fallen asleep from sheer exhaustion. Her sleep was restless, though, filled with terrors that sometimes made her cry out. Small escape. Or maybe no escape at all. While she had slept, Valerie had grabbed naps as she could.

Valerie stood at the front window, watching the day brighten to an almost hard brilliance. Full of promises that ought to be painted in black, not blue.

She heard stirring behind her and saw that Kerri Canady was waking in the chair she'd used most of the night. Beside her, her service dog also stirred, sitting upright. On duty.

"Coffee?" Valerie asked.

"Love some, if you don't mind."

"I don't. I need it. Fuel."

Kerri smiled faintly. "The best kind."

"No news?"

"You've been there all night. You'd have heard my radio."

Valerie knew it to be true, but sometimes fear could make a person ridiculous. She was being ridiculous. She was also feeling resentful, angry and impatient. What the hell were all those people doing out there? Looking? Or getting too weary to see? Her stomach churned.

When the coffee finished brewing, she carried two cups to the living room and handed one to Kerri. "I should have asked if black is okay."

"It's great. Thank you."

Valerie resumed her watch of the street outside, waiting for some sheriff's vehicle that wasn't going to show.

She spoke again. "When does Gage Dalton get to the office?"

"Usually around eight."

Valerie nodded and glanced at her watch. Fifteen minutes. Her decision made, she dumped her coffee in the kitchen sink.

"I'm going out," Valerie said to Kerri. "If she wakes, tell May I'm checking on things."

Kerri simply nodded.

Dressed in a fresh black slack suit, one free of dog fur, she set out for the sheriff.

Gage Dalton's story was known all over town and Conard County, even to people who had been too young to have remembered it when it had happened. A former undercover agent for the DEA, he'd seen his wife and kids blown up by a car bomb that had been intended for him. That had also burned him badly.

When he'd arrived in Conard County, apparently a friend of the old sheriff, he'd been a man lost in a bleak abyss.

Living in a room above Mahoney's bar, he'd established a nightly routine: one drink followed by an endless walk along empty night streets. Hate and despair had burned in his dark eyes, frightening away anyone who might have spoken to him.

Back then the locals had called him *hell's own archangel.*

Then Emmaline Conard, the local librarian, had drawn him steadily back into the light. Into the world of the living. Had brought smiles to his face.

Valerie was certain the grief had never left him, the guilt must have remained, but he'd reconstructed his life.

Now he was known as the new sheriff, despite all the years he'd held the position, but this county had loved the old sheriff too much to let go of him entirely. Now they loved their new sheriff, too. They certainly admired him.

But this would be the first time they met on equal footing, her being a cop, too. A detective.

One who wasn't going to sit on her hands, able to do nothing but try to comfort her sister.

One who was determined to get involved or there'd be hell to pay.

GUY REDWING SAT in the mobile command post, radios crackling around him, questions coming at him like annoying mosquitoes. No news yet.

He sipped the coffee someone had brought him. It was cold now, as cold as his heart. The little girl still hadn't been found. No trace of her anywhere.

A local Amber Alert had gone out yesterday, but no one held any hope that it would bring news. The child couldn't have wandered *that* far, far enough that someone who didn't know her might see her. The worst fear was that she was alone in the range that surrounded Conard City.

The sun was rising and hope was dying as a new day dawned. They'd keep looking but he was beginning to believe that they'd find Lizzie Chamberlain's body out there. When they found her.

But the longer the little girl remained missing, the more he began to have a darker thought: kidnapping. Like it or not, they were going to have to start looking at that possibility, even without a ransom note or phone call. And there could be other reasons besides a ransom for stealing a child, all horrifying to contemplate. As soon as he got to the office, he was extending the Amber Alert if Gage hadn't already.

He rose after the day became fully bright. He shook off fatigue and turned to his second-in-command, an experienced deputy named Connie Parish. "I need to get home and change. I probably smell like a wet dog that's been rolling in poop."

Connie smiled faintly. "Not quite that bad, Guy. But go. You'll be back just in time for the food train."

And train it would be, Guy thought as he stepped outside into the chilly air. People from all over would be showing up with food to lay out on long folding tables. As searchers switched out, coming in for a break, they'd be starving and cold. Exhausted, too.

And Maude, the owner of the City Café, would be arriving with yet another truckload of insulated carafes of coffee. Bless her.

At home in his small apartment, he showered and changed into a fresh uniform. He tied his long black hair back with a leather thong. One thing he refused to get rid of.

Despite his promotion to detective, he still wore the uniform of a deputy. He was Native American and had met prejudice all his life, but that uniform helped a bit to grease the wheels in his professional dealings with the people he was sworn to protect. People he was sworn to serve who hated him merely because he wasn't White. The irony didn't escape him.

Nor did a bitter anger, which he tamped down as far as he could. It rose again when he faced overt prejudice, but he'd learned to keep a smooth face even when he wanted to punch someone. Life's lessons well and painfully learned.

Some among his own family didn't approve of him either. They saw him as a sellout.

Straddling the fence could be painful sometimes.

Then he shook his head, grabbed his windbreaker and headed for his official Suburban, a tan monster covered with road dust, in need of a good washing. The words *To Serve and Protect* seemed to mock him from where they were painted on the vehicle's side. Yeah. Okay then.

He rubbed grit from his tired eyes and told himself to quit the pity party. He'd made his choices and he lived with them. This BS was emerging only because he was so weary and worried.

Before he'd even backed out of his driveway, his radio crackled to life with his call sign. He was too tired to feel even a small lift of hope as he heard the dispatcher, Velma.

"You better get to the office," Velma said in her smoke-roughened voice. "Seems like there might be a little problem. I just know Gage wants to see you yesterday."

"Hell," he said, not caring if Velma heard it, not caring if every police radio for miles around heard it.

What now?

VALERIE WAS CERTAIN that she was adding to the unpleasantness of Gage Dalton's morning, but she didn't care. She was past caring about anything except getting her niece back from the clutches of wild nature, or the clutches of some kidnapper.

Because she couldn't ignore the possibility of kidnapping, not when so many people were out there looking at the area around the town and into the scrub that surrounded it.

Her niece wasn't out there. Lizzie was lost, all right, but after the cold night just past, the idea of a kidnapping offered some hope, meager as it was. If anyone found Lizzie out there now amongst the grasses, in the uneven and treacherous terrain, they weren't apt to find her alive.

"It's got to be a kidnapping," she said, aware of Detective Redwing sitting beside her as they both looked at Sheriff Dalton across his desk. "No one's seen any sight of her. No clue as to her whereabouts."

Dalton's face had been burned on one side, shiny with old scar tissue that kept him from moving one side of his mouth and the eyebrow above one eye. It was a constant, scalding reminder to those who saw him. It was the face that must remind him every morning, as he stood before the bathroom mirror, of the wife and children he had lost through betrayal of his true identity.

But Gage had clearly learned to live with it. Learned to live with the pain that made him wince sometimes when he moved.

"You know we're doing everything we can, Detective." Acknowledging her experience.

It wasn't what she wanted to hear. "I know about the search parties. They've come up with nothing. What about kidnapping?"

He leaned forward, wincing, and picked up a pencil, tapping the eraser end on his desk. "There are a few problems with that."

"There's one hell of a big problem with all of this." Her hands tightened. She was not about to be sidelined or dismissed.

"I don't disagree. But there's no evidence of an intruder in your sister's house. None. So we're left with a problem, as in how did anyone remove that child from her crib?"

Good question, much as Valerie hated to admit it. "We need to investigate the possibility anyway. And I want to be part of that investigation."

"You're talking about some truly ugly things here. You're a detective. You don't need me to tell you that."

She closed her eyes briefly, hating what he hadn't said. That mothers *do* sometimes kill their own children. That fathers too often kidnapped them after a divorce. To get even. To assuage the bitterness and anger that could come from both rejection and from losing full custody. There would have to be an investigation of both May and her ex-husband.

His voice gentled. "You also don't need me to tell you that you're much too involved in this. That you could wear blinders and not know it. Like right now, you're sitting there convinced that neither May nor Chet could be involved."

He was right and she prickled a bit, but she knew something else. "I'll look under every rock. Right now *everyone* is a suspect."

Gage nodded slowly and turned his attention to Guy Redwing. "How do you feel about Valerie becoming involved?"

Valerie looked at the face of the man beside her. A strong face with high cheekbones that broadcast his ancestry. She didn't think about what that might mean for him. Didn't give a thought to the fact that he might feel she was in some way denigrating him by insisting she become involved in his investigation. Never thought he might attribute her determination to a prejudice against the Indigenous people. Never thought that he might believe she was questioning his abilities *because* he was Native American.

Since yesterday, she had gone far past any kind of political correctness.

Guy Redwing paused a few moments. His expression remained stoic. "All help is welcome, Gage. We need to find that little girl."

"Well then," Gage said, dropping his pencil. His dark gaze bored into Valerie. "You need to understand one thing, Detective Brighton. *Guy* is the detective in charge of this case."

Outside on the street, a cold breeze freshened the air with threat. The unfeeling blue sky remained.

Guy Redwing put his uniform Stetson on his head. Tan like the rest of his uniform except for the dark green official jacket. Tall. Standing straight.

"You're a detective," she said to Guy Redwing. "Why do you still wear a uniform?"

"Look at my face," he said flatly.

It was then she began to understand. But she still didn't care. "No other detective to help with this case?"

"Not right now. Our other detective, Callum McCloud, is away in Boston. You're stuck with *me*."

She gave a short nod. "How much experience do you have?"

"In law enforcement? Quite a few years. As a detective? I'm sure it's not as much as *you* have."

THE ANGER BURNED in Guy once again. Questioning his ability to manage this case by himself? There could be only one reason.

She was a tall, slender woman in crisply tailored clothes that were very much out of place here. Blond-haired, blue-eyed and pretty, the epitome of White.

Now he'd have to deal with her sense of superiority, especially given her longer experience with being a detective. He'd have to deal with her emotional involvement in this case. As if the case weren't difficult enough. He squared his broad shoulders, reminding himself that this was all about one small child. That child mattered more than anything.

"As for kidnapping," he said, "I've been considering it. But the search is going to continue whether you think it's a waste of time or not. No stone unturned. You said it yourself."

She answered with a brisk nod. "I wouldn't want the search stopped. There's always a chance…"

He drew a deep breath and blew it out between his lips. "We've got to question the people most directly involved. Are you up to it?"

"I'm not sure May is up to questioning, honestly. As for Chet, I have no idea. He's been out searching, I was told."

"He is. But what about *you*?"

She didn't answer him.

Now came the part Guy had spent the better part of yesterday and last night hoping to avoid. Questioning the parents. *God!*

He spoke again. "I'll take the lead. It'll be easier on you." It would make it easier for him, too, not having her intervene, perhaps encouraging certain answers.

Again she didn't reply to him. He hadn't expected her to.

CHET CHAMBERLAIN WAS a man of moderate height with a thick head of brown hair and eyes that were often gentle. As an OB-GYN, he had a great many opportunities to be gentle. Usually he was impeccably dressed for this area, in neatly pressed clothes that were Western enough to fit in.

Right then he was grungy, his jeans covered with blades of dry grass and small twigs, his chiseled face smeared with some dirt he must have gotten on his hands. As he sat on the black leather couch, one arm wrapped around an ashen May, he looked like a man reaching the end of his tether. And May looked like the spitting image of her sister.

"Anything change?" he asked Guy Redwing as soon as Guy crossed the threshold. Then he spied Valerie. "Hi, Val. May was hoping you'd come."

"Nothing's changed," Guy answered. He didn't sit until Chet waved him to a nearby chair, also black leather but with chrome legs. "Except that we're considering a new line of inquiry."

Valerie had already taken another chair. Her hands were twisted together, Guy noted. Why had she wanted to be part of this interview? It was going to tear her apart.

"I need to ask you both some questions," Guy said, returning his attention to Chet and May. "I know this will be difficult, but I've still got to ask them."

Chet nodded, his jaw tightening. "Ask. Val?"

"She's part of the investigation now," Guy answered. "Working with me. Any objection?"

May spoke, her voice tremulous. "I want her to be part of it if she's willing."

Guy managed a faint smile. "She demanded it. Her willingness isn't in question."

"What are *your* questions?" Chet demanded. "Do you want to know if one of us did something awful to Lizzie?"

May drew a sharp breath. "Are you kidding me?"

"We're looking into the possibility of kidnapping," Guy answered, evading the ugliest question now that May had brought it up herself. He had his answer to that one, for now. "The questions aren't going to be pleasant for you, but we need every possible bit of information to help find Lizzie."

May sagged again into the crook of Chet's arms. "I'd never hurt my baby. Neither would Chet."

Guy looked at Valerie Brighton. Her face had grown paler, but he saw no anger there. Okay. At this point she wasn't going to interfere with necessary questions. He turned back toward the couple on the couch. *He* needed to ignore the ache in his heart for these parents—to focus instead on his ache for the child caught in all of this.

Chet spoke. "Saying it isn't going to be enough, May. They have to ask questions, if there's any possibility that Lizzie was kidnapped. Or…"

He left the thought unfinished, but Guy realized the doctor was getting the full picture of the possible suspicions that might be directed their way. Chet's face had hardened, and his posture had grown more protective of May.

Guy changed tack. "Has anyone gotten seriously angry with either one of you recently?"

They both shook their heads.

Guy continued. "Anyone at all who might hold a grudge?"

Chet answered. "Not that I know of. May?"

"I can't imagine. Anything's possible, I guess." Tears began to roll down her face again. "Why would anyone steal our little girl?"

"That's what we need to find out," Valerie said, speaking for the first time. "Anything at all you can think of."

Apparently neither of them could.

Guy changed tack again. "When did you last see Lizzie, Mrs. Chamberlain?"

"I already told you that!"

"We need to go over it again. We're looking at everything from a different angle this time. So please, just tell me when last you saw her."

"When I put her to bed at eight. When I sat reading her a story and singing a lullaby. She was asleep when I left the room. I checked in on her maybe an hour later before I went to bed."

She shook her head and another tear trickled down her cheek.

"And you, Dr. Chamberlain?"

Chet's face had grown even harder. "Three days ago, when I stopped by to see her."

Guy nodded. "Is that your usual visitation schedule?"

This time Chet's voice cracked a little. "No. I took a chance. May and I disagreed about me just dropping in, but it was nothing major. She understands that I love Lizzie. May?"

"It's true. I felt like he was disrupting Lizzie's schedule. I can't have this pop-in-and-pop-out happening any old time. I told Chet he should at least call first."

Guy nodded. "Raising a child, especially one who's still not yet three, can be challenging and tiring."

May went from teary-eyed to angry. "Who cares?"

"It's a full-time job, and I hear the Terrible Twos can be fatiguing."

"She wasn't terrible. Ever."

"But when do you have time for *yourself*?"

LISTENING TO THESE questions filled Valerie with both anger and sorrow. She knew why they needed to be asked, but she hated that they were being directed at her sister as if May were capable of mistreating Lizzie.

"You know when it was hard?" May demanded. "Her infancy when she had colic. When I felt like a failure because there was nothing I could do to help her. When I walked the floor for hours in the middle of the night listening to her cry."

"Difficult," Guy agreed. "But time for you?"

"Day care for four hours three times a week. It gives me time to do the things I need to do, it gives me time to exercise my mind, to just relax or whatever. Oh, I had my own time, Detective."

Guy pulled a notebook from his pocket and flipped through a few pages. There was more, Valerie knew. Much more. Her hands ached from clenching them. From fighting the urge to go to May.

"You say you discovered she was missing at around seven a.m. Is that right?"

"God, yes. The instant I opened my eyes I knew something was wrong. She always woke me around six. She never lets me sleep late."

"So you heard nothing at all? No one moving in the house, no unusual sounds from Lizzie?"

"Nothing," May said, her voice stretched tight. "Not one peep." She shook her head. "Not a thing. I don't understand why! I should have heard her making some kind of noise. If someone took her, she should have made *some* sound at being disturbed. She's at the point where she's afraid to be away from me, even when I take her to day care. She always cries."

"That's a normal stage," Chet said. "Normal. Right now she cries when I take her home with me. It doesn't last long, but she *cries*."

Oh, God, Valerie thought. This was getting worse and worse. It sounded as if May might be concealing something. Then came the most fearful question of all.

Guy asked it. "But you said yesterday that you have a baby monitor, right? Could it have been turned off?"

"It's on all the time!"

And there it was, a hole in her claim to have heard nothing at all, not Lizzie crying or any other sounds. God in heaven. Guy would be suspicious now, and justifiably so. Now Valerie was clinging to the hope that her sister couldn't be a monster.

"How often do you change the batteries?"

"The units are rechargeable. They beep to tell me the charge is getting low."

"So none of that?"

May shook her head. Now Chet was staring at her as if doubt were creeping into him as well.

Guy rose. "Mind if Detective Brighton and I take a look at them?"

May shrugged. "Go ahead."

Valerie rose with Guy and walked with him to Lizzie's room. The bedding in the crib was rumpled, the blanket thrown back as if the girl had been *taken*, not as if she had climbed out on her own. She pointed to it with a finger and Guy nodded.

God, she hoped she wasn't helping to deal a blow to May.

He found the monitor near the crib and lifted it, studying it. Then he summoned Valerie over with a crook of his finger. He'd slid the back off the monitor and Valerie stared into an empty space.

"Someone took out the battery," she murmured. "Oh, sweet Mother Mary."

She looked into Guy's strong face and for the first time saw past his impassivity. Pain filled his dark gaze.

"Kidnapping."

VALERIE GAVE HER sister a hug before she and Guy departed. He spoke.

"I'm going to send my team to knock on doors. They got nothing from the neighbors yesterday, at least the ones who were still home. A lot of folks were out in the search parties. But maybe someone will have remembered something if we jog them again."

"Maybe. Listen, I need just a minute to make a phone call."

"Go ahead." A phone call? At a time like this when he could almost feel the pain and anger that enveloped her?

Then she surprised him when she lifted her cell phone to her ear.

"Hi, this is Valerie Brighton. I brought in a small black-and-white dog yesterday. The stray hit by a car? How's he doing?" She listened, then said, "Do it. I'll cover it." As she disconnected, she saw him staring at her. "A dog I found by the roadside. Broken hip. He's going to need surgery."

Well, that gave him a whole new spin on this woman who seemed both demanding and dubious of him. In the midst of all that must be tearing her apart, she had rescued a dog, had brought her to the vet and was now ensuring he received proper treatment.

Maybe there was a generous soul beneath all those roiling emotions, a soul that could save a dog despite everything. That, however briefly, could spare a little attention for an injured animal.

His opinion of her climbed a notch or two. "I'm going to check in with the command post. Then let's get some coffee while we discuss next steps."

She gave him a brief nod.

MAUDE'S DINER, AS the City Café had been known for years, wasn't very busy. Just a few retirees too old to join the search. Coffee was easy to come by, delivered in thermal carafes that recently had replaced the individual cup-by-cup service. Maude's daughter Mavis, a clone of her stout and usually angry mother, had insisted on it. No time to waste pouring bottomless cups of coffee at all the tables.

Guy shoved a menu toward Valerie. "Get some breakfast. You'll need the energy. When was the last time you ate?"

"None of your business." But she hadn't eaten a thing since her departure from Gunnison. Fear and worry were good appetite suppressants. She took the menu, seeking something that wouldn't roil her stomach more.

Guy chose a double serving of biscuits and gravy. Valerie selected pancakes, the only thing that looked bland enough to swallow. She couldn't even face eggs. It was all about energy anyway.

She was surprised when she received a double order of the pancakes. She looked up into the face of Mavis. "I didn't order a double."

Mavis frowned. "I heard you. Eat as much as you can. Long day ahead." Then she stomped off.

Valerie stared at the heap of pancakes then looked at Guy. He shrugged. "She's right."

Then she studied her overly full plate, evading his gaze, which reflected concern, and she was sure some of it was about her. Of course. He didn't want her on this case and he had no idea what kind of problem she might become. Too bad.

For her own part, she honestly wasn't certain how objective she might manage to be. It was a good thing, though she hated to admit it, that she wasn't the lead on this one. Even though she wanted to batter her way through every obstacle at any cost.

Which made her a loose cannon.

She forced herself to eat despite all the worries and emotions careening around inside her. With each mouthful her stomach began to fill and the sugary syrup hit her bloodstream, energizing her.

"Okay," he said when he'd cleaned his whole plate and Valerie had eaten three quarters of hers. He poured them both fresh cups of coffee. "How many kidnapping cases have you worked?"

"None." But she *had* worked on a case where the mother had killed her child. She suppressed a shudder. *Not May.*

"Tell me more about Chet," he suggested. "He's a doctor, right?"

"Obstetrician. He shepherds mothers through their pregnancies and delivers their babies. He's fond of saying that his are the first hands that hold a newborn."

"He's proud of that?"

Valerie bridled. "He should be. Delivering a baby is an important role."

Guy shrugged one shoulder. "I didn't say anything was wrong with it."

Valerie sat sipping the hot coffee. Mavis stomped by to remove their plates.

Guy's gaze remained steady. This man, Valerie realized, wasn't going to give an inch.

"So," he said presently, "what brought about the divorce?"

It was Valerie's turn to shrug. "They'd been married five years. They seemed happy. Then May got pregnant."

"Joyous?"

"At first." Val took a napkin from the dispenser and began folding it aimlessly. God, she hated to talk about this. To become a witness, rather than a detective. But there was no escaping it. She shredded the napkin, trying to suppress her inner turmoil.

Guy spoke quietly. Almost gently. "I know this is hard."

"I was on the outside looking in," she told him defiantly. "Anything I say isn't gospel."

A brief nod. "Got it."

Valerie sighed, then stuck her toes in the water. "Chet's job has irregular hours. Babies don't get born on a schedule. He's not, as he's said, one of those doctors who will set up Caesarians to make a convenient schedule either for himself or the mother. He wants those babies to come to a natural full term. Unless there are complications, of course. So he can be called out at any hour of the evening or night for a delivery or a problem with a pregnancy."

Guy nodded again. "I can understand that."

"Well, May didn't seem to have a problem with that. At least not until she became pregnant. Then she started complaining to me about how little he was home."

"Okay."

Valerie's jaw had clenched. She forced herself to relax it before she gave herself a major headache. "It got worse after Lizzie was born. Chet had his regular office hours, of course, but he also had all those urgent calls to deal with. May felt she was the *only* one taking care of Lizzie. The *only* one who paced the floors at night with a colicky baby."

Valerie grabbed another napkin and began to treat it like the first. God, this was killing her. Her niece was out there somewhere but here she sat playing witness. With every word she felt as if she were betraying her sister.

"It wasn't true, of course," Valerie said, her hands tightening until her knuckles turned white. "Chet was there as much as he could be. But I guess that was the problem. Anyway, she felt abandoned and divorced him."

"There was a custody fight? I heard something about it through the grapevine."

"Double damn," Valerie said vehemently, hating this man and his questions. "When do I get to stop being a witness?"

Guy leaned back in his chair, his gaze unwavering. "Would you ask these questions in a similar case that didn't involve your sister?"

The words felt like a slap in the face, all the worse because she knew he was right. It mattered now, all of it mattered. He was just being a good detective, despite her initial doubts, and she should give him credit for that.

"All right. There *was* a brief custody fight. Chet wanted joint custody. May argued against it, talking about Chet's hours and how he'd have to hire a nanny to take care of Lizzie. She didn't want her daughter being raised by a stranger. She didn't want Lizzie's life to be upended every six months."

"And she won."

"Obviously."

Valerie closed her eyes, feeling her chest squeeze until

she thought she might not be able to breathe. She'd done it. She'd given both of them a motive, especially Chet. She hated herself.

Then her eyes popped open and she looked straight at Guy. "So tell me, Detective Redwing, just what good would it serve either of them to kidnap Lizzie? How hard would it be to conceal my niece in this town? Impossible. And if either of them put Lizzie in another's care, how often could they see that child? What's more, May's statement in court mitigates against that. She doesn't want Lizzie being raised by a stranger."

NONE OF IT mitigated against murder, however, Guy thought as they left the restaurant. Revenge? A deep grudge? Especially on the part of Chet. Gentle obstetrician he might be, but he'd been denied joint custody. Then to be told he didn't have the right to just drop in to see Lizzie? That had to have angered him. But enough to kill a child just to deprive May of it? *If I can't have it, neither can you.*

It wouldn't be the first time.

Anger churned in him. But he had to give props to Valerie Brighton. She'd given him as much as she knew because, as a detective, she understood its importance. Even though she had known where it might lead.

"Thank you," he said as they crossed the street toward the sheriff's office. "I know that wasn't easy." It hadn't been. She probably displayed a totally impassive face when she was working, a detective needed one, but she hadn't been impassive as a witness. He'd seen the play of terrible emotions run across her face. The awareness of what she might be doing. She was a strong woman.

"I need to go out to the command post," he said. "Check up on things."

"I'll come along. I'd like to see."

Of course she would want to make sure they weren't handling the matter like a bunch of rubes. That must be her opinion or she wouldn't have forced her way into this investigation. As a detective, she'd known better than to do so because she was personally involved.

Then he caught himself. More eyes, more ideas, might be useful.

THE MOBILE COMMAND CENTER, such as it was, had been positioned not far from the Chamberlain house in a grassy area, still browned from winter. He led Valerie inside and introduced her to Connie's replacement, a deputy named Sarah Ironheart. Sarah had a bit of a storied background, too, having years ago broken up a bar fight started because some locals objected to the presence of a Native American man. Sarah, herself partly Indigenous, had broken up the fight with a well-timed shotgun blast into the air. Later she had married the man, Gideon Ironheart, who was the long-lost brother of Micah Parish, also a deputy. Micah had his own stories to tell about the bigotry around here, although it had lessened somewhat since his day. Lessened but not vanished.

The extensive Parish family, however, had achieved a measure of acceptance through their long years in law enforcement. Connie, who had been in the command post earlier, had married Micah Parish's eldest son.

That acceptance did not entirely extend to Guy, a relative newcomer whose roots lay in a reservation. He figured he'd always be something of an outsider around here but had long since resigned himself to it.

It is what it is.

"Good setup," Valerie remarked after she and Sarah had been introduced.

Sarah smiled. "It's pretty good, Detective."

"Valerie, please. Or Val if you prefer." Valerie pointed to the screens, one in particular. "What's that?"

"A GPS map of where the searchers have been. Cell phones are good for something besides calls, texts and surfing the web. I'm sure you know that. Anyway, all the searchers have been advised to turn on their mobile data so we can track them."

Valerie pulled over a chair and looked. "The search area looks blocky."

Sarah nodded. "Uneven ground, uneven pace. Guy?"

"We're extending the radius again today. Have the K-9s found anything?"

Sarah shook her head. "Not a trace."

Valerie exchanged looks with Guy. He returned a brief nod.

Kidnapping.

FEELING ALMOST ILL, Valerie left the command post with its monitors and humming, crackling radios. Outside, she paused to draw several deep breaths.

"Are you okay?" Guy asked quietly.

"Trying to be. At this point the only damn I give is for my niece. For Lizzie. And I'm not liking the chances."

"There's always a chance," he said firmly. "A better one if she hasn't been in the dark and cold all night. Someone could well be giving her decent care."

She looked at him from eyes that felt swollen, although no tears fell. "But *why?*" The obvious question.

"If we knew that, we'd know where to look."

"The obvious answer," she retorted. "Maybe this person will get in contact soon. Give us some kind of direction."

"I hope to God he or she does. The sooner the better."

ETTA MARGOLIS FOUND an envelope in her mailbox that afternoon. She regularly walked the half mile to the rural mailbox at the end of her rutted drive to collect the mail, mostly advertising flyers and the few monthly bills. This time there was a hand-addressed envelope. She barely looked at it and curiosity touched her only slightly.

She lived on a small piece of land outside of town, a parcel cut from a larger ranch, originally intended for the family of the rancher's son.

That family no longer lived there, having skedaddled to a bigger city with more opportunity. The rancher, who'd fallen on tough times, had been only too glad to rent the house to Etta and her ex-husband for a song. A property he now didn't have to maintain.

Etta had lived there alone since her divorce, and the maintenance was more than she could handle alone. She lived in expectation of being evicted.

She also lived with terrible grief over the loss of her only child, a boy who'd been stillborn. Her grief and her husband's drunken anger, an anger that blamed her and her doctor both for the child's death, had ripped them apart. He had offered her no comfort as she'd wept and ached— just his fury. For two years they had had no contact and she wanted it that way. His anger, his blame, had been intolerable in the midst of her bottomless grief.

Once back at the ramshackle house, she recognized her ex's handwriting on the envelope. God, she wanted nothing to do with that man ever again. She tossed it unopened into the trash can outside the house, where it would disappear beneath coffee grounds and food scraps and eventually into the compost heap.

Like the rest of her life.

Chapter Four

Valerie stopped by her sister's house. May, her blond hair now stringy, was surrounded by friends again. She looked up eagerly as Valerie entered.

"No news," Valerie told her immediately, wishing she could offer more. Her sister's anguish was unbearable, her own nearly so. "I'm sorry. We're working every angle. I just came home to change into better shoes before we start pounding the pavement. Do you need anything?"

"Only my baby," May answered, her voice breaking.

Valerie knelt before her, taking her hands, aching so much for May and Lizzie that she didn't dare let it show for fear of upsetting May even more. Someone *had* to offer hope. "Everything is being done. I can promise you that. Where's Chet?"

"A delivery needs his attention," May said almost bitterly. "There's always somebody else's baby." The unspoken words were there, though. *Never enough time for* our *baby.*

Valerie wondered how Chet could even manage to deliver a baby under these circumstances. Or maybe he was escaping into work? Or escaping May's grief and fear?

She didn't know Chet well enough to judge.

She exchanged her dressy black shoes with two-inch

block heels for black flats. Police shoes. Her feet didn't always like being shoved into the toe box of ladies' shoes and coming events might require her to run or travel over rough terrain.

When Valerie emerged from her bedroom, she found that Kerry Canady and her dog had been replaced by another liaison officer, a pretty young woman named Artie Jackson.

"Artie is short for Artemis," the deputy said as she rose to shake hands with Valerie. "I'll do my best to take care of May."

"I know you will." As would May's friends, who kept coming as if in shifts.

Then she stepped outside and found Guy Redwing waiting, leaning against his Suburban. Under other circumstances she might have thought he was an extremely handsome man. Under the current ones, she barely noticed.

"There are other people who might have a motive," she said as he pulled the vehicle away for the curb.

"Plenty, I imagine, once we start thinking about it."

"May and Chet know a lot of people, what with him being a doctor and her being a schoolteacher."

"Absolutely. Then there are all the day care workers. It doesn't take much to create a grudge in some people."

She felt his glance touch her briefly.

"It's going to be a long day," he remarked. "Even with other deputies helping with the questioning."

A long day indeed, especially when accompanied by worry and fear.

BY FOUR THAT AFTERNOON, they'd talked to a lot of people, from neighbors to other acquaintances and the day care staff. All professed to be unaware of anyone who disliked

May or Chet. Anyone who might have reason to nurse a grudge. No one had seen or heard anything.

No threat for ransom had arrived either, no phone call, no note.

Almost reluctantly, Valerie joined Guy for coffee and a meal at the diner. She didn't want to eat but knew she must. Lack of sleep was beginning to catch up with her. As well as anyone, she understood the importance of a clear head.

"We're stuck," she said bluntly as she finished a meal she hardly tasted.

"At the moment," he agreed.

Weary or not, Valerie still possessed her temper. "At the *moment*?" she demanded. "We've got nothing, no leads at all. Even the K-9s couldn't find a trace."

"We have a whole lot of people who all said the same thing, as was to be expected. Any one of whom might be lying or shading the truth."

She dropped her fork and nearly glared at him. "How the hell do we find that out? Are you going to do background checks on everyone in this town, in this county?"

His jaw tightened. "Those checks have already begun. Do you take me for a fool?"

He spoke mildly enough, but Valerie could see the anger burn in his dark eyes. After a few moments, she looked down at her half-empty plate. "No," she said finally. "No."

"Good, because I'm not. You may be a big-town detective, but I know this county, this town. I've been policing it for years. How long have you been away from here, *Detective*?"

Except for brief visits over the last twelve years, she'd lost touch with this area, especially the people. She barely remembered even her high school friends. Presently she said, "I apologize, Detective."

"Try calling me Guy. And I'll call you Valerie. Maybe we'll get some equality going here. As much as you can give an Indian, anyway."

Ouch. She turned her head to look out the big window beside them. People walking by as if everything were normal while May's life was one of torture. The whole world should be weeping. "I wasn't thinking that."

Or had she been? God knew prejudice against Native peoples was strong in this part of the country. Had she been harboring some without realizing it? But bigotry was an insidious thing, invisible to those who didn't suffer due to it.

She looked at him again, wondering about herself. "I'm sorry if I made you feel that way."

"I'm used to it."

A part of her pried itself away from her reaction to Lizzie's disappearance. She nearly winced at how Guy must be feeling. "What I was thinking, consciously anyway, was that this is a small department compared to what I work with now."

"Inexperienced," he corrected.

"Maybe."

"We deal with everything here," he said. "Everything. Maybe just not the quantity of cases you're used to."

Valerie nodded slowly. "I'm not exactly an expert on kidnapping."

He shrugged one shoulder. "Who is? With the possible exception of the FBI."

"Maybe they should be called in?"

"Not yet. A bunch of suits out here wouldn't be welcomed. The clams would rather suffocate."

In spite of herself, she smiled faintly. "You're probably right."

"I know I am." He picked up the check. "On me. Expense account. Then you should get yourself back to your sister's and try to get some sleep. I know it won't be easy, but we'll do better with fresh brains."

Valerie couldn't disagree, but she wondered if she'd be able to sleep at all.

GUY WATCHED VALERIE walk into the Chamberlain house. Well, the woman hadn't been as much of a pain as he'd expected. Professional in every way during their interactions with folks around here. But she needed to ditch that suit. Everyone looked at her dubiously, as if she wore a stamp that said *outsider.*

Instead of heading home himself, however exhausted his brain might be feeling, he went to the office to check in.

Gage Dalton was still there, keeping an eye on everything. Apparently he couldn't give up and find his bed yet either.

"No luck?" Gage asked when he saw Guy.

"Not a damn thing. If anyone has any suspicions, they're not saying a word."

"Must be the first time in this county's history that the grapevine hasn't been working overtime." Gage rubbed his eyes. "How's this Valerie Brighton working out?"

"Totally professional. Impressive under the circumstances."

Gage nodded. "I was concerned about that. I bet you were, too. Unfortunately, other than her personal involvement, I couldn't find a reason to tell her no. I suspect she'd just have gone off on her own. We don't need that."

Guy shrugged. "No one would have talked to her anyway. They don't know her anymore."

"And she sticks out in that suit," Gage said, echoing Guy's

earlier thought. *Not one of us*, it would appear to folks. "I hoped that her connection to May and Chet might get her somewhere, though. Sympathy."

"Nope. Not yet anyway. And there's a downside to that connection. Who'd want to tell her that someone hated her sister or former brother-in-law? Some things might be said elsewhere, but not to her face."

"Too true." Gage raised his one mobile eyebrow. "You need to hit the sack. Hell, *I* need to hit the sack. We'll be no good to anyone."

Reluctantly, Guy headed back to his small apartment. Just big enough for a bachelor. Needed some work, though. Maybe he'd get to it eventually.

Sleep eluded him for a while. He put on some soothing music and settled into a recliner, hoping his brain would stop spinning at high speed. He didn't want to let go of the problem. He couldn't stop thinking about Lizzie. That poor little girl.

He closed his eyes, willing himself to find the trancelike state that always preceded sleep for him. At last it found him, relaxing him, slowing down his thoughts. Drifting away steadily.

His last waking thought was of Valerie Brighton. A pretty woman. A confident woman. A smart woman with a great deal of self-control. A dedicated woman, especially to her family.

But attractive. Sexy. That image of her almost shocked him awake.

A White woman. Hell, he knew better than that. His one foray into that kind of relationship, many years ago, had made him wise to the reality of this world.

But he sank into dreams anyway, too many of them about Valerie Brighton.

VALERIE ENTERED THE Chamberlain house to find May stretched out on the couch. A new liaison officer occupied the chair across from her. She offered a smile to Valerie but didn't speak. Her name badge said she was Deputy Benton.

May's sleep was less restless than last night, probably because she was too exhausted to toss and turn. Maybe because pleasanter dreams tried to protect her for a little while.

The revolving friends were gone, of course. Much as they wanted to support May, they had husbands, children, household tasks such as making dinner that couldn't be ignored indefinitely. All those things that May now lacked.

Valerie debated only a second or two. Bed or coffee? She opted for the coffee, reluctant to sleep without mentally going over the day's interviews.

Not a bad word anywhere about May or Chet? That seemed so unlikely that she tried to remember more closely. Had anyone seemed evasive? As if they might be lying?

But the day had managed to turn into a blur, and all she had was a small notebook tucked into the pocket of her suit jacket. She studied it as the coffee brewed, wondering if she'd scribbled something there, something that had caught her attention or made her uneasy.

She finally slapped it shut and got her coffee. She carried an extra mug out to Benton, who nodded gratefully, then returned to the kitchen. At least this room hadn't given over entirely to black, chrome and stainless steel. That was probably next on the list.

She wondered vaguely whose idea the decor had been. May's? Chet's? Or both of them? The rest of the house looked like something pulled out of a magazine. It wasn't as if Valerie hadn't seen all this on earlier visits, but she'd never thought about it before.

But even the kitchen was on its way to coldness. A stainless-steel refrigerator. A black and stainless-steel induction stove. A black dishwasher.

Amazing that the counters hadn't been turned white or metal. They still gleamed with blue tiles left from times past.

For all its elegance, this home felt almost monastic.

Why?

And what did it matter?

Only Lizzie's room defied the rest of the house, with pale pink walls, dashes of bright color from toys, bedding a patchwork of red, blue, green and white diamonds. An island of color.

She couldn't help wondering if May and Chet's relationship had started cooling well before their divorce, maybe before Lizzie's arrival. It might have. How would she have known?

At last she gave in to her body. She switched the coffee off and headed for bed.

As she rested her head on the pillow, she thought of Guy Redwing. He seemed capable enough. Steady enough. And he'd made her wonder.

How much unknowing bigotry did she harbor?

Chapter Five

Day three. Too long.

Oh, God, Valerie thought as she showered and dressed for the new day. This time she chose jeans and a warm blue sweater over her preferred suits. She hadn't been blind to the way people looked at her.

May was awake, looking miserable as hell, staring at the coffee table where someone had set a pastry before her, ignoring a cup of coffee.

Valerie pulled one of the chairs near the couch where her sister seemed to have planted herself. The liaison officer remained, looking sleepy. Soon the friends would start their daily rotation.

Valerie reached to hug May. "You hanging in there, sis?"

"What else can I do?" May's voice sounded wobbly. Then her blue eyes, so like her sister's, met Valerie's.

"We're running out of hope, aren't we?"

Forty-eight hours, so crucial, had passed. But Valerie wasn't about to say so. "Of course not," she replied firmly.

"You'll keep looking for her? Please?"

"I wouldn't consider anything else." She gently pushed the pastry May's way. "Come on. You won't be much good to anyone if you starve yourself to death. Heck, you won't even be able to hold Lizzie when we find her."

May's eyes closed briefly. "Please, God," she whispered. Then she reached for the pastry and spoke listlessly. "Want some?"

"I'm going to grab something quick at Maude's. Meet up with Guy." She reached out to squeeze May's hand.

May spoke again. "I'm glad you're on the case."

So was Valerie. She'd have gone stark, staring mad if she'd had to sit on her hands. "Where's Chet?"

"He called. He should be here soon."

"Good." Maybe. Something had torn these two apart. Maybe something more than May had ever mentioned.

With too many questions zinging around inside her head, Valerie made her way to the diner to find Guy. He'd taken a booth near the front window, a view on another cloudless day and a street that was growing busy.

He nodded to her when she sat across from him. He'd been nursing coffee from an insulated carafe that Valerie didn't remember from years ago when she'd visited Maude's. She touched it.

"New?" she asked.

"Quite recent. I heard it was Mavis's idea."

"Wouldn't have been Maude's for certain."

Guy offered a faint smile. "I'm going to have breakfast and so should you."

She didn't need the reminder and felt a brief spurt of irritation. God, another man, another member of the patriarchy that didn't think a woman could take care of herself. Then her irritation passed. Maybe she was being unfair. Yet again.

Eggs, rye toast, bacon. Calories. Cholesterol. Any other time she might have shuddered at her choices.

While they waited, Guy brought the conversation back to the kidnapping. "Did you catch anything yesterday when we talked to people?"

She shook her head. "Nothing I bothered to note."

"Then maybe we need to repeat the interviews, look for any discrepancy."

The next step to be sure, although whether it worked on this kind of crime she didn't know. It couldn't hurt though when they had no leads. "There's got to be something somewhere. What good would it do for a stranger to take a child so young?"

"Beats me. This whole thing stinks to high heaven."

Mavis banged her plate down in front of her. At least that hadn't changed in all these years. She'd sometimes wondered how Maude and her daughter managed to do that without breaking a whole bunch of crockery. The bang, however, seemed more like an announcement.

Stinks to high heaven. She knew where Guy's thoughts were turning and everything within her rebelled. Neither Chet nor May could possibly have disappeared their daughter. Nor did either of them have any reason to, not as firmly rooted as they were in this town. Where could they possibly hide a child? What good would it do either of them? The same questions kept roiling in her, like a rat on a wheel.

The thought that occurred to her next made a cold chill run down her spine, a vision of Lizzie buried in a shallow grave somewhere. She'd thought of that, maybe even mentioned it to Guy, but now it struck her forcefully and tried to consume her with sickening terror.

Could there be that much animosity between May and

Chet? Could either of them hate that little girl so much? Could anyone?

She nearly pushed her plate aside as her stomach churned. "Guy, I can't think they…" She trailed off, unable to voice her own thoughts.

"We're police officers," he reminded her. "We have to think of *everything*."

He was right. She couldn't dispute that. No police officer could.

She managed to eat. It wasn't an option.

When they were almost finished with breakfast, Guy spoke again. "I want to take a closer look at Chet."

She pushed her plate aside, hating the direction all this would take her. "Why?"

"Because he didn't get joint custody. Because just a few days before Lizzie disappeared they had a disagreement about whether he could just drop in. You heard what May said."

"But is that enough?"

"Maybe not. We have to look more closely. Something tore that marriage apart. Do you really think it was his work hours?"

She'd begun wondering about that herself. She felt a great deal of liking for Chet but she didn't know him very well. Nor was it likely that May would have told her everything about her decision to file for divorce. Some secrets were better kept for any number of reasons.

Grief and fear slammed her again and she turned quickly away to look out the window once more. She'd already learned that Guy was an astute observer of facial expressions. She didn't want him to read her face right now.

And once again she hated the growing bustle of people

outside. Normal lives untouched by a tragedy of this magnitude. The whole damn world should have frozen in its tracks.

GUY HAD WATCHED the flow of emotions across Valerie's face. He wondered if she had any idea how much she betrayed, yet she could become totally impassive on the job. How many times a day did she have to lock away all her emotions in order to be a detective? As many as he did?

Even here in this small town being a cop could get incredibly ugly. For all this was a friendly place where neighbors helped each other out, it was still full of human beings. And human beings could get downright horrible. Some of those smiles out there probably hid dark things: hatred, malice, envy, anger. There were even a few longstanding feuds, but these days they played out mostly in court, unlike past times when they might be settled with guns. Yet the surface around here remained tranquil and pleasant. Most of the time.

Then there was the grapevine. Gossip was a popular activity in these parts. A way to fill some empty hours and maybe play a quiet game of one-upmanship. Like the game of telephone, however, stories stretched and changed along the way. It was usually harmless, but occasionally that grapevine would get clogged with maliciousness and outright lies. One thing was for sure—it was never silent.

But on this matter, at least, the gossip had gone still. Which was interesting in and of itself. By now someone should have started a story about May or Chet. Some ugly tidbit that would grow as it spread. Maybe some little fact that got twisted. Maybe a fully made-up story.

But nothing.

That alone disturbed him. He had no doubt that Gage was right about it. His wife, Emmaline, was plugged into everything in the area. As the head librarian and daughter of a founding family, the Conards, she had deep enough roots to be in touch with it all. She'd know if there were any whispers about the Chamberlains.

The lack of whispers might be speaking loudly. Did it mean no one harbored any ill will against the family? Or did it mean that for once nobody wanted to stir up any kind of trouble because a missing child was involved?

If anyone knew anything that might be helpful but didn't want to say it to anyone else, that would hinder the investigation.

Valerie returned her attention to him. "Have the search parties quit?"

"Not yet. The number of searchers has diminished, though."

"I'd expect that." She frowned. "We're losing precious time."

"Hour by hour," he agreed. And so far they had no damn way of speeding this up. It twisted his gut into a knot when he looked at the problem that way.

He noticed Valerie had begun to aimlessly fold a paper napkin, creasing it sharply. "What?" he asked. Her nervous habit. She'd done it yesterday.

She looked up. "Huh?"

He pointed to the napkin. "What's troubling you apart from Lizzie's disappearance? Because something obviously is. We're not going to get anywhere if you hold anything back. Did you remember something that bothered you about the interviews we did?"

She shook her head slowly. "No. Not exactly." She bit

her lower lip, worrying it. "The cop in me is probably getting too suspicious."

"Maybe. Share it anyway."

She suddenly looked stricken. To his surprise his own heart responded to her distress. God, he didn't need that.

She spoke at last. "What Chet and May both said about Lizzie crying when she's taken from her mother?"

"Yeah? The baby monitor had been shut down."

Valerie shook her head slightly, and her eyes reddened just a bit. "May should have heard her cry anyway."

Guy felt gut-punched. It took him nearly a minute to find his voice and when he did he had to clear his throat. "What do you mean?"

"I could be wrong. God, I hope I'm wrong!"

"But?"

"But Lizzie's room is right next to May's. Those walls aren't soundproofed. Lizzie cries loudly. Monitor or no monitor, May would have had to have been drugged not to hear her. Monitors aren't for hearing from the next room but for being somewhere else in the house."

VALERIE FELT SICK enough to vomit. She resumed folding the napkin, trying to focus on that one little bit of clarity. But the detective in her had fully wakened and she couldn't ignore what she had just figured out.

"That means one of two things," she continued, her voice ragged with squelched emotions. "Either May was drugged somehow or someone did something else to get that child out of the house without crying." She shuddered, unable to hold it all in.

"Or…" Guy let the word hang. He knew he wasn't going to state the unspoken part: that May had gotten rid of her own daughter.

Chapter Six

They left Maude's together, climbed without a word into his Suburban and sat in silence for a century or two, or so it felt to Valerie.

Her chest squeezed so tightly that Valerie doubted she would ever breathe again. Her stomach threatened to eject the food she had just eaten, and with the nausea came a cold sweat.

Words finally burst out of her. "May wouldn't hurt her. Absolutely would not! She adores Lizzie."

"She's also a single mom with an ex who seems unable to accept the terms of the custody arrangement. Or maybe she's being unfair to him, given his irregular hours. That bit sounded a little cruel to me."

Valerie hated to agree, but it had struck her that way, too. Did she want to deprive Chet of all contact with his daughter? Was she that angry and bitter? What had brought on that divorce? Something so ugly that May had never told her own sister?

Guy spoke again after a minute or so. "You need to question her about that."

"I know," Valerie answered, her voice thick. "I know." She stared through the windshield at the offensive, sunny, normal street. "I'm beginning to wish I'd never insisted on getting involved in this."

Guy snorted. "As if you wouldn't have been thinking like a detective anyway even if all you did was sit this out with May. You're doing it right now even if it's killing you."

Her hands clenched into fists. "I don't know if I can do this, Guy."

"No one else can."

His words dropped into her like hot lava bombs. He was right.

GUY LEFT VALERIE at May's house. She stood on the sidewalk, looking up at the large brick house, feeling almost crushed under the weight of what she needed to do.

More anguish, fear and guilt than she could imagine lay inside that house, a lurking beast. No one, not even Aunt Valerie, could possibly experience the depth of pain that May was feeling.

Now she needed to enter that house in a way that would only make May feel worse. Valerie hated herself.

But it had to be done. Squaring her shoulders, seeking the stability and detachment that had carried her through some truly upsetting cases, she headed for the door. She felt like a high-wire walker with the gaping Grand Canyon beneath her. A misstep might hurt May, it might permanently damage their relationship, and she might fall to an internal death all her own.

God, that was her beloved sister in there. Friends all their lives. The best of buddies, sharing everything.

But maybe something hadn't been shared this time. Something that might help find Lizzie.

Or something that would damn her sister or Chet to eternal fire. She couldn't believe it. She didn't *want* to believe it, but for the next while she *had* to force herself to believe it was possible. Butterflies in the pit of her stomach fluttered so wildly it felt as if they were locked in some kind of battle.

When she entered the house, she found May all alone. Her sister had curled up on the couch and was staring blindly into space.

"May? Where'd everyone go?"

May stirred only slightly. "I told them to leave," she answered dully.

"Why?"

May's voice rose and she sat up. "Because that damn cop was useless. She was sitting there by the hour with nothing to report. Because I can't stand another person trying to tell me it'll be all right."

Valerie shut up, letting her rant, awash in pain for her sister.

"Because," May continued, "I'll scream if one more person offers me tea or coffee or pastry or some sloppy casserole. Because I want to scream every time someone tells me I need to eat something! I'm living in hell and I can't stand anyone telling me that it's going to be okay."

May drew a shuddery breath. "It's not going to be okay. It's not. My baby's out there somewhere, all alone. Frightened. Maybe being mistreated. Maybe *dead*! And no one's helping. No one!"

Then May dissolved into wracking sobs, sobs that threatened to tear her apart. Valerie eased down onto the sofa beside her and wrapped her arms around May, holding her tightly, letting the storm tear at her sister.

Helpless. God, she was so damn helpless and useless. And now she needed to ask questions, awful questions, questions that might tear May apart more. She squeezed her eyes shut, trying to steel herself from the minutes ahead.

When May's sobs began to ease because of fatigue, and she started to sag, Valerie asked quietly, "Where's Chet?"

"Where he always is," May answered wearily. "With some patient who matters more than I do."

So no time with Chet was better than some time with Chet? But hadn't that been the reason for the divorce in the first place?

She stroked her sister's hair. "But he went out with the search parties."

May's voice strengthened, laced with fury. "Big deal. He took a week off when Lizzie was born. One lousy week. His partner couldn't handle the patient load alone. She has a *family* to get home to. Chet covered evenings and nights for her all the time. But not for *his* family. So *I* had to handle it all alone. God, the people in this county must be breeding like rabbits!"

"Did you have a problem with that before Lizzie was born?" Valerie couldn't remember any complaints before then.

May sniffled, drew back and grabbed a tissue from the nearby box to dab at her eyes. "I didn't notice it as much. I had my teaching job. I was bringing home my work all the time. I was *busy.*"

Valerie drew a breath. "So Lizzie changed all that."

"Of course she did. It's different with a baby. I stopped working because I needed to take care of her and I didn't want to be sending her to day care five days a week. I wanted to take care of my own baby, not let someone else do it."

Valerie nodded, taking it all in, feeling May's words

pierce her like knives. She steadied herself with a deep breath. She couldn't afford to give in to her own anguish. *Not now.*

May spoke again. "At first it wasn't so bad. I was walking on air. Then it changed."

"How so?"

May didn't answer for a while, then: "I started to feel bad. Resentful. Dulled by it all. Chet said it was postpartum depression. He wanted to give me a pill for it. A pill! Like that would change anything about the situation. I was basically locked up in this house with an infinite sea of diapers and a kid who needed me all the damn time. Sure, friends would stop by, but conversation gets pretty dull when all you have to talk about is diapers and babies. And it left me feeling left out as they shared all *their* stories of the day."

Valerie took her sister's hand and held it snugly, stating the obvious. "I can't say I understand how it was for you."

May turned her head, looking at Valerie from wet eyes. "I loved Lizzie all the time, though. You need to understand. No matter how miserable I was feeling, I always loved her. I *do* love her."

"Of course." Valerie had begun to feel she was swimming in unfamiliar waters and couldn't find her footing. She didn't know how to reach out. She'd never had to reach out to anyone in this state of turmoil. She was also getting a better idea of what May had been going through.

May wiped her nose with the tissue. "Chet was here when he had the time, just like always. But I started to feel he wanted to get away from me. Like he was working more than usual just to escape my moods, to escape all the work involved. Maybe that wasn't fair, but I began to believe it. Then came the colic."

Valerie waited. She wanted May to tell the story her own way.

"Do you know anything about colic? It can go on for months. There's no help for it. It lasts three or four hours at a time, usually, and you feel so damn helpless walking a screaming child you can't help. Night after night. It seemed like it would go on forever."

"And Chet?"

"He helped when he was here," she said fairly. "But he wasn't here very much. An awful lot of babies were being born during the nights. Then there were his office hours." She sniffled again. "Do you think he was running away? Or having an affair?"

Valerie felt shock all the way to her toes. Chet having an affair? That had never entered her head. He didn't seem like the type. "Only Chet can answer that question," she answered carefully.

"Like he ever would. I demanded to know and he denied it all. Work was his everlasting excuse. If I was going to have to deal with it all alone, so be it. I divorced him. The only thing he fought me about was custody."

"How did *you* feel about the divorce?"

"Free." May wiped her eyes again and spoke fiercely. "He was no longer a problem for me. Whatever his reasons he was gone and, without worrying about what was going on with him, I started to enjoy Lizzie even more."

May fell silent for a while, her tears dried up, her breaths growing calmer. When she spoke again, she said, "He was rejecting me so I rejected him."

EVENTUALLY MAY AGREED to eat something, to drink some coffee. Valerie found the refrigerator overflowing with well-

meaning gifts of food. Plenty to choose from. Given May's
state her sister needed some hefty fuel to keep herself going,
so Valerie chose some sweet, fatty pastries to go with the
coffee. She carried plates and mugs for them both and placed
them on the coffee table. This time May reached for the pastry without being prodded.

But Valerie had gotten the clearer picture she'd needed.
Roses hadn't turned to ashes because anything had changed
except May. She faced it squarely. May said she loved Lizzie,
had never stopped loving her, but was that true?

Given the situation and how May had come to feel about
Chet, fairly or unfairly, the divorce made sense. She wondered about Chet's version of events and whether she could
get him to talk about it.

When May ate half the pastry and appeared inclined to
eat no more, Valerie asked gently, "Your life changed dras-
tically with Lizzie but Chet's didn't."

"Exactly. That's it exactly. Plus I didn't feel I could trust
him anymore."

It all made sense, Valerie thought as she watched May
wipe her fingers and mouth on a napkin.

But she was haunted by a memory. A woman she'd known
years back had commented on a news story about a mother
who'd killed her own son. *There but for the Grace of God*,
she'd said.

Valerie had asked her what she'd meant.

The friend had looked at her and replied, *You have no
idea how far up the wall a kid can drive you, especially as
they get older. I once got so angry, worn out and sick of
the constant arguments that I had a vision of banging my
son's head against the wall. It shocked the hell out of me.*

Then the woman had added, *The only difference between her and me is that one split second of clear thought.*

Well, Valerie had seen plenty of that during her years with the police. When that one split second of clear thought never came it resulted in horrific crimes. The pleas—*I didn't mean to do it.* Too late.

May could have missed that instant of clear thought. Some people did.

Valerie again felt sick enough to throw up.

ON THE OFF CHANCE that someone they'd interviewed the preceding day might have remembered something, Guy went back to question some of the people. Besides, while he'd thought Valerie's presence might loosen tongues, her being May's sister, she might just as well have silenced people who didn't want to criticize May in front of her sister. But he'd had that thought before and all that mattered was that it propelled him.

He hoped he wasn't wasting valuable time, but what other leads did he have?

Besides, Valerie was doing the hard part, talking to her sister. He didn't envy her that task at all. Much as he didn't want to give the woman any props, he had to about this.

His initial impression of her was changing. He no longer saw her as an interloper who looked down on him. She seemed determined to be professional. Neither had he noticed anything else that might indicate she was a bigot.

Although a lot of people could succeed in concealing bigotry when it suited them, at least for a while.

He shook his head at himself as he worked his way through the interviews again, briefer this time because he only needed to know one thing: if anyone had heard any-

thing about enemies of the Chamberlains or something un-
flattering about either of them. He gently prodded them to
think more closely.

He got no further than he and Valerie had the day before,
which frustrated him no end. There was nobody on this
planet who didn't have an enemy somewhere. The Chamberlains weren't saints. No one was, at least among the living.

He stopped by the command post again and found Connie Parish back on duty. The search teams had thinned out
and the hope that they'd find the child anywhere in the vi-
cinity had just about died.

Which might be a good thing, he thought as he returned
to the Chamberlain house. If Lizzie had been kidnapped—
and it was beginning to look as if she had—then she might
still be alive. It just widened the search area, though only
God knew by how many miles.

Lizzie's photo and description had gone out on the extended Amber Alert Gage had issued that morning. Prior
to that, however, there'd been absolutely no evidence that
the child might have been taken. Now every policeman in
a four-state area was on the lookout. So were caring members of the public.

But nothing yet.

Guy pulled over to the side of the street, needing to gather
himself before seeing Valerie or her sister. Life had hardened him in a lot of ways, but he wasn't hardened to the
plight of any child.

This case had pierced his heart.

Chapter Seven

Chet Chamberlain had moved into a small house in a subdivision nearer to the hospital. The subdivision, so unlike much of the rest of Conard City, had been built because of the GI Bill after the Second World War. The houses were aging and basically graceless, but most had been maintained well enough over the years.

They were also small houses. Conard City didn't boast a huge number of large ones, although during boom days the wealthier citizens had constructed mansions along Front Street and nearby. Or at least mansions compared to everything else around here, Chet thought.

Not that he truly cared. The small place he lived in now was big enough for him. Two bedrooms, one of them an office for him, a basic kitchen and living area. It was enough room, and a place where he didn't spend much time.

It also didn't hold memories and dreams, unlike the big house he had deeded over to May. *That* place had once been full of dreams that he and May had shared. Now it held only pain for him. He wondered if May felt the same pain but doubted it. She'd been the one who had demanded a divorce.

The situation with Lizzie was eating him alive. The house he hunkered down in no longer felt like a hidey-hole. When he walked in there now, he could only hear Lizzie's laugh, hear the sound of her running feet. He kept turning, expecting to see her. He wondered if May felt the same way in that big house, or if the sea of agony had swamped her.

It hadn't quite swamped him yet, but he was holding it at bay by diving into his work. He couldn't think of one damn useful thing to do about his daughter, and he couldn't offer comfort to May. There was no comfort to be offered, not when the whole thing was tearing him to pieces, too—not when she'd thrown him out. He wondered briefly if she knew he felt the same fear and worry she did, then cast the stupid question aside. Of course she did.

He'd been cut off and with the severing of that tie he was left alone in a situation that made him want to rend the very heavens. Why would May even think about what *he* was feeling?

He had just come back from the hospital and poured himself a finger of whiskey, shutting his ears to the sounds of Lizzie, already imprinted on this place from her too-short visits. He couldn't bear to think of where she might be now, how she was.

It was almost a relief when Valerie knocked on his door and told him she needed to talk with him. He let her in, asking immediately if there was any news. Hope's tendrils tightened around his heart along with the agony that wouldn't quit.

Val shook her head. "I'm sorry, not a word. But I need to talk with you, Chet. If you can stand it."

Chet waved her to a chair but remained standing himself, glass in hand. "Want a drink?"

Val shook her head. "This wouldn't be a good time."

"No, it's not," he agreed, looking at the whiskey. "But

it's all I have right now." Unable to hold still, he paced the small living room with its sofa, recliner and TV. "You've come to play detective, I suppose."

He heard her sigh and finally looked at her. Really looked at her. "What did I say?"

She gave him a small shake of her head. "*Detective* isn't something I play at."

"Oh, for God's sake, Val, you know I didn't mean it that way. What's wrong with you?"

"Only the same thing that's wrong for all of us right now."

He saw her eyes redden and realized Lizzie's disappearance was hurting her almost as much as it was hurting May and himself. A new ache slipped through him as he wondered why he hadn't considered Val's feelings in all of this. Maybe because she always seemed so self-possessed? So confident? Or maybe he wasn't as empathetic as he believed?

"I'm sorry," he said after another swig of his whiskey. "I'm a mess. I'd claw something to death if I could. Scream. Chew nails. Shoot myself."

That got her full attention. "Shoot yourself? Why?"

"Because this has to be my fault somehow! Ask May, everything's my fault!" His voice had risen and he fought to force himself back into the zone where he could treat patients who were in the worst of crises. Patients who needed him to remain calm no matter what. It wasn't easy in this situation. Not that it ever was, but Lizzie being gone? That was whole orders of magnitude worse than anything he'd ever faced.

"You think May's blaming you?" She tilted her head, then rose and headed for the small table where the liquor bottle sat along with a few highball glasses. "She's not blaming you," she told him as she poured a small amount of whiskey for herself.

"If she isn't, she will eventually," he answered, bitterness replacing everything else inside him. "God, it got to the point where I couldn't do a damn thing right. May turned into someone I could hardly recognize. But I'd have waited it out, Val. She would have gotten past it all. Despite what she might say, I wasn't the one who changed."

Holding her glass, Val perched on the edge of the recliner. "I heard May's side of the divorce, but what about yours?"

He glared at her and drained his glass. "Are you blaming me for this?"

"I'm not blaming anyone," she said gently. "I just want to understand."

"Understand what? I already told you. May *changed*."

"Okay. How did you feel when she told you she didn't want you dropping in to see Lizzie?"

He felt his mouth twist. The detective was here, and her kid gloves would come off if necessary. "It made me feel godawful. *She* was the one who argued I shouldn't get joint custody because of my irregular hours. So what am I supposed to do? Stick to a weekend here and there when I might have to run out to work? Leave Lizzie with a babysitter? The babysitter she didn't want me to get?"

Val nodded slowly. "I see your point."

"At least *you* do," he said bitterly. He turned away to look out his front window at the deepening night. Lizzie was out there somewhere. Terror gripped him.

"Tell me, if you can, who might have a grudge against you? Anything that springs to mind."

He continued to stare at the window, and now ice filled

him. "A lot of people," he said eventually, his mind springing them up like weeds in a badly kept lawn.

He heard Val move behind him. "Who?" she asked.

"Dozens of people. Maybe more." Now he turned to face her, the ice in his veins hardening. "Do you have any idea why obstetricians and gynecologists carry the most expensive malpractice insurance in the medical field? It's so bad a lot of medical school graduates look for any other area of practice."

"Why is that?"

"Because," he answered harshly, "we get blamed for everything that goes wrong. We get blamed for stillbirths, genetic defects. Mother Nature doesn't get the blame even though we don't cause the problem. No, *we* get sued. How the hell am I to blame for Down syndrome or cystic fibrosis? Or any of a million things that can go wrong with a fetus? How can we be blamed if a mother doesn't take her prenatal vitamins and has a child with spina bifida? You want the whole list?"

"That's not necessary," she said quietly. "I'm sorry, Chet. It shouldn't be that way."

"No, it shouldn't, but insurance companies find it cheaper to settle a lawsuit than to fight it. So there you have it."

He poured himself another whiskey.

Valerie spoke again. "Think about it, Chet. Please. Anyone you can think of who might want to hurt you through Lizzie. We need all the help we can get, okay?"

"I'll try. As if I can focus on anything except Lizzie."

"Can you go through your records and see if anyone stands out? That might be a real help in this search."

"Okay." He gritted his teeth. "Okay. I'll look. I'll get some

medical people to help looking at the files to speed it up."
His face sagged. "It won't help."

Now her voice developed an edge. "Why not?"

The detective was here, he reminded himself. Not the
Val he knew as a fun sister-in-law.

"HIPAA," he finally answered savagely. "Patients have a
right to privacy under federal law. I can't tell you *anything*!"

He stared down at the glass in his hand, then hurled it
across the room at the wall, where it shattered into pieces,
just like his heart.

"She's my baby," he said as the tsunami washed over him
again. *"She's my baby."*

GUY REDWING WAITED outside in his official Suburban. Valerie felt almost weak as she walked toward his car, her legs
shaking as if they could no longer support her. He climbed
out and met her halfway.

"Valerie?" he asked.

"It's not him," she said brokenly, then did something
she hadn't done in her entire career. She collapsed against
him, tears pouring out of her, grateful when his strong arms
wrapped around her and held her close. She needed him
desperately.

GUY HELPED HER into his vehicle, then drove away from
Chet's place, not sure what to do. The strong woman in the
passenger seat was breaking down, understandably, but the
situation was awkward beyond belief. She might well hate
him for seeing her weakness. He'd already figured out that
she was a woman who hated to show weakness. Powerful.
Strong. Capable. That's the image she projected and most
likely the person she was.

Until this. He shook his head a little as he drove aimlessly. This would kill just about anyone, he thought. Not only worrying about her niece and her sister but needing to be a detective through it all. He couldn't imagine.

But he didn't need to imagine it. It was happening in the seat right beside him. When the storm passed, she was probably going to hate him for seeing her like this. Hate herself.

So what now? How could he shelter her without making her feel worse? Damned if he had any idea.

"Want to go back to May's?" he asked when she seemed calmer.

Her voice was thick. "No! Not yet. I don't think I've ever felt so helpless in my life, Guy. I'm not ready to prop up my sister, not yet."

He thought of Chet Chamberlain. "Maybe someone else should do a little of the propping. Like Chet."

"He seems to be convinced she doesn't want him around. That she's going to start blaming him for whatever has happened to Lizzie."

His interest perked but he let it slide for now. He didn't think pushing her was going to be any help to her just then. Let it rest until she was ready to talk about it.

"How about I pick up something at Maude's? Then we can go to my place for a bit. Just to give you a break."

"I shouldn't need a break. I'm just doing my damn job."

"Right," he said sarcastically. "Under any other circumstances, I'd probably agree with you."

He didn't wait for her to come up with any more objections. He drove to Maude's, grabbed some steak sandwiches and salad, and returned to his vehicle with a couple of bags. Valerie sat quietly, staring out the passenger window. He doubted she was seeing anything that wasn't inside her.

Chapter Eight

Over all these years in Conard County, Guy had rented an apartment in the complex that had been built so long ago by a short-lived semiconductor plant, but was now used primarily for student housing. He'd done little to improve it, just a recliner and a second-hand dinette set. A single wall-hanging of a rug his mother had woven. A bed, of course.

And on the one battered side table a photo of his immediate family. A reminder of those he loved, some who barely spoke to him since he'd put on a badge.

He placed their boxed dinners on a rickety kitchen table, started some coffee, and pulled out a few chipped plates along with some scratched silverware.

He saw his quarters with fresh eyes as he led Valerie inside. It wasn't much.

"I like the blanket," she said. "Beautiful."

"My mother made it."

He felt her gaze on him as he set out the utensils and opened the box. "Grab a seat. The chair will hold you and the table won't collapse."

She looked around the small kitchen, then sat. "You like it like this?"

"It's better than where I lived on the rez."

Her face changed infinitesimally as he put food on the plates, then poured two mugs of coffee. At least the cups weren't chipped.

She took a small bite of the sandwich. "These are still as good as they used to be."

"As reliable as Maude."

When she swallowed a second mouthful, she asked, "Was your childhood awful?"

"No. The winters could be hard, though, when we couldn't pay for enough heating oil. But by and large it was good. Plenty of loving family and friends."

She hesitated visibly. "I thought the government built houses on the reservation."

"If you can call boxes with poor insulation and dirt floors houses."

"God, Guy!"

He finished his sandwich and started on the salad before he spoke again. "Try finding a job when you're a redskin."

"But…" She bit her lip. "Isn't that an awful word?"

"Just the one I heard a thousand times. We all got labeled drunks and layabouts. Indigent instead of Indigenous. Especially hard for the women."

She pushed her salad around her plate. "How so?"

"Have you ever heard of MMIW? Missing and Murdered Indigenous Women?"

She pushed the salad aside and looked at him from a pale face. "Tell me."

He waved a hand. "When Indigenous women turn up missing or murdered, the cops barely investigate. For rapes it's even worse."

She leaned back and drew a shaky breath. "I don't have words. Is that why you became a cop?"

"Yeah. That's it. I swore I was going to change things in my small part of the world. Some of my friends and family don't get it. They think I went over to the dark side."

"God! How do you stand it?"

"Because I have to."

Telling her all this had only roiled up feelings he'd spent years burying. That clawing rage filled him once again. To distract himself from it, he went to get them more coffee.

She looked at the mug. "I could do with a drink."

"Sorry, I don't touch alcohol."

Her expression filled with sorrow. "Because of the labels?"

"Because Indigenous people are genetically prone to alcohol addiction."

She drew a sharp breath. "But how…"

He shook his head. "The Aztecs knew it. They had rules about it. Only small children and the elderly and sick could drink alcoholic beverages. The rest of the time it was off-limits. Anyway, I hear they found the genetic reason. I don't know for sure. But I've seen enough of my people succumb. Never a drop for me."

He sat again. "You wouldn't believe the number of liquor stores around the edges of a reservation. Even though it's not allowed on the rez, plenty of people go off the rez to buy it. The Whites love it."

His hands clenched. "We try to protect ourselves and get sabotaged. The Navajo Nation is better about it. They'll arrest anyone, Whites included, if they're found with alcohol on the rez. Not everyone has a big enough police force to stop it. That costs money, which a lot of nations don't have. What does it matter anyway if some of the cops are addicted, too? Why should they care? Anyway, it gives them a good excuse to crack down on drunken Indians."

"I never thought about it," she admitted. "Never."

"Why would you? Easier to think of us as drunks."

She shook her head, falling silent. Then, "Is that why you wear your uniform instead of plainclothes?"

"Believe it. Like I said, it greases the wheels. That uniform puts me in a special category. Folks might not like it when I'm the responding officer, but they don't hassle me. Not often, anyway."

"I can't imagine, Guy. I just can't imagine."

"You don't need to." Shoving his anger back down into his box of private furies, he forced himself to relax. "I'm lucky I got the job here. To *be* here. Micah Parish paved the way a long time ago. Then there's the vet. Mike Windwalker. A few little steps, among others, toward acceptance."

Once again she fell silent.

Eventually he spoke. "I shouldn't have dumped all that on you. You've got enough on your plate right now."

"I'm glad you told me. There's so much I don't understand. Now I'll know to be on the lookout for this crap."

Nevertheless, he felt like a jerk for letting all of that ugliness out, and worse for speaking of it to Valerie. No way to make amends for it. He'd spewed it and now he had to live with it. The way he always lived with the consequences of his actions.

But he moved away quickly from his own problems and back to hers. More important right now. "So you really think Chet couldn't have had anything to do with this?"

"Not directly." Now she reached for her cooling coffee and downed half of it.

"Need some water?" Guy asked. "You look thirsty."

"Please."

He went to the fridge and pulled out a bottle. "Mind drinking it like this or do you want a glass?"

She gave him a faint half smile. "I'm not a hothouse flower. Gimme that bottle."

In spite of himself, he nearly smiled as he passed her the bottle. She drank half of it before setting it aside.

But now it was time to deal with the *other* difficulty. He repeated the question. "You said you think Chet had nothing to do with Lizzie's disappearance?"

"I don't. I don't think May did either. I listened to them, Guy. I couldn't mistake their pain, and I believed what they both said. There's a wrinkle, though."

He stiffened, expecting her to give him bad news. "What?"

"I asked Chet to check his records for anyone who might bear a grudge. He said he would, but it wouldn't do any good. HIPAA. He can't reveal any personal health information under federal law."

"Damn it!" He drummed his fingers on the table, a moderate reaction to the surge of fresh anger he felt. Hell, he hated this case. He hated what it was doing to so many people. He hated that every twist and turn took them nowhere. He hated that a child was at risk.

She spoke. "I feel the same. I don't know what kind of trouble Chet might get into if he flouts that law. Federal penalties, certainly."

"Penalties he might not care about if he develops a strong opinion about who might be involved."

She drew another deep breath. "Maybe."

"That's a thin thread to cling to." He rose, pacing every inch of this tiny apartment. "There's got to be something somewhere. I know some people disappear into thin air, but a small child? A kid who's hardly more than an infant?"

"Damn it, Guy, I don't even want to think about how that could happen!"

He stopped pacing. "I'm sorry."

Finally, she shook her head. "We're cops. We've got to think about it."

Horror filled him when she spoke the dreaded words. "Does this county have any cadaver dogs?"

Chapter Nine

"No," he answered heavily. "No. Some trackers but not that. And the K-9s couldn't even pick up a scent around the house."

Tears began to pour down Valerie's face. "We've got to."

"I'll find one. Some department in this state must have one. Or maybe more. But are you sure you want to do this? It's basically giving up hope."

"You think I don't know that?" She jumped up, hugging herself, her tears growing more copious. "But there has to be a resolution of some kind. This can't go on forever!"

That she would even think of a cadaver dog told him how deeply she had sunk into the horror of this situation. Almost beyond rescue. Or maybe far beyond it unless they found Lizzie alive.

She turned toward him, and without thinking about it, he wrapped her in his arms again, wishing he could be a bulwark rather than merely a companion as she walked through this fire.

He had no words to offer, no clues to help the situation, nothing but a pair of arms to let her know he cared, that he was there for her. Other than that, he was totally useless.

He'd solved many cases over his career, but never had he

wanted more to solve one. To bring relief to Valerie and her family. Helpless, he offered all that he could.

WITHIN GUY'S EMBRACE, Valerie felt herself softening. The tightly coiled spring inside her eased, letting her go until she relaxed deep within.

But she felt ashamed and humiliated by her uncharacteristic reaction, by revealing herself as weak and worn out. She'd had some tough times as a cop; she carried hideous memories that often disturbed her sleep until they faded into an ugly background. But never before had she broken down.

She *didn't* break down. Never had. Yet here she was, clinging to a man as if he were a lifeline. She disgusted herself.

Yet she couldn't move away. She'd found a haven and didn't want to leave it. When he loosened his hug just a bit, a sense of panic filled her, but then in his gentler embrace he began to rub his hands over her back. Soothing her. Calming her even more.

"Like a horse," she said suddenly, her voice raw.

"Huh?"

"You're soothing me like a horse."

A snort escaped him. "Cripes, Valerie, I've never hugged a horse in my life."

She tilted her head in order to see his chiseled face. "Are you sure?"

He shook his head slowly. "I'm sure. And I've been around plenty of horses. Damn, Valerie, you don't remind me of a horse at all."

"I hope not." Then she forced herself to back away, dashing away those embarrassing tears on the sleeve of her sweater. As soon as she did, the pain started to return. She could get through this, though. On her *own* two feet, not his. She *had* to or she'd lose her sense of self, her confidence in her ability to take it all on the chin.

With each step she took away from him she felt as if she were ripping her skin off, returning to the raw nerve ending she seemed to have become. She resumed her seat at the rickety table.

"Sorry about that," she managed to say. But she wasn't, not really. A part of her, disgusting as it was, had found a few minutes of calm in the hurricane of horror that buffeted her. Had, perhaps, given her a clearer mind.

Guy stared at her for a couple of minutes, then went to the wall phone to punch in a number. "Gage? Sorry to disturb your evening, but Valerie and I want you to find a cadaver dog. Maybe a team of them."

Once again Valerie tightened like a coiled spring. All of it was back, cloaking her like wet, dead leaves.

"Yeah. Thanks." Guy hung up. "Gage knows of a private group. He'll get them."

She whispered, "I can't believe I asked for that."

"You walk down every avenue you have on a case. You know that. So we'll walk down this road and God willing these dogs won't find any more than the K-9s did." He sat across from her, studying her as if waiting for another emotional outburst.

She wouldn't give it to him. Wouldn't feel guilty about another one. With difficulty, she forced herself back to her detective self.

"I can't believe the K-9s didn't find anything at all."

"Me neither. You'd have expected them to catch Lizzie's

scent outside the house. Or the scent of someone else who'd been in her bedroom with her. Nothing."

"How is that possible?" But she knew it was possible. And that was the only reason she'd asked for a cadaver dog.

She jumped up, pacing as Guy had such a short while ago, although she felt as if she'd climbed ten mountains inside herself since then. Now she simply couldn't hold still.

"My sister," she said. "My former brother-in-law. Will I ever be able to see them the same way again? All this suspicion. It stains things forever. May sure won't see me the same way again. Ever."

"You can't know that."

She turned on him, feeling her face twist. "Really? The minute those cadaver dogs show up, she's going to know exactly what we've been thinking about. She's going to *know*. Our relationship will never recover."

"If she gets closure..."

"That's an overused pop psychology word. Closure? How can there be any real closure to something that will cause you pain for the rest of your life? Knowing isn't really enough. Like in a book, it's the hook at the end of a chapter to pull you forward. But it doesn't pull you out of the story. You don't get any closure to the book until you read the last sentence. Until you finish your life."

Guy shook his head. "That's bleak."

"It's also true. Tell me I'm wrong."

Clearly he couldn't. His usually impassive face revealed little, but she could still sense hidden emotions playing across it. She just couldn't read him. That could get frustrating, she realized. It was frustrating right now.

Wrapping her arms around herself again, she resumed

pacing. "The hours are passing. The precious forty-eight are gone."

"If it's a kidnapping there might be more hours."

"So where's the ransom note, Guy? Where is it?"

THAT BOTHERED GUY, TOO. There had to be a motive for Lizzie's kidnapping, if that's what it was. So why no note? Why silence?

The first thoughts that occurred to him were so despicable he refused to entertain them. "Maybe somebody just wants a baby."

She froze midstride, then faced him again. "It's happened," she said hoarsely.

"That's why hospitals have such stringent security precautions these days."

She sat with a thud. "You're right."

But how did they trace that one? "We should start searching for someone who suddenly has a child Lizzie's age."

"Maybe so," she answered. "But how? A little kid could be explained away as a niece who'd come to visit. Or as a child from a previous marriage. Or the kidnapper could live in a place isolated enough that no one would see."

"It won't hurt to send out a bulletin. Maybe the Amber Alert isn't enough. Maybe it needs refreshing."

Valerie nodded, hope pricking the agony in her heart. Just a little prick she didn't dare nourish.

Guy continued. "This kidnapper would have to eventually buy something for a kid that age. A toy. Most likely clothes. This kind of kidnapper wants to treat a child as his or her own."

"Wants to enjoy parenthood," Valerie agreed. "That might be enough, but how long will it take?"

"Conard County isn't the only place in Wyoming with a grapevine. I don't know how long it might take, but sooner or later someone is going to notice something. Maybe as a result of the Amber Alert. Or maybe just because they find it suspicious."

She began to rub her upper arms and Guy asked, "You getting chilled? I can turn up the heat."

Valerie shook her head. "I'm a wreck, that's all. Self-comfort, I guess." She dropped her hands.

Not knowing where else to take this, he asked, "Want some fresh coffee? Or a bed? You can have mine. I can sleep in the recliner."

"I'm not sure I'll ever sleep again. I should go back to May, but I'm still not ready. After the way I questioned her, I don't think she'll be happy with me. Regardless, the state I'm in, I'm not sure I could be supportive enough."

But then she rose.

"Enough. She's probably sitting there all alone. I can't leave her that way just because I'm having a crisis."

Guy rose, too. "I'll take you."

And maybe he'd go inside with her. Handle the tough questions May was bound to ask. Spare Valerie as much as he could.

He'd expected this partnership to be a whole lot different. Instead her grief was welding them into a tight team.

A White woman. Damn it all to hell! Hadn't he learned?

WHEN THEY ARRIVED at May's house, Sheriff Gage Dalton was limping toward the front door. He paused as Guy and Valerie pulled up.

He greeted them with a short nod. "Anything?"

"Ideas," Guy answered. "Nothing we want to discuss in

front of May unless it appears it might help her. I'll let Valerie be the judge of that. Otherwise, we'll tell you later."

Gage looked at the house. "I don't like what's happening in there. That poor woman. That poor child. Lizzie's old enough to be terrified out of her mind. Just let me get my hands on the perp."

"And you'll arrest him," Valerie said. "Or her. Another wrecked life won't help anything."

Gage gave her his half smile. "At least one of us has a clear head."

"Not really," Valerie said. "Hearing you say it, well, I feel the same so I can hand *you* the advice. And remind myself."

Valerie opened the door for them. No knock. May wasn't in sight.

"May?" she called, her heart starting to race. She hoped May hadn't done something stupid.

But then May appeared from the bedroom area. She looked haggard. "I was just sitting in Lizzie's room." In her hand she held a small blanket. "It's all I have left."

Valerie hurried to her and hugged her tightly. "We're working on it, I swear."

"Yeah," May said wearily. She pulled away and dropped onto the couch, holding the blanket to her face. "I can still smell her. But it's not enough!"

"Of course not," Valerie answered, sitting beside her.

May looked past her at Guy and Gage, speaking on a rising note. "Both of you? Bad news?"

"No news," Valerie answered swiftly. "Not yet."

"But when? Oh, God, when?"

"We've got some leads," Guy answered. "We're working

on them." He took a chair facing her and after a brief hesitation Gage took the other.

"I may need help getting out of this chair," he remarked absently. Then he turned his attention to May. "We're calling in some extra dogs. Maybe that will help."

Valerie was grateful for the way he phrased it.

"Help how?" May demanded. "Do you know how long she's been out there?"

"We do," Guy answered gently.

"Then she's dead! *Dead!* I can't believe that. I won't believe that!"

"That's not what we're saying," Valerie interjected quickly. "Extra dogs might pick up a scent where the others failed."

May's eyes had grown watery again, but tears didn't fall. She probably didn't have a tear left to shed, Valerie thought. "We're thinking it might be a kidnapping."

May's head jerked. "Your questions weren't about that. I listened."

"Then maybe you didn't hear me quite the right way. I can't promise that's what happened, but we're seriously thinking about it, okay?"

May nodded stiffly and looked at the blanket she was holding so tightly. "Lizzie," she murmured. "Who would steal her? Why?"

Well, those were precisely the right questions, Val thought miserably. Questions without answers like everything else in this disappearance.

Gage spoke. "May, we've got everyone working on this. And not just in Conard County. Everyone wants to find Lizzie. *Everyone.*"

May sighed and sagged, letting her head fall against the

back of the sofa. She continued to clutch Lizzie's blanket. "I don't know how much more of this I can take. God help me, I can't stand this."

WITH LITTLE MORE to offer, Valerie followed Gage and Guy out the door.

"Well?" Gage asked. "And *cadaver* dogs?"

"I thought of it," Valerie said, not wanting Guy to take any heat about it.

"*You* did." Gage studied her carefully. "Why?"

"Because it needs to be done. I'm still a cop, much as this mess is tearing me apart."

Gage nodded. "I agree, although I didn't want to say so to you. I contacted a couple of teams and they should be here tomorrow."

Valerie couldn't bring herself to answer. She was having enough trouble dealing with what this might mean.

Guy spoke. "Valerie talked to May and Chet again today. I reinterviewed everyone we'd already spoken to. No dice."

Gage sighed and rubbed his chin. "May and Chet?"

"They didn't do it," Valerie said with conviction. "Neither one of them is playacting. Chet said he'd go back through his medical files to see if there's anyone who might bear a grudge against him, not that it will help. He can't reveal any information. HIPAA."

Gage swore. "Another dead end. I'll have to see if we can't get a warrant to look at any files he considers possibilities, or even just get names." He paused. "I'd be damned surprised if we can't get a warrant to review the files. Okay, that's next on my list."

Valerie felt a tide of relief. More possible leads. At this point she'd settle for just one.

"Thank you, Gage."

"I wish I could say it was my pleasure but nothing about this is a pleasure. Catch up on your rest, both of you. You're going to need clear heads tomorrow. I hope we're not all destroyed when those dogs start searching. I can't bear the thought that Lizzie isn't still alive and I don't care how far or how long this takes." He looked at Valerie. "That's a promise."

After Gage left, Valerie turned to Guy. "You know I can't possibly begin to thank you."

"No need. My job."

"It's more than that and you know it." She looked down. "It's not normal for me to break down."

"It's not normal that you're investigating a case involving your niece and your sister. Take it easy on yourself."

She managed a small smile for him. "Still, I'm grateful."

They said good-night and Val walked back into the house, into the hurricane of her sister's grief and the storm of her own anguish.

FAR OUT ON a ranch, Etta Margolis looked at another envelope from her ex, Phillip. Why wouldn't he just leave her alone? He'd sure left her alone in the aftermath of the still-birth of their child. His ranting, his anger, most of it had been directed at her because it *had* to be someone's fault.

She knew from listening to her doctor, Chet Chamberlain, that often there was no explanation. Nature made mistakes. Not the mother, not the doctor. Things went wrong with babies at any time during their development. Their son had been one of those mistakes.

But Phillip had been impossible, making her sorrow all

the greater with his accusations, refusing to believe that her grief mattered compared to his fury.

She'd almost thrown the envelope in the trash like the first one, but the arrival of a second letter troubled her. They hadn't passed a word in all this time. The letters were so out of character for him that a smidgeon of curiosity awoke in her.

Maybe she should read it, just to see what was going on. If he wanted to get back together she'd write and tell him to shove it. The idea of rejecting him in no uncertain terms gave her a quiver of pleasure, the first she'd felt in a long time.

So she ripped the envelope open and got a huge shock.

Etta, I found a baby for us. She's about the same age our son would have been. Doesn't that make you happy?

She crumpled the note and threw it on the compost like the first one. The man was truly insane. Then she buried the brief note with pitchforkfuls of more compost.

How could he adopt a child? He was a divorced man with a police record for having beaten Etta, even though she hadn't dared to follow through.

Yeah, Phillip had tipped over the final edge. Putting it from her mind, she turned on the TV.

It was good to be free of Phillip. Maybe the best thing about her life in the last two years. She wasn't going to let him worm his way back in. Miserable and lonely as her life now was, she didn't want him to fill any part of it.

Satisfied with her decision, she put on some sitcom. Even canned laughter sounded good these days. But never the news. Never. She had enough reality to cope with inside herself.

Chapter Ten

Guy returned to his ratty apartment, seeing it through Valerie's eyes, then wondering why he should. It was *his* place, damn it, and it sufficed. Why should he care about her approval?

The fact that he might troubled him.

Then there was his outburst about life as an Indigenous person. Why had he felt the urge to tell her something so personal? It wasn't as if she could help change the reality of it any more than *he* could.

So much for his belief that working inside the system might help his people. Maybe he should just quit and go home apologetically to his family.

But no. Regardless of whether he changed this small bit of the world, the job needed doing and he took a great deal of pride in his work. It satisfied him. It also gave him some control, though not enough. More than he'd had on the rez.

How could he even think of quitting at a time like this anyway? His detachment as a cop was beginning to desert him big-time. As had happened with Valerie, although she had a better excuse than *he* did.

He made some instant cocoa, unable to face another cup of coffee, and headed for his recliner, his mind shifting gears to all the interviews he'd repeated. He still couldn't believe that no one had any unkind words about the Chamberlains. Nobody was *that* good.

There ought to be at least some envy out there. The Chamberlains were relatively well-off for these parts. Big fancy house, new-model cars, maybe even some exotic vacations.

And what about Chet? Had no woman ever made a play for him? A woman whose advances might have been rejected? The same thing went for May, a beautiful woman. Although women with babies were less likely to interest men. Usually.

Had one of them been cheating? Given Chet's apparent hours, he was the likeliest one to have a second relationship, one easy to conceal.

Time to get to Chet's coworkers, to get beyond the teachers, the preschool, and neighbors. So far they'd been too busy to get to that obvious arena.

Tomorrow, he decided. It had waited long enough, and the longer Lizzie was gone the more likely it was for someone to speak about matters no one wanted to mention. Matters that might not be relevant but still had to be checked.

God! He put his cocoa on the end table and rubbed his eyes. Someone had to talk. Someone always did. The criminal himself often told someone.

But what if the kidnapper—or killer—didn't talk to anyone around here? Spreading the search over four states made it even less likely that they'd hear anything. Too many people, some of whom wouldn't have a reason to care or wouldn't tell for a variety of reasons, like not wanting to get involved with the law.

Staring into the bleak reality of this case was like going

down a black hole into nothingness. Staring into that empty hole eventually dragged him into a restless sleep. The black hole followed him into his dreams.

NOT FOR THE first time, Gage Dalton was finding it impossible to sleep. This time he didn't lie to his wife, Emma, claiming it was his back.

"The missing baby," she supplied without even asking him what was wrong. "For heaven's sake, Gage, you can't keep this up. Find a way to sleep or you'll be dead tomorrow."

He shook his head. "You go to bed. I'll manage."

"Then I'll stay up with you. Unlike you, I can call in sick tomorrow. Nora Jackson can handle the library."

He looked at Emma, taking in her beautiful face and thinking about her loving nature that had dragged him out of the dark pit his life had become all those years ago. Since then, life had touched her only lightly, making her all the more beautiful in his eyes.

"Do you suppose Nate would be up at this hour?" he asked suddenly. Nate Tate, the sheriff who had preceded him. The "old sheriff" as everyone referred to him, as they referred to Gage as the "new sheriff" even after all this time. That didn't bother Gage. It was a mark of respect this county continued to show the old lawman.

Emma looked wry. "Need a brainstorm, huh?" She glanced at the clock. "It's late but I'm sure he won't mind being dragged out of bed. He's that kind of man and he still hates being sidelined."

"Tell me about it. Besides, he knows this county better than I ever will. I swear he could name every person off the top of his head."

"He probably could, but he was born here, unlike you. Call him. If it bothers him he won't hesitate to tell you to get lost. He's never been one to withhold his opinion."

Gage finally rustled up a half smile, then reached for the landline. Every wise person out here kept one. Cell communications could be disrupted by any number of things. Which was why all his deputies carried satellite radios. SAT-COMS. Everything seemed to have an acronym.

Nate was on Gage's speed dial and the man sounded only mildly sleepy when he answered the phone. "Tate." Just as he had for years while he was sheriff.

"Gage," he answered. "Spare me some time?"

"The Chamberlain case, I reckon. Get your butt over here. I'll put on the coffee."

Gage kissed Emma goodbye with the always repeated "I love you." Because they both realized there was always a chance that one of them might not come home. The passing of years only strengthened that awareness. It might be the last time the words were spoken. The final memory.

Then he went out the door, pulling on a light jacket. The spring leaves were beginning to pass the feathery stage and become fuller. Beautiful in the daylight, creepier at night as the wind rustled them.

He had no room in his head to really notice, though. His thoughts, his worries, pushed him to Nate's house through the dark night, his official vehicle the boss of the roads he drove over. No traffic to argue with him tonight, however.

He made it to Nate's house in ten minutes over town streets toward the subdivision on the outskirts. Built after the Second World War in response to a pressing housing need and the GI bill, most houses here were small though well-kept. Nate's house was the exception. With six daughters, he'd long ago expanded to create space for his girls and all their friends. Practically a mansion compared to his neighbors' homes.

The porch light was on, as were lights inside the front of the house. As Gage pulled into the driveway behind the two family cars, Nate opened the front door, ready for him.

Age had added some lines to Nate's face and his dark hair had changed to silver but overall he looked like a man in great condition. He greeted Gage with a shake of hands. "Head for the family room. Still take your coffee black?"

"My stomach wishes I wouldn't, but yeah. Thanks."

The huge family room hadn't changed much over the years, even with the girls moved out. It had lost the bean bag chairs, however, replaced by some recliners that faced a large flat-screen TV. Gage sank carefully into one of the recliners and nearly sighed with relief. It eased his damaged body.

Nate returned with two large mugs of coffee. "Never thought I'd watch so much TV," he remarked, then took the other recliner. "Lousy case," Nate added. "I'm glad I'm not working it. How's Guy Redwing doing?"

Which meant that Nate still had his feelers out, was in touch with everything including who was leading the investigation. That gave Gage a probably exaggerated sense of support. He had sometimes thought this man would know if anyone sneezed in Conard County.

"Guy's doing great from everything I can tell."

Nate nodded. "I thought he would. Fine officer. I hope things are better for him. I remember when I hired Micah Parish, an old buddy of mine from Special Forces. Man did he get a load of BS around here. Well, until the day he took out a sniper in the bell tower of Good Shepherd Church."

"That would make a difference, all right. I'm not sure about how it's going for Guy along those lines. He doesn't talk about it at all. I suspect he's getting some bull, though."

Nate nodded. "Speaking of Good Shepherd, I just got a ping tonight. Pastor Molly is returning early from her trip, should be here tomorrow."

"That's good. We could use her pastoral comfort right about now." Pastor Molly Canton was now married to the other detective in the sheriff's office, Callum McCloud. Callum had some business in his old hometown and Molly had taken some well-earned vacation time to accompany him. "Callum, too?"

"Just Molly. Woman's got a backbone of steel along with that gentle nature. Anyway, I'm sure you didn't come to discuss Molly."

Gage shook his head. "Heard any other whispers?"

"I wish. Never heard the grapevine so quiet in my life. Reckon Emma's told you the same."

"She has. It's strange."

"I'll grant you that. Never saw tongues quit wagging. Which I guess means that everyone is so shocked by all this, so disturbed, that nobody wants to be responsible for any rumor that could turn ugly."

Gage nodded. He sipped coffee and watched Nate do the same. Then he sighed. "Nobody's talking about anything, even in our interviews. You know as well as I do that the Chamberlains can't be perfect. No one is."

"Damn county's going to hell in a handbasket," Nate remarked. "Been saying that for years. When I grew up here, we didn't have the kind of crime we've been seeing the past years. Now a baby might be kidnapped or dead?"

Nate drained his mug then leaned back. "So tell me. What's going on and what do you want from me?"

"Ideas," Gage said bluntly. "Are we missing something? Are we going about anything in the wrong way?"

"You did the search, right? You're questioning people about anything they might have seen or heard about the Chamberlains. Tried to find if they have any enemies."

"And we've called for cadaver dogs."

Nate looked away. It almost seemed he winced. "Not good."

"No choice. Valerie suggested it." He paused. "You know who Valerie Brighton is?"

"Hell yeah. Now, *that* got the tongues wagging, including in the department. Some folks claim it shows that Guy ain't good enough."

Gage shook his head. "Bigots will find any excuse. Thing is, given she's a detective with a personal stake in all this, there's no way I could keep her out. Better to team her with Guy than have her trying to investigate on her own."

"Couldn't agree more. And folks'll simmer down once this case gets solved. I researched Valerie."

A crooked smile escaped Gage. "Why am I not surprised?"

"Well, I figure I got more time to look into her than you got." It was Nate's turn to smile. "So I did. Using access I'm not s'posed to still have."

Gage chuckled. "I didn't hear that."

"Figured you'd go deaf. Now Valerie. She's got a brilliant record. Highest solve rate in robbery-homicide. A record most would envy."

Gage nodded. "That's good to know."

"Might could be this is a little different. She's *involved*."

"Thought about that. But *she's* the one who wanted the cadaver dogs. Cop thinking."

"True." Nate rose. "More coffee?"

"Natch."

Nate returned a minute later with freshened mugs. "Been thinking about this whole mess."

"I thought you would be."

"Any ideas I might not have heard?"

"Valerie asked Chet to look over his records for anyone who might have reason to hold a grudge against him. HIPAA is a problem. You wouldn't know if I can get a warrant?"

"Never had cause to get one, but law enforcement is probably allowed. Same as they can read your online chatting or phone info with a warrant. No damn privacy anymore."

Gage cocked his one functioning eyebrow. "You think that's bad?"

"Not for law enforcement. That's all I'll say, except you couldn't pay me to use any of them online social groups."

"Off the grid, are you?"

Nate snorted. "Like I said. So you think Chet might find something?"

"I'm hoping. You probably heard we're looking at kidnapping, too."

"No shock there."

"No ransom note, though. Strange."

"Somebody could have a different reason for taking the kid."

"That idea sickens me."

"Yeah." Nate fell silent. "Hell and damnation."

"We need just one thread to pull and we're not finding it."

"I'll think on it, Gage. Right now I ain't seeing a thing

you ain't done. But if I come up with something, I'll let you know. And you keep me in the loop, too."

Gage had to be satisfied with that, but he was more satisfied they now had an additional brain, a good one, thinking about all this.

Another strand of hope, albeit slender. But just hope, not a lead.

He swore as he drove home and banged his palm on the steering wheel. He'd lost his kids to a car bomb intended for him. He'd nearly lost his mind. He knew how that felt to a parent.

And now he was losing his cool on this one.

HE WASN'T THE only one losing his cool. Not that Valerie had been totally cool since Lizzie disappeared, but it was getting harder to squelch her own grief even though it might hinder her in the investigation.

After she finally got an exhausted May into bed, she couldn't sleep herself. She paced the dimly lit house, her mind racing. Poking at everything they'd learned, trying to shake out more info. Seeking any hole they hadn't peered into.

She stared out the front window into the darkness and felt despair washing over her.

"God," she murmured. "Just a clue. Please, just one little clue to help us."

Chapter Eleven

The cadaver dogs arrived in the early morning. They were trained by separate owners but evidently willing to work together. Their owners looked a bit fatigued, having driven most of the night.

At nearly the same time, Kell McLaren arrived with his own K-9, both of them retired from the Army.

"Bradley," Kell said, "isn't a trained cadaver dog but he's damn good at chasing a scent. Any scent. Let him smell the baby's dirty clothes or a blanket. And let him sniff around for any other scent in that room. Won't take him any time to sort out a useful odor."

Guy didn't think that Bradley could do much more than the department's own K-9s, but he had to admit Kell's dog had a lot more experience. There wasn't much call for K-9s around here, except for searching for some idiot hiker who'd lost his way or managed to get himself injured. Or the occasional fool who tried to fly his small plane over the mountains.

"Go for it, Kell."

He took Kell and his dog into Lizzie's bedroom. May at once grew worried. "Another dog? He isn't…"

She clearly couldn't bring herself to speak the words.

"Nah," said Guy easily. "This one's Army trained. Probably better than ours." Maybe.

May looked relieved. "But the other dogs?"

"Same thing, but with more experience than ours."

May accepted it and returned to her living room, where she sat beside Valerie, who appeared washed out. Guy didn't expect much from her today.

"I've sent Connie Parish over to the hospital to do some interviews." He was past caring if May heard it. Besides, he reasoned, it wouldn't make Lizzie's disappearance any harder to take. Might even ease her mind to know something of what was being done.

Valerie nodded. A moment later, May nodded as well. The two were images of worn-out anguish.

"It's been too long," May said woodenly. "She can't be alive out there."

Guy sat facing the two women, controlling his expression. "Maybe we can find the exact place she disappeared."

May shook her head. "What good will that do?"

"We're trying everything, May."

"Yes," said Valerie. "We are."

May looked at her sister. "I know," she said finally. "I'm glad you're helping, Val."

Ouch, thought Guy, even though it wasn't fair. Why wouldn't May trust Valerie more than anyone else? Valerie had a bigger stake than the rest of them.

Besides, he was just a redskin cop. And how many times had he heard that in these parts? Or everywhere else.

Also not fair to May. He reined in his ugly thoughts that wouldn't help anyone, least of all himself. Instead he focused on the crushing burden May was placing on Valerie's shoulders.

He waited a few minutes, then when no more questions arose, he stood and looked at Valerie. "Get yourself some rest, Detective. You won't be much help right now."

She didn't argue, merely nodded.

That troubled him, too. He'd seen her fire, her determination. Was she giving up?

Kell McLaren's dog stood outside Lizzie's room, off lead now.

Kell said, "I don't know how much he found in addition to the baby's scent, but Bradley seems raring to go."

"Then let him." Although how Kell read that much in the dog, Guy had no idea. He had to trust Kell's experience.

The two went out the door. Unlike the cadaver dogs, also off lead, who were searching a wider area, Bradley kept lifting his head, sniffing, then sniffing the ground. He was searching for something different from the other dogs and he appeared to be seeking a scent apart from the others. He certainly didn't head toward *them*.

Maybe they'd get something out of this. He just hoped it wasn't the cadaver dogs who found it.

THE SEARCH CONTINUED throughout most of the day while Guy kept badgering the office about whether they'd gotten any kind of response to the widened Amber Alert. He knew they'd call him if they got even the slimmest lead, but he kept calling in anyway.

Connie returned from her expedition and motioned to him. He moved away from the house, hands tightening against disappointment. Not even the barest spark of hope ignited in him now.

Simple fact was he had begun to think about trying to

find a psychic, because they sure as hell weren't getting anywhere this way.

"Well?" he demanded of Connie.

"Maybe something. Some of the PAs at the hospital know several people who got angry with Chet over the last few years. They won't say who, of course."

"Of course. Gage said he's looking into a warrant to break the HIPAA barrier. Don't know how long that will take."

"Judge Carter doesn't waste time when it's important."

"Never known him to. But there might be some difficulties here. Look, I'll stay here in case any of the dogs alert. You go over to see Gage and tell him what you learned. Maybe that'll be the probable cause the judge needs for a warrant."

"It can only help. Anyway, I haven't interviewed everyone. Gotta go back after shift change."

Guy watched Connie stride away then resumed waiting. There was too much waiting in this case. He wanted some action.

He wanted a child back in her mother's arms and his hands around someone's throat.

A good solid punch would help, too, help exhaust some of the fury he dealt with. Except that it would be stupid beyond belief to hammer a tree and break his hand. Never had he wished more for a punching bag. But he couldn't afford the time to hunt one up.

He was involved in an endless hunt that required every ounce of patience he had, but he didn't have enough time.

Neither did that little girl.

IN THE LATE AFTERNOON, he went into the house. Both women looked as if exhaustion had dragged them into sleep for a little while. Valerie's color had improved.

And sitting with them was Pastor Molly Canton, wearing her clerical garb of black shirt with white dog collar and black slacks. Molly was something of a bone of contention around this county, being a woman, but acceptance of her had grown after a few years. It was obvious she wasn't going away, no matter how much resistance she met.

Sort of like him, Guy thought.

"Listen," he said, "I'm gonna send Artie Jackson to Maude's. You folks want something to eat that doesn't come in a bakery box or a casserole dish?"

Molly smiled. Valerie managed a small one. May's face remained flat.

"We all need to eat," Molly said kindly. "Especially you, May. You have to keep up your strength for Lizzie."

At last May nodded.

With a little coaxing, Guy put together an order then went to hunt up Artemis Jackson, who was reaching break time from her shift in the trailer. She hated her first name, preferring to go by Artie. An athletic young woman, she wore her uniform well.

"Okay, Artie, here's the list for Maude. Throw in a meal for yourself. Chilly as it is, you need extra calories to stand out here."

Artie smiled, as much as anyone could in these circumstances. "Thanks."

"No thanks necessary. Trust me, the department is paying."

With a small laugh, Artie headed for her vehicle. Moments later she drove away.

Which left Guy pretty much alone, except for the deputy in the command trailer who was monitoring the location of the dog handlers.

Thinking about those cadaver dogs, Guy realized he'd never hoped so hard in his life that nothing would turn up.

AFTER DINNER, WHICH even May had eaten most of, Guy left the three women and stepped outside, mentally beating his head for ideas, solutions, anything at all in this intractable case.

He wasn't surprised when Valerie joined him a few minutes later.

"I'll go over to the hospital," she said. "Do some more questioning."

"You'll do no such thing," Guy answered.

She turned on him, blue eyes sparking. "How dare you?"

"Look, the people over there know who you are now, at least some of them. We're running up against a problem here, Valerie. I bet a lot of them don't want to talk because of your relationship to Chet and May. How could they say anything critical in front of you that might get back to the Chamberlains?"

She compressed her lips and turned her head away. She couldn't argue with that, thank God.

Damn, this woman was wrestling him into knots. And they weren't all about Lizzie. Her feelings were beginning to become his own. He felt her frustration, for sure. She needed to be doing something and right now couldn't. Well, neither could he.

After a bit, he said, "I told you I was sending Connie Parish over there. Everyone around here knows her. Spent her whole life here. What's more, they trust her discretion. Much as you don't want to admit it, Valerie, you've been away for quite a few years. They don't really know you anymore."

"Val," she said quietly.

"What?"

"Just call me Val. Everyone who knows me does."

So he knew her now? Maybe that was a compliment? Hell if he knew. He still wasn't sure he could trust her. His own form of bigotry, he supposed, a one-eighty from what he'd faced his entire life. Right now, though, he needed to get her mind on something else.

"So what's happening with that pup you rescued?"

She turned her head back to him. "I haven't checked."

"Then check. Seems to me you're in the process of adopting it."

Her lips curved upward ever so slightly. "I wish. My hours wouldn't be fair to a dog, though."

Well, he could understand that. "So think about a cat. It could probably endure your hours. Anyway, check on that dog. Might make you feel a bit better."

She nodded and pulled her cell phone out of her pocket.

Relief eased him, but only briefly. What could he come up with for another distraction? But distractions were far from his own thoughts.

Except her mouth. Man, that tiny smile. He closed his eyes. What was it they said about men thinking about sex six times an hour or more? But not right now. Absolutely not right now. Right now it felt loathsome.

"He's doing okay," she said when she disconnected. "Out of surgery and recovering. They're going to try to find someone to adopt him."

Sad, that. "It's amazing you rescued it. Considering you probably drove hell-for-leather to get here."

Her eyes widened. "How could I leave it, Guy? How could any feeling person?"

"Well, someone sure as hell did. Guess it was one of those

people who don't have feelings at all for anything but themselves. Most folks around here know the value of animals. Most people depend on them one way or another."

"But not everyone. This is no utopia."

"True." Sad to say, but humans didn't seem capable of creating one.

He rocked on his heels, trying to think of something else. "You ever hear about the big program to colonize other planets?" He now had at least some of her interest.

"No, not really. Something about visiting Mars?"

He snorted. "Yeah, with plans to terraform it. Make it into another planet like our own. But that's not what I'm talking about. I'm talking about the bigger plan. The one that says we'll eventually have to escape Earth to save the human species."

"Wow," she said quietly. A spark of interest showed in her eyes.

"Yeah, I read an article about it recently. And all I could think was, what makes us think we're worth saving? Then they talked about how one of the biggest problems would be getting the thousands of people on a huge spaceship not to develop all kinds of problems with each other. You know, feuds, fights, all that."

"Wars," she said quietly.

"Exactly, because we all get along so well right now."

She nodded, that small smile appearing again.

"Anyway, I was getting more disgusted by the piece, then this one scientist asked the question I was waiting for. He asked what makes us think we're so special that we need to be saved from extinction. He said there are eighty-eight million species on this planet. They don't deserve to survive?"

"Good point."

"So he concluded by saying we ought to just cram a small spaceship full of the most viable bacteria, send 'em out and let 'em evolve. Just the way they did here. In a few billion years they might evolve into us. Or into another species." He shrugged.

"That's a thought." Val's smile widened a shade.

"Sure is. On the other hand, how can we be sure we or the bacteria will arrive on completely dead planet? How can we be sure we won't become an invasive species that destroys all the life already there? Look what happened in the Americas when Europeans arrived."

Now her smile became broad. "I like the way you think."

He shrugged again. "Or maybe I see the whole world upside down."

"Maybe you have a right to, given your experience."

That observation took him by surprise. "Well, we haven't done such a great job taking care of *this* planet. Land us somewhere else and we'll do the same thing all over again. We don't seem to learn from our mistakes."

He let it go, aware that he was ranting, however quietly, a rant that came from his own culture. Should he even try to explain that to her? Nah. She wouldn't understand. She'd probably think those beliefs were weird, or worse.

After a bit, Val spoke again. "Just more human superiority. When we're only a gene or two removed from chimpanzees. Have you ever seen them in a zoo?"

Guy shook his head.

"I did. Calm females looking rather disdainfully at a couple of male chimps that were acting pretty much like wild teenagers trying to impress the girls. I couldn't help seeing similarities."

Now it was his turn to smile. "Given what you see on the job, I'm not surprised."

She looked down, then glanced at the watch she wore. "I'm going in to get a drink since you've got me off duty. Want some coffee or tea while we wait here for what feels like forever? I'll bring it out."

"Thanks. Coffee if you don't mind."

Which left his own thoughts spiraling into the very real problem that wasn't going away, distractions notwithstanding. He called the office yet again. "Anything from the wider world?"

Velma's scratchy voice answered him. "We're doing what you said, calling every department we can find. Surprising how many there are in a state with so few people. Anyhow, nothing yet. All the federal and state forest rangers are on the lookout, too. Woods and brushland being searched everywhere. And we're just getting ready to start calling surrounding states."

"Tell 'em I don't care if it's just a wisp of something unusual. *Anything.*"

"I think they know that, Guy. But if you want, we'll call all of them again."

"Call. I need *something.*"

"Like I said, we're just getting on to neighboring states, too."

"Maybe it's time to start calling airlines. Except they probably see so many infants boarding there's no reason any would have stood out." He swore. If you looked at the numbers it was amazing how many people just vanished, never to be seen again. One little kid could do that even more easily.

VALERIE CAME OUT of the house carrying a tall coffee for Guy and two fingers of bourbon for herself. She rarely drank because she could be called out on a case at any time. But Guy had made it clear that she wasn't working right now. The waiting made it even more difficult.

She held her glass up to Guy. "Does this bother you?"

"Why would it? Never wanted the stuff. It's not like I'm a recovering anything."

She tried to smile but fear was rising in her again, like a tidal force that couldn't be denied.

Just then Guy's radio crackled with his call sign. He answered immediately. "What's up? Tell me it's not the cadaver dogs."

Valerie heart hit top speed, leaving her nearly breathless. God, no!

Then came the answer. "Kell McLaren's K-9. He's found the point where Lizzie Chamberlain disappeared."

Chapter Twelve

They got to the spot in less than five minutes. There was Kell, Bradley sitting right at the edge of the road, not all that far from the Chamberlain place.

Valerie and Guy jumped from his vehicle and trotted over to man and dog.

"Here," Kell said. "Right where Bradley is sitting. The child's trail vanishes."

Valerie felt her knees grow weak. Guy instantly reached out a steadying hand.

Guy spoke. "How can you be sure it's Lizzie's scent he's been following? If she was being carried, how could she leave a scent trail?"

Kell simply looked at him. "A million ways. Ask Bradley how he does it, not me. I just know he can follow scents that are days old. Maybe fuzz from a blanket drifted to the ground. Maybe the guy had to set her down occasionally."

"Well, that settles it."

Valerie drew a shuddering breath. "Kidnapping. At least she's not dead. We've got to tell May."

Guy scanned the area. "Not all that far from the Chamberlain house. What, a mile?"

"A little more," Kell agreed. "Whoever it was followed a

circuitous route, though. Like he was afraid of being seen even in the dead of night."

"Or maybe the kid was crying," Guy said.

Valerie had thought of the same thing. Because Lizzie always cried when she was away from her mom. But why hadn't May heard a thing?

The question that had plagued her nearly from the beginning haunted her now.

GUY AND VALERIE returned to the Chamberlain house, a house that felt as empty as a tomb except for May and Pastor Molly.

May looked up immediately, her hands twisting Lizzie's blanket. "Anything?"

Valerie answered. "Kell McLaren's K-9 found where Lizzie disappeared. It definitely appears she was kidnapped."

May sagged and murmured. "Thank God. Thank God. She's not dead."

Valerie and Guy exchanged looks. There was no proof of that. None.

Valerie slipped outside with Guy and they held another brief meeting beside Guy's Suburban.

"No crying?" Guy said.

"No." Valerie's fists clenched and her neck appeared to stiffen as she turned her head to look into the deepening night. "She might already have *been* dead."

Guy blew a long breath between his lips. "Don't even think that way."

"Then why didn't May hear her cry? Why, Guy?"

He gave a short shake of his head. "You giving up?"

Her eyes blazed. "No, damn it. But all possibilities…"

"Have to be considered," he interrupted. "But how about you let *me* worry about the worst ones. Let's just find that little girl."

Val bit her lip. "Okay. Okay."

"Meantime shut your cop self down for just a little while. Give yourself a break. Hell, I don't know how you're walking this tightrope without falling."

"Funny, I had that image myself a day or so ago. I'm doing it because I have to."

He nodded. "Life's that way sometimes." He waited, knowing he was the only person she could share her fears with, all the million images and ideas that must be roiling her.

When she didn't speak, he turned to get into his vehicle. Then her voice stopped him.

"Guy?"

He faced her.

"I don't want to sit in there with May and do nothing at all. It'll make her feel worse if I'm sitting on my hands. Can I come with you?"

A new tension coiled in him, but he answered simply. "Sure, Val. Climb in."

VALERIE FELT AS if she was abandoning her sister, but she had to get away, just for a while, the need all the stronger because the investigation was turning up nothing. Because Lizzie had vanished into thin air and they had no idea where to look.

Because sooner or later May would begin to wonder why her sister was doing nothing. Because there'd be anger and confrontation, neither of which would do either of them any good.

She felt awkward about asking Guy to take her with him, but he hadn't seemed reluctant. She knew she was infringing on a professional relationship but it seemed a minor concern considering the entire situation. There'd been times in the past when she'd needed to be a cop with another cop. One who understood the worst sides of human nature.

Once she stood in Guy's small apartment, she wondered if she'd made a mistake. She hadn't thought about how this might affect him, the kinds of gossip that might make the rounds.

"You want me to go?" she asked him. "People might talk."

"People talk anyway, sometimes about things they know nothing about. I can offer you coffee, instant cocoa, or orange juice."

"Cocoa, if you don't mind. Maybe the milk will help me wind down."

"Sure." He stripped off his gun belt and headed for his bedroom. When he returned he'd shed his uniform for a chambray shirt and jeans. "Take a seat." He pointed to the recliner.

"But you…"

"Trust me, I can sit. So just relax as much as you can while I make cocoa."

It was a comfortable recliner, inviting her to put her feet up. She resisted. Leaning back and closing her eyes didn't strike her as relaxing at all.

Ten minutes later he returned with a cappuccino cup full of aromatic cocoa. "I added some cream." He set it on the end table beside her. "And so much for instant. Takes a whole bunch of time to dissolve that powder."

He turned and dragged one of his two kitchen chairs over,

then got his own cup of chocolate, putting it beside hers on the single end table. He straddled the chair.

"You're gonna reach a breaking point, Val. I don't know how you can handle all this. Your personal concern, your need to be a cop in the midst of it. It's going to crush you."

She sighed and reached for the cocoa, sipping carefully. It was hot. "I've gotten near there a couple of times. I don't like feeling weak."

"Weak is the last thing I'd call you. And unfortunately I think you're right about your sister. At some point the blaming starts."

"Yeah. And that can leave permanent scars. I don't want that between us, although it probably can't be avoided if we don't find Lizzie soon."

She sipped more cocoa while staring into her personal hell. Lizzie. May. The fruitlessness of their hunt.

Guy spoke. "Connie said earlier that a few PAs remembered patients getting really angry at Chet. She's gone back to the hospital to interview people after shift change. Haven't heard any more yet, but at least we've got one good reason to get that warrant."

"Thank God. I'd hate to think that a clue could be buried in patient confidentiality."

"I think Judge Carter will agree. He's always struck me as sensible."

"I seem to remember he's a good judge."

Clutching at straws, Valerie thought. All they had to cling to right now. Frustrating. Maddening.

"Gage went over to talk with the old sheriff. You remember Nate Tate?"

One corner of her mouth lifted. "How could I not? The man's a legend."

"Seems like. Anyway, Nate says you have an enviable rate of case resolution."

She shrugged a shoulder. "I'm not counting."

"You should. You should *trust* yourself, hard as it is right now. Your instincts are good. You're facing things you can barely stand to think about."

She shook her head. "The cadaver dogs?"

"Widening the search area tomorrow, but given what Kell found, those dogs are going to come up empty."

"God willing."

But another dead end. Someone had apparently taken Lizzie away in a car. She hated to think how many hundreds of miles the kidnapper might have traveled by now. "I'd give just about anything for a ransom note."

Guy's answer came slowly. "I'm not sure I would."

"Why?"

"Because any kind of ransom note implies violence."

"Against Lizzie," Valerie answered reluctantly. "No matter whether they get the ransom or not."

EVENTUALLY VALERIE DOZED off in the recliner. Guy waited a while, saw that at first she was restless but then calmer, more settled. More deeply asleep.

He chanced taking a shower, but when he looked in she was still asleep so he went to lie down on his bed. Meditation seemed to be his only possible escape into sleep but it didn't come easily.

Morning was creeping closer and he saw no help on the horizon. The sun would rise and nothing would change. Not unless some alert person or cop reported something unusual from somewhere.

But he couldn't afford to think that way. While the situation grew worse with every passing hour, he needed the hope that would keep him moving forward.

Maybe they'd get some useful info out of the hospital. He was counting on it.

But the first clue came with a knock on his door at nearly 4:00 a.m. Not his radio, but a knock.

Still half-dressed, he jumped out of bed to answer it. He saw Val starting to sit up, her eyes bleary.

Then he opened his door and saw the tall older man standing there. "Gray Cloud!"

The two men hugged with the affection of many years.

Gray Cloud entered, his presence seeming to dominate the entire room. No silver touched his long black hair, but the lines of wind and weather had marked him with their wisdom. His jeans were worn nearly white in places, his red jacket looking newer.

Guy made introductions. "Gray Cloud, this is Valerie Brighton."

Gray Cloud nodded. "The detective from Colorado. Sister to May Chamberlain, right?"

"Yes," she answered, rubbing sleep from her eyes. "Sorry if I'm intruding."

Gray Cloud shook his head and sat in the chair that Guy had earlier vacated. Guy pulled up his other one.

Then he explained to Valerie, "Gray Cloud is one of our elders, like a father to me. He's the guardian of Thunder Mountain."

A million questions filled Val's face but she didn't ask them. Good, this wasn't the time. A visit by Gray Cloud to town was rare. He certainly hadn't made his way here to speak about tribal or religious matters.

"Coffee?" Guy offered.

Gray Cloud shook his head. "I came to tell you one thing. A man with a small child was seen by one of our people. Out at the farthest reaches of our reservation. We sent a party to keep an eye on him but he was gone and hasn't come back." He looked at Guy. "I can take you there but it'll be on horseback."

"No problem, as you know."

Gray Cloud looked at Valerie. "You ride?" It was clearly an invitation.

"Yes."

"Then meet me at the old sawmill at dawn. I'll have horses and we'll set out. Maybe you can find a clue out there."

Then he rose and left with a farewell.

Valerie sat there, clearly wide awake now. "A clue? We have a chance at a clue?" She jumped up. "And who was *he*?"

"I told you, an elder. A nearly legendary one." He stood, too. "Let's get you back to the house. You'll want to get cleaned up and put on some clothes that will be better for riding, and warm enough in case we have to go up into the mountains."

AN HOUR LATER they were driving away from the early glow of the soon-to-rise sun and getting close to the old sawmill that hadn't functioned in over seventy years.

"What did you mean about that guardian thing?" Valerie asked.

"Guardian of Thunder Mountain," Guy answered, aware that he might make her see him in a different light than as simply another cop. An Indigenous one maybe, but still a cop. He hoped that didn't shift.

"Why does the mountain need a guardian?"

Well, he wasn't going to lie. "You must know something about Thunder Mountain."

"A little," she confessed. "There's an old gold-mining town up there, abandoned long ago."

"And the thunder?" he asked.

She hesitated. "A few times when I was in high school we went up to the mining town, even though we weren't supposed to. I...heard thunder a couple of times. Really loud thunder."

"Exactly." Guy hoped she'd leave it there. But of course she didn't. Every little detail mattered to a cop. To a good cop, anyway.

"What's this all mean, Guy?"

Here we go. He wasn't about to lie. "The mountain speaks to us through that thunder. After the Whites came to mine the gold, our forefathers decided the mountain needed protecting. Gray Cloud is the current guardian. Has been most of his life."

"I won't even ask how he protects it. I'd probably never understand. So it's holy ground?"

Guy nearly winced at the familiar White perception. "*Everything* on this planet is sacred to our way of thinking. Every rock. Every tree. Every animal or plant. It's all sentient. Thunder Mountain stands out the way some places do, but this mountain *speaks*. Let's leave it at that, okay?"

"I'd never understand anyway," she said quietly. "And I'm not being critical, just curious."

He could live with that, he supposed. It wouldn't surprise him, though, if she dismissed it all as superstition. Just about as superstitious as their churches.

Hell, it did no good to think this way. So what if this

woman was peeling him open like the layers of an onion? Someone would have gotten around to it sooner or later, and he didn't mind that it was Valerie. Val.

When the sawmill came into sight, he forgot everything else. Gray Cloud stood there as promised with three pinto horses.

Gray Cloud spoke as soon as they got out of the Suburban. "We'll meet up with Jimmy Two Hands along the way. He's the man who saw the stranger with the small child."

They rode away from the sawmill as the sun began to brighten the day, although they still rode through deep shadows beneath trees.

VALERIE ENJOYED THE ride despite everything. The sway of the horse beneath her, the woods so redolent of evergreens with an earthy smell rising from the duff beneath their horses' hooves. Their saddlebags were full and she wondered what was in them but didn't ask. Gray Cloud carried a rifle in his saddle scabbard, Guy his pistol on his belt. Protection. Against bears or mountain lions maybe?

She found a measure of peace in those hours, admiring the beauty of nature, the beauty of the pintos, which were clearly well-kept. A rare space in time when she could draw a deep breath without aching. The tightness in her chest eased as it hadn't since before she heard the news about Lizzie.

They followed no road, but instead seemed to be riding along game trails. Gray Cloud certainly knew his way through these deep woods. Valerie had no doubt that she could get herself lost in ten minutes out here.

She also knew that the only thing that restrained her impatience was the hope that they'd find something useful at the end of this ride.

Guy drew up beside her a few times to ask how she was. He looked iconic, she thought, astride the horse as if he'd been born in that saddle. His long hair was caught at the nape of his neck in the way she'd become familiar with even though she wasn't used to seeing it on a cop.

"I'm fine," she always answered even though she knew that she was apt to become saddle-sore if this ride went on too long. She didn't care.

What wasn't fine was that she couldn't entirely let go of worry. The man and the child were gone now, Gray Cloud had said. They might find nothing useful at all.

Why the hell would the kidnapper have come to these mountains and woods anyway? Because he felt they would conceal him better? But why did he want to hide so far out of the way with Lizzie?

Questions. Too many questions. Her sense of peace slipped away.

After about three hours, which grew increasingly chilly as they climbed the slope, they came upon a mounted man who was waiting for them on his own pinto.

"Jimmy Two Hands," Gray Cloud said, then introduced Valerie and Guy.

"I know Guy," Jimmy said and didn't sound totally approving. Then he turned his attention to Gray Cloud. "The man is gone. The child with him. They were staying in an abandoned cabin a mile from here. There's some sign."

Sign? Valerie's attention perked.

"Why kind of sign?" Guy asked.

"You'll see."

More riding as Valerie's impatience grew, as any peace

she'd found deserted her. After this they'd have to ride back to Guy's vehicle. Too long, especially if they found anything.

"Any news from Connie Parish?" she asked as Guy drew up beside her again. His radio hadn't crackled once so she knew there was no news. She needed to ask anyway.

"Not yet. She's probably found only more of the same. Mentions but nothing specific. I hope Judge Carter issues that warrant today."

She hoped so, too. Then there'd be so many records to examine. More information, she hoped.

At long last they saw the cabin in the distance, a decrepit box of logs. A small clearing filled with brush surrounded it.

"Whoever lived out here?" Valerie wondered.

"Some old guy," Guy answered. "A hermit who lived off the land."

"An ascetic," Gray Cloud corrected. "Forsaking all civilization to pursue inner knowledge and peace."

That sounded like an interesting story, Valerie thought. She wanted to ask Gray Cloud if he spoke with the mountain, but didn't dare. It was none of her business. Besides, she already felt as if she'd been permitted to know secrets and didn't want to press.

Nothing like a nosy White woman, she thought wryly. Which was probably how they saw her. White. She got it. Guy had been teaching her.

When they reached the cabin, Jimmy Two Hands dismounted and the others followed suit. Apparently these horses didn't need to be hitched or hobbled to keep them from wandering off. Reins were draped over their necks and they were allowed to browse.

Guy pulled two collapsed leather buckets out of his saddlebags and filled them from liter water bottles. For the horses. Well, that probably explained the full leather panniers.

"Before we go in," Jimmy Two Hands said, "let's walk around out here. There's information."

He pointed. "Off-the-road vehicle. He must have come up through that break in the trees. See?" He pointed out faint tracks leading that way.

"That would be an expensive vehicle," Valerie remarked. A clue in itself, perhaps?

Guy shrugged. "He could have rented it. We'll have to check into it."

Gray Cloud spoke. "He's also not allowed to use it here. How long ago, Jimmy?"

"Two days. See how the green parts of the brush are already straightening out?"

A whole lot of info from something that was barely visible to Valerie's eyes. Once it was pointed out to her, faint as it was, she could see it. She'd never have noticed by herself. Her impression of Jimmy Two Hands skyrocketed.

Once the trail of the vehicle had been marked by everyone's gaze, they approached the cabin's single door. It didn't even have a window, although a window would have been madness, given the winter.

Jimmy spoke. "There's not much inside, but enough to make me wonder. We heard about the missing child."

He retrieved a tactical flashlight from his own saddlebag. Gray Cloud pointed to Valerie's horse and she opened one of her own saddlebags, finding three flashlights in there. She passed them out.

"Move carefully," Guy warned. "Disturb nothing."

Jimmy gave him a nod of approval.

Inside, they found a wooden bench and a rustic lumber

table with enough dust to suggest that it had been unused for years. A few empty cans and food packets. Then Valerie drew a sharp breath.

The dust had been disturbed on the bench and the table. Then Guy pointed. "The dirt floor has been messed with in that corner."

"SOMEONE STOPPED HERE," Gray Cloud reminded them. "It might mean nothing."

It might or might not. Narrowing the beam on her flashlight, she began a minute inspection of every part of the cabin, as did Guy. As if they were a forensics team.

Guy hoped for any clue beyond that someone had been here. He was particularly interested in the area of the dirt floor that was a mess of boot prints, and the rough logs around it. He wanted any sign that a child had been here even though a witness had reported it.

He wasn't finding any though and cussed silently. A clue, damn it. A clue. He didn't know how much information it would give them except that Lizzie might have been here. If she had been, that wouldn't tell them where she might have gone, any more than Kell's dog's discovery had. But maybe they'd have something more useful to consider.

Then Jimmy spoke again. "Do you smell it?"

Valerie straightened and sniffed. There it was. "Soiled disposable diapers." Faintly she detected the smell of feces, ammonia and baby powder.

"Buried," Guy said and eyed the disturbed dirt. "Here maybe." He turned to Gray Cloud. "Any kind of shovel?"

Gray Cloud nodded, then went outside to whistle. One of the pintos trotted over. A minute later he returned with a collapsing shovel.

"Here," said Guy, pointing. "He trampled it for a reason." Then he took the tool from Gray Cloud and began digging. He imagined Val's heart was in her throat, as was his. They might find something worse than diapers in here. If the odor *was* diapers.

Val and Gray Cloud kept their flashlights on the area while Jimmy moved around the cabin, continuing to search.

"Lizzie's too old for diapers," Val said, her voice trembling.

Guy answered. "And maybe the kidnapper didn't know any better way to deal with the problem. I doubt he was lugging a kiddie toilet."

Then thunder clapped above them. A clear day but thunder clapped.

"The Chamberlain girl was here," Gray Cloud said, sounding as if he made a statement of fact.

GOD, VALERIE THOUGHT, was the mountain speaking to him? That thunder sure as hell shouldn't have happened. Her world began to spin as it tried to cope with a different reality but her gaze never left the hole Guy was digging.

Then it appeared: a dirty disposable diaper that was folded over. Soon Guy found more.

"The missing girl was here," Gray Cloud said again.

Valerie didn't doubt him for a moment although the diapers may have caused his statement. Her heart thundered as the mountain had. Now what?

She watched as Guy stopped digging and looked at Gray Cloud. "What else?"

God, Valerie thought again. Guy was asking for paranormal information from an elder. As if it were natural and right. Would he act on it?

Gray Cloud tilted his head. "Look east, Guy."

The return journey was faster. As if once having followed the path the horses felt comfortable in trotting back down it.

Her mind was totally blown but that hardly mattered. They'd found possible evidence that Lizzie was still alive. That was what truly mattered.

When she and Guy reached the Suburban, Gray Cloud led the pintos away. For their part, they sped in the vehicle down the nearly abandoned dirt road as fast as they dared.

Valerie, clinging to both hope and a fearful wonder, finally asked, "What happened in that cabin? God, the world just tilted. I can't..."

"Believe it?" Guy asked. "You don't need to. Soon enough you'll find a rational explanation or you'll forget about it. It doesn't fit in your world."

She bit her lip and fell silent. *Something* had happened. Eventually she returned to it. "The mountain spoke?"

"I heard it. Didn't you?"

"The thunder, yes. But how could it carry a message?"

"For those with ears to hear, it does. Does it really matter, Val? We found those diapers. Are you going to ignore what Gray Cloud said about Lizzie being to the east? Do you dare?"

No, she didn't dare ignore it. That much was true. There could be other explanations, for example that when they found the diapers it was easy enough for someone to say Lizzie had been there.

Guy was right. She was going to rationalize it away. She made herself stop. It wasn't respectful of her to dismiss his beliefs. Nor was it fair to Gray Cloud, who had taken the trouble to come to Guy about the stranger and child at the cabin. Whatever had happened, the part about Lizzie being to the east narrowed their search. Since they were finding nothing else, what harm could come from moving their search out to the east, away from the mountain slope?

But there had been that thunder, so sudden and out of nowhere. *That* was hard to explain.

Giving up, she returned to the most important matter: Lizzie.

GUY FELT VAL'S internal struggle as she sat beside him. He had no doubt where it was going to end and told himself it didn't matter.

There were two kinds of non-Native people. First, those who sought out Indigenous teachers to take them into a more mystical world. Sadly, most of those teachers were charlatans, claiming to be something they weren't, claiming an access to knowledge they didn't have. Not to mention that it insulted the beliefs of the Indigenous peoples. A week of sweat lodges and campfire stories in a haze of marijuana or the peyote that was legal only for Natives to use in religious practices. Plenty of money in it for these so-called teachers.

Then there was the other group of non-Natives, the researchers who studied lore and legend then dismissed it all as lore and legend without any basis behind it. Never giving any credence to the idea that those stories might not be apocryphal, but instead carried truth in stories that would easily pass down generation to generation.

He figured Val was going to settle firmly into the latter camp.

Oh well. She had *her* reality. He walked in it daily and understood it even though he didn't entirely lose himself in it.

Crossing a bridge of beliefs could never be without peril.

All that mattered was that they heed Gray Cloud's statement that Lizzie was to the east.

That couldn't be ignored in *any* reality.

Chapter Thirteen

They arrived back in town by late afternoon and stopped first by the sheriff's office. Inside there was a buzz of activity, and without preamble Guy asked, "Anything?"

"Connie's zonked," Artie Jackson replied. "She *did* get enough information at the hospital to get the warrant in front of Judge Carter. We're hoping to have it issued in a couple of hours. You guys?"

Guy answered her. "Lizzie and her kidnapper seem to have been hiding in a cabin at the edge of the reservation. We found used diapers buried there. It was suggested that they're not far to the east of the cabin. I need to make up a new plan of action. Get operations ready to move in the morning. The cadaver dogs?"

"Nothing. Except some old bones that might have belonged to a long-ago miner or an Indian. No one knows how old, yet. Archaeologists are on their way."

"Okay then." He glanced at Valerie. "We can't start much until we have that warrant and we can't act on a new search plan until tomorrow. So I think Val and I are going to get some coffee and dinner from Maude's. I'll have my radio on in case anything turns up, but we both need a break."

"Long ride?" Artie asked.

"Long enough that I think Detective Brighton may well find it hard to move tomorrow."

Valerie was already stiffening up after the drive home, and her thigh muscles and seat were unhappy with her. As were a few other muscles. She sort of limped down the street to the diner.

She spoke just as they were about to enter Maude's. "Do you mind her using the word Indian?"

"Not as much as I mind redskin and Injun. It's okay, however untrue it is."

"Untrue?"

They found a booth near the back.

"Untrue," he repeated. "All because Columbus thought he'd found the West Indies. A slight correction was made with the name Amerindians, but not a good enough one."

"I can get that." Now it even hurt to sit, and she squirmed a little. He must have noticed.

"A hot bath," he suggested. "And some sports cream. We can hit the pharmacy for it after we eat."

"Longest time I've ever ridden a horse," she admitted. "I used to be a regular visitor to a stable where I could pay by the hour to ride. It was actually great, not just the riding but all they taught us about horse care, then made us do it ourselves. I loved it."

"But you don't do it anymore?"

She screwed up her mouth. "I became a detective. There's a huge downside to that promotion."

"On call 24/7," he agreed. "Kinda makes a hash of things."

"I wouldn't trade the job for the streets, though. Patrol cops spend more time being bored than I do."

He smiled faintly. "I spent a lot of hours driving around

out there in a patrol vehicle. I sure got a good look at the countryside, though. Nights spent under the stars or sleeping in the back of my Suburban when I was too far out to return to the office."

"That sounds beautiful. I remember I could see more stars out there than any other place I've visited, except possibly Mesa Verde National Park."

He raised a brow. "I guess you didn't often sleep in the remote areas of the mountains."

She gave a small laugh. "You'd be right. It's a little unnerving when it's so dark you can't see the ground in front of your feet."

"Hence flashlights, lanterns, torches and campfires. Or moonlight."

"I love the moonlight."

"It'll sure wake you up if it hits your eyes while you're sleeping."

Val was trying, Guy saw. Trying very hard to tear her mind away from the pain and worry that tormented her. Well, he wasn't doing much better. He hated that they could do almost nothing right now.

"You know," he said as they finished eating, "it won't help to serve that warrant tonight. They'll be on night staff at the hospital, administration gone for the night. And what will we get anyway? A handful of names to eliminate because I'll bet my badge that the man we want won't be much easier to find than he is now, even with a name. He's gone."

She looked down at her nearly empty plate then pushed it aside. "Let's get some coffee to go. Then I need to get to my sister. God, I can't imagine what she's going through."

"I think you can," he said as he picked up the bill. "You're most of the way there yourself."

Guy dropped Valerie off at the Chamberlain house, ignoring a wish to take her back to her place. Just so he could keep an eye on her, he told himself. But he was getting past the point of believing that was all it was.

"I'll sketch out a search plan for tomorrow," he assured her.

He watched her limp up toward the front door. That woman was going to find it almost impossible to walk tomorrow.

Then he drove to the office to study maps. Online mapping wasn't going to work for this.

INSIDE, VALERIE FOUND that Pastor Molly was still there, dozing in a chair. Molly stirred the instant Valerie entered.

"May is in bed," Molly said. "She's so worn out it's a wonder she wakes up at all. Chet was here for a while, then got called in for a delivery. Complicated, he said."

Hardly surprising, Valerie thought. Chet was always being called in. At least he had something to focus on other than his worry and anguish. May had no such escape.

Valerie sat on the couch with the latte Guy had bought her. "I'm sorry. I didn't think of getting one for you."

Molly looked wry. "I know my way around a coffeepot. Even that fancy espresso maker your sister has. I'm fine and caffeinated to the gills."

"We didn't have any coffee on the ride today. I'm making up for it."

Molly tipped her head. "How'd the trip go?"

"It was long. We *did* find diapers buried in this old log cabin. Reasonably fresh. And tracks of an off-road vehicle that came in and left."

Molly nodded. "I guess that helps. You know when they were there?"

"Left a couple of days ago, Jimmy Two Hands said."

"That long ago? I mean, getting the word here…"

"It's a long way out," Valerie answered. "Took us three hours to get there on horseback. Given the location, I doubt it would have been any faster on an ATV."

Valerie sipped her latte, grateful for its warmth, its flavor. Caffeine started to wake her up. "God, I'm sore from that horse."

Molly laughed quietly. "I've heard about it, but never tried it."

Valerie drank more coffee, then chewed her lip, hesitating. "Molly?" She had a question that wouldn't go away.

"Yes?"

"You're a religious person. I think…" Again Valerie hesitated. Molly waited patiently.

"I don't know if I'm supposed to talk about this," Valerie continued a minute later, her heart tapping nervously. "But while we were out there, we heard a loud thunderclap."

"That's strange. There isn't a storm in sight."

"Which made it astonishing. Then… Gray Cloud spoke. He said with certainty that Lizzie had been the child in the cabin, and that she was east of there."

Molly frowned faintly. "What are you trying to say, Val?"

"That Guy believes that the thunder speaks to Gray Cloud, who is, by the way, the guardian of Thunder Mountain."

"And that troubles you?"

"I don't know what to think. Guy said the thunder speaks to those who have ears to hear it. How do I process that? Is it even remotely possible?"

"You're asking either the right or the wrong person about that depending on your beliefs." Molly smiled. "I believe God speaks to us through our hearts and minds. Sometimes it pops into my head as clear as if I were being spoken to. Not often, but it's happened to me a few times. Not just a feeling, but clear *words*."

Valerie leaned forward, listening.

"You can believe me or not," Molly continued. "Does it fit your own beliefs? It fits into mine. So about Gray Cloud? I'd say that thunder speaks to him. I'd say the breeze breathes secrets and the creaking of trees may be filled with meaning. I suppose that would shock my parishioners if I said it that way, but ears to hear? Yes."

Valerie blew a long breath and leaned back. "Thanks, Molly. I guess Gray Cloud might hear the thunder speak."

"It's all God's creation. Who are we to limit the Almighty?" Molly rose. "I'm going to make myself some coffee."

Halfway to the kitchen, she paused and looked back. "Val?"

"Mmm?" Valerie was still trying to absorb what Molly had said.

"I told you that sometimes I hear God as clear as the spoken word. Wasn't so long ago that I had one of those experiences."

Valerie raised her head. "Yeah?"

"Yeah. I was praying about whether I should take this job. Praying hard, I might add, feeling deeply pulled toward it but resisting the tug, not sure I was strong enough or worthy enough for this task. I kept begging for guidance. Then, as clear as anything, a voice in my head said *I'm telling you but you're not listening.* So here I am."

Wow, Valerie thought. Just *wow*.

Chapter Fourteen

Guy had spent hours poring over terrain maps, determining the possible paths the kidnapper's ATV could travel, figuring out where search parties should move and whether they should go on foot or by horse or their own ATVs.

He wasn't going to leave even a square yard unaccounted for, but plans still had to be made, as did a decision about whether to start with a wide cordon moving in toward the log cabin or whether they should spread out from it.

He snagged a couple of hours of sleep in one of the cots at the back of the building, then dove in again. The list of searchers he needed was massive.

He counted up horses and ATVs, as well as seasoned hikers who would be prepared for the sudden weather changes that could happen in and around the mountains. Prepared to take care of themselves if they became injured.

The numbers were staggering, especially considering that if the kidnapper had ditched the ATV and driven away in an auto, he could have traveled quite a distance. But he hadn't yet. What was holding him in the area?

If they could find an answer to that question this hunt might get a whole lot easier.

But they had more questions than answers and had since the outset. Even the Amber Alert was bringing in no hints.

Well, plenty of people were looking in more distant areas. He had to concentrate on his own patch.

Given the massive numbers of horses, vehicles and people he needed, he started a phone tree going at dawn, each person contacted asked to contact two more and so on. The surrounding ranches sure had plenty of horses and vehicles. The park and forest services might have lists of regular hikers.

He settled on a staging area and arranged as best he could for supplies anyone might need. He ordered the command trailer moved to it along with its generators.

He didn't know if this county had ever organized such a large operation, but the knowledge wouldn't help him now.

This was a whole new ballpark, and not even Gage, with all his experience, seemed to know if this had happened before. If it had, he had never heard of it, nor had the old sheriff, Nate Tate.

A first. He almost wished he wasn't spearheading it.

VALERIE AWOKE SO stiff that when she tried to sit up to get out of the bed, she groaned. Somebody lead her to the ibuprofen, please.

And here she'd thought she was in such great condition. Not.

She found ibuprofen in the medicine cabinet and popped three, regardless of the directions. She could barely wash herself in the hot shower, had trouble toweling herself dry. Pulled her clothes on with more stifled groans.

Sheesh. She left the bedroom hoping the ibuprofen would start working soon.

She found May sitting on the sofa once again. Molly was

there, freshly dressed so she must have found time to slip away during the night. Today she wore an ankle-length skirt instead of slacks.

Coffee smelled fresh in the air, so with a mumbled "Good morning," Valerie headed straight for it. With her mug full, she limped back to the living room and joined the two women.

May looked at her hopefully. "Molly says you found something?"

Ack. No way to be sure except for Gray Cloud's declaration and she still didn't know if he was right. She looked at Molly, then felt her own certainty. She had to share it with May.

"We're pretty sure the kidnapper had Lizzie in a small log cabin on the slope of Thunder Mountain. Guy is working on a new search plan."

"Had?" May repeated. "He took her away again?"

"He's hiding," Valerie said gently. "He doesn't want to be found."

May closed her eyes. "I can't believe someone would do this for no reason. Why no ransom note?"

"It's not for money," Valerie said with conviction. "This guy's got another reason but we don't know what. What we *do* know for sure is that as of two days ago Lizzie was alive."

"How can you know that?" May demanded, her eyes moistening.

"Because we found diapers. Fresh ones."

"Diapers? Lizzie doesn't wear diapers! It can't be her!"

Valerie reached for her sister's hand and quoted Guy. "And this guy can't be carrying a kiddie toilet around with him. Can he?"

May drew a ragged breath. "I guess not. But Lizzie won't

like it. She's so proud of having grown-up panties. Oh, God, she must be so scared! Hating it all. Wondering where I am and why I don't come for her!"

There was no way to dispute that. And no way to evade the likelihood that once they got Lizzie back she was going to be scarred. Maybe for life.

Valerie shoved that aside. Years of counseling might be ahead for Lizzie but all that mattered right now was getting her back healthy and safe. The *only* thing that mattered.

Molly spoke. "May, wherever Lizzie is right now, she knows you love her. She hasn't forgotten that."

"But she must be wondering." May dropped her head. "I can't take this anymore. Lizzie probably can't either."

Molly answered. "Children are a whole lot more adaptable than adults. More accepting of the way things are. You're probably having a far worse time than she is."

Valerie looked at Molly, thinking the pastor couldn't possibly know that, even if it sounded likely given that the kidnapper was taking care of Lizzie well enough to have provided and changed diapers.

But they were apparently the right words for May. She lifted her head. "I hope so. Oh, God, I hope so."

GUY ARRIVED A short time later, looking like a man who was pushing past the limits of fatigue. His voice, though, was as strong as ever.

"A new search party is gathering," he told them. "We're going to have a hundred people or more with horses and ATVs arriving soon, along with a bunch of experienced hikers. And Connie Parish is taking the warrant and a team to the hospital. Administration will begin searching records."

"Oh, thank God," May whispered.

Guy turned to Valerie. "Want to come to the staging area with me, or would you rather join the team at the hospital?"

Valerie didn't hesitate. "I'll go to the staging area."

OF COURSE SHE'D come to the staging area. There'd be more action out there and she couldn't bear the thought of shuffling through mounds of paper, looking for a needle in a haystack. Even though that was often a part of her job, it was a part she didn't want to do just then.

Lizzie was out there. If she took Gray Cloud at his word, as Guy apparently had, then east was the best place to look. Guy was right about the paper search, too. The kidnapper was hiding and a name wouldn't help them much. They still had to find him and Lizzie.

The ibuprofen had begun working and she carried a small bottle of it with her. In case she needed to move quickly, she couldn't afford to be hampered by aching muscles. Although if adrenaline kicked in for some reason, she'd move anyway. And fast.

The staging area took her breath away. It was already a jumble of horses and riders, ATVs and backpackers, all apparently waiting for directions. It wasn't long before Guy had the terrain maps laid out on a long folding table, and with men and women around, separated by means of transport, he began pointing out the directions he wanted them to take.

Valerie got the feeling that these searchers knew the area well enough to simply nod when Guy told them where he wanted them to head.

Valerie turned around slowly, surveying the land she could see. Here the rolling hills that filled most of the county had grown much steeper as they butted up against the mountain. Still full of woods. Ravines and gullies sliced through them. The seemingly gentle roll of the land was deceptive only because the slope of the mountain itself looked so much more treacherous.

As groups of searchers began to spread out, the police K-9s arrived along with Kell and his dog Bradley. Only a few dogs when all was said and done, probably because the sheriff couldn't afford to have very many. K-9s were expensive.

No, not very many K-9s, but each would be an important help. The dogs were assigned to mounted groups, which might easily miss something. Their handlers mounted and went with them.

But the ATVs went alone, something that worried Valerie. If they moved too fast, they could easily miss something. Then there were the hikers. How much terrain could they cover?

Still, the group was impressive in its size, and Valerie tamped down her worries. She was impressed that so many had turned out to help, taking themselves away from other duties and pursuits. All of them set out for rough terrain, places where a child or an ATV could be hidden.

Except that Lizzie was so tiny. And what if the kidnapper had abandoned his vehicle?

It didn't bear thinking about.

Coffee urns had been set up, plugged into the generators, and mounds of dried foods had diminished as the searchers stuffed them into their saddlebags, backpacks and ATV compartments. Then Valerie watched as they disappear over hills and into woods.

So many of them. She still felt a sense of disbelief. And

she desperately wished she was physically capable of going with them.

Then Guy nudged her. "Look."

A new group of at least a dozen mounted men approached, among them Jimmy Two Hands and Gray Cloud. Gray Cloud drew rein in front of Guy. "We're not the only ones among us who are searching. Where do you most need this group?"

Guy looked up at him. "Where are the others?"

"We've been combing the reservation since yesterday morning. Dozens of us. But this team? Where would we be most useful according to your plans?"

Gray Cloud needed only the quickest look at the map and where Guy pointed. With a nod he heeled his horse. With him, fifteen men rode away.

"I can't believe…" Valerie started to say, then sank onto a folding chair.

"What? That so many people give a damn about what happens to a small child they don't even know?"

She shook her head. She didn't know how to explain her incredulity. It was amazing. Overwhelming. Something she had never expected to see and would probably never see again.

Guy disappeared into the operations trailer while Val remained outside. It was a beautiful morning, crisp, clear, perfect. An army had just headed out in nearly every direction to seek Lizzie. An army of volunteers.

The only reason she was sitting here rather than going out with one of the groups was that she'd killed herself riding yesterday. She couldn't mount a horse yet. She doubted she'd do more on an ATV than hang on and groan. As for hiking…well, she was still limping.

Maybe she should have gone to the hospital after all. Reading through patient records would be more useful than where she was now. She hated the feeling of uselessness.

Guy eventually returned and sat in a folding chair beside her. "How are you holding up?"

"Angry that I got so saddle-sore yesterday that I'm no help today."

He shook his head a bit, adjusting his tan uniform Stetson on his head. "There are plenty of people out there. You wouldn't be able to add a thing. Anyway, the cordon is starting to narrow. Nothing yet."

Valerie wasn't surprised. She would have expected him to burst out of that trailer if there'd been any news to share with her.

"If they don't find her..." She let the words trail away. They were obvious.

"Connie says they've managed to get a few names out of staff members and their files are being examined."

Valerie sighed. "Like you said, how much good will that do?"

"Depends," was all he answered.

Eventually she said, "I'm sorry I doubted that Gray Cloud could understand the thunder."

He turned his head, looking at her. "What brought that on?"

"A story Pastor Molly shared with me. Maybe more importantly, something she said along with it."

His gaze grew more intense, those dark eyes pinning her. "Which was?"

"She believes the wind whispers and the trees creak, and those with ears to hear understand. Like you said."

"Anything else?"

This seemed important to him and she understood why. She had doubted his cultural beliefs and now he wanted recognition from someone outside it. "She said it's all God's creation and asked who are we to limit the Almighty?"

Guy nodded and returned his attention to the forest that reached up above him. She noticed for the first time that the evergreens cradled hardwood trees that were just beginning to burst with spring life.

"Life," she said, her mind wandering as it noted the trees, "is both important and precious. *All* of it."

"But right now Lizzie is the most important of all."

Tears pricked her eyes but she didn't give in to them. "I can't thank you enough, Guy. I really can't."

"No need. Look at all the people who are trying to help. Every one of us wants to find that little girl."

"I see that." Her heart nearly burst in a way very different than from grief and fear and anguish. "I don't think I've ever been filled with so many conflicting emotions."

"You're on one hell of a roller coaster ride."

He offered a hand and Valerie took it, nearly clinging to the comfort of his touch, feeling less alone, less tossed on a stormy sea.

Guy glanced at her repeatedly from the corner of his eyes. She was nearing something, he thought. Nearing a breakdown? Or something else? All he knew was that he was worried about her. The rapids they rode in this river could crush her. No amount of experience and training could overcome how personal all of this was to her.

He squeezed her hand gently but didn't let go. If she needed a rock to cling to right now, he would be that rock for her. Whatever it took.

"Lizzie's safe," he said presently.

"I haven't heard the thunder."

He eyed her sharply. "I just know it, Val. I *feel* it. Whatever is going on, this man doesn't want to hurt her. Those diapers prove it, but you don't need me to tell you that."

"No," she agreed quietly. Once again Guy was right.

"So she's safe," he said. "Alive and well, although she's probably not happy right now. She's being sheltered by a sick mind but sheltered regardless."

The wind quickened suddenly and she looked up for the first time. "Oh, God."

Guy followed her gaze. "A storm. A freaking storm." Overhead, gray clouds roiled, coming nearer.

"That'll end the search."

"I doubt it. I seriously doubt it. Those folks out there are determined."

This time she could only hope he was right. "How are the searchers being tracked? Or are they?"

"In this part of the world, satellite phones are common. We're tracking them."

She nodded, hanging on to the reassurance. What else did she have?

Thunder rolled down the mountain and he heard her catch her breath. Rain couldn't be far behind and would chill the kidnapper and his precious burden if they had no shelter.

"God," Val said. "Can it get any worse?"

It could. Guy knew that and was sure she did as well.

He stared up into the boiling clouds and wondered if Gray Cloud heard anything this time. He hoped so.

A COUPLE MORE hours passed fruitlessly. Then Guy's radio crackled. It was Connie.

"We've got a dozen names, Guy," she said. "I'm sending people out to question them now."

"Read me the names," he said to her, and listened to the list.

Then she said, "Margolis. Phillip and Etta Margolis."

Guy rose instantly to his feet. "The Margolis place is closer to us than to you, Connie. I'm heading that way."

The rain began to fall, just gently. It was going to get worse.

As if summoned, Gray Cloud and his pinto emerged from the growing mist of rain. Guy waited impatiently for the elder to draw close.

Sitting straight in his saddle, Gray Cloud pointed. "That way. One of us found the ATV in a ditch hidden beneath tumbleweed. The girl is alive." He slid from his saddle and approached the maps that were still laid out on the table. He bent over them, studying them, then pointed to a spot with his index finger. "Here." Then he mounted again and headed in that direction, off the rez into a world more hostile to him.

Guy's heart sank. That wasn't in the direction of the Margolis place. Gray Cloud had indicated ranch land, wide-open spaces of brush and greening grasses.

For once he chose to ignore Gray Cloud. He poked his head into the ops van and said, "I'm going to be away from the staging area for a while. Radio me." Without another word, Valerie in tow, he headed for his Suburban.

They had to start somewhere and the mention of the Margolises might be the only concrete information they could get.

He knew exactly where the Margolis couple lived. In the

past he'd been called out there several times for domestic disturbances. Phillip Margolis was a slimeball.

ETTA MARGOLIS SAT at her kitchen table, a cold cup of hot chocolate in front of her. She didn't want to walk to the mailbox, fearing another note from Phillip. Instead she used the growing storm as her excuse. When rain started to fall, her excuse became a good reason.

She had long since grown to distrust her ex-husband. Over the years she had learned that he was willing to lie and cheat, and that he could become violent, oftentimes with little reason that she could tell.

She was well rid of him. She never wanted to see or hear from him again.

But those notes niggled at her. What the hell was Phillip up to now? And how did it involve her?

That stuff about having found a kid for them increasingly bothered her. Surely he hadn't done something wrong. Not something like that. Beating her, throwing things, cussing, conning, stealing when he could, justifying every horrendous thing he did? Yeah, that was Phillip.

But she still believed there had to be some things he wasn't capable of.

They had already lost one baby. Etta didn't want another.

Chapter Fifteen

Guy and Valerie reached the end of the forest service dirt road and turned onto a county road that was in little better condition. County funds had managed to pave a lot of outlying roads, but maintaining them was expensive, too. Guy had to steer around a lot of potholes, the result of winter, slowing the trip more than he would have liked.

Valerie spoke as they jolted along. "What's with the Margolises? Why did you jump into high gear when you heard the name? It's not just that it's closer for you to reach, is it?"

He gave a slight shake of his head as they rose over another sharp bump. "I know that couple in all the wrong ways. Too many calls for domestics."

"Hell," Val said quietly. "So they're dangerous?"

"In this way? I don't know. I'm sure it's not Etta, but her husband, Phillip? I'm not as sure about him." He paused, steering them around a pothole. "That man is violent and it doesn't take much to set him off, near as I can tell. Full of rage."

Valerie didn't speak, but a glance at her told him she had paled.

"Listen," he said, "this is probably a wild-goose chase,

but I *can* get there faster than anyone else. Keep in mind that whoever has Lizzie is taking care of her. Okay?"

"Okay."

"I just want to clear the plate of this one item. That's it."

"I understand. And then?"

"Then we'll see."

VALERIE STARED OUT the Suburban's window at the countryside that jolted by. They were leaving behind the location where the search was ongoing, and driving away from the area that Gray Cloud had indicated. Had the kidnapper really moved again? Now Gray Cloud and his team had found the ATV. Why was Guy ignoring that?

Was she clinging to the thinnest of straws, a man who heard thunder speak and said Lizzie was alive?

She turned her head to look at Guy. His strong face had settled into lines of stone. He was holding himself in tightly.

Guy was a cop, she thought. Following the most important hard evidence rather than his elder. She judged the tug between two worlds must be hard for him, but he still chose the path of a true investigator.

The gentle rain was falling here, too, enough of it to make Guy lean forward to see obstacles in the road. She heard another roll of thunder and wondered almost wildly if that would change the direction of the search again. She felt as if she were becoming untethered from reality and tried to convince herself it was just stress and lack of sleep.

Then she looked again at the man beside her and realized that Guy was firmly tethered to reality, even if they were two slightly different realities. She gazed at him, envying his strength. He straddled such a fine line while remaining steady. Steadfast.

She wondered what she would have done without him.

The wipers continued to *thwap* and the rain grew heavier. Lizzie was out there somewhere. In the cold and wet. She could only hope the SOB had her inside and protected.

When she saw a few flakes of snow begin to drift down, she nearly wanted to scream. Did it have to keep getting worse?

"Not much farther," Guy said almost abruptly.

He seemed to be getting angry.

"Do you think Lizzie will be there?"

"I don't know. I'd like to think Etta would have acted if Phillip had showed up with a kid. But I don't know for sure. He damn near killed her a couple of times."

Val knew such situations intimately. "She'd be terrified."

"She's *lived* terrified. Never could get her to press charges, though. I tried. Kerri Canady tried. It seemed all she wanted was to put an end to the abuse, temporarily anyway. But fear still held her prisoner."

Valerie had often thought the story of abuse to be a sad one. People wondered why the abused spouse didn't just leave. Those people didn't know how such terror could become an iron cage.

"There's the road. I guess you'd call it a driveway." He swung the vehicle sharply to the left and they began bouncing down an even worse road, at the end of which waited the Margolis house. About a mile away, Valerie judged. A lonely house in the middle of nowhere.

Her hands knotted into fists. *Please let Lizzie be there.*

GUY PULLED RIGHT up to a battered porch, tugged a rain cover over his cowboy hat and hurried to climb out. Valerie joined him, heedless of the growing downpour.

Guy pounded on the door. No gentle knock of announcement, but a full police banging that demanded attention.

Half a minute later the door opened, showing a thin, bedraggled woman who bent as if she were old.

"Deputy Redwing," she said dully. "I didn't call you."

"Let us in, Etta. We need to talk."

Etta nodded and stood back from the door, giving them entry. Inside, the small house spoke of deep poverty, everything worn out, the walls peeling, the wood floors warped.

"This is Detective Valerie Burton," Guy told Etta. Then he waved a hand. "Etta Margolis."

"I got coffee," Etta said nervously.

"No thanks," Guy answered. "Where's Phillip?"

"I don't know." Etta sagged into a chair at a battered kitchen table that was part of what might be called the living room. Behind her was a stove, a small slab of counter and a sink with a hand pump. "I don't know."

"Why don't you know?"

Etta shook her head. "Ain't seen that bastard in more'n two years."

Now Guy pulled out two chairs, taking one himself and waving Valerie to the other. "That's good, Etta."

"Damn straight," the woman said more firmly than Valerie would have expected, given that she looked as weak as a frail bird. "I swear if he shows his face around here ever again, I'll get the shotgun. I shoulda got it years ago."

"I wouldn't have blamed you," Guy answered. His voice had grown kind, as if he felt badly for this woman.

"The rest of the law would've." Etta regarded him. "Why you want Phillip?"

"Just need to ask him a few questions."

Etta shrugged. "Ain't got no idea what that man's up to now."

"I guess not." Guy paused. "You know we're looking for a little girl who disappeared a few days ago. Chet and May Chamberlain's daughter."

Val saw Etta pale even more, if that were possible. Her heart started galloping when the woman's eyes slid away. Etta knew something.

"Didn't hear. Their baby's gone?"

"Somebody took her."

It seemed a long time before Guy spoke again. "I heard you and Phillip got really angry when you lost your baby."

Etta sagged a bit. "*Phillip* got angry. He hit me a lot. Blamed me and the doctor for it."

Valerie leaned forward, needing to hear more. She spoke carefully. "But *you* didn't get angry?"

"I was too busy hurting. Grieving. That man wouldn't give me no space to cry, just blamed me until I couldn't find a tear left."

God, what an image, Valerie thought. What an awful, horrible image. How terrible this woman's life had been. "I'm so sorry," she said.

"It's done. Gone. That man took to his heels cuz I said I'd shoot him in his sleep if he didn't stop. Guess he believed me." Then Etta looked at Guy. "The baby was kidnapped?"

"That's how it looks. Thought I'd check with you in case Phillip…"

Etta interrupted him. "He might coulda."

GUY HEARD VALERIE draw a sharp breath. Now she'd be hanging on tenterhooks, not that it would do any good.

Sadly, he believed Etta when she said she didn't know where her husband was. No help in that.

But he pressed ahead with questioning her. "You have any reason to think that? Any idea at all?"

Etta gave a jerky nod. "Got two notes from him. First one just upset me, but I didn't make nothin' of it. Threw it in the compost without reading it. Then I got another one and thought he'd lost his mind. If he ever had one."

Guy heard Valerie breathing quickly now. They were on the edge of something. How much good it would do he couldn't yet know.

"The second note," he prompted gently.

Etta looked at him, and for the first time expression creased her face. Alarm? "Said he found a baby for us. Couldn't think how. Thought he was lyin' again. Nobody'd let that man adopt a kid. But..." The word trailed off.

Now Guy was leaning forward a bit, his deliberately relaxed posture gone. "Where'd the note come from? Do you still have it?"

"Out with the compost like the first one."

"Did you see a postmark?"

"Don't recall." Then Etta started shaking her head and her whole body began to rock. "Shoulda kept 'em. Now they's on the compost heap. Ain't nobody gonna find 'em now." Then tears started to roll down her face.

"Kidnapping a baby," she mumbled. "Sweet Mother Mary, that man's eviler than Satan hisself."

As soon as they were back in the vehicle, Guy reached for his SAT phone.

"I need two things yesterday," he told dispatch. "I need an urgent bulletin put out on Phillip Margolis. He might have

Lizzie Chamberlain. Then I need three or four people out here to go through a compost heap looking for envelopes he might have sent to his wife. I need a postmark."

An affirmative answer crackled back to him.

Then he added, "Oh, and a third thing. Tell ops to start reeling in the search parties. I have information that's going to redirect us. I'm headed that way now."

Val looked at him. "What Gray Cloud said? I thought you were ignoring him."

Guy shook his head. "Never wise to ignore that man. I prioritized. We got our information, such as it is, and the gear is ratcheting even higher."

He pounded his hand on the steering wheel.

"If we hadn't found those diapers yesterday, I'd be scared to death for Lizzie now. Phillip Margolis. A damn grenade just waiting for someone to pull the pin."

Then he jammed the Suburban into gear and they took off again, this time with less respect for the condition of the roads and the heavily falling rain.

Thunder boomed again, louder and more threatening. Overhead, the skies darkened and wept copious tears.

PHILIP MARGOLIS HUNKERED down in the remains of a sod hut built ages ago by some settler. It didn't have much inside it, but at least it still had a roof.

He'd never have guessed a kid could cry so much. The sound was driving him out of his gourd. Changing her diapers didn't help. Wrapping her in stolen blankets, including a ratty one he'd had for himself, didn't help. Mashed canned food didn't help.

If he hadn't promised the kid to Etta he'd have left it somewhere for the coyotes.

He could hardly believe now that he'd ever wanted a kid so much that he'd raged like an angry bull when they lost it. If a kid this old could make such a ruckus, he figured a brand-new one would be even noisier and unhappier. And every bit as stinky.

He'd have to get to a store soon. All the food he'd stuffed into his beat-up old truck was getting sparse. He needed more of those damn diapers, too. He wondered desperately if candy would make that kid shut up.

For the first time in his life, Phillip Margolis pondered whether he'd made a bad plan. All to get that damn woman back, a woman who made him mad but at least took care of him to his own specifications. The only good thing he could say about Etta. How had he figured she'd come back to him just for a shrieking kid?

That kid now renewed its hollering with a particularly high note that caused him to want to rip out his ears.

Coyotes were beginning to sound better by the minute.

Chapter Sixteen

Before they reached the staging area, Valerie spoke. "I'm thinking."

"Tell me," Guy said, his voice threaded with steel.

"If Phillip wants to give Etta a baby, he'd have to be circling closer to her, wouldn't he?"

Guy was silent for all of two seconds. "That's brilliant, Val. Why didn't I think of that?"

"Probably because you're so worried about Lizzie."

"Like you aren't?"

Valerie saw his hands tighten around the steering wheel, his knuckles turning white. It'd be a wonder if he didn't leave depressions in that wheel.

Valerie's heart was shredding even more than it already had. A man who was like a grenade waiting for someone to pull the pin? She shuddered, thinking of little Lizzie in his hands.

She spoke again. "We'll have to be very careful if we start to close in on him."

"No kidding."

Because that man, if he felt he were losing his last hope of getting Etta back by way of a child, might do anything.

Become like a cornered animal. What might he do to Lizzie then? "Why would he want Etta back?"

"Because he's missing his punching bag? Because he's missing his docile little caretaker? Because he wants total power over someone? Hell, I don't know. I never know what makes people like him tick."

Nor did Valerie. They had all kinds of excuses, these abusive people. Bottom line, it was always someone else's fault that they lost control. They'd *had* to do it.

She'd heard that excuse from murderers, too. They hadn't *meant* to kill. It wasn't *their* fault. Of course, she'd met those with another kind of excuse, too. *Someone told me to do it. I was afraid not to do what I was told.*

Rarely did you get one who'd admit he got his jollies from the power over life and death. That it was a high for them. Most of them were braggarts, proud of themselves. Many of that type bragged to too many friends, giving the cops a prime suspect.

She shook her head, realizing she was wandering useless corridors in her mind. Trying not to think about what could happen to Lizzie in the hands of someone like Phillip Margolis.

It was just too much.

When they reached the staging ground again, searchers were beginning to regather. Valerie wouldn't have blamed them for calling it a day, not in that constant rain with the deep chill it brought along. They sure looked a lot more tired than early that morning and were guzzling coffee from white foam cups.

A tarp had been erected over the coffee urns and a long table. Someone had hauled in more boxes of dried foods. Getting ready for another round.

Guy pulled out the terrain maps again, spreading them on the table, this time looking at the area around the Margolis house. He pored over them with the aid of a bright lantern. Valerie looked closely as well, trying to sort it all out herself.

Guy put his thumb on the map. "This is the Margolis house, right about here. Now we've got to consider Phillip might be circling in on it. But how far out would he go first?"

He raised his head, clearly thinking. "To the east, Gray Cloud said. But that was earlier. Assuming the elder was right, what would that tell us about where he's traveling? He's already come quite a distance from the Chamberlain house. If he's slowly closing in…" Guy bent to the map again.

Valerie spoke. "The Chamberlain house is where?"

Guy stabbed at it.

"And the cabin?"

Again his thumb pointed. "Here."

"And the ATV?"

She looked at him and saw his eyes widen a shade. He traced the map from May's house to the cabin then to the general area Gray Cloud had said was to the east. Then to the abandoned ATV. Which put that area north of the Margolis place. "To the east all right, but a big circle, far from a direct line to his house."

Then he lifted his head. "You did it, Val."

She guessed she had. Somehow.

Guy spoke. "I've got a plan."

That was the best thing she'd heard all day.

IT WAS AN hour or more before searchers headed out. They fueled up first. Some departed from the group apologetically, but livestock needed tending no matter what. Others began to trail in from their morning searches, having gotten so far out.

But new searchers had arrived, too, and hearing Guy's plan they were eager to get going. Again the search areas were sectioned, but everyone got the same message. "You see anything, report it, but don't try to get close to the guy. We don't want him to feel cornered."

And then what? Val wondered, chewing her lip until it started to feel sore.

Guy surprised her by reaching out and touching her lip lightly. "You're going to shred yourself. Find a different nervous habit."

His touch was welcome and despite everything she had to smile faintly. Somehow he always managed to drag her out of the pit, just a little. He had a gift for that.

"This is awful," she said needlessly.

"Just remind yourself of all the times you've had to wait for reports to come in from the streets, from door-knocking. That's what this is."

"Obviously it feels different."

"No shock there."

More thunder boomed hollowly. People were risking lightning strikes out there, risking their necks in more ways than one in this storm. Valerie rubbed her neck, trying to ease the tension that made it ache. "Why did we have to get a storm?"

"Ask the mountain," Guy said with a shrug. "It makes its own weather, like a lot of mountains."

She turned toward him. "Can you hear it?"

"Hear it speak, you mean?"

Valerie nodded.

"When I was a kid, I thought so a few times. Didn't know if I imagined it and haven't heard it since so maybe I did."

She hesitated. "Maybe you shut it down."

He snorted. "I had a lot of more important things on my mind at the time, it's true. Besides, I never had the makings of a medicine man."

Whatever that meant, Valerie thought, but didn't want to probe into places she might not be welcome. She didn't want to do a single thing that might make Guy uncomfortable. He was an admirable man in so many ways.

The chill was beginning to reach through her clothes so she took a package of beef jerky. A good way to chew off anxiety while fueling her body. And it *did* need fuel. "What's that?" she asked, pointing to a paper-wrapped package.

"Deer jerky. You should try it."

"I accept beef as part of the food chain. I haven't quite gotten to deer."

That pulled a short laugh from him. "Deer look cute, don't they? But they sure can be nasty if they get afraid or annoyed. It's like a horse. You don't want to be at the back end if something scares it." Then he shrugged. "We're blessed with all kinds of food, we're grateful for it, and never take more than we'll eat, at least not directly from nature. I won't say anything about packaged foods."

That tugged another small smile from her. "They get on the reservation, too, huh?"

"Hell yeah. We're not saints and no way can we make a Cheeto. Like everyone else, we got polluted." He winked. "Just normal folk."

Mostly, she thought. Except for people like Gray Cloud. Then she remembered Pastor Molly's story.

Okay, then. Just like everyone else on this planet. *Her* world was sure full of people who thought they had a direct line to the Almighty. Or at least claimed to.

"I'd like to know more," she said to Guy.

"Maybe another time. When all this is settled. Then we'll see."

Except that she'd be on her way back to Gunnison, leaving behind what she had begun to think could be a marvelous journey.

Leaving Guy behind.

GRAY CLOUD RETURNED ALONE, water dripping from his oilskins. "He's still out there," he said to Guy. "Hasn't moved. Keep looking."

"Got a pinpoint on him?"

Gray Cloud shook his head, looking surprisingly wry. "Little is given, much has to be learned, usually the hard way." Then he rode away.

Valerie sighed. "Not helpful."

"You're wrong," Guy answered flatly. "He just told us the guy isn't moving. And he didn't say anything about Lizzie. She isn't dead."

"How can you know that?" she demanded, once again on the edge of screaming. "You can't *know* that!"

He regarded her stolidly. "He'd have known if she wasn't."

Valerie walked away, hardly noticing that the rain was beginning to let up.

Nothing. Every damn move in this hunt turned up nothing. What the hell good did it do to believe that Phillip Margolis was behind this? It didn't get them anywhere.

They still had to *find* that bastard.

GUY WATCHED HER walk away. He'd have given his life to put Lizzie into her arms, into May's arms. But they still needed to find her, to find Margolis. There was an awful lot of land out there. Too much, maybe.

He rubbed his brow and adjusted his Stetson. Wearing his uniform sure wasn't greasing the wheels on any of this. Except for Gray Cloud. He wondered if the elder would have come forward with what he heard in the thunder if Guy hadn't been leading this hunt.

Or maybe he would have, despite expecting to be dismissed or thought crazy. Gray Cloud cherished life, all life. He'd have done what he could have, even risking scorn. Guy knew him well enough to believe that.

The rain was lessening, but that wouldn't change the conditions out there for the search parties. The land was a mire protected only by brush and wild grasses that might ease their movement. Maybe.

It was his turn to pray, and he prayed to all the gods he'd ever heard of. The One God.

Inevitably he remembered what Pastor Molly had said. *Who are we to limit the Almighty?*

He decided that he might make an effort to get to know the pastor better. To discover more about that woman and her broader beliefs.

He might like her a whole lot.

But then his thoughts returned to Lizzie. Of all the people to have taken her... Phillip Margolis. A monster.

PHILLIP MARGOLIS COULDN'T stand the crying anymore. He stepped out into the lessening rain to escape. The only thing that ever quieted that brat was riding in the truck. As if it somehow soothed her. The only thing that did. He had to get out of here.

But the idea of taking the truck and moving right then proved impossible. The sod hut had kept out the rain, but when he stepped out he saw the small rivers running downhill along the side of it.

His truck would just get mired. He cussed. He swore every ugly word he knew, then cussed them all over again.

And then, out of the blue, came the memory of Etta threatening to shoot him while he slept.

Maybe his plan to get her back was stupider than he thought.

Being stuck here with that kid was a nightmare. The only consolation he had was that no one could know *he* was the one who had taken that screaming kid. He could abandon that brat and head for the hills as soon as the ground dried a bit.

And that didn't sound like the worst idea he'd ever had.

But what about getting that woman back? Etta. She belonged to him. She was his property as he'd proved countless times. She'd do anything he said.

Including coming with him and that kid as far as he wanted to take them, far beyond detection, to a place they weren't known at all.

She might even be able to quiet that squalling. That was what mothers did, wasn't it?

He stomped down on his own frenzy. He had to get to Etta as soon as possible. Had to get them all away from Conard County. Soon.

If only the ground would dry enough that his truck wouldn't get stuck in mud. Getting stuck would be enough to make him want to kill.

VALERIE RETURNED FROM the mist, walking straight toward Guy. Some of the searchers were returning, carrying
bad news about the sogginess of the terrain. Some of the
ATVs were finding it impossible to continue. Another strike
against this whole idea.

Guy turned from the men and women he was talking to
and looked at Valerie. "You gonna be okay?"

"I don't even know what okay is anymore. I need to do
something, Guy. Sitting around like this isn't helping. I've
got to *act*."

He understood. He wasn't far from feeling the same way
himself. "But how?" he asked reasonably. "You're just one
person, and if you join the search how much will you add?"

"How can you be so calm?" she demanded.

"Because someone has to be. Someone needs to oversee
all this." He balled his fists. "Someone, Val. You know that."

She looked away, giving herself a little shake. "I still need
to do more than sit around waiting for news."

He drew a long breath and expelled it between his lips.
"You got an idea?"

"I'll go to Etta's place. Wait *there*. He has to come eventually."

"You might be spotted by Margolis."

She shook her head. "If I am, he won't know who I am.
Most people don't know yet that I'm a cop. I haven't been
around long enough. Anyway, I'd be surprised if the grapevine traveled to Etta. She's as isolated as anyone I've ever
seen."

He couldn't argue against that, especially considering that
Etta hadn't even known about the kidnapping. "I warned
you about Margolis. He's unpredictable and dangerous. You
should be armed."

She pulled back the left side of her jacket, revealing her waist holster. "I have my service pistol. But if you think I'm going to shoot anywhere near Lizzie, you couldn't be more mistaken. I'll find another way to deal with him."

Guy reluctantly nodded, completely unhappy with her decision but knowing there was probably no way to stop her. "You can't go alone."

"What, am I going to drive up to that house in your official vehicle? Make a grand appearance that'll keep him away if he's anywhere in sight?"

"Then how are you going to get there?"

She looked around, waving her hand at all the pickups scattered around. "I'll borrow a vehicle."

Guy thought about it for little more than a split second. "I'm going with you. I won't go in the house, though. I'll wait somewhere out of the way in case he shows up. Promise me one thing, though. You'll arrange for Etta to get Lizzie out of his arms before he knows you're there."

She nodded. "Fair enough. I thought about that, but I still won't go in a cop car."

She was right, of course. He considered the problem for a minute or so, then keyed his radio. Static answered him, so he reached for the satellite phone.

"Joe?" he said. "Cal?"

"Yo," came an answer from Joe.

"Can you lend me your truck?"

The answer was prompt. "Keys are still in the ignition. Help yourself."

"Thanks. I take it you haven't seen anything else?"

"One of our group seems to remember an old sod hut about three miles from here. We're closing in on it. Carefully, like you said."

Guy stepped inside the command trailer and looked at the maps on the video screen. "I see you."

"Then come on down if'n you want."

Guy disconnected the call and emerged from the trailer to find Valerie looking sodden and forlorn. She sure as hell couldn't ride a horse. She was still moving gingerly.

He told her what Joe had said.

"Maybe," she answered, "we ought to go to that hut."

"Maybe. But what if he's already moved again? What if he sees us coming?" He knew he kept throwing up roadblocks but he had to consider every possibility.

She chewed her lip again, staring out into the deepening dusk. "It's got to be the Margolis house then. He *does* want to bring Lizzie to Etta."

As good an answer as any. He turned operations over to Artie Jackson and Mark Alton, both adequately experienced to take over now.

"I'll keep in contact," Guy told them, "but at some point I'm going to have to go dark. Don't worry, but I can't risk the sound of a radio or phone."

Then he joined Valerie at Joe's truck, a crew cab in silvery gray, with high suspension and four-wheel drive. It looked as battered as any working truck out here.

"You're going to freeze to death," was all he said to Valerie as they drove away. As soon as he could he turned the truck's heater to high. The blast felt good to his own cold skin. To hers, too, he imagined.

"I didn't exactly come dressed for a downpour," she answered. Nor did she sound as if she cared.

THE JOLTING OF the truck over the bad roads reminded Valerie that she still hadn't recovered from her trip on horseback. Pawing in her pocket, she found the small bottle of ibuprofen and swallowed the pills dry. This truck didn't have soft suspension, and each jolt reminded her of her overworked muscles, some of which she probably hadn't used enough over recent years.

"I need to find time to get back to the gym," she remarked, again trying to distract herself even as her nerves ratcheted up.

"I don't know how much that would help saddle-soreness."

Maybe nothing could, except riding for hours nearly every day. "I feel like a wimp."

"That's the last thing I'd call you."

Small comfort.

SHE TOOK AN opportunity to call May. Guy listened, wishing he could help as he heard Val's side of the conversation.

"Everybody's out looking," Valerie said to May. "Damn near the whole county, as far as I can tell. It's amazing, May."

A pause. Then, "We think we might be closing in on the kidnapper. But I can't be sure. Still, the guy seems to be taking care of Lizzie. Count on that, May. I'll let you know as soon as we have anything."

As unsatisfactory a call as Guy could imagine, but a few scraps for May to cling to. That woman *needed* to cling to hope.

"How's she doing?" Guy asked when Valerie disconnected.

"About as well as anyone could, I guess. She's still breathing, anyway."

"And Chet?"

"Somehow he's managed to be there most of the day. I guess the Conard County birth rate has temporarily dropped."

Guy heard a touch of bitterness in her voice. "Big problem, huh?"

"Not until Lizzie came. Not until May quit her teaching job to become a full-time mother."

"That'd be a heck of a change."

"Too much, I guess. I read that some men get resentful because they're no longer the center of attention for their wives. I don't know for sure because I didn't get Chet's side of the divorce. Not really."

"Some men need to grow up," Guy said sharply.

"Yeah."

He allowed the silence to dominate, along with the *thwap* of the windshield wipers and the creaks from a truck that was getting old from rough use. Eventually he tried to distract her again. Little else he could do.

He spoke. "I guess you study up on human psychology."

"Like Gray Cloud said, some of it we learn the hard way. But yeah, I'm kind of a student."

"Me, too. Always looking for answers for why people behave the way they do."

"Biggest mystery of the universe, as mysterious as black holes and the big bang."

"Those are two things that blow my mind."

She answered with surprising wryness, given the circumstances. "Seems physicists and cosmologists would agree with you."

Another window into this woman, one he liked. They read the same things, were fascinated by the same things. Another link. One he wasn't at all sure he wanted.

THEY REACHED THE Margolis homestead. Rain still fell dismally, although much more lightly. Valerie climbed out and walked to the front door. As soon as Etta opened it and let her in, Guy drove away. She had no idea where he was going but was certain he'd do the wisest thing. She trusted his experience and knowhow. Maybe more than she trusted her own.

Etta was surprisingly glad to see her.

"I didn't want to sit here alone," Etta said. "Not all alone and waiting for Phillip. God knows what he'll do to me. Or that baby. Let me make coffee and soup. You look cold to the bone."

Valerie noticed that the shotgun now stood beside the door. Ready. A change seemed to have come over Etta, too. She no longer looked as shrunken, as hopeless. Maybe she was looking forward to putting two loads of birdshot into her husband.

That wouldn't be surprising.

Etta soon served her hot coffee and a big bowl of canned chicken soup.

"I can't thank you enough for this," Valerie told her.

"Least I can do. I'm grateful you came. Because he's coming. I feel it in my bones. That man would never let me go. I shoulda known that a couple of years wasn't enough for him to get the message."

Etta faced her across the battered kitchen table. "Those deputies didn't find much in the compost heap. Didn't think they would. I buried the damn stuff good."

"How come?"

"Because I was pissed. Crawling back like the slime he is. A snake, although maybe that ain't fair to snakes. Somehow I knew he'd never let go. I was just beginning to hope."

God, this woman still had some fire in her. It was almost as if these events had awakened her from despair.

Valerie's phone rang and she pulled it out of her pocket. Guy.

"I'm in position, Val," he said. "I'm going dark now."

"That's a good idea," Valerie answered. "I'll do that, too."

"Just remember, this puts you on your own."

"I'm not alone. Etta's locked and loaded and ready to shoot."

Guy's laugh was genuine but brief. "Give that woman kudos for me."

Val disconnected and turned her phone off. "Guy's out there. Ready. He said to give you props."

Etta smiled faintly. "Nothin' I ain't wanted to do for years. Just get that little girl away from him, then look out."

Valerie reached across the table, covering Etta's cold, bony hand with her own. "Not unless there's no other choice, Etta. You don't want to go to jail."

"I been in jail most of my grown life. At least in jail I wouldn't be worrying about *him*."

GUY HAD DRIVEN up the road until he'd found a short turnout that ended in barred fence facing a cattle chute. The chute would guide livestock straight into the back of a waiting truck.

He checked his GPS, recalled the terrain map from memory and set out at a slow jog. He had a good idea of where he needed to go.

Finally he hunkered down behind a low hillock that gave him a view of the Margolis house through his night vision goggles. Here he felt no one would be able to come up from behind him without him knowing first. Soggy as the ground was it might deaden footsteps, but on high alert he was sure he wouldn't miss the smallest sound.

Considering the problem, though, he decided that Phillip Margolis would have to come by truck. He couldn't possibly intend to slog his way over so much open ground with Lizzie in his arms. Besides, he'd need his vehicle, whatever it was, to make a quick escape.

He had little doubt that Phillip intended to abscond with both the little girl and his wife. Not if he meant what was in his note.

Nope. Margolis intended to make a clean getaway with them.

He wondered if the cordon was closing in tightly enough to worry Margolis. If he'd caught wind of the search. That might complicate everything. Might put Lizzie in greater danger.

Hell and damnation.

THE WAIT WAS no easier at the house, Valerie thought. Nerves crawled along her skin. This might conceivably take days, especially the way the weather had been today.

Etta seemed okay with the waiting. Naturally she was. She didn't want to see that man again in this lifetime.

"Remember," she said more than once to Etta, "you want to pretend you're happy about the baby. Take Lizzie from his arms. Can you do that?" The question seriously worried her. Most people were lousy actors.

"'Course I can," Etta answered. "Been pretending with that man for a long time. Could never let him see nothin' but fear. He never guessed how I really felt, not until I said I'd shoot him."

Then this might work, Valerie thought. It might. "He can't know I'm here."

"You don't have to tell me that. Get the baby, then you take care of him. I hope you shoot him."

Valerie surely wanted to. Then they both settled back into the endless wait. Etta dozed on a battered, nearly shredded sofa in the main room. Valerie sat in the dark on a chair in the tiny bedroom. No way could she sleep on it because it was like sitting on hard lumps.

But she didn't want to sleep. Someone had to remain awake.

At least Guy was out there somewhere, although he might not be able to do much from where he was.

But if her plan in this house went awry and Margolis got away with Etta and Lizzie, Guy would take care of it.

With that, for now, she had to be content.

Except contentment was not part of her basic mood. No, she kept thinking about Guy in ways that felt awful in the present circumstances. How could she let desire run through her *now*?

She had Lizzie to worry about. So why was she thinking about a tall, strong man with an unmistakable Indigenous face, a man in whom she sensed a deep-rooted anger? Why was she thinking about how sexy he was, how fascinating?

About how much better she wanted to know him.

She ought to feel disgusted with herself under these circumstances, but disgust refused to come.

All she felt was a longing, a yearning. One that could never amount to anything. Not when she had to leave. Not when he had every right to scorn her world.

And, by extension, to scorn her.

God, she was a flaming mess.

THE STORM HAD PASSED. Phillip Margolis stepped outside the tiny hut. At least the brat had fallen asleep, the only escape he got. This was a stupid idea. He wanted to kick his own butt.

At least the ground felt firmer now. The little rivers were slowing down as they passed the hut. Soon he'd dare to move. Probably not until late tomorrow when night might provide some cover.

Not that he expected anyone to be interested in his place. No reason. They didn't know about him.

The moon peeked between scudding clouds, giving him some light to see by. Dawn was almost here.

He turned around to go back inside when he caught sight of movement atop a nearby hill.

His heart nearly stopped. Two men on horseback. Were they hunting for him? He swore under his breath. What now? He was sure he'd left no trail.

But then the two men turned their mounts away, disappearing behind the hill.

Margolis began to breathe again. Just a couple of cowboys checking out the range after the storm. That was all they could be. Because no one on this damn planet could know *he'd* taken the kid. Or where he was hanging out.

No one. He'd made damn sure of that.

But once again he thought about leaving that kid behind and just getting out of here.

Then he thought about Etta. He wanted that woman back where she belonged, and the brat was the price of taking her back.

She'd want the kid. Of course she would. After they'd lost their own, she'd never stopped sniveling no matter how many times he hit her. That had been almost as infuriating as that kid inside the hut.

Settled in his own mind, he went back inside to enjoy a little quiet. He'd have liked a fire, but that was too dangerous, smoke coming out of an abandoned hut.

He was too smart to make that mistake. Then he decided he was a pretty smart man.

There was no way on earth that they knew who had taken the kid, and they had no way to find him.

Satisfied, he even let himself sleep in an ancient chair. The silence from the brat was a relief.

Chapter Seventeen

Morning's gray light began to glow dimly in the east. Guy rubbed his eyes to clear the grit out of them, then returned to watching the house.

Soon the sky grew brighter, a crystalline light purified by yesterday's storm. Probably pretty, but he was in no mood to notice. The night's cold and damp had made him ache a bit, and he longed to stand up and move around, but didn't dare for fear of being spotted.

Instead he had to work on squirming a limb at a time. It wasn't enough, but it had to do, at least until the sun began to warm him.

He wished he dared turn on his radio, to see if he could get any news, but if Margolis was anywhere nearby that would be as stupid as standing up in case he heard it. He trusted his people, but even trust had its limits when you hungered for information.

He wondered about Valerie, about how miserable she must be as well. He doubted she'd slept any better than he had. Something had to happen soon or they'd both become useless.

But given all the empty time, all the time when his immediate concerns weren't enough, he thought about Valerie in a different way.

She was beautiful. No question. But she was more than just a sexy woman. A confident, experienced cop. A woman full of a determination that he admired. A woman who shared some of his own interests.

A woman who'd found a way to cross a threshold that was important to him. She'd found a way to believe Gray Cloud.

But was that enough?

He reminded himself that once this case concluded she'd head back to Gunnison. No reason for her to stay here.

So maybe it was okay to while the time by having thoughts he shouldn't be having. Neither of them would be in danger from *that*.

But she was still a woman he wanted to hold close. To cradle in his arms. To claim with both his mind and body. He remembered as if it were etched into his mind the one time he'd held her to comfort her. Not the same at all, but his body kept wanting to remember anyway.

Had he ever felt this way before? He couldn't say he had. Not like this. Not even with his first girlfriend so long ago. Indigenous like himself, making her a much wiser choice, a woman who shared his culture.

But she hadn't drawn him the way Val did.

Hell's bells.

THE HOURS CONTINUED to drag. The perfectly blue sky seemed to sneer at Valerie. She wanted to step outside and look around but knew that wouldn't be sensible. Her tension, already bad enough, rose even more.

Worse, now that she wasn't at the staging area, she'd

give almost anything to know what was happening there. News of any kind?

Instead she shared a breakfast of stale cereal and coffee with Etta.

"I eat it without milk," Etta said apologetically. "I don't get to town often and milk spoils too fast. That Pastor Molly takes care of a lot for me. She brings me bags of groceries when she can. A few times she took me to the store. She's a good woman."

"The cereal's okay," Val answered. "It tastes good anyway." She was hungry enough to think *hay* would taste good right now. "So you get television out here?" She pointed to the ancient tube TV on its stand across the room.

"Satellite," Etta answered. "Since Phillip left I ain't been able to adjust it, though. Picture's getting snowy."

"Maybe after all this is done I can get somebody to fix it for you."

Etta nodded. "Sure would be nice. I used to have a kitchen garden. When I was out there working on it...well, that was the only time Phillip left me alone. He liked them fresh veggies, too. So I could be out there and for a little while I could be safe."

Valerie's heart squeezed. "But you don't do it anymore?"

Etta shrugged. "Too hard for me to keep up the compost pile. Needed Phillip to turn it over with the pitchfork. But I still throw scraps on it anyway. Habit, I s'pose."

Etta stared off into space and Valerie wondered what she was thinking about. She didn't feel she could ask, though. Etta's thoughts were her own, and Valerie had no right to pry.

Etta scooped up the cereal bowls and put them in the sink. Then she poured more coffee. "I'm gonna be leavin' soon."

Val drew a sharp breath. "Why?" Her mind was already scrambling, dredging up awful ideas.

"Cuz I can't to keep the place up. Ran out of money a while ago so I don't do the repairs. The rancher who owns it, Mr. Dawson, all he asked was for us to keep up the place. One of these days he's gonna notice I ain't doing it. He'll be wanting to get some other folks in here."

"But where will you go? What will you do?"

Etta shrugged. "Don't make no mind."

But it *did* matter, Valerie thought. This woman had reached the end of her rope in every way possible. If she hadn't been so worried about Lizzie, she'd worry a whole lot about what was going to happen to Etta Margolis. Her life appeared to be on a permanent downward spiral.

"I wish that man would get here," Etta said angrily. "I want this over. I want *him* over."

"Me, too, Etta."

The woman eyed her. "Bet you do. As much as me. She's your niece, huh?"

"She is."

"Then maybe you ought to shoot him more'n once."

"Don't tempt me."

MARGOLIS WOULDN'T BE traveling on foot across rough ground with Lizzie. Not unless he'd tipped over his own mental edge.

Guy knew that in his bones. However the man approached, he was going to need to do it in his vehicle. Whether he drove by road or over land made no difference. Unless he left Lizzie behind for some reason.

Like he wanted to get rid of the little girl. A band clamped around Guy's chest. Or maybe the guy would want to scout first. Also a possibility.

But there was no reason for Phillip Margolis to suspect they knew he was the kidnapper. Maybe he'd drive up to Etta's door bold as you please.

Finally, as the day's breeze woke in the sun's heat, he dared to turn on his radio and contact the operation trailer. The voice that answered was Gage Dalton's, to Guy's surprise. Apparently the sheriff couldn't sit this one out at his desk.

"How's it going?" Gage asked without preamble.

"Nothing yet."

"Same here, so far. The cordon you set is tightening around the Margolis house. Reckon he's got to move soon. He's been getting closer."

"He *was* getting closer. Now we don't know. Has anyone seen that sod hut someone thought they recalled yesterday?" Not that he had much hope it'd be easy to find a sod hut. After a hundred and fifty years, grasses and brush would have grown on it, concealing it.

"Not a peep," Gage replied. "Valerie still in the house with Etta?"

"Yup."

"Good. Just let me know if you want eyes in the sky."

Oh, man, would he like a helicopter searching out there. "I don't want to scare him, Gage. He might do something to Lizzie. You know what Margolis is like."

Gage's sigh was audible over the airwaves. "Too much risk at this point," he agreed finally. "Hard to be so close yet so far."

"Tell me about it. I'm going dark again."

Then he switched off the radio and took another scan of

the area through his binoculars. No sign of any vehicle. No sign of anyone crossing the open ground.

Guy was getting tired of the sound of his own smothered cussing. Nothing creative or helpful there.

Nothing helpful from the heavens either. Just so deep, clear and blue that it hurt his eyes to look up at it.

Regardless, Guy rolled on his back to stare up into it anyway and pulled a piece of deer jerky from his pocket. His jaws ached as he chewed it.

Well, hell, what *didn't* ache? His heart sure did.

VALERIE TRIED TO practice some deep breathing and muscle relaxation, almost like meditation, but she was having trouble keeping at it.

She kept eyeing that shotgun beside the front door. It would be too deadly in this confined space. It would spread its load everywhere, endangering everyone. She wondered if she should conceal it somewhere and rely on her own semiautomatic.

But removing that gun might scare Etta. She obviously felt a strong need to be able to protect herself from her husband. Facing him filled her at once with terror and a strong urge to kill him.

What if she didn't take Lizzie away from Phillip? What if she just reacted to her own instinct to kill that bastard?

So once again she reiterated the plan to Etta, who managed a scornful look.

"You think I'm stupid? I want to kill that man but I don't want to kill no baby. Gotta be able to live with myself, even if it's in jail for the rest of my livelong days."

Valerie appreciated the sentiment. She'd spend the rest of her life in jail, too, if it meant taking out that SOB. Pay him back for all he'd done to Lizzie and May. Never before had she felt such a strong murderous urge. She'd always relied on the law to take care of the monsters, even if it never seemed like enough payback.

But she'd had to face the fact, a long time ago, that these monsters were human, too. Not another species. Just one of the worst expressions of the human race. Perfectly human, in other words.

But like most people, she still thought of them as monsters. Other than human. Still, it was no excuse for the rest of the people who occupied this planet. Some crimes were heinous, but that didn't mean others weren't capable of them.

That ugliness dwelt in everyone, rarely evoked, rarely acted upon. Just look at her right now. She wanted to kill and hoped she'd find some justification if the chance arose.

Feeling a whole load of self-disgust, she walked from window to window, standing far enough back that she wouldn't show through the glass.

What was happening out there? What was Guy doing?

GUY WAS BELLY-CRAWLING closer to the house. He'd decided to get into a better range to act when Margolis showed up. Needing a place where he couldn't be seen through one of those windows.

He felt some self-disgust, too. He'd fallen asleep on watch. Not for long. Probably eased by the conviction he'd hear any kind of motor approach.

No excuse anyway, even though the nap had freshened his mind, made him feel stronger. The only part of this he really hated was that he was probably leaving a clear trail in the soggy ground behind him. Giving himself away if Margolis happened along here in his truck.

He didn't want the man to hightail it.

But there was always the chopper. Even if Margolis tried to run, they'd be able to follow him. Small comfort.

And Lizzie? Tossed from a moving vehicle to cover the crime?

Guy's stomach churned then settled into a tight, leaden knot. He felt hamstrung.

MAY HAD BEGUN to feel even more frantic. No word from Val since yesterday. No news from the police except they thought they were closing in.

How could they be sure of that? How could anyone? Then one of the people who again started filling her house turned on the TV. As soon as she saw the bulletin about Phillip Margolis, she knew. Knew with absolute certainty.

"I'm going out to his house," she announced.

More than one of her friends said she couldn't.

She glared at them. "Are you going to stop me? How?" Into her panic, into her determination, came one calm voice.

"May?" said Pastor Molly. "May, you shouldn't do that."

"Why the hell not?"

"Because you might interfere with the police operation."

May shook her head. "What operation? They haven't found her yet."

Molly nodded to the TV. "Now they know who they're looking for. Trust them to take care of it. Trust your sister."

"Oh, God," May wailed. "Trust? I don't trust anyone at all!"

The people around her froze.

Molly approached her and took her into a gentle hug. "Yes, you do. You trust Val."

At last May started to sag against Molly. "I've got to do *something*!"

"But you don't want to risk getting in the way. To risk complicating things by involving yourself. They've got enough to worry about with Lizzie and that man. They don't need to be worrying about you, too."

JUST THEN, CHET walked into the house, his eyes seeking May.

May straightened, pulling away from Molly. "This is all *your* fault. All of it." Then she stormed away to her bedroom.

Everyone in the room stared at him, apparently agreeing with May. Except for Pastor Molly. At least she didn't offer some anodyne that wouldn't have worked. Clenching and unclenching his fists, he looked from face to face, taking in the silent accusation.

He left, but not before he saw the bulletin on the TV screen. Standing out front under a brilliant sky, trees rustling in the breeze, a memory grabbed him.

Phillip Margolis. Chet remembered that case all too well. The fury he'd endured from Margolis, the threats. The wild grief from Etta. Those godawful moments when he'd had to deliver unthinkable news and then withstand the reaction.

One of the times he wished he hadn't gone into obstetrics. One of the many times he'd been sure it wasn't his fault. Not that the knowledge helped him deal with their pain, or his own.

His fists clenched again as he stared into the past.

He wasn't at all sure that May wasn't right. Maybe it *was* all his fault.

PHILLIP MARGOLIS WAS getting far past the end of his tether. The brat was screaming again. She spat out the mashed peas he tried to give her.

He changed a stinky diaper again, a diaper that was stinkier that the first ones, trying to ignore the crying that drilled into his brain.

Even his inexperienced eyes could tell the kid was losing weight.

Damnation. He had to get this kid to Etta or he wouldn't get a chance with her. What if the kid was sick and died? Then what?

His aching head couldn't think about the *and then.*

Go! his brain was shrieking. *Get the kid out of here and to Etta. Make* her *take care of this.*

Riding in the truck always made the brat shut up. Always put her to sleep. Besides, nobody'd be looking for *him.* He could just drive up to his own front door. Which maybe he should have done first thing except he'd been afraid of leaving a trail. No, he wanted to be sure no one was on his tail.

Desperate, he stepped outside and looked around. No one in sight. He checked the firming ground and made up his mind.

Running around to the back of the hut, he pulled the clay-stiffened brown tarp from the old pickup. Rusty and ancient, it ran good, which was the whole reason he'd stolen it from a scrap yard. Perfectly good engine in there, with a little tweaking.

Four more miles and he could dump the kid on Etta, who'd get what she'd always wanted. A baby. A squalling brat. A pain in the head and neck. She could take care of it and him, too.

She'd get that crying to stop.

Then he went back around front and saw the kid halfway out the front door.

He should have gotten one that couldn't walk yet. But Chet Chamberlain didn't have a slew to pick from.

He grabbed the kid, wrapped it in a filthy blanket then went around to stuff her in the truck. For some reason he suddenly recalled the baby seat that had been given to them by the sheriff's department. A freebie, coming with a bunch of instruction and warnings about how it was important to use it for the child's safety. How thrilled Etta had been with it, how often she had touched it. Then he shrugged it off and put the struggling bundle on the truck's floor in front of the ratty passenger seat.

Chamberlain deserved everything he got. Then Margolis looked at the drying ground again.

Now or never.

Chapter Eighteen

Now that midday approached and with it the breezy sounds that would help cover the radio, Guy checked in again. Gage was still out there at the operations trailer.

"One of the searchers spied a truck headed south on the county road in the direction of the Margolis place. Moving slow."

Adrenaline hit Guy like a punch. "We're ready." He wished he could give Val a heads-up, but she was still dark. No sounds that might warn anyone. Because she had no way of knowing for sure that Margolis wouldn't come on foot.

Guy was sure now. He disconnected, turned off the phone, going dark again.

But now he had a direction to guide him. The bastard was going to pull up to his own front door, deluded into thinking that no one was looking for him.

Guy prayed that Lizzie was with Margolis. That he hadn't left the little girl somewhere to draw Etta out.

Hell if he'd let Margolis leave unwatched. If the guy didn't carry a kid into that house, then it would be time for the chopper. Or to get someone to follow Margolis to wherever he went with Etta.

Guy swore again, aware of how many ways this could

all go wrong. How many ways Lizzie's life could be risked. How many bad things might happen.

But some decisions had to wait until he knew if Margolis had the child with him.

He belly-crawled closer to the house, to a place where he could step in if he had to.

At this point he'd have put a gun to Margolis's head if necessary to find out where Lizzie was.

If there was one thing he knew about Margolis's type of bully it was that they were all cowards at heart.

AT THE CHAMBERLAIN HOUSE, May emerged from her bedroom to all the kindly faces that waited for her. They all meant well, but she was past caring about it. Other than getting Lizzie back, she wanted just one thing.

"Where's Chet?" she asked.

"He left," Janine Baxter said.

May's face, all swollen from crying more tears that she would have ever believed anyone could shed, said, "It's not his fault."

Janine replied, "It's Chet who needs to hear that, not us."

STILL STANDING OUTSIDE, hating his helplessness, hating himself, Chet squeezed his eyes shut. There was only one baby he wanted to hold in his hands right now. Just one.

His phone rang and he automatically answered it.

His office assistant was calling. "Mary Pringle is on her way to the hospital."

Another delivery. He couldn't deal with that right now. "Tell Lucy to take it. She can fit it in somehow. I can't... Not right now."

"She'll understand."

"She damn well ought to." He'd been making all kinds of excuses for Lucy because she had a young family. He was through. He'd made excuses for her when he had his *own* family to care for. He'd failed.

What had made him do that? A sense of responsibility to his patients? Or a need for control? After this, if there was an *after* worth living for, he needed to deal with himself.

Then, stunning him, he heard May call him. Wondering if he was hallucinating, he turned slowly and saw her standing in the doorway.

"Chet," she said, her voice wobbly. "I was wrong. I need you."

With no reluctance whatsoever, he walked toward her.

PHILLIP MARGOLIS TOOLED down the road slowly, mainly because the kid had shut up. The minute he stopped, that little brat would start up again. He needed some time to prepare for shrieking, even if he meant to dump the kid on Etta.

But God, he was enjoying the quiet. Nothing but the rumble of an engine and the creaking of the truck's aging frame.

Yeah, he'd get them far away, because if he didn't someone would notice him and Etta suddenly had a child. He'd make his wife come with him. Easy to do with the kid.

Visions of Denver or Billings filled his worn-out head. Places with things to do. Bars. Living here at the back of beyond, he'd missed going to bars whenever he wanted.

He'd missed a lot of things, he suddenly realized. All because of Etta. All because he couldn't trust her by herself.

His anger at his wife began to surge. Damn woman was to blame for all of this. *All* of it.

As soon as he got her away from here, he would teach

her a lesson she'd never forget. Threaten to shoot him? He'd make sure she'd never even think of that again.

Visions of vengeance replaced visions of bigger towns to hide in. Yeah, he'd teach her good.

GUY SWORE AS another rock poked him in the ribs. He'd be black and blue all over when this was done. Not that he cared.

He hoped Val was okay. This wait had to have been harder on her than him. Hunkered down inside that house, unable to do anything at all, with no idea what was happening. If anyone knew where Margolis might be. If they had a hope in hell of rescuing Lizzie soon.

All Guy wanted at this point was to see Margolis in cuffs and Valerie walking into her sister's house to put Lizzie safely in May's arms.

It didn't seem like such a big thing to wish, but it was *huge*.

ETTA MARGOLIS WAS growing increasingly stressed, increasingly afraid.

Valerie slipped her arm around the woman's shoulder. "Just remember you won't be alone with him. I'll be here. You know that. Just get him to give you Lizzie. I'll take care of the rest."

Etta's eyes drifted to the shotgun.

"No, Etta," Valerie said firmly. "You don't want to hurt the baby."

Etta shook her head. "I told you I don't. It's the last thing I want. But then let me plug Phillip. Please."

Valerie squeezed her a bit. "No, Etta. Let the law take

him away. We will, I promise. He'll go away for a long, long time."

Etta's pallid face turned to her. "But he'll be getting out someday, won't he?"

Oh, God, Valerie thought. This woman was on a hair trigger. Not fully trustworthy. She took Etta by the shoulders. "Please, help me save my niece, hard as it might be. Please."

Etta squared her shoulders a little. "Yeah. We gotta save your niece. We gotta."

There was still some hope that this woman wouldn't fall apart at the crucial moment. But now Valerie had another thing to worry about: Etta's state of mind.

Then Etta went to get the shotgun, putting it nearby.

Valerie closed her eyes briefly. That shotgun was Etta's only lifeline. Or at least she perceived it that way.

But if Etta took Lizzie from Phillip, she'd have to abandon that protection. She wouldn't be able to shoot with a child in her arms.

What Valerie had believed might be getting better was steadily getting worse. She struggled for a way to break Etta out of her spiral.

"Do you want to hear about the puppy I rescued on my way up here?"

Slowly Etta's eyes focused on her. "A puppy?"

"Yes. Hit by a car. I found him on the roadside, but he needed surgery. He's getting better now. He also needs a home. Would you like to adopt him?"

"He got a name?"

"Not yet. That's for you to decide, if you want him."

Etta nodded slowly. "Never dared have a dog before. Always wanted one."

"Then let me tell you about this little guy."

GAGE WAITED AT the staging area, following the search. Many of the people had been reeled in as the cordon tightened. Others had been instructed to keep their eyes on the truck without being seen.

And still that truck rolled slowly down the county road. Too slowly as far as Gage was concerned.

Connie popped her head out of the trailer. "Boss?"

He turned, wincing a bit. "Yeah?"

"Two of the guys found the sod hut. Don't know if that's much good now, but they said it's been occupied recently. Food cans, diapers, that kind of thing. Lizzie isn't there, though."

"Good. More evidence. Tell them not to touch a thing."

More evidence? He hoped they didn't need it, that Margolis would pull up at his own front door. It was good, though, that he hadn't abandoned the girl there. All the good Gage could see just then.

He wondered how Valerie Brighton was doing inside that house. If she could trust Etta Margolis to cooperate. And how close Guy might have managed to get.

Three people to depend on, one of whom might not be trustworthy at all.

Waiting was never easy, even though he'd had to do plenty of it in his undercover days with the DEA. Experience didn't help, though. Impatience grew and, along with it, inescapable tension.

VALERIE HEARD THE engine in the distance. She had to tell herself that it could be any vehicle, but her heart raced anyway.

Soon. Very soon.

She sought internal calm, aware that she might have to deal with Etta, too. Complicating the whole thing.

She looked at Etta. "He may be coming. Remember, Lizzie first."

Etta glared. "You don't haveta keep telling me."

Valerie hoped that was so.

GUY HEARD THE engine, too. He crawled even closer to the house. Adrenaline still spurred him.

Picking up his binoculars, he looked as best he could down the driveway and saw a truck turn in.

This was it. Now just let the man get out of the truck with the baby. Let him take Lizzie inside where Valerie was no doubt ready.

Nearly holding his breath, Guy watched the truck approach. Then he saw Margolis climb out and walk around to the passenger side. The man looked impatient but didn't look around as if he thought he might be observed. Then he reached inside and lifted out a bundle.

The bundle started screaming.

VALERIE, PULLING HER pistol out, said quietly, "I'll be right here, just around this corner." One of the few corners in this house.

Etta gave a tight nod but her hand reached out to caress the butt of the shotgun that stood right beside her.

Valerie felt every muscle in her body tighten with apprehension. If that woman reached for that shotgun, she'd be the first one to go down. The very first.

Then would come a mess beyond description. Margolis would still have Lizzie. Would he try to run or use the little girl as a shield?

Be out there, Guy. Be out there nearby.

GUY WAS OUT THERE, all right. As close as he could get without revealing himself. For the first time he wished he had a rifle. A pistol wasn't nearly as good for aiming. Too easy to miss a target. Too easy to shoot Lizzie.

Not that he wanted to shoot anywhere near the child. He'd far prefer to charge in there like a raging bull.

THE TRUCK STOPPED in front of the house. Valerie heard a car door slam. Then she heard Lizzie start to cry. Still alive. A breath of relief whispered through her.

From where she stood, she could still see Etta but not the front door. Her hand tightened on her pistol grip. She released the safety, held the gun in both hands, barrel down. Ready.

MUCH AS PHILLIP MARGOLIS had come to hate the kid who writhed against him and screamed, he still felt a sense of triumph as he approached the front door.

The latch was still as useless as it had always been, so he simply kicked it open. It wouldn't matter since he planned to leave with Etta and the brat just as soon as he could get her packed and into the truck. He'd never need that damn door again.

He immediately saw Etta in the interior gloom. Saw the shotgun beside her.

"Look what I done brought you, Etta. You don't wanna be hurtin' our kid, do ya?"

Etta, that dried-up woman, shook her head jerkily. "Ours?" she croaked.

"Yeah, a pretty one, too. 'Cept she won't shut up. You can shut her up, Etta. You're the mom now."

He walked toward her, holding Lizzie forward for Etta to embrace. She took an unsteady step toward him. He was more relieved than he wanted to admit when she moved away from the shotgun.

"Is she pretty?" Etta asked, extending her arms.

"Yeah. Really. But you gotta make her stop cryin' or I'm ditchin' her. Up to you."

"I'll take her," Etta said with another unsteady step. "How'd you get me this baby?"

Lizzie was setting up her usual ruckus. Just as soon as he got Etta to take hold of this brat, he was going to tell her to pack. And while he waited he was going to step outside again, just to escape that screaming.

VALERIE HAD TENSED until every single muscle in her body felt like overstretched steel. Her hands held the butt of her pistol as she peered around the corner. She needed Etta to get Lizzie clear of Phillip, but as they met with the baby between them, she clamped her teeth together.

Just get on with the exchange!

OUTSIDE, GUY WATCHED Margolis disappear inside. The sound of Lizzie's shrieking tore at his heart. He moved even closer, getting into a position that would allow him to spring at the first opportunity.

What was going on inside? His heart thudded in his chest like a blacksmith's hammer.

NOW FIRMLY HOLDING the little girl, Etta stepped away from Margolis. "You poor little baby," she murmured. Then, "Damn it, Phillip. You don't know a thing about caring for a child."

"I changed her diapers, didn't I? She won't eat, neither. You take care of that from now on."

Two steps away. Turning her back to Phillip. "I'll just do that now. You got diapers?"

"In the truck. But first you get your own stuff together. We're leaving."

Etta turned around again, rocking the baby. "Where to?" Then she started singing a soft lullaby. Lizzie hiccupped and her cries began to ease.

"Somewhere ain't nobody gonna find us. Somewhere you can raise that damn kid without interference."

"Except you," Etta said sharply, then resumed rocking Lizzie and singing. Another step away.

Valerie tried to judge if the two were now separated enough that she could act before Phillip could grab Etta and Lizzie and turn them into hostages.

One more step, Etta. Please. Just one more step.

GUY WAS AS close as he could get without warning Margolis that he was out here. He wanted to be closer, much closer. But again he had to wait. He figured he must be grinding his teeth to nubs.

FAR ENOUGH, VALERIE DECIDED. And now the quickest way to protect Etta and Lizzie was with her gun.

Sliding around the corner, gun raised in both hands, she saw Phillip Margolis's eyes grow wide.

Then she pulled the trigger. Right in the thigh as she'd wanted. Margolis fell, screaming.

And Valerie didn't care if he bled to death.

AT THE GUNSHOT, Guy vaulted from the ground, onto the front porch and inside. Etta stood holding the baby, her eyes tightly closed. Valerie stood in a marksman's stance, her face white.

Then he looked down at the man lying on the floor, writhing in pain, bleeding heavily. He keyed his radio. "I need an ambulance at the Margolis place. Now. He's been shot."

Without another word, he went to Valerie and gently lowered her hands, taking the gun from her. Then he wrapped her in his arms.

"It's okay, Val," he said. "It's okay now."

A shudder ripped through Valerie. "He needs a tourniquet."

"Like I give a damn."

Unfortunately, given the spurt he saw from Margolis's leg, he knew an artery had been hit. He'd bleed out fast. Hating the world for just an instant, Guy shredded an old sheet to wrap tightly around the guy's upper thigh.

"You should've hit him in the chest," he said to Val.

"Too easy. I want the bastard to suffer."

At last she moved, approaching Etta and taking Lizzie into her arms.

"Lizzie," she said softly, then began to weep.

Chapter Nineteen

Guy stepped out onto the front porch and keyed his radio, reaching Gage. "We've got her. Lizzie seems okay but needs a look-over, maybe the hospital. Tell May. Send two ambulances. Margolis has been shot in the leg."

Then he went back inside to keep an eye on Val. She had to be on a ragged edge, given the past days, the surge of adrenaline that must be draining, given that she had just shot a man. Given that she finally held Lizzie in her arms, apparently safe and sound.

Two ambulances raced up the rutty drive and paramedics jumped out as soon as they stopped. They attended immediately to Margolis, then put him on a stretcher and carried him out.

Through it all, Valerie stood holding Lizzie, tears running down her face. She rocked the baby and finally looked at Etta.

"Thank you."

Etta offered a brief nod, then a smile. "Did my heart good to see that man shot. Too bad you want him alive."

Guy spoke. "Imagine him spending years and years in prison."

Etta's smile widened. "Might go visit him just to enjoy it. Them other prisoners ain't gonna be nice to him."

"Not when they hear he kidnapped a young child. Even the worst of them have limits."

Etta nodded again, then looked at Valerie and Lizzie. "It's a good thing," she said presently. "Best damn thing I ever done in my whole damn life."

THE OTHER TWO paramedics checked Lizzie over head to foot. Valerie didn't want to let go of her niece but knew she had to. All she could do was shake her head as they uncovered the small child and began to examine her.

One looked at Valerie. "She needs to go to the hospital. Some dehydration. A bad diaper rash. Maybe underfed." Then they wrapped the child in a fresh, clean blanket.

Lizzie had grown quiet, unusual for her with strangers. As if she were too weak to cry anymore. Val drew a deep breath, trying to steady herself, fearing for Lizzie in a new way.

She turned her attention to Guy. "Let May know."

"I'm sure she's already getting a call."

She nodded and climbed aboard the ambulance with Lizzie.

GUY WATCHED THEM GO, wishing he could follow, but there was still some cleaning up to do.

He turned to Etta. "We're going to find a way to help you, Etta. Some way to get you out of this ramshackle house and in among people who'll care."

Etta sagged into that rickety kitchen chair looking drained. "Been thinking about leavin' but I been livin' this way too long to change."

"You might be surprised. The sun doesn't have to be only outside. It can be inside, too."

Etta dragged her gaze to him. "And some folks call you a stupid damn redskin." She shook her head, then looked down. "Damn fools everywhere. What do I need 'em for?"

Sometimes Guy wondered that himself.

THE TRIP TO the hospital seemed to take forever, the ambulance jouncing over the rutty road.

"Sorry for the bumpy ride," one paramedic said.

"Like you pave the county roads," Valerie answered.

At last they turned onto smoother pavement. Flashing lights but no siren. No real urgency. That relieved Valerie just a little. She needed assurances from a doctor, treatment for Lizzie.

Lizzie looked so tiny on that huge stretcher. One of the medics was on the radio, describing the situation. Except for dehydration, it didn't sound that awful. Not yet, anyway.

When they arrived at the hospital, she climbed out of the ambulance to make way for the stretcher. The first thing she saw was May and Chet standing just outside the entrance. They both rushed toward the stretcher.

Moments later, Lizzie and her parents were whisked away. Valerie stood alone outside the ER, suddenly aimless. Lizzie didn't need her now, needed only Chet and May. Later she could see her niece.

Right now, Valerie needed something else. Someone else. Someone who'd walked through this fire right at her side.

She turned around, wondering how to get to Guy's apartment. She couldn't remember. She hadn't paid much attention when he'd taken her there. Maybe she could get directions from someone.

Then she saw the Suburban squeal up, lights flashing.

Guy jumped out and came running toward her. A muddy, grassy mess from his night crawling overground.

She didn't care how dirty he was when he wrapped his arms around her. Held her tight.

"You're coming home with me," he said.

It was the only place she wanted to go.

GUY PRACTICALLY MOTHERED VAL. He steadied her up the stairs. Put sugary food in front of her and a sweet cola in her hand. Told her to drink. Got her a blanket when she started to shiver.

Sat beside her, holding her hand. "Drink. Eat. Don't argue with me."

She felt no desire to argue with him. Instead she obeyed his orders, draining half the cola in one draft. Eating a cinnamon bun as if her life depended on it.

He reached for the same for himself. A short time later he pressed another bun into her hand. "You need the sugar," he reminded her. "But you know that."

Yes, she knew that. After all the adrenaline, she *did* need every sugary morsel. Licking the stickiness off her fingers, she accepted another soft drink.

"I'll be okay," she finally said.

"You will," he agreed. "You're tough. Tough as ten cops."

"I doubt that. *You* were there."

"It wasn't *my* niece."

"She might as well have been. I've been beside you all the way through this. You never cared less than I did."

"Just doing my job."

Right, she thought. *Right*.

AN HOUR LATER, May called. Guy waited while Val talked to her sister, then disconnected.

She looked at Guy, smiling. "Lizzie's okay. She's going to be fine. They want to keep her overnight, though. I can visit once they get her into a regular room."

"Want me to come with?"

"Of course. You did as much as anyone to bring Lizzie home. Then I gotta figure out how to thank most of this county."

"I think the news will be enough."

Val finally sagged into the recliner and fell into a deep sleep.

Good, Guy thought. He took the opportunity for a long, hot shower to wash away the infinite filth that covered him in the last stages of this case. He wished he could as easily shower away the ugliness in his brain. Then he dressed in a fresh uniform.

Still a lot of cleaning up to do with the case. T's to cross and i's to dot. There'd be a whole lot of forensic evidence to review, too. Not that they'd need much after the scene in the Margolis household, but charges other than kidnapping could probably be leveled against Phillip Margolis, too, charges like child abuse. Guy wanted to throw the entire book at that monster.

He wished he'd been the one to shoot Margolis. Val didn't strike him as the type who'd be able to brush it aside. She was the type who'd carry that single shot with her for the rest of her life, no matter how justified it had been. He'd rather carry that burden himself.

He sighed quietly, wiping his face. He saw an Indigenous

face in his mirror and he'd always been proud of it, even when others tried to steal that pride.

He brewed a pot of coffee while Val continued to sleep away her exhaustion. Glancing at the clock, he figured it wouldn't be long before Val wanted to go to the hospital.

Reluctantly he carried a mug of coffee toward the recliner, then shook her gently.

She came instantly awake, instantly alert.

"Coffee," he said, handing her the mug. "Then I'm taking you home so you can clean up before we go to the hospital."

She offered him a faint smile. "I guess you already took care of that for yourself."

"Hell, yeah. That damn brush was prickly."

At long last she laughed. "Bet I had an easier night than you did."

"That depends on your perspective."

An old towel in the trunk took care of wiping the dirt and dust from the driver's seat in his vehicle. The outside was splattered with mud. Well, Gage wouldn't like that. All official vehicles were supposed to gleam.

Then he chuckled quietly. As if Gage would care this time.

The end of this long siege was beginning to get to him, too. After all the fear, all the worry that they'd never find Lizzie, after all the effort they'd put out to find the little girl, it had started to sink in that Lizzie was okay, the job was successfully concluded.

Odd, he couldn't remember ever having felt at loose ends before.

He drove Val to the Chamberlain house, then waited outside for her. Unfortunately, that gave him time to think about Val. About how much he'd started to dread the day when she returned to Gunnison. About the hole she'd leave behind in him.

Then he started counting all the reasons he shouldn't feel this way. There were probably a dozen or more, but he stopped at a few. Her job was elsewhere. She wouldn't quit to stay here. He wouldn't want her to either. What would she do here?

He wouldn't quit to follow her. Not that she'd want him to.

Nope, there was that huge cultural and possibly even racial divide. Separate lives intersecting only because of a crisis. He needed to remember that.

Val emerged from the house thirty minutes later, wearing one of those business suits he'd first seen her in. Resuming herself. Resuming her own life.

Maybe sending a message. And maybe he should read it. The hole inside him began to grow.

AT THE HOSPITAL, May and Chet were clearly so happy that they could barely contain their joy. Both of them profusely thanked Valerie and Guy.

"You saved her." May beamed at them. "And, Val, I knew you'd help."

"I couldn't have done it without Guy. He gets most of the credit." Then a tear ran down Valerie's face. "I'm so glad she's okay. Can I see her? Can *we* see her?"

"Of course!" Both May and Chet spoke at once.

Chet reached for the door. "She's sleeping," he said. "Poor tot needs the rest."

"I'm not surprised," Valerie answered.

Stetson in hand, Guy followed the three of them into the room. Lizzie lay in a large raised crib with net topping over it. An IV ran into her arm.

"The IV will come out soon," May said. "Then we can

take her home. Plenty of food, the doctor said. That man didn't feed her enough."

Guy got his first good look at Lizzie. To think all this time he'd known her face only from photographs. She was even more adorable in life.

Adorable? That didn't sound like a word he'd usually use. Hah. This whole experience had changed him in unexpected ways.

He stood for a while, looking at the child whose plight had consumed him for so many days, and felt good about himself.

Then he moved quietly. "I need to get to the office. This case needs winding up."

Valerie hesitated. "I'd like to come along, Guy. I want to know everything."

He nodded. "Come on. And when we're done with this, I gotta find a way to help Etta."

Val followed him out the door. "You're right. It's wrong to leave her out there all by herself on the edge of poverty."

"It's wrong for a lot of people, but she did a great thing, didn't she?"

"It wasn't easy for her either." Val smiled. "Remarkable, when you think about all she's been through with that beast."

"She said it was the best thing she's done in her life." He didn't mention how glad Etta had been to see Phillip shot. No need to bring that up, not when it was probably raw for Val.

Phillip Margolis was still in the hospital, under sedation, under guard. Not that the coward was likely to try anything, not when it might cost him his leg.

What they wanted were the rest of the details, details that might lock his prison cell even tighter.

And eventually they wanted to know why he'd chosen Lizzie Chamberlain to give to his wife, although they had a good idea about that. Still, they needed the creep to say it. To brag.

Guy suspected the man would brag quite a bit.

Valerie again looked out of place in the front squad room, as out of place as she had upon her arrival. But this time she was greeted with nods and smiles. Those who spoke called her *Detective*.

She had become a recognized part of the team. Guy wondered if she realized that.

After they'd wound up the paperwork with as much as they had learned, Guy suggested he drive Val home.

Once in the Suburban, she spoke wearily. "I want to hear that man tell it all. I want him to nail himself with his own mouth."

"Me, too," Guy agreed as he pulled up in front of the Chamberlain house. "A full confession."

"Yeah." Instead of climbing out of his vehicle, she leaned her head back and turned it to look at the house. "There's still one thing I want to know."

"What's that?"

"Why May never heard Lizzie cry."

The question slammed Guy. Val had mentioned it before, but he'd forgotten all about it during the hunt. Answers tended to come later when a case was solved.

"Yeah," he said reluctantly. "Yeah." But maybe neither of them truly wanted to know.

The question hung there like a huge loose end.

Then Val looked at him. "Can I come to your place, Guy?"

Chapter Twenty

"Sure," Guy answered, slipping his vehicle into gear. He tried to sound nonchalant but wasn't sure he succeeded. His heart began a slow, steady throbbing as he drove through town. It continued as they both exited the vehicle and headed for his apartment. The stairway had never seemed so long.

Inside, he asked her if she wanted coffee, or just to sleep.

She smiled faintly and gestured, the movement taking in the entire place. "You haven't committed, have you."

He stilled, surprised by the comment. "What do you mean?"

"Oh, you're committed to the job, all right. I've seen it. Total commitment."

"Then what?" He scanned his own apartment. Only partly furnished.

"I mean this place. You may be committed to your work, but you're not committed to staying here. Some part of you believes you'll be moving on. To what, Guy?"

He remained quiet as he looked around again. Maybe she was right. What did that mean about him?

"At home," she continued, "I have plenty of furniture. So

I can entertain. So I can be comfortable all the time. I hung pictures on the wall. I have some appliances on my counter. It looks like a home, not a waystation." She studied him. "It's obvious you don't have friends come over. Do you feel you don't have any?"

He blew a long breath.

She looked into his eyes. "All you have on the walls is that beautiful blanket your mother made. Do you think about going home to your family all the time? Or something else? You don't feel permanent, do you?"

He felt stripped uncomfortably bare. He wanted to ignore her questions, dismiss them lightly. The problem was, there was truth in them. Maybe a truth he needed to face.

"I don't know," he said finally.

She shook her head and looked pained. "You've built walls around yourself. As clear as the boundaries of your reservation. You just don't believe you belong. You view everything through the lens of how you've been treated by Whites all your life."

He tried not to wince in response to words that struck him painfully. "Maybe so. With good reason."

She nodded, then sat on the edge of the recliner. "I'm sure you have reasons. You've shared some of them with me."

"So?"

"So maybe you need to commit yourself. To this county. To the place where you work and live your days. To the people around here. They can't *all* be jerks, can they?"

No, they weren't all jerks. Problem was that he was always steeling himself against meeting another one. They showed up. Boy, did they show up, and too many of them did it overtly.

But he was also trying to steel himself against Val, wasn't

he? Wondering at some level what his family would think if he got more involved with her. Some of them already objected to him being a cop. How would they react to Valerie?

"Maybe," she said slowly, "you ought to wear the plainclothes you're entitled to wear now and stop worrying about the bigots. You know who *you* are. If they can't deal with it, tell them to shove it. You're a *detective* with the Conard County Sheriff's Department. Have more confidence in yourself. You deserve to."

He didn't know what to say. She didn't understand. Or maybe she understood more than he wanted to believe. He wanted to ask who she was to criticize him.

But deep inside he knew it was a critique he deserved. Maybe one he needed.

"Val…" But he didn't know what to say. Home truths. He needed to think about them. But Val didn't give him time, not then.

She smiled at him. "Take me to bed, Guy."

His head exploded as if light burst through him. For a split second his world turned brilliant, so bright he couldn't see anything.

Then he took a long breath and reached for her hand. "Val, come with me."

"All the way, if you want." Her smile lingered as she took his hand and rose.

All the way? But he couldn't question her, not then. His pulse pounded through him, the desire for her that he couldn't ignore, that he no longer needed to ignore, rising in him as he led her to his bed.

"I hear the thunder," he said.

Her smile broadened. "Me, too."

SHE WAS EXQUISITE. Val didn't wait for him to undress her, but slowly shed her jacket, then reached for the buttons on her creamy blouse. Still smiling.

"You, too," she said huskily. "Or I'll do it myself."

He wouldn't have minded, but neither did he want wait.

All at once they sped up, clothes flying everywhere.

Falling together, they landed on the bed. Their hands began to move in a journey of discovery. Her skin was as smooth as silk and when she writhed against him, her hips rising, he felt the blaze rise in his own body along with zings of lightning.

Oh, he heard the thunder all right. It hammered in his ears, filling him with its power.

He caressed her breasts, their nipples pebbling beneath his fingers. He ran his hand down her side and finally reached her center. She arched against him, then closed her hand around his staff.

Her voice was breathless. "Now, Guy. Fill me now."

He couldn't have waited a second longer. Sliding into her hot wet depths felt as good as a homecoming. She moaned and tightened around him as her hips began the rhythm as old as time.

He rose and fell with her, riding the storm of desire. Higher and higher until at last thunder clapped a final time.

Together they found deep contentment. Deep satisfaction. *Together.* As one.

THEY FELL ASLEEP, wrapped in his comforter, wrapped in each other's arms. Val had no idea how long she slept, but when she woke all she wanted to do was snuggle closer.

Guy. His warmth. His strength. His kindness. His determination. So much to admire.

Then there was his sexiness. She had to stifle a giggle for fear of waking him, of him pulling away. She squeezed her eyes closed, remembering their lovemaking. As far as she was concerned it had been perfect. She hoped he felt the same.

Desire had been running like a current all along, beneath her fear and anguish. Buried because it was out of place. The wrong time.

But the time was wrong no longer. She didn't want to think about what might come. About all the problems. Their jobs, so far apart. Their cultures creating a distance that wasn't measured in miles. Reasons for a new fear and she wasn't sure how she'd handle any of it.

But in these special moments, cradled against him, she pushed the worries aside. They'd arrive when they couldn't be ignored. Just accept the now. The gift.

GUY AWOKE TO the miracle of Val snuggled against him. He knew by her breathing that she no longer slept. He hugged her closer, aware that they'd opened a can of worms they wouldn't be able to ignore. He forced the thoughts away.

He shifted his head so that he looked into her face, seeing her drowsy smile. He wanted to keep that smile there forever.

Then his stomach growled loudly. She giggled.

"Embarrassing," he said, "but when was the last time we ate?"

She answered with certitude. "I had some dried cereal with Etta yesterday morning."

"For me it was during the night when I ate deer jerky."

"Too long," she agreed.

"I can run to the truck stop and get something. Or you can risk your life with whatever I might have lying around here. I don't cook for myself often."

"How about we both go to the truck stop? Sounds much safer to me. Easier, too." Then she laughed.

It was the most beautiful sound he'd ever heard, except maybe her moan of completion.

He jumped out of bed and grabbed for his clothes. "I'll beat you."

"Just you try."

Laughing like kids, they pulled on their clothes, more rumpled this time. He wore jeans and a sweatshirt. She pulled on her suit again.

The suit that announced another barrier.

Hell!

The drive to the truck stop diner didn't take long, and soon they were inside. Only then did Guy see the clock and realize it was 4:00 a.m. They'd gotten some real sleep.

Valerie ordered eggs, bacon, a side of home fries. Guy doubled the same order for himself.

They faced each other across a table in a booth. The dark night beyond the window was punctuated by rumbling trucks beneath vapor lamps. You couldn't see many stars from here.

All Guy wanted was to look at Valerie anyway. Beautiful had become gorgeous in his eyes. He wondered how she saw him, but from her smile decided her view of him couldn't be that bad.

The coffee was rich and dark, waking him up more. It appeared to have the same effect on Val as she held the mug in both hands.

After they were served and had eaten in silence for a few minutes, Val looked up from her plate.

"You know we're going to have things to talk about," she said with uncharacteristic uncertainty.

"Yes." Things he didn't want to talk about at all.

"That is," she continued, "if you don't want it to end here."

The words burst from him, barging past his usual restraint. "I *don't* want this to end here. Do you?"

She shook her head, looking down again. A sigh escaped her. "Maybe we can deal with one issue at a time."

"It's possible. Or we can deal with them all at once and let the straws fall where they may."

She looked up and her gaze locked on his face. "What do you mean?"

"I want to marry you." He spoke with conviction. "To hell with all the rest of it. We'll deal."

She stopped breathing. Her eyes widened. "Guy?"

"I mean it." He'd never meant anything more in his life. It had crashed in on him during the night just past. He wanted this woman forever under any terms. Now all he had to fear was her answer.

"Your family?" she asked quietly.

"They can live with it the same way they live with me being a cop. You were right. I need to stop erecting barriers. This one comes down *now*. I love you. Will you marry me?"

Her face suddenly glowed like a rising sun. "Yes, Guy. Oh, yes. Come what may." Then, "I love you, too."

He smiled the broadest smile he had in ages. He felt like he was walking on air.

Then, just to keep himself under control, he said, "Finish eating or I'm going to drag you out of here right now. The bed might still be warm."

She laughed, a pure, clear sound. "What a difficult choice. You're impossible."

He laughed, too. God, had he nearly forgotten how to laugh?

REALITY RETURNED AS it always did. Morning came too soon. Bright sunlight filled the world, for once not feeling like an affront.

Guy swung Val by the Chamberlain house to clean up and change. Again she emerged wearing one of her suits. Today it didn't feel like the barrier it had seemed just last night.

She'd agreed to marry him. It didn't get better than that.

When she slid into his Suburban, she said, "They aren't home from the hospital yet. I should check in on Lizzie."

"Absolutely."

She chewed her lip as they drove. "I think it's too soon to question May."

He thought about it, dreading the answer she might get. "Yeah, give her a day or two to get used to having Lizzie back. Maybe it's not really important." He ached for Val in expectation of the pain she might soon feel.

"It's important," she answered. "I *have* to know."

THE CHAMBERLAINS WERE still at the hospital, both of them in Lizzie's room. Nobody tried to halt Val or Guy, to limit the number of visitors.

May and Chet looked weary but happy. Lizzie still slept.

"How is she?" Valerie asked.

"She's fine," May answered with a smile.

The IV was gone, Valerie noted. A good sign. A good sign that Lizzie slept so peacefully.

"A few more hours," Chet said. "Then we'll take her home."

We. Valerie noticed that but didn't want to press. Were her sister and her husband patching it up? Coming together again? She hoped so. She'd always liked Chet, had always believed until two years ago that May had made the right decision in marrying him. She wanted to see that contentment in May again.

Chet rose and extended his hand to Guy. "I haven't thanked you yet."

Guy returned the handshake but shook his head the tiniest bit. "No thanks necessary. I wanted Lizzie safely home as much as you did."

Then Chet turned to Valerie and hugged her. "You came when May needed you. I'll always be grateful to you."

As if she could have done anything else, Val thought as she returned his hug. Was Chet beginning to realize that he hadn't been there enough when he was needed before?

May spoke. "Chet is going to let Lucy handle more of the workload."

Chet nodded as he stepped back. "Belatedly it occurred to me that Lucy isn't the only one with a family to care for."

So he *was* thinking about it. Reordering his priorities. "Good for you," was all Val answered. About time, too.

She let her question go for now. In a day or two, when the Chamberlains had settled back in together, she'd ask. She needed to know why May hadn't heard Lizzie cry.

Maybe May had an answer. Or maybe the answer lay entirely with Margolis.

She summoned her patience, but it wasn't as hard as when Lizzie was missing.

SHE AND GUY went by the sheriff's office again and found a squad room looking weary but happy. They'd all exhausted themselves in the hunt for Lizzie and Valerie tried to thank them.

They were having none of it. "What?" asked Sarah Ironheart. "Like we'd have ignored it?"

Connie Parish laughed. "After we all catch up with some sleep we're going to throw a party. You gonna join us, Detective?"

"Call me Val. And yes, I'll be there."

Guy asked, "Where's Gage?"

"Emma made him come home," Mark Alton answered. "She worries about him."

"And Margolis?"

"Still knocked out. Doc says we might get some sense out of him tomorrow. Guess he lost a whole lot of blood."

Guy looked at Val. He saw her jaw tighten. No, she wasn't happy about shooting the man, much as he deserved it. He'd have wondered about her, though, if she didn't feel it. No one should ever be immune to that. To being responsible for pulling a trigger.

"I'm not even going to *try* to cook," Guy said as they emerged into the sunny day. "We've got better things to do. I'll ransack Maude's menu. How's that?"

That smile danced across Val's face again. "You make me happy, Guy."

As happy as she made him, he hoped.

LATER, THOUGH, WHEN they were sated with food, and temporarily with their hungry bodies, Val took the recliner and Guy pulled up one of his kitchen chairs, reaching for her hand.

"Well?" he asked reluctantly, unusual nerves filling him. "Changing your mind?"

"God no! But how are we going to do this? Who do we tell and when? What about your family? Our jobs?"

Guy looked down, facing the justice of her concerns. "I love you, Val. We've got to find a way."

"Yeah, we do." She leaned back and closed her eyes. "It's not enough to just let things fall where they may. I don't want you to be unhappy for any reason. But…"

"Yeah, but." He sighed. "Tell you what. We'll meet in the middle at some hotel or other when we can both get away."

She nodded slowly. "I want to get as much of you as I can. But there's no room for another detective here. And I don't think I can go back to patrol."

"No, of course not." He wouldn't ask that from her ever.

"And you can't move to Gunnison. Too far from your roots, your family, your people. I don't want that either." She needed her job and the sense of purpose he gave her. He'd even sacrifice himself to save her from losing that.

She opened her eyes. "We'll manage. I love you too much not to try."

"That's it then. Tomorrow you get May to answer your question. And I'll take a trip out to the rez. We'll go from there."

THE NEXT MORNING, Guy dropped Val off at the Chamberlain house, then headed out to the rez. A satellite phone call had prepared the way for him.

At the Chamberlain house, happiness filled the air. Lizzie was curled in her father's arms, viewing her world from her safe vantage point. Val managed to hold the little girl for a few minutes before her crying became too much.

She grinned. "That crying must have driven Margolis crazy."

May laughed. "I hope so."

But the moment had come. Every inch of Val's body tightened. God, she didn't want to do this. "May, can I have a few private words?"

May looked at her sister, her smile fading. "Sure, Val."

They went into the master bedroom and closed the door. May had grown stiff, her hands tightening, her gaze on her sister. "What's wrong, Val? What's wrong?"

Valerie drew a deep breath, hating the words she was about to speak. "May, why didn't you hear Lizzie cry the night she was taken?"

May dropped down onto the edge of the bed, her face paling. "Oh, God, Val." Then she started crying quietly.

Val promptly sat beside her and wrapped her arm around her sister's shoulders. "May, I'm sorry. I have to know, just for me. No one else needs to. No one else is wondering." Except she'd share whatever it was with Guy. She wasn't about to start anything by lying to him.

Tears dribbled down May's face. "I'm awful. Just awful."

"How so?"

"I had a few drinks. Some nights I'd have a few just so I could sleep. But Lizzie's cries always woke me up. *Always*. I swear."

"But that night was different. How?"

May put her hands over her face. "Oh, God!"

"May?"

May scrubbed her face with her sleeve. "Oh, all right! I didn't drink. I took sleeping pills. Prescription sleeping pills! I started doubling the dose."

Valerie felt shock all the way to her toes. "May..."

"I'm awful, just awful!"

Val hugged May even tighter. "You've got to stop that before you get addicted."

"I know. I know! I'll never touch them again, I swear."

But now Val had another question even as she ached for May. "Did anyone know that you did that regularly?"

May wiped her face. "A few. I was worried about it, so I told some of my friends."

And that explained a whole lot, Valerie thought. *The grapevine.* The one little piece of information that no one had shared out of loyalty to May. Because it seemed irrelevant to Lizzie's disappearance.

Only it hadn't been. Not that it would have helped much in finding Lizzie.

She held May, rocking her gently. "It's okay. It'll be okay now. If you need help, ask Chet. Please."

May nodded. "I will. I promise I will. Maybe I should have taken those antidepressants he wanted me to. God, this whole mess has been terrible. Postpartum depression then this. I can't blame anyone but me."

"I wouldn't say that at all. There's no one to blame but Phillip Margolis. No one."

With her eyes closed, Val wondered though. If May had awakened and found Margolis in her house, with her baby? Matters might have taken an even worse turn.

GRAY CLOUD WAITED for Guy in his small shed on the side of Thunder Mountain. A foothold he retreated to for peace, to keep an eye on the mountain. It was an infrequent break from tribal councils and other matters that needed the attention of an elder.

Gray Cloud sat cross-legged by a fire, a tin coffeepot resting on the rocks that made the fire ring. He smiled and waved Guy to sit with him. "It's a beautiful day. Coffee?"

Guy accepted. A strong, rich brew with a few stray coffee grounds in it. As near as he could tell, Gray Cloud had never abandoned all the old ways. A keeper of the tribe's history and wisdom.

"So," said Gray Cloud, his dark gaze kind. "What brings you?"

"You've been more of a father to me than my real one."

Gray Cloud nodded. "Sometimes that's the way of it. I gather you have a knotty problem you want to discuss?"

Guy chuckled. "I came knocking, didn't I?"

"It's usually why. I might not be able to help. I'm not the smartest man on the earth, you know."

"I wouldn't expect you to be." He remained silent and so did Gray Cloud. He let the heat and richness of the coffee pour through him as he enjoyed the peace of the woods around him. A squirrel hopped by, unafraid.

"Okay," Guy said presently. "I want to marry Valerie Brighton."

"Why would that be a problem?"

"My family. You must know they don't approve of me being a cop. They're going to disapprove even more about this."

Gray Cloud raised an eyebrow. "You played with my children when you were young."

Guy nodded. He vividly remembered those childhood

days. Days of freedom and fun, the bunch of them running around, playing games.

"And you knew their mother," Gray Cloud said.

Guy remembered Gray Cloud's wife, too. A wildlife biologist who had come to Thunder Mountain to study wolves. She had died too young. "But you know my family, what they're like."

"You know that my wife was non-Native. The disapproval didn't stop me. Will that stop you?"

Guy waited, sensing there was more. Some reminder he wanted.

"I don't know everything, Guy, but I know one thing."

"What's that?"

"No man has the right to decide the course of another man's life. Follow your heart. But you didn't need me to tell you that."

Maybe he *hadn't* needed to hear it, Guy thought, but he still felt better when he went down the mountain to meet his parents. An elder hadn't disapproved. Now his parents could just deal with it.

They'd have to anyway.

VAL AND GUY met again late that afternoon at his apartment. She burst with curiosity. "How'd it go?"

Guy nodded. "It went. Gray Cloud gave his blessing."

"Would that have made a difference?"

He smiled. "Nope. But it was still good to hear from a man who's like a father to me."

"I'm sure it was. You're still very much a part of your people. Besides, it's always good to feel that people we care about aren't against us. And your parents?"

Now he laughed. "About what I expected. As if I'd taken a

dump on the doorstep. They'll get used to it. Or they won't."
He shrugged. "I knew what I was going to do and nothing
would have stopped me. Bottom line."

"Like becoming a cop."

"Like becoming a cop," he agreed. "Now you. What did
you learn?"

"Oh, it wasn't good." Her face saddened and she perched
on the recliner. "Damn it, Guy, get another decent chair.
This is ridiculous."

He grinned. "I hear you, Detective Thunder. What about
May?"

Sorrow whispered over her face. "This is a secret, Guy.
Totally."

"Lips sealed and all that. Tell me."

"May's been taking sleeping meds. Doubling the dose."

He dragged the kitchen chair over and sat as close as he
could get, his concern for Val deepening until it nearly hurt.
"Other people knew?"

"Evidently she got worried enough to tell some friends.
After that, I suppose one of them mentioned it outside the
small group and the grapevine did its work. Margolis must
have heard."

"That would explain a lot. How's May doing?"

"Feeling ashamed. Blaming herself. I told her she needs
to talk to Chet. I hope she does."

"Sounds like she's going to need some help."

"Yeah." She sighed. "Yeah."

Eventually she shook her head. "Let's get back to us, Guy.
I want to feel the happiness and love you give me. I want to
get rid of the rest of the whole damn world, at least for now."

In total agreement, he scooped her up and carried her
toward the bed. She laughed at last.

"The grapevine's working again already," he murmured huskily. "Guaranteed."

"Then let them talk. They'll just be full of envy."

He laid her down, then sank beside her, hugging her close. "I love you, Detective Valerie Brighton."

"I love you, too, Detective Guy Redwing. Forever."

"Forever won't be long enough."

* * * * *

THE EVIDENCE
NEXT DOOR

JULIE MILLER

Prologue

Three months earlier

The visitor waited patiently until the prisoner was shown into the room. It wasn't the first prison the visitor had been to, and though the age of the building and the uniforms might be different, it was still a prison. The blank expression on the prisoner's face, carefully revealing nothing but hatred and distrust, was familiar, too.

Although it was an accepted rule that the inmate remain handcuffed during the interview, the visitor refused the guard's offer to chain him to the table, as well. "I'm looking for cooperation, not to make his stay here any more miserable than it already is."

"You know what he's in here for, don't you?"

The visitor nodded before waving the guard away. "I've done my homework. You may go."

"Your call." The guard shrugged, as though he didn't think that was the best choice. But the visitor wanted something very specific from the man sitting across the table, and that wasn't going to happen if a guard who was armed and wearing a flak vest hovered over them. "I'll be right outside that door. Watching. You got ten minutes."

The visitor didn't bother thanking the guard as the door closed and locked behind him. The prisoner didn't bother with introductions and niceties, either. "Cooperation? Who are you? My new attorney?"

The visitor studied the man's shaved head and brown eyes. In another world, he would probably be considered handsome. But rage, frustration and a focus on surviving versus the opportunity to settle into a successful, free life had given him hard edges. It had taken a while to find this man, and the visitor was counting on them sharing a need for retribution. "I can't offer you legal absolution. But I can offer you something you might find eminently satisfying."

"All I want is to get out of this place. I intend to keep my nose clean so I don't get any time tacked on to my sentence."

"You won't have to lift a finger and jeopardize your time here. I just have a question for you."

"I'm no snitch, either. I intend to stay in one piece until I do get out of here."

"There won't be a sign painted on your back, Mr. Boggs."

Boggs puffed up, wanting to correct the *Mister* appellation. But perhaps the skills from his mandated anger management class had kicked in—or maybe he was simply curious enough to know why a stranger had come to see him. He dropped his cuffed wrists onto the table and leaned forward. "Then what the hell do you want from me?"

The visitor set a photograph on the table and pointed to the image. "I want you to tell me everything you can about this woman."

Chapter One

"Your arms and shoulders are too big."

Grayson Malone wobbled over the prostheses attached just above each knee and grabbed the balance bars on either side of him to steady himself. He'd made it up and down the rehabilitation center's ten-foot walkway all by himself, thank you very much, before the physical therapist with the long, honey-blond ponytail stepped up beside the railing. She crossed her arms and smirked up at him as if she was challenging him to prove her wrong.

"Too big?" He looked down into her gray-blue eyes and arched an eyebrow to meet her smirk. "They fit inside my T-shirt okay."

"Very funny."

Like him, Allison Tate was a veteran integrating back into the civilian world in Kansas City, Missouri. Although they'd served in different branches of the military, in different parts of the world, and in different capacities, he seemed to have more in common with her than any of the other therapists he worked with here at the clinic. Shared commiserations, pride and a sense of duty gave them plenty to talk about—as did the fact that they both lived in the same apartment building where veterans got a bit of a break on the monthly rent as a benefit of their service. In fact, they lived on the same floor, and had had several opportunities to connect outside of PT over the past few months. She was easy to talk to, and she was a good physical therapist. Allie knew when to push him and when to pull back as he adjusted to life in a wheelchair or walking on his new prosthetic limbs.

She was pushing now. "Seriously, Gray, the reason you're back here for PT is because you've pushed your recovery too hard. Yes, we finally have your new prostheses adjusted to fit the changing musculature of your thighs, which should even out your gait. But you're going to keep getting those spasms in your back and hips if you don't give your body a chance to adapt. You've been doing more than your PT exercises when you work out at home, haven't you?" she challenged.

"I was in the Marines for eleven years, Allie. I'm used to working out every day." He lifted his leg another shaky step and continued down the walkway. If he walked slowly enough and concentrated, he didn't need the rails, his crutches or the damn chair to be mobile. Although his wheelchair was still his fastest mode of travel, and his go-to when he needed to rest his back or give his residual limbs a break.

"There's a difference between being physically fit and having too much muscle." She moved along beside him. "You're top-heavy. It's throwing your balance off. Plus, it's more weight to carry on those joints." She flattened her palms at either side of his waist to steady him as he turned, and the skin beneath his T-shirt leaped at even that impersonal touch. "You need to take dancing lessons, relearn where your center of gravity is."

"Dancing?" Gray chuckled, chasing her down in swaying slow motion as she backed along the railing. He was fourth-generation military, a man's man. At least, he used to be. He wasn't sure exactly where he qualified on the macho scale now. He hadn't been man enough to keep his ex-girlfriend after shipping home on a medical discharge. Brittany had barely been able to look at him below his chin, much less help with his recovery. Despite her teary apology and professions of love, she'd confessed that lying in bed beside a man with no feet "*freaked her out*" and she'd broken up with him. Now he qualified for geekdom as a chemist and blood analyst for the Kansas City Crime Lab. Not exactly the catch he used to be. "I don't think I'm exactly the ballet or ballroom type."

Allie ducked beneath the railing and planted herself in front of him, forcing him to grab the railing to stop himself from plowing into her with his forward momentum. Instead of backing up to avoid a collision, Allie took a half step toward him. She braced one hand on the waistband of his sweatpants and splayed the other at the center of his chest. "Overworking one part of your body at the expense of another skews your balance. Dancing helps with coordination and mobility, too." She nudged his chest back, squaring his weight over his hips before sliding her hand up to his shoulder. Then she pried his left hand off the bar and rested her fingers lightly in his palm. "Put your other hand at my waist," she instructed.

Gray hated that he had to squeeze her arm for a moment until he found his balance over what used to be his legs and settled his hand above the flare of her hip. "Like this?"

"There you go. Let's hold this position for sixty seconds. You're a tall guy. Own it. Get used to the feel of your upper body centered over your hips, not leaning forward on your crutches or the bar. I want your legs and core to do the work, not your arms." She adjusted her own stance, moving closer so that he had to hold the posture or risk toppling over onto her. "That's it."

As they stood there in the mockery of a ballroom dance pose, with Gray tightening his core muscles and keeping his shoulders back like a good Marine, he breathed in Allie's scent—a blend of something antiseptic, likely her hand gel, with something flowery and more intimate underneath. He wondered at the hints of femininity beneath her tallish, tomboy facade. She was always confident and strong. Sure, her pink scrubs and thick, gorgeous hair reminded him that she was a woman. And like the women he'd served with or who worked with him at KCPD, she was a pal—a valued, respected colleague. Before holding her in his arms and standing close enough for the heat of her thighs to reach his, he'd never realized Allison Tate was also a girlie girl.

She squeezed her hand in his and retreated a step, urging him to move with her, while maintaining his posture. "That's it. Again. I know you're lifting weights in the gym at our building. You need to find something to exercise your lower extremities."

Urges that had lain dormant inside of Gray for nearly two years woke at the unintentionally suggestive words. First, she was an assault on his senses, and now his brain was filled with naughty ideas about the kind of exercise he'd like to do with her. Make that *used* to do. Make that… Gray stumbled. But Allie was there, holding him until he recovered his balance. Hell, how was he supposed to make love to a woman anymore? Although he'd discussed it with his counseling therapist, they didn't exactly cover the nuts and bolts of that in physical therapy.

"Maybe you should walk more at work," she suggested, "and not spend so much time in your wheelchair, hovering over your microscope and equipment in the lab."

"Crimes aren't going to solve themselves. I have to work. People can't wait for me to get from my lab to a meeting. The lab is a big building. There's a lot of ground to cover." Now he was just getting frustrated with himself for being less than the man he used to be—literally. Every time he thought he'd learned to accept his fate and settle into his new normal, a cruel voice laughed inside his head. *So, you think you're attracted to this woman? Ha. What are you going to do about it?*

Nothing.

He'd be her neighbor. He'd be her patient. He'd be her friend.

But he wasn't going to jeopardize any of that or embarrass himself by trying to be something more.

But Allie's teasing reprimands and positivity weren't going to stop. "Maybe you could leave the lab and go work actual crimes scenes."

"I've worked crime scenes. When my chair or the possibility of dropping my crutches won't jeopardize the integrity of the evidence." That didn't give him as many opportunities to get out into the field as he liked, but he wouldn't jeopardize his work or that of any of the other criminalists he worked with by adding his own tracks or trace to a scene. "Besides, the bulk of blood analysis is done in the lab. I can evaluate blood spatter or spray patterns from the pictures other members of my team bring me."

"Okay." They reached the end of the walkway, with Allie still holding him like a dance partner and encouraging him to move with her. "Then take up running," she suggested.

He snorted at that, scarcely aware that he'd turned without having to grab the railings or lean on her. Then they were *dancing*, step-by-step, back down the walkway. "Seriously. Look into a pair of prostheses with curved blades. Like that runner from South Africa. Who supposedly murdered his girlfriend. And I'm guessing someone like you from their crime lab helped put him away."

She stopped moving and her voice trailed off. Her hand slipped from his shoulder down to the crook of his elbow, and he could see her thoughts turning inward to a sad or troubling memory. Had the mention of a dangerous boy-friend triggered something she'd rather forget?

"Allie?" Gray squeezed the hand he still held.

She shook off those troubling thoughts and moved her free hand back to his shoulder, giving him a nudge to straighten him back into place. He hadn't even realized he'd leaned toward her. He did realize it took several seconds for her gray-blue gaze to tilt up to his again. But she was smiling. Maybe she was simply empathetic to what had been a tragic news story. "I run several times a week. It's a great stress reducer for me. That's the time I'm supposed to think through my to-do list and solve all the world's prob-lems, but I find it's usually thirty to forty minutes of not thinking about anything at all. Mentally, I find it very re-laxing. Plus, it keeps my lungs and leg muscles strong, and allows me to indulge in the ice cream I love without put-ting any more weight on my hips and butt. You might find it helpful, too. It gives you those exercise endorphins you must crave, and keeps you from being a grump. But you won't get top-heavy."

Gray's gaze dropped to said hips and butt, not seeing anything he didn't like about those curves. Then he realized he was eyeballing her, and that she'd danced him back to the opposite end of the walkway before he saw another man's hand reaching toward her. He instinctively slipped his hand to the small of her back and tightened his grip, pulling her hips into his. But the impulse to turn and put himself between Allie and the perceived threat didn't come fast enough.

"You flirtin' with my patient, Tate?" Another physical therapist, dressed in nylon running pants and a polo, settled his fingers atop Allie's shoulder.

Doug Friesen seemed oblivious to the way Allie flinched away from his touch and ducked beneath the railing to the opposite side of the walkway, releasing Gray, as well. "I was keeping an eye on Gray while you were helping Ben. Mrs. Burroughs still has a few minutes left on the stationary bike. Maeve is watching her now. Her patient was a no-show." She glanced over to the striking older woman with gray streaks in her dark hair, sighing at the woman's responding wink and thumbs-up, which seemed to imply there was something romantic about her impromptu *dance* with Gray. Allie shook her head at the shameless matchmaking before patting Gray's arm. "I know this guy is a perfectionist. I could see his posture flagging, and I knew that exercising in that position wasn't going to help those back spasms he's been having."

Doug studied Gray's alignment and frowned. "Are you saying I'm not doing my job right?"

Allie shrugged at his mildly defensive tone. "I'm saying

we're a team here, and since we're understaffed and usually have to cover more than one patient, we help each other out where needed." She nodded toward the medically retired Army sergeant at the dexterity table who was adjusting to his new life with one hand. "Your session with Ben was running long. Maeve is keeping Mrs. Burroughs from trying to set me up with her son and every man in the room between twenty and eighty. In return, I keep your patient moving when you're otherwise occupied. Plus, I'm covering for Maeve a couple of hours on Saturday morning."

"Of course. Thanks." Doug thumbed over his shoulder to the table where he'd set up a new puzzle block challenge for Ben Hunter to practice with the prosthetic hook on his left arm. "You sure you don't want to trade with me? Sergeant Hunter is in a snit about something. Said he'd rather work with you than anybody else. It took longer than I expected to convince him to stay for therapy today and work with me. Sorry about that, Captain." Even though he'd asked him to use his given name, Doug had once told Gray that his service in the Army National Guard had ingrained in him the habit of calling the veterans he worked with by their rank. "Let me see you make the walk one more time, and then I'll get you on the massage table for a few minutes to put some heat packs on you."

Ignoring the knots in his hips and back, Gray dutifully retraced his steps. But his gaze was focused on Allie. Her butt formed a perfect heart shape as she bent over to pick up a towel that had fallen to the floor. That woman did not need to worry about her love for ice cream. Those curves were somehow both athletic and lush. Between their hips and chests brushing against each other, her willingness to touch him and that particularly lovely view, his manhood had perked up with a distinct interest in the friendly blonde who lived in the apartment next to his. But he was certain that having sex with his funny, smart, delectable neighbor wasn't the sort of lower body exercise the PT had in mind.

Gray and Allie were friends. Neighbors. He hitched a ride with her to physical therapy on the mornings he had a session before work, or carpooled home when he came in afterward, like today. Sometimes they ran errands together since he was still getting comfortable driving the van with hand controls he'd been trained on. He'd opened a pickle jar for her and disposed of the mouse trap she'd set for the little friend who'd invaded the cabinet under her kitchen sink this past winter. They'd bonded over the fact they were both veterans, and they both loved thin-crust pizza and Kansas City Chiefs football.

Even before today's overt awareness of all things Allie Tate had caught him off guard, he'd considered asking her out on a date. But what was the point? He'd occasionally seen a man *walk* up to her door to take her out. He couldn't do that. He enjoyed her company, admired her self-sufficiency and appreciated her humor so much that he felt like a creeper for fantasizing about taking their friend-zone relationship to the next level, like any normal man would. But Grayson Malone, who'd left his legs and two of his best friends back in the Middle East, wasn't a normal man. He needed metal rods and suction cups, or that damned wheelchair, to get around. Hell, he wasn't even sure how he would make love to a woman anymore. The plumbing still worked, judging by his body's stirring interest in Allie, but rods of cold titanium and a patchwork of scars around both stumps were hardly a turn-on. What if she physically recoiled like Brittany had? Or even politely glanced away? How was he supposed to brace himself without hurting her? Or even put himself inside her when he needed both hands to stay upright? Not to mention how studly his appeal must be after plopping down on his butt or landing on his face because he'd tripped over his nonexistent feet.

"Gray? Malone!" Allie's touch on his arm interrupted his deep thoughts.

"Huh?"

"You were a million miles away."

Actually, his thoughts had been right here in this room. On the woman standing beside him, her eyes narrowed as if his preoccupation worried her. "I'm sorry. It's been a long day. What did you ask me?"

"Do you need a ride home this evening? I'm not sure how you got here from work. I didn't see your van out front. I was going to order some takeout and pick it up on the way home. Otherwise, I'm heading straight there."

"Jackson dropped me off."

Allie's eyes widened, maybe trying to place his friend from the crime lab. "The big guy?"

Gray nodded.

"He's hasn't been waiting for you this whole time, has he?"

Jackson Dobbs? Sitting in a room surrounded by this many people he didn't know? Not likely. "I sent him home. I've got a car scheduled to pick me up."

"You didn't drive your van?" she asked.

Man, he had been lost inside his head. When had Doug circled around behind Allie? True, the brown-haired guy was retrieving Gray's metal crutches, but generally, Gray was hyperaware of his surroundings. Observing the people around him had been too deeply ingrained in him by the Corps.

"I'm not a hundred percent confident with my reflexes," he answered honestly, meeting Allie's gaze. "So, I try to avoid rush hour traffic. Especially after dark."

"Then let me drive you," she offered. "Save the money. We're going to the same place."

He shook his head. "It's enough of an imposition getting me here to PT. You don't need to be hauling me around the city."

"It's *not* an imposition. If I've ever made you feel like that, I'm sorry."

There was a difference between not being an imposition, and actually being needed. Wanted for something more than opening pickle jars and disposing of dead rodents.

Gray accepted the crutches Doug handed him and slipped them on to his forearms. The tension around Allie's mouth hadn't been there a few seconds ago. It made him want to lighten her mood. "Not to worry. I've got PT again on Friday morning. I could use a ride then."

Her smile felt like a hell of a reward for a simple carpool invitation. "How about you drive on Friday," she suggested. "It'll give you more practice with the hand controls. And since the days are starting to get longer, you won't be driving at night on the way home. I get off work early on Friday, so you could pick me up, and we'd get there before sunset."

The tension returned as Doug touched the small of her back. "I thought you and I could catch dinner and a movie on Friday night. You said you'd like to do that sometime."

"I'm sorry, Doug." She turned and retreated a step from her coworker, a step closer to Gray. "Thanks for asking.

But I'm working Saturday morning, so I don't want to be out late."

"I'll give you a ride home Friday if you need it," the other man offered.

"It's more convenient if Gray does it. We live in the same building, down the hall from each other. You live across the city. It would be hugely out of your way."

Even with his rusty people skills, it was easy to pick up on Allie's discomfort with Doug and her attempt to let him down without hurting his feelings. Gray leaned his hands into the grips of his crutches and stepped up beside her. "If you trust me to drive you, I'd be happy to chauffeur you around. I could use the practice."

Her delicate nostrils flared with a sigh of relief. "I don't mind riding in your van if you don't mind squeezing into my Accord. Gas prices are nuts right now, anyway. Let's carpool and save money. I'll drive tonight—you take Friday."

"You having money issues?" Doug asked. Even Gray cringed at the tactless question. "All the more reason for me to give you a ride."

"You'll do no such thing." She smiled as she said the words, but Gray wasn't imagining the way her hands fisted in the towel. "I'm trying to save the planet. Help Gray with his occupational therapy. And—" she glanced up at Gray again "—have someone to talk to during the boring commute. You know, like friends do?"

"I can talk to you friendly-like," Doug insisted.

Gray read the silent plea in her eyes. There was something else besides a neighborly favor between friends going on here. But whether Allie was trying to avoid Doug, specifically, or something else, he couldn't tell. He wouldn't avoid those instincts that told him something was off with his next-door neighbor. The last time he'd ignored that little warning voice that said something wasn't right, he'd come home to Kansas City a double amputee.

He might not be a fully functional warrior anymore, but he could be a friend and help Allie out. Even if all she needed from him was an excuse to avoid Doug.

"All right. I'll cancel my car tonight. We're getting takeout for two, though—and I'm paying for it. Also, I'd appreciate the backup when I drive on Friday—just in case my coordination is off, or I get distracted making sure I'm doing everything right."

Allie's smile of relief bloomed across her face. "I'd love to ride shotgun with you."

Doug's noisy grunt made him sound like he was about thirteen years old. "Looks like Sergeant Hunter is about to have a meltdown. I'll get him started on the treadmill—let him run off that temper." He eyed the young woman with the short brunette hair chatting with Mrs. Burroughs before nodding to Gray. "I'll see if Maeve is free on Friday. Don't leave before I get those heat packs on your back and do today's exit survey."

"I won't."

Once Doug was out of earshot, Allie groaned beside Gray. "Why do I feel like I've just thrown Maeve under the bus?"

"I'm happy to help out with whatever that was. But will my wheelchair fit in your car? I'll still give you the out and stick with my car service."

"We'll make it fit. Possibly in the back seat if it won't go in the trunk." Allie smiled up at Gray. "I appreciate the help more than you know." She glanced back at Doug before squeezing Gray's arm and excusing herself. "I need to rescue Maeve and get Mrs. Burroughs through her electric-pulse treatment on her hip. See you in about twenty-five minutes. I owe you one, Gray." She tilted her gray-blue eyes up to his. "You're my hero."

Chapter Two

Allie carried Grayson's crutches onto the elevator and held the doors open while he rolled his wheelchair inside. The entire ride home she wondered how the friendly—and dare she say flirty?—vibe they'd shared at the PT clinic had become dark and closed off. The many moods of Grayson Malone were as confusing as they were intriguing. What had she said or done to send him so deep inside his head that the only words he'd spoken on the drive home had been to give his order to the Chinese restaurant where they'd stopped to pick up dinner?

As much as his unexplained silences ticked her off—after all, she was a medical professional and a veteran, to boot, who had some experience helping vets deal with reintegrating into civilian life and post-traumatic stress—something twisted in her heart to imagine the pain or frustration or flashback or regret he was dealing with all by himself right now.

Although she would have happily walked beside him at his pace from her car through the parking garage, he'd insisted on removing his prostheses and using his wheelchair. He'd said his back was hurting after the physical therapy session, which probably wasn't a lie. But she suspected he was self-conscious about his awkward gait and moving slowly with his prosthetic limbs as much as any kind of physical pain he might be feeling. Her tall, broad-shouldered neighbor with the intelligent green eyes and dark blond hair still cut in its high and tight style from his Marine Corps years wasn't the first disabled veteran she'd worked with at the physical therapy center.

But he was the only one who'd ever sparked any interest. The only one she'd ever seen as something more than a patient. The only one she'd *danced* with.

That thought should have scared her.

But she'd still turned to him for help this evening.

And he'd been in a brooding, distant mood ever since.

"Thanks for the save," she said after they entered the elevator, while she waited for Gray to spin his chair to face the front. Then, she pushed the button for the third floor and tried once more to generate a neutral, neighborly conversation to get them back to where they'd been less than two hours ago. "There are only so many ways I can say no to Doug, and I've tried them all. But he keeps asking me out. Plus, he's the handsy type. He finds ways to touch me at work all the time. It's always impersonal, nothing overtly sexual, but it doesn't stop."

"You don't like Doug?" Gray adjusted the bags of Chinese takeout over the gym bag on his lap.

She tried not to jump at his astute response, then realized this conversation was heading into her own dangerous territory.

"I'm kind of off men and dating right now," she admitted without explaining why. "I moved to Kansas City for a fresh start. I haven't even been here a year yet. I want to stand on my own two feet and settle into this new version of my life now that I've left the Navy behind me."

The Navy wasn't the only thing she'd left behind in Florida.

"You don't want to be tied to anyone right now," Gray clarified.

"Not the way Doug wants. I'm willing to be friends. But my patience is wearing thin. I can't tell if he's clueless or doesn't care that I'm not interested the way he is. Maybe he thinks persistence will change my mind." Allie shrugged. "I don't even think he's that into me. It's the thrill of conquest he likes. Hence his eagerness to hit on Maeve seconds after I shot him down."

"You need to flat out tell him no."

Allie shook her head with a wry smile. "I have to work with him. I don't want to make things awkward between us."

"It's already awkward for you." She heard the innate command of an officer in Gray's tone. At least, that clipped authority was better than the perfunctory silences they'd shared on the ride home. "That's not fair. Tell him no."

"Maybe if I told him I had a boyfriend, he'd back off." She sighed at how high school that solution sounded. "But then I'd have to come up with someone to play the part."

Allie eyed the prime candidate across from her. For one wild second, she considered asking for his help with that, too. The idea of Grayson Malone claiming her as his woman wasn't repugnant. Even with his mood swings from sexy protector to mysterious grump, it wasn't repugnant at all. But *she* was the one who didn't want to be in a relationship—real or fake—right now. The last one had nearly killed her.

Oh, God. She hoped she wasn't attracted to Gray because

some subconscious part of her brain thought his wheelchair or prosthetic legs made him seem weaker than Noah Boggs had been—like she could take him in a physical fight if she had to. Allie shook her head, dismissing the thought as soon as the possibility had flitted through her brain. Standing upright, Grayson Malone was a man who made her feel petite, sheltered, feminine. And that upper body strength was no joke. Even with part of it missing, his body was in better shape than Noah's had been. Allie's skin prickled with goose bumps at the thought of sitting in Gray's lap, snugging herself against his hard chest and feeling those arms wrap around her. And though there was a bleakness to those dark green eyes right now, she'd seen kindness there. Alertness. Humor and intelligence, too. Noah's eyes had been cold and smug, and at the end, full of rage.

No, she wasn't attracted to Gray because he was weak or controllable. She was attracted to him because he was interesting and intelligent and handsome. She was attracted to his strength—be it physical, character or intellectual—and the certainty that he'd never use that strength against her.

She curled her fingers into her palm, resisting the urge to stroke them across Gray's lightly stubbled jaw. The elevator filled with the delicious scents of cashew chicken and crab Rangoon, along with the more subtle scent of Gray—slightly musky from working out, slightly spicy from his soap or shampoo, and completely masculine in a way that woke feminine impulses in her that she didn't want to acknowledge.

Besides, she had a feeling his answer to faking a relationship would be no, if not *hell no*, judging by the way Gray stared straight ahead at the steel doors.

Deflecting any concern he might have for her relationship with her coworker, Allie broke the awkward silence and switched topics. "Carpooling on the days we're going to the same location at the same time makes economic and environmental sense. And I'm serious about you practicing your driving. You've had that van for four months now. I know the snow and ice we had this past winter made it tricky to learn. Theoretically, though, you could drive a regular car as long as you have your prosthetic legs on. It's time for you to own how far you've come in your recovery."

The doors opened onto the third floor, and he gestured for her to precede him out. "I worry that I'm more of a menace to other people than myself."

"Why do you do that?" Getting a little fed up with this particularly negative mood, she turned on him the moment he rolled up beside her. "You always deflect compliments and words of encouragement. Why do you make light of the fact you survived a war zone? Transitioned into a cool new civilian job? Come through countless surgeries and psychological therapy? Mastered your chair *and* walking *and* driving again? I know you're still dealing with post-traumatic stress, mourning the guys in your unit you lost and getting used to your new normal. But you've conquered more in two years than most men tackle in a lifetime. I'm in awe of you, Gray. I see your success, not your shortcomings."

His eyes locked on to hers for several charged moments before he dismissed her vehement speech and rolled past her toward their apartments. "Therapy session is over, Allie. I'm your neighbor, not your patient, certainly not your *hero*. Let's eat dinner and call it a night."

Was that what this mood swing was all about? Because she'd been grateful enough to thank him for stepping up when she'd needed a friend? She rolled her eyes before following. Stubborn man. For a few minutes at the clinic when he'd put his hand on her waist and they'd practically danced, and then when he'd pulled her body flush with his to avoid Doug's touch, she thought they'd made a connection beyond being neighbors. Certainly, the interest she'd felt stirring behind his zipper meant he wasn't completely immune to her. She'd even imagined what it would be like if they were really dancing. At five-nine, she was on the tall side for a woman, and was still as fit and athletic as she'd been on active duty, maybe even more so after her dealings with Noah. But Gray stood half a foot taller, making her feel feminine and almost delicate when she stood close to him. He was the perfect height for her to lean in and tuck her forehead against the juncture of his neck and shoulder. And then he'd answered her silent plea for help. Like a real hero, he'd had her back when she'd needed someone. Allie swore she'd felt something a little like lust and a lot more than affection stirring deep inside her.

She'd needed an excuse *not* to accept any favors from Doug Friesen. He already made working at the clinic uncomfortable with his innuendos about wanting to be more than coworkers. But she didn't want to tell him to go suck an egg, or to break his wrist if he touched her one more time, because she'd still have to come back and work an eight-hour shift with him the next day.

Allie had already had her fill of men who wouldn't take no for an answer.

Even more than a practical desire to avoid any awkwardness at work, especially around the patients—Doug didn't spark any frissons of lust or affection in her. She supposed he was good-looking in a preppy, class president sort of way. He was a skilled therapist, had a good rapport with his patients. But he didn't draw her eye when he walked across the room. He didn't challenge her with his wit and intelligence. He didn't make her tingle.

She had male friends, from both her time in the Navy and here in Kansas City. Since moving to the Midwest, she'd forced herself to go on a few dates—some good, some bad—but none were memorable. She'd gone into the Navy to get her medical training and see something of the world. In some ways, she'd seen far too much, and had been ready to move closer to her folks, who lived in a small town in central Missouri, when her commitment was up. She had a solid, rewarding career. But she wasn't going to settle for a guy like Doug. Nice, maybe, but blah. Boring. Inconsiderate. She wanted more.

Allie desperately wanted to tingle.

Inhaling a deep breath, she watched Gray unlock the door to the apartment next to hers. Damn. Look who made her tingle. A moody, wounded Marine whose protective alpha nature snuck out when he wasn't thinking about his legs and scars.

More than that tingle of awareness, Allie wanted to feel safe.

She wasn't sure any man could pull off that miracle anymore. Doug didn't make her feel safe. Her ex-boyfriend certainly hadn't. Even restraining orders from both the Navy and a civil judge against Noah Boggs didn't make her feel completely safe.

She couldn't say that Grayson Malone made her feel safe. After all, he was a patient of hers, theoretically making her the stronger member of their relationship. Yes, he was a decorated Marine, but he used his brain more than his fractured body now. She wasn't certain he could stop the threat she felt lurking in the corners of her life.

But she trusted him.

Grayson was a good man. He was a criminalist at the crime lab, specializing in blood analysis and chemistry. And yeah, with those muscular shoulders, close-cropped hair and piercing green eyes, she could see traces of the Marine he once had been. His self-confidence might have taken a serious hit, since he'd clearly been a physical man before his injuries. But he was funny and considerate— when his demons and self-doubts didn't shut him down. And he'd caught on to her plea to not leave her alone with Doug on Friday night.

She'd embrace that trust. Let her guard down for the hour or so they'd share over dinner and be grateful that there was at least one man in this world she didn't have to worry about hurting her.

Allie reached her own door and inserted the key before speaking again. "I'm going to change out of my work clothes and wash my face. I'll be over in about ten minutes to eat." Or, since he'd done her a favor with Doug, maybe she'd do him the favor of letting him brood all by his moody self. "If you still want the company. Otherwise, I can take my food now and say good night."

"No." With deft precision, he spun his chair in the open doorway and faced her. "Sorry I turned into such a downer. Sometimes, I wish my emotions were as easy to process as a piece of evidence is." Those green eyes drilled into hers. "But I'd like the company. If you can put up with me."

Eloquence aside, as apologies went, that one was pretty sweet. "I've put up with worse than you, Malone," she teased.

"In your line of work, Tate, I bet you have." The harsh

line of Gray's mouth softened with the hint of a smile, and he rolled his chair into his apartment. "I'll stick the food in the microwave to keep it warm. See you in ten."

Relieved that they seemed to be on friendly footing again, Allie opened her door...and froze in her tracks. Her jaw gaped open at the utter devastation that greeted her.

Payback.

The single word was written in crimson paint—at least she hoped it was paint—over and over, across her TV screen, the front of her grandmother's hutch, the bank of cabinets hanging above her kitchen peninsula, and in varying sizes and designs across every wall.

So much rage. So much destruction. The blood seemed to drain from her head to her toes, leaving her shivering in its wake.

Blips of memory—fear that she was losing her mind, harsh words, hard fists, cruel humiliation—flashed through her brain. Not again. She'd done her part. She thought she'd left her nightmare behind. But this twisted...sick...rage...

Allie swallowed hard and searched for her voice.

"Gray?" The word came out on a strangled gasp. She pushed back her fear and retreated from the gruesome sight. She was a fighter. That was why she was here now. That was why she was alive at all. Because she fought back. "Gray?" Air finally poured into her lungs, and she screamed. "Gray!"

Allie stumbled down the hallway. Gray was already out his door, pumping his wheelchair toward her. "Allie? What's wrong?"

She met him halfway, digging her fingers into the shoulder of his fleece hoodie. He wrapped a hand around her forearm, his narrowed eyes demanding an explanation. "Someone's been in my apartment. It's…awful."

"Is the intruder still there?" He pulled his cell phone from his pocket and pushed forward.

"I don't think so. But I didn't get past the entryway. And I didn't stick around to look."

"Get inside my apartment. Lock the door behind you."

Instead of obeying his orders, Allie fell into step behind him, still clinging to his shoulder. "You can't go in there by yourself. If he's still there, you'll need backup."

Besides, she didn't want to be alone, not when she was on the verge of forgetting every bit of training she'd had and panicking.

"You think I need backup?" he asked, hesitating.

"This doesn't have a damn thing to do with your legs." She flipped open the can of pepper spray she carried. "Every soldier needs backup."

Every sailor did, too.

He nodded sharply, his green eyes meeting hers. "All right. But you stay behind me. And don't accidentally shoot me with that stuff."

Allie scanned up and down the empty hallway. "I won't."

Gray nudged open her door and cursed, looking at the blood. Something that looked like blood. It was still awful. Still unsettling. Still so full of hate.

"Eyes on me, Lieutenant," Gray ordered. Startled by his command, she automatically obeyed. He rested his hand over hers, forcing Allie to retreat from the horrific sight as he rolled away from the opening. He punched in 911. She kept her gaze locked on his as the dispatcher picked up. He quickly identified himself as an adjunct of KCPD, gave their address and asked for the police. He squeezed her trembling hand in his. "I'm going to need a team from the crime lab here, too."

Chapter Three

"It's blood." Gray watched the end of the swab turn pink, confirming his suspicion. He dropped the phenolphthalein reagent into his kit beside his chair, then secured the swab with the trace he'd swiped off Allie's living room wall in a sterile evidence tube before labeling it and stowing it in his evidence kit, as well. He looked over to his team leader, Lexi Callahan-Murphy, who was numbering and photographing the impressions in the carpet and on a sofa cushion that could indicate the size of shoe, if not an actual shoe print, worn by the intruder. "Every sample from every surface I've retrieved—it's all presumptive positive for blood."

Lexi tucked a strand of the light brown hair that hung from beneath her CSI ball cap behind her ear and looked up from her work. "Human blood?"

"I'd have to type it at the lab to confirm. There may be some animal blood mixed in. Just from the sheer volume— the perp would have to have cleaned out a blood bank to get this much. But again, I want to run these samples in the lab before making any definitive conclusion."

Zoe Stockman, the rookie on the crime lab's C team, plucked a fiber from the carpet near the baseboard with her tweezers and studied it in the beam of her flashlight.

"This is too thick and coarse to be a human hair. It looks like it has blood on it, though." She clenched the flashlight between her teeth to secure the fiber in an evidence envelope. "Could have come from a paintbrush," she suggested.

Although she still hadn't developed the confidence the rest of the team shared while processing a scene, especially after a disastrous experience with the former criminalist who'd been her mentor, Gray believed in Zoe's technical proficiency. "I suspect you're right," he agreed. "Looks like a lot of this was painted on. Some of it was thrown, obviously," he said, nodding toward the spatter of red droplets on the couch and wall. "Whoever it was had to have had plenty of uninterrupted time to make this big a mess."

Ever the team builder, and attuned to the needs of the criminalists she supervised, Lexi smiled at Zoe. "Good work, Zo. One fiber isn't a lot to go on, but you might be able to trace the make and manufacturer, and then give us an idea on where our perp might have purchased it."

A faint smile replaced the flashlight on Zoe's lips. "I'll make it my priority back at the lab tomorrow." Her gaze darted briefly to his. "You know, since Gray's a friend and all."

He offered her a curt nod. "Appreciate it."

Gray rolled his chair back a couple of feet to take in the damage and violation of what should have been Allie's safe haven from the world. He wasn't a detective, but he'd learned to read the enemy well enough in his time with the Marines in the Middle East and other hot spots around the world. Whoever had done this was very angry and extremely obsessed with Allie.

Payback was a personal message.

But what could his pretty, practical, strong-willed neighbor have done to anyone that would warrant this kind of threat?

It was late, and hunger gnawed at the walls of his stomach from the dinner he'd missed. But Gray's analytical brain was running on all cylinders, cataloging the movement of criminalists and police officers around Allie's once-tidy apartment, as well as thinking back to his worst day in the Corps and a more recent trial where his expert testimony had helped put away a disturbed young man who'd murdered three women. When the rocket-propelled grenade had hit his convoy carrying weapons and explosives from the base to the front line, there'd been plenty of blood to go around— the scattered body parts of his dead and wounded buddies, the shredded muscles and arteries hanging from his own shattered bones. In court, he'd explained how the young man had drained the blood from his victims, much like a coroner preparing a body for a funeral. It was his analysis of the jars of blood stored in the suspect's basement, and the trace amounts of embalming chemicals he'd found in them, that had linked Jamie Kleinschmidt to the three women and secured his conviction. He suspected there had been even more victims, but three confirmed kills were enough to secure a place for Kleinschmidt on Missouri's death row.

Allie's apartment wasn't a murder scene or a war zone. But there was a hell of a lot of blood here, too.

And a hell of a lot of questions he needed answers to.

Gray rubbed at the sweats covering his muscular thighs, willing the phantom pain that sparked through the nerves at the end of his stumps to recede. The fact that he was feeling anything there at all had become a signal that something was off. About the crime scene? About Allie? With himself? Something was nagging in the recesses of his brain that he needed to check before he lost the effectiveness and objectivity necessary to complete his mission—er, to do his job.

Usually, Grayson possessed a clinical mind that allowed him to separate his science from his emotions. He'd survived on that battlefield by being able to separate his pain and fear and grief from the medical training necessary to keep himself from bleeding out and dying until another team could get to him. But the threats painted on Allie's walls and furniture bothered him more than the sounds and smells of battlefield triage or the gruesome collection of trophies he'd cataloged in a serial killer's basement. He was a wounded Marine who'd seen and dealt out death. A chemist and criminalist who analyzed the aftermath of a victim's worst day.

This should be just another crime scene he needed to process.

Only, as he watched Allie hugging her arms beneath her breasts, her hips rocking against the edge of the countertop in her kitchen like the nervous tapping of a foot while she dutifully answered questions from the dark-haired female officer assigned to the case, Gray knew this was anything but another crime scene.

The urge to protect Allie tightened the muscles across his arms and chest, while his hands fisted around the wheels of his chair. Grayson wanted to go to her. He wanted to be her champion the way he had been earlier that evening at the clinic when Doug Friesen wouldn't keep his hands off her. In the elevator she'd even hinted that he could pretend to be her boyfriend to help keep Friesen's unwanted attention at bay. But Gray didn't want to do *pretend* with a woman. He didn't know whether to feel flattered that she saw him as a worthy candidate to be her partner or insulted that she believed *fake* was the only kind of relationship he could handle. Hell, he shouldn't even be considering a relationship—real or pretend.

Allie was a veteran Navy lieutenant, strong both physically and mentally. She didn't need a man to take over, but she could use a friend to stand beside her, a fellow veteran to have her back while she dealt with the job in front of her. Gray could see that today had taken a toll on her, and his moodiness hadn't helped. Despite the healthy natural glow of her skin, he could see the shadows beneath her eyes, and read the tension bracketing her mouth as she discussed the break-in with Officer Cutler.

The reality was Grayson Malone wasn't anybody's champion. Not anymore. He forced his grip to relax. He couldn't take his chair through her apartment, as the wheel tracks might compromise the foot impressions and blood spatter in the carpet. If he avoided the taped-off path they suspected the intruder had taken from one bloody message to the next, he'd have to move furniture to maneuver his chair. And with the other members of his CSI team, Officer Cutler and Allie herself watching, Gray wasn't about to crawl to the kitchen on his arms and stumps the way he often navigated his own apartment.

His newly fitted prosthetic limbs were in their bag, down the hall, inside his apartment. By the time he'd considered retrieving them and putting them on so he could move around more like a normal man, the moment that Allie needed support and comfort had passed. Now she was striding out of the kitchen ahead of Officer Cutler, heading toward the open door where Lexi's husband, Officer Aiden Murphy, and his K-9 partner, Blue, were patrolling the hallway to keep the scene clear of curious neighbors.

Like his, the apartment was small enough that there were no private conversations unless someone whispered. "I've been gone since early this morning," Allie explained to the shorter woman. "Went for a run and then drove to work. I showered and changed into my scrubs there."

Officer Cutler did the math. "That gave our perp about thirteen hours without interruption to do this." She jotted the information in her notes. "I'll check with the neighbors and building staff to see if anyone heard any activity during that time frame." She glanced past Allie to Shane Duvall. The bearded and bespectacled single dad was dusting the door locks and frame for prints. "Any signs of forced entry?"

"None." Shane snapped a picture of a print he'd found on the doorknob before lifting the print with tape and sealing it. "The intruder had access. I don't even see pick marks in the lock."

Jackson Dobbs, a big, quiet man, and probably Gray's best friend at the lab, was working beside Shane. "We'll need your prints, ma'am."

Gray rolled a few inches closer. "You'll need to exclude mine, too. I opened the door after Allie noticed the break-in."

Jackson simply nodded.

"Could you have forgotten to lock your door this morning?" Officer Cutler asked.

Allie's ponytail whipped back and forth against her shoulders as she shook her head. "I don't forget that. Ever."

Gina Cutler paused a moment at Allie's vehement denial before making a note. "So, we're looking for someone who has a key. Or who had the opportunity to make a copy of yours."

"I haven't given a spare key to anyone." Allie's gaze

darted to Gray's. "Not even a neighbor if I should get locked out. I keep my keys in my bag at work in a locker with a combination lock. Otherwise, they're on me."

"*Is* there a spare key?" Gina asked. "Where do you keep it?"

"It's taped inside my mailbox downstairs."

"Shane." Lexi ordered her teammate to process the second key.

Shane closed his kit and headed out the door. "I'm on it." He held out his hand for Allie's mailbox key. "I'll dust the key and mailbox for prints. And I'll see if the tape has been replaced recently or has any trace on it. I should also be able to tell if a copy was made."

Allie removed the mailbox key from her key ring but seemed reluctant to hand it over. Had Gray ever realized how paranoid she was about restricting access to her apartment? Seeing her hesitation, he brushed his plastic-gloved fingertips across her forearm, hating that she startled at even that light touch. "You can trust Shane, Allie. I'll vouch for him."

Her lips curved into a brief smile, and she handed over the key. "Of course. You're just doing your job."

"Yes, ma'am," Shane assured her. He clasped the key in his hand. "I'll bring this back, I promise. And I'll let you know if I see any signs of tampering with your mailbox."

"Thank you." She exchanged a nod with Shane, and he headed to the stairs at the end of the hallway.

"The building super has a master key," Gray pointed out, inching his chair closer to Allie's side before turning to face Officer Cutler. "You should check out who has access to that set of keys, as well."

Gina made that note, too. "Just a couple more questions, Ms. Tate. Does it look like anything's missing?"

Allie heaved an impatient sigh. "You asked me that already."

"And now that you've had a little time to think about it, I'm asking you again." Gina made no apology for doing her job well. "Oftentimes, after the initial shock of something like this wears off, the person I'm interviewing can remember more details."

After holding the other woman's gaze for a moment, Allie dutifully surveyed her apartment again. While the main rooms of her apartment had been vandalized, nothing of conventional value, like the big-screen TV, the laptop on her kitchen table or what looked like some genuine antiques inside her hutch, had been taken.

"Nothing that I've noticed." Allie pulled her hands inside the sleeves of the fitted running shirt she wore under her scrub top, tugging the ends down past her fingertips and poking her thumbs through the wrist holes.

Was she cold? Was the fear and feeling of violation getting to her? Were those subtle, almost constant movements of her fingers and arms and swaying posture her way of dispelling nervous energy so that she could hold on to her patience and rational thought? Or were they signs of a crack in her protective armor?

Instinctively needing to support her in some way, to let the fellow veteran know that he had her back when she needed him, Gray unzipped the gray hoodie he wore and shrugged out of it.

"Can you tell if anything new has been added?" Gina asked.

Allie frowned at the question. "New? Like what?"

"A hidden camera? A love letter? A more specific threat?" Gina Cutler was a pint-size dynamo who'd been a top candidate for KCPD's SWAT teams until getting shot on a routine patrol call took her out of the running. But she'd honed her empathetic instincts and street smarts to become one of the department's most skilled investigators. "Most of the cases I handle now are women and minors who've been victimized. We obviously don't have the whole story yet, but this doesn't feel like a robbery to me. Or random vandalism. It feels very personal."

The color drained from Allie's cheeks as she fisted the end of each sleeve in her fingers and hugged herself. "There's a camera on my laptop, but it's turned off right now. How would I know if I have a hidden camera?"

Jackson Dobbs, ever a man of few words, volunteered. "I'll look." He pushed to his feet and crossed to the back of her apartment to begin his search.

"No notes. No threats—beyond the obvious." Allie shrugged. "No spare body parts in my freezer or knife stuck in my great-grandmother's doll or men's boxer shorts in my lingerie drawer." Was that her idea of dark humor? Or was she speaking from some kind of experience? Gray couldn't read past the brittle shell of sarcasm surrounding her. But he could see her fingers shaking as she tucked them into her body for warmth or self-comfort.

"Here." Gray handed her his hoodie to put on. When she hesitated to take it, he pushed himself up onto his thighs to drape it around her shoulders. "You're shivering."

"Thanks." For a brief, charged moment, she looked him straight in the eye, as if she was surprised to see him at her level. Then Gray sank back onto his seat, and she shoved her arms into the sleeves of his jacket and zipped it up. "It's probably my adrenaline wearing off rather than being cold."

More than he had for the past several months, Gray wished he was standing on his own two legs so that he could wrap Allie up in his arms and take her away from this scene that so obviously upset her. But what he couldn't do physically, he could still do verbally—take control of the room. "Gina, you done asking her questions?"

"For now."

Gray touched Allie's elbow and nodded toward the doorway. "You should head next door and hang out there while we finish processing—"

"Whoa. Who's cleaning this mess up?" A short, stocky man in tan coveralls appeared in the doorway.

Allie spun around at the interruption, tripping on the wheel of Gray's chair. She would have landed in his lap if his hand on her back and at her waist didn't catch her to keep her upright. Gray tried not to make anything of the fact Allie made no effort to move away from him. Perhaps she wasn't aware of how his hands lingered against her, or how her leg still butted against the end of his thigh. "What are you doing here?"

Before the man who'd startled her could step inside, a warning growl from Aiden Murphy's Belgian Malinois *encouraged* him to raise his hands and back away.

"Easy, Blue." Aiden Murphy warned his K-9 partner to sit. "I need you back in the hallway, sir. This is an active crime scene."

The building superintendent Gray had just mentioned kept his hands in the air, but only retreated beyond the curious poke of Blue's nose. "I work here. This is my building," the thirtysomething man with short, thinning hair explained.

"Allie and I are friends." He peeked around the doorframe. "You all right, Al?"

Allie summoned a weak smile. "Yeah, Bubba. I'm okay. I wasn't here when the break-in happened."

Gina clicked her pen to add information to her notepad. "You are…?"

Allie made the introductions. "Officer Cutler, this is our building super, Bubba Summerfield."

"Bubba?" Gina arched a skeptical eyebrow.

"My real name's Jim—James. No one's called me that since I was a kid." Once he realized Blue wasn't going to take a bite out of him, he finally dropped his arms to gesture with them. "This is a good neighborhood. Stuff like this doesn't happen here. This building is filled with veterans and their families. Everybody here are good people. Unless one of them is messed up in the head. Or lost his temper or something. Some of our guys who've been in combat have post-traumatic stress."

With that comment, Allie took a step toward Bubba. "You're not talking about Mr. Malone, are you? He would never hurt me."

"I didn't mean nothin' personal by that, sir." Bubba peeked around her to offer Gray a quick apology before smiling at Allie. "I'm just sayin' I wouldn't expect anybody around here to do something like this." Ignoring both uniformed officers and the dog, Bubba reached for Allie. "You don't need to be afraid, okay? I'll keep a better eye on things. I promise."

Before his grubby fingers ever touched her sleeve, Allie cringed away from his touch. "Please don't."

Gray wasn't the only person in the room who could see that Allie was nearing the end of her rope. With a nod to

Gray, Gina shuttled Bubba out of the apartment. "Mr. Summerfield, I'd like to ask you a few questions. Have you been on duty all day?"

"Yeah. Well, I worked my regular nine-to-five shift, and then I've been on call this evening." Bubba spun his finger in the air, indicating the apartment behind them. "Seriously, who cleans this up? Am I going to have to repaint..."

By the time Officer Cutler had steered Bubba down the hallway to continue the interview, Allie had pulled her purse off her shoulder and dug through the contents. "Where is my phone?"

But her shaking hands made it difficult to latch on to things and she was getting more and more frustrated. When her sunglasses and a bag of tissues tumbled out onto the floor, she muttered a curse. Gray scooped up the fallen items, then captured her hand in his firm grip when she reached for them. "Hey." Finally, the tremors he felt in her dissipated and her gray-blue eyes locked on to his. "You're usually cool as a cucumber. Tonight, you're rattled. Talk to me."

"I'm not rattled." She followed his glance over to the bloody *Payback* painted on her kitchen cabinets. "Okay, I'm a little rattled," she admitted, dropping her gaze back to his. "I'm tired. Hungry. And rattled."

"You have a right to be," he agreed. He stroked his thumb over the back of her knuckles, urging her to explain whatever she was hiding from him.

"I just need to make a phone call. It could be important." She pulled away to deposit the items back inside her purse before resuming a less frantic search. "Is it too late to call Charleston?"

"Charleston, Missouri?" Gray frowned at the seemingly

random question. "That's clear on the other side of the state. Down in the Boot Heel."

"Charleston, South Carolina," Allie clarified, still searching.

"What's in South Carolina?" he asked, still not understanding the urgency of her actions.

"NAVCONBRIG CHASN."

Ah, hell. Not so random, after all.

Brig. Navy prison. Gray sat straight back in his chair. What did that have to do with Allie?

Lexi closed up her kit and joined them at the doorway, no doubt reading the wary concern in Gray's posture. "NAVCONBRIG what? What's that?"

Gray answered. "The Naval Consolidated Brig. It's part of a joint base with the US Air Force in South Carolina." But his gaze never left Allie. "You were stationed there?"

She shook her head. "I was stationed in Jacksonville, Florida, before my separation from the Navy and coming here to Kansas City."

The brig in Jacksonville would only house prisoners for a year or so. She was talking about a prison where military hard-timers served out their sentences.

"Who's in the brig in South Carolina? Someone who would do this to you? Someone with friends on the outside who would do this to you?" Lexi exchanged a look with her husband, then met Zoe and Jackson's curious stares. They were all waiting expectantly for her answer. But Allie's eyes stayed focused on Gray. This was not the lead any of Gray or his team had expected to find here tonight. But Allie had been out of the military for less than a year. It was definitely a lead he intended to pursue. He turned his head to Lexi. "Call Chelsea." The crime lab's computer guru could find just about any information any of them ever needed. "Have her look up the number."

"There's no need." Allie had finally found her phone. She pulled it out of her purse and held it up as if she was making a confession. "I have the brig number programmed in my cell."

Chapter Four

"Thank you, Sergeant. Yes. I'll do that." Allie disconnected her phone, shoved it into the pocket of her scrub pants and cursed. "I hate this."

If she hadn't inhaled the crisp, almost icy scent of Gray just then, blended with his own subtle musk on the hoodie she still wore, she might have hurled the phone across the room. But the unfamiliar, blatantly masculine scents reminded her that she wasn't in her own apartment. This wasn't her own space, her own things to take her frustration out on.

But not knowing, not being able to plan a course of action, feeling lost and helpless while she waited to be blindsided by something else—something worse than threats on her apartment walls—left Allie crawling inside her skin. She needed to go for a run—the physical exertion and mind-numbing endorphin release would do her good. She needed to be able to check out from the stress that was eating her up alive for a little while.

Only, the clock on Grayson's stove was ticking past midnight. It was too late for a woman alone to safely dash through the streets of Kansas City. Sneaking down to the treadmill in the building's workout room didn't hold much appeal, either. With the break-in, she clearly wasn't safe in her own space. Besides, she'd promised Gray she'd stay put so she wouldn't get in the way of the work his team from the crime lab needed to do. And, she'd stay safely locked behind his door so he wouldn't worry, and he could focus on the science that might give her the answers that her phone call to South Carolina had not.

Allie picked at the veggies in her Snow-White Chicken, wishing she had something to contribute to Gray's team besides staying out of their way. After he'd settled her into his apartment, pointed out where the necessaries were located, and encouraged her to make herself at home, he'd locked her in and gone back next door. He and his team had to finish processing her apartment and other parts of the building they thought might provide a clue as to who'd broken into her sanctuary and defaced it with the vile, blood-soaked threats.

Her phone call to South Carolina had only ratcheted up the tension inside her to the point that, five hours after discovering the break-in, she ached from stress. She'd gotten the party line in military speak—but no answers. The hour was late. The office staff had gone home for the evening. She needed to contact the staff of the Marine Corps colonel currently serving as the warden during office hours or try to do some research online. Depending on national security issues, the information she wanted might not be public record, anyway. After setting the alarm on her phone to call the brig office back at 9:01 a.m. Eastern time, Allie resigned herself to a sleepless night like the ones she'd known back in Jacksonville.

The layers of command sounding concerned and supportive, all while covering their asses and doing nothing, felt far too familiar. She'd lost so much and fought so hard to do the right thing two years ago. She thought she was stronger now—physically and mentally. But that sense of violation—that powerless feeling of standing alone against the enemy when she'd opened her door and read the bloody threats—had taken her right back to the nightmare she thought time and distance had erased.

With her body running on fumes, but her brain unwilling to shut down, Allie busied herself cleaning up Grayson's kitchen. She was surprised to discover that he was a bit of a slob, with a couple days' worth of dishes stacked in his sink and on the stove. A mystery sauce had hardened on one pan and a plate like glue, but she needed to keep her hands busy. So, she loaded the dishwasher and ran it. She even washed the pan and a steak knife and spatula by hand and left the items on the placemat on his table to dry.

Stay busy. Don't think. Don't feel. Just get through tonight. Don't let him get into your head and take anything else from you. You can fight again tomorrow.

It was a mantra she'd learned in therapy. That one-day-at-a-time self-talk had gotten her through the worst moments of her life. She'd gone a couple months now without preaching the words of survival to herself. But she needed them tonight. She was supposed to be safe here in Kansas City. Safe in her own apartment. Safe in a new job where her past couldn't find her. This was supposed to be a new beginning. A new life.

Allison Tate didn't scare easily.

But she was scared now.

"Payback" had awakened a whole hell of a lot of fear in her tonight.

Stay busy.

Allie scooped up Gray's bag from beside the front door and carried it into his bedroom where she laid it and the crutches she didn't think he truly needed across the foot of the bed. The clean laundry piled there demanded she take the time to fold it and stack it neatly in the basket. There it was again. Gray's scent. Distracting her. Clinging faintly to the towels she folded, even after a trip through the wash. She buried her nose in the soft, cotton terrycloth, and imagined the cool, fresh scent came from his shampoo or shower gel. She imagined it in his short, crisp hair. On his skin.

It was an irresistibly manly smell, a soothing smell. She didn't need to stress. She was safe here in Gray's apartment. Gray made her feel safe.

No. Gray made her *tingle*.

Allie's eyes popped open at the silent admission. Being attracted to a man right now was so not safe. Grayson Malone had his own demons to fight. He didn't need her issues dumped on top of his. She should go. But that was an irrational response. She'd stood her ground and fought the last time her life had turned upside down. She was a trained Navy lieutenant. She was physically stronger now than she'd been two years ago, thanks to all the running and defense training she did. She was more stubborn than any of the patients she dealt with. Besides, where would she go? Home to her parents? And possibly put them in danger? Bunk on a friend's couch? Who were her friends in Kansas City? Whom could she trust to handle the kind of trouble she'd be bringing with her?

Doug Friesen? She snorted through her nose at the idea of trusting that man with anything.

Maeve Phillips? No, she wouldn't subject her young co-worker to this kind of threat.

One of the men she'd gone out with? There was a reason she hadn't agreed to a second date with any of them.

Ivy Burroughs? Although they chatted and worked together several times a week, the sweet older woman was a patient, not a friend.

Someone from her last duty station back in Jacksonville? Hardly. The people she'd called friends there had distanced themselves and left her to fight her battle on her own.

There was only one name on her list of trusted friends now.

Grayson Malone.

Handsome green eyes and short, high and tight hair she itched to run her palms over flashed through her mind. Did she really want to drag him into her troubles and use him as an ally?

Allie cursed. This wasn't fair! Why couldn't she enjoy a few lusty impulses with her Marine-next-door crush? Why couldn't she get the answers she needed tonight? She wanted to go back home and continue playing her flirty little games, trying to get Gray to wake up and notice her as something more than a friend. But she was afraid to go home now. To be alone. Why did she have to be afraid?

Because she knew just how bad things could get when she had no allies. No backup. No safe place to land.

Don't think.

Allie shook off the downward spiral of her thoughts and looked for another distraction. Gray's bedroom was as masculine and sparsely furnished as hers was feminine and full of pictures and meaningful tchotchkes from family and friends. Was his lack of decor a bachelor thing? A conscious, clutter-free choice that made life in a wheelchair or walking on fake legs easier? Then why let the dishes overflow the kitchen sink? Did he not have family and friends and good memories to fill up the empty spaces in his life? She wanted to give that man a hug. She wanted to dance with him again. She wanted to make memories with him that would bring smiles and colors and stories to his life.

Stay busy.

Finding the linen closet in the master bathroom, Allie gathered the armload of towels and set them inside. The hints of Grayson's scent she found so mesmerizing increased tenfold in the small room. She lingered in the doorway and breathed in the scents she associated with Gray until she started to feel a bit like a creeper. Heaven help her, she wanted to curl up in that scent and be surrounded by it.

Don't feel.

Moving on, she gave herself a tour of his spare bedroom, which he'd set up as a home gym, perused the books and Blu-ray collection stored in his entertainment center around a flat-screen TV, plumped the cushions on his sectional sofa—the only other piece of furniture in the living room—and finally returned to the kitchen. With nothing left to do to pass the time, Allie tested her now cold food and reheated their meal from the Chinese restaurant. She found a second plate for Gray and set the table for a really late dinner.

She forced down a bite of soggy egg roll while pushing the rice around on her plate. She was about to toss the whole thing into the trash when she heard the key turn in the door lock.

Logic told her no one but Grayson could be coming into his apartment. But raw nerves and wary survival instincts had her reaching across the table for the steak knife. Once she saw his broad shoulders and familiar green eyes, she eased her grip on the knife's wood handle. "Is your team finished with my apartment?" She pushed her chair back and stood. "I'll get out of your way."

"Sit, Allie." Gray's weary gaze locked on to her hand, but he made no comment about arming herself. "You can relax for now. At least, finish your food." He bolted the door behind him and rolled his chair through the apartment. "My team will take the evidence we gathered back to the lab and start processing it in the morning. Your place is taped off, and there's an officer stationed outside."

"Sounds secure enough."

"Not safe enough for you to be sleeping there," Gray insisted. "Besides preserving the crime scene, there's the risk of contaminants from all that blood. Lexi is already putting together a list of volunteers to come over to clean up and repaint anything we need to once the scene is released."

"You and your friends don't have to do that."

"It's done." He washed his hands as he continued. "It's not good for your mental health to be surrounded by reminders like that. Take it from someone who knows a little bit about recovering from trauma. Eventually, you'll have to face it again." He grabbed a towel and dried his hands. "But not tonight. Some time and distance can help you rebuild your strength and cope with the aftereffects." He hooked the towel over the edge of the sink before facing her again. "I have a feeling you already know that, though."

"I just need answers. An explanation. Then I can move on." *Stay busy.* Allie pulled his dinner from the microwave and set it on the table. "You must be starving. Here."

He tilted his face to hers, refusing to take a bite until she sat and picked up her fork again. Once she swallowed a mouthful, he dug into his cashew chicken. Between bites,

Gray reached into the pocket of his sweats and set her mailbox key on top of the table. "There were no signs that your spare had been removed—no minute shavings to indicate it had been through a key cutter, either."

"How did he get into my apartment?" Allie dropped the key into her purse hanging over the back of the chair.

"That's the million-dollar question. My best guess is he somehow got a copy of your key while you were at work. Or some other place where you lost track of it."

"I don't lose—"

"You don't lose track of your keys. Just like you never forget to lock the door."

"I'm a woman alone in the city. I'm always careful," she insisted.

Allie shivered. Clearly, she'd slipped somewhere along the way. At least, someone wanted her to think she hadn't been as diligent as she should have been.

"Maybe they weren't with me twenty-four seven." Allie reached into the pocket of Gray's hoodie and pulled out her ring of keys. "How can you tell if it has been copied?"

Being careful to touch only the edges, Gray inspected the key. Then he pushed away from the table and rolled over to what turned out to be a junk drawer. He tore off two long pieces of scotch tape and stuck one to each flat side of the key. He studied it carefully under the bright light above the sink, then gently peeled off each piece of tape and inspected them, as well. Allie was curious enough to find out what he was seeing that she joined him at the sink. She braced a hand on his shoulder and leaned over him to see the results he pointed out. "I only see one thumbprint—yours, I'm sure. No trace of metal dust. If a copy was made, it doesn't look like it was from this one. Or it wasn't done recently. Any trace is long gone."

Although she liked seeing how focused, thorough and resourceful he could be, Allie wasn't thrilled with Gray's answer. "You think someone's been planning that break-in for a long time? Stalking me to be there if I lost track of my keys? Or distracting me so that someone else could gain access to them?"

He tossed the tape in the drawer and returned her keys. "I deal in facts, not supposition. If it means anything, I don't think you made a mistake. I'm not sure how the perp got into your apartment, but this isn't on you. This was a highly planned attack. We'll figure it out."

"Of course. Thank you." When she tucked the keys into her pocket, she realized she still wore the hoodie Gray had loaned her hours earlier. She unzipped the jacket. "I forgot I had this on. I suppose you'll want it back."

"No." He wrapped his hand around her forearm, stopping her from shrugging out of the hoodie.

"No?"

"If you're cold and need it to stay warm, you're welcome to it."

"I don't want to take advantage—"

"You're not taking advantage of me, Allie. Your home was violated. You're second-guessing whether or not you could have prevented the break-in. If wearing my old hoodie makes you feel better, it's the least I can do to give you some comfort tonight."

He gently squeezed her arm before releasing her, and Allie wondered if he was aware of just how much they'd touched each other today. She certainly was aware. With every touch—as impersonal as his strong hands keeping her from falling, or as intimate as her fingers gently clasped in his as they danced—she felt a buzzing like fizzy soda dancing across her skin, leaving bubbles of warmth in their wake.

Tingling and dancing bubbles. Where were these romantic notions coming from? She'd always liked Gray. They had a lot in common—a shared military background, working together at the clinic, living in the same building and knowing a lot of the same people. But events tonight seemed to have knocked down whatever walls of professional detachment and self-reliance she'd kept between them, and she was *very* aware of the man. Not the neighbor. Not the friend. The man.

She hugged the hoodie more tightly around her and realized she was falling hard and fast for the Marine next door. This jacket smelled like him. Yeah, it made her feel better. Its warm, oversize bulk made her think he was holding her in his arms. She should be distancing herself from him, but she wasn't strong enough to do that right now. But it wasn't in her to lie about her feelings. "Gray, you've given me more comfort than you know tonight," she admitted. He paused midbite, frowning in confusion as she sat across from him. "You might want to rethink that 'taking advantage' thing, though. You said to make myself at home, and I did."

"You washed the dishes. I appreciate that." He glanced over to the counter. "The sink is a little high for me to be comfortable, so I usually put off that chore until there's nothing left to cook in."

"It wouldn't be too high if you wore your prostheses. And you wouldn't need your crutches here." When his eyes narrowed at her opinion that he wasn't as broken as he seemed to think he was, she hurried to change the subject. "Full disclosure. I went through *all* of your apartment. I needed to keep busy. And, I was curious. It was…a distraction. Sorry I invaded your personal space."

"I've got nothing to hide from you." For a moment, he studied her as intently as he had her key. Then the corner of his mouth crooked up. "Did you roll around on my bed and mess it up?"

"No. But I folded the laundry that was there."

"Put things away where I won't find them?"

"I don't think so."

"Did you move the bookmark in the book I was reading?"

"No."

He pointed his fork at her and grinned. "I know. You threw out my girlie magazines."

"I didn't find any… Oh." Allie sat back, shaking her head. "You're teasing me. I didn't think you did teasing."

"I didn't think I did anymore, either." She wondered why that confession seemed to surprise him. He stuffed a fork-ful of food into his mouth. "You have a beautiful smile. You don't use it often enough."

Allie's cheeks warmed at the compliment. This unexpect-edly fun side of Grayson Malone interrupted the malaise of her thoughts, giving her a momentary reprieve from her nightmarish fears. She gave the teasing right back. "Prac-tice what you preach, Captain Grumpy Butt."

He reached across the table and picked up her fork, en-couraging her to eat. "I invited you here. I told you to make yourself at home. I wanted to give you a respite from all that crap you had to deal with next door."

"I'm used to dealing with anything that comes up on my own." She stabbed a snow pea. "I'm also *not* used to letting things get under my skin like this."

"I suspected as much. Think of it as a favor from one

veteran to another. Letting you hang out here, touching my stuff, looking through all my things—"

"I didn't look through all—"

"—is me having your six."

"My six?" Allie inhaled a deep breath and nodded. Yeah. Knowing someone had her back right now felt good. "I haven't heard that phrase for a while. I was never in combat, but we dealt with enough of the aftermath in the hospital and therapy clinic that I appreciate being part of a team." Knowing someone she trusted had her back was the thing she'd missed the most when her life had gone south back in Jacksonville. She'd had no one to plan a survival strategy with, no one to give her a respite when she needed a break from all the stress, no one to still be her friend when she became a pariah. Allie swallowed the pea pod and speared another. They ate for a few minutes in silence before she asked, "Are the police done asking me questions?"

"For tonight."

"And your crime lab teammates are gone?"

Gray nodded.

"Am I allowed to go back in there and pack a bag? FYI, you didn't have to warn me off. I don't intend to stay there until Bubba can get the locks changed. But I would like to check into a hotel before it gets too late."

"You really want to stay alone in a hotel room?" Gray polished off the last of his meal. "It's late and you're exhausted. Crash here tonight and we'll figure out the next step in the morning. The officer will escort you inside your place if you want to grab some toiletries and pack an overnight bag. Or you can use what I have here." He gathered his utensils, picking up the steak knife, too. "Officer Chambers will keep an eye on my place, too. You don't need to sleep with this. No one will get to you here tonight."

Of course, he hadn't missed that she'd been ready to defend herself against whoever came in that front door. "Thanks. But I already told you, I searched every room. You don't have an extra bed."

Gray nodded over his shoulder. "The sectional is a comfortable place to sleep. I've crashed there many nights, after staying up too late watching a movie or ball game. You can take my bed."

"If the sectional is so great, I'll take it," Allie insisted. "All I need is a pillow and a blanket."

"Deal." He cleared the table around her, encouraging her to continue eating. "Why did you check on the location of a known felon?"

"How did you know that was what I was doing?" Maybe Grayson Malone was a little *too* smart for her. Allie tossed her fork onto her plate and pushed it away. "There goes what little appetite I had left."

"I can fix you something else. Sandwich? An omelet?"

Carrying her plate to the sink, Allie shook her head. "I'm good."

"You said you were hungry earlier. You need to keep up your strength. I have ice cream."

The man didn't miss a detail—she'd mentioned her love for ice cream at the clinic. But the thought of putting any other food in her stomach right now was worse than skipping a meal altogether. "You wouldn't have a cup of tea, would you?"

"Sorry. I'm a coffee guy."

"Maybe just some water?" She turned on the faucet to rinse their plates.

But Gray reached around her to turn it off. He tugged on her wrist and turned her to face him. "Enough stalling. While I appreciate the help, you are not my maid." Even though he had to tilt his head to hold her gaze, because his upper body was so long and his shoulders so broad, he made her feel surrounded by him. "Are you going to answer my question about NAVCONBRIG CHASN, or are you going to make me find the connections for myself?"

Allie looked down into his handsome green eyes, then had to look away—had to pull away because the intensity of those eyes seemed to pierce right into the heart of her. She headed into the living room and settled on the edge of his sectional couch. "I know you need me to talk about this. But I don't want to. The criminalist needs to hear the facts." She hugged her arms around her waist and buried her nose inside the collar of his jacket, breathing in the scent she was beginning to crave. "But I'm not sure I want my friend to know."

"Nothing you tell me is going to change the way I feel about you." He had feelings about her? Probably friendship. Maybe a sense of camaraderie since they'd both served in the military. Maybe gratitude since she didn't let him cut any corners when it came to his physical therapy and healing. She heard him moving behind her. "To be honest, it's a relief to know that I'm not the only one facing a problem that seems too big to surmount."

"You're glad my apartment was vandalized?"

He rolled his chair around the end of the couch and handed her a bottle of water from the fridge. "That didn't come out right. Someone threatening you doesn't make me feel better. But it gives me something to focus on besides wallowing in my own self-pity."

"You have nothing to feel self-pity about."

He slapped his thigh. "Missing my legs, my buddies from my unit and the self-confidence I used to wear like a second skin when it comes to anything outside of work?"

"Grayson—"

"Talk to me, Lieutenant. Distract me." He dismissed her argument without giving her a chance to think about shoulders and scents, teasing, dancing, hand-holding and unexpected tingling.

"You sound a little bossy to be doubting that self-confidence of yours."

This time, the teasing wasn't going to work for either of them. "Tell me first. It'll be easier to tell Officer Cutler later."

She pulled the sleeves of the hoodie down over her fingers. "I don't want you to see me as a helpless, fragile female."

He looked at her as though she'd spoken gibberish he couldn't understand. "Fragile?" He surprised her, reaching out to grasp the tab of her zipper, and cinched the jacket closed beneath her chin, tucking her into its warmth. "Maybe for about two seconds tonight. But you're entitled. Feminine? Always. Being tough with your patients and keeping yourself in fighting shape doesn't change that. And *helpless* is the last word I would ever associate with you." He captured both of her hands and gently chuffed them between his. Resting his elbows on his knees, he leaned toward her. "Your hands weren't this cold when I held them at the clinic this evening. Confirms my theory that you're pretty shaken up about what happened tonight. But you didn't run screaming out of your apartment or collapse in a pile of tears. You armed yourself with pepper spray and reentered the premises with me."

"I felt safer with you."

"You remembered your training. You kept your head despite your fear. Nothing you've done tonight makes me think you're weak or helpless." His nostrils flared as he inhaled a deep breath. "Accepting help does not mean you're helpless."

"Something your therapist said to you?"

He grinned. "Something my *physical* therapist said to me."

Allie wanted to answer that wry smile, but she couldn't. Not if she was going to talk about her past. Time to practice what she preached.

"Chances are, I could outrun or fight off a threat that was pursuing me." Her grip pulsed within his. "But to have some unseen enemy sneaking around me, messing with my things, watching me—and I didn't even know the threat was still there? That unnerves me a little bit."

"'Still?'" Was there any detail this man missed? Gray went on. "It gets in your head. Makes you doubt yourself. You want to put a name to that threat and take care of it. I'm guessing that name has something to do with a Navy prison." When she would have pulled away, he tightened his grip. "I already have Chelsea O'Brien, our crime lab computer guru, on standby to look up any threats you have lurking in your past. But if I knew how to direct her search, we'd get answers a lot faster." His eyes demanded her gaze. "Why do you have a prison number on speed dial?"

Allie could see the men in Gray's platoon obeying that stern, narrowed gaze.

She could see women responding to the intense maleness

of it. It made even an Amazon warrior like her feel like she was womanly, cared for, protected.

"I was checking on the status of a prisoner. Making sure he was still incarcerated there. I want to make sure he hasn't escaped or been paroled for good behavior—which he could totally fake."

"Sounds a little like a sociopath. If he's out, you think he'll be coming for you?"

"He'd certainly want payback." Her gaze darted to the wall separating their two apartments before facing him again. "But the NCO on duty tonight couldn't help me. The base commander's office is closed until morning. I'm to call back after 0900 to confirm he's still locked up."

"If he's still there, it'd be a good idea to get this guy's visitors' log, too. He could have called in a favor or hired someone to terrorize you." Gray pulled his cell phone from the pocket of his sweats and typed in a text. But he looked up, seeking the answer to his unspoken question before he hit Send.

"Noah Boggs. The name you want to research is Noah Boggs. He was a doctor at the base hospital where I worked."

"Chelsea can find answers online that we mere mortals can't." He typed in the name Allie spelled out, sent the text, then set his phone aside. "Now, what's the *payback* for?"

"Could you...? Would you sit with me?"

"It's easier to talk about this if you don't have to look me in the eye?"

Oh, yes. Mr. Intensity was in crime-lab mode right now. This conversation would be easier if she had her neighbor/ friend/crush to lean on, instead. "The body heat doesn't hurt, either."

"That's your reaction to stress? The blood stops circulating to your extremities, and you get cold?"

"Something like that. Please?"

A shadow dimmed the rich green of his eyes as his gaze dropped to the cushion beside her. Then he gave a curt nod, set the brake on his chair and easily pushed himself up onto his thighs like he had in her apartment. He flipped around and plopped down onto the sofa beside her. "Can't have you freezing on me. I don't have that many blankets in the house."

Again, she was struck by the size of the man. Gray mistakenly thought his wheelchair or prosthetic limbs diminished his presence. But Grayson Malone overwhelmed her senses. Allie's forehead barely cleared his shoulder as he sat beside her. Sitting this close, she could see the individual hairs of the wheat-and-bronze stubble that shaded his jaw and neck. Even through the layers of shirt and scrubs and hoodie, she could feel the heat coming off his body. And yeah, there was the scent she would always associate with sexiness and security.

He fussed with the cotton jersey of his sweatpants, tucking the pinned folds beneath the end of his stumps and smoothing the material over his tree-trunk thighs.

Allie toed off her work clogs and curled her legs up beneath her. She purposely let her knees rest against Gray's thigh and pulled his left hand into her lap. "Relax. I won't bite. I promise."

Gray's laugh held little humor. "My last girlfriend didn't like my legs touching her. Freaked her out."

"Stupid woman."

Now, *that* was a real laugh.

"It's her loss." Allie wrapped both hands around Gray's

and butted her arm against his, making sure he understood that his touch was exactly what she wanted. "You're a furnace. I like that about you."

He splayed his fingers, then laced them together with hers, holding her hand as tightly as she'd latched on to his. "All right, Lieutenant. No eye contact. A little body heat to warm you up. A kind boost to my ego. Enough stalling. Tell me about Noah Boggs."

"It's complicated. But basically, my testimony sent my ex-boyfriend—a fellow Naval officer—to prison."

"For what?"

Allie traced the length and strength of his fingers intertwined with hers. "We worked at the same hospital in Jacksonville. He launched a harassment campaign against me after I went out with him a few times and then decided we weren't going to be a good fit."

"Why not?"

"It was always about him. He was good-looking. Fun to flirt with. At first, I thought he was funny and kind. But if I wasn't in the mood to laugh or I didn't show enough appreciation, he got weird."

"'Weird' how?"

"He'd be critical. Demanding. He'd praise me with one sentence and put me down the next. Like, I was a strong woman. I could take whatever he dished out. I should learn from my mistakes and be even stronger."

"'Mistakes?'" Grayson growled a curse. "And anything that didn't stroke his ego or serve his needs was a mistake?"

Allie nodded. "I was late getting off work one time, and we were supposed to have dinner with the hospital administrator and her husband. He went without me so my tardiness wouldn't embarrass him. Or, I kissed him wrong. I needed to let him control our physical contact." Gray's hand squeezed around hers. "I told him I wanted our relationship to be a partnership. There should be give as well as take. I wasn't there to be his verbal punching bag. I told him he was the only mistake I'd made, and that it wasn't going to work out between us."

"He didn't take rejection well?"

Understatement of the year. "He made a token effort to win me back, but I knew things would get worse, not better. I gave him a firm no."

"And that set off whatever landed him in prison?"

"We were both still in the Navy. He was completing his residency at the hospital where I worked in the physical therapy department. He commanded the patient treatment team we served on together. After I made it clear I wasn't playing hard to get, and we weren't getting together, he wrote me up for a couple of stupid infractions. Gave me crappy assignments. He'd say and do inappropriate things for a working relationship. I tried to distance myself, but he was always there."

"Like Friesen. That's why he gets under your skin when he hits on you at the clinic. It pushes a hot button for you."

"Imagine Doug with a mean streak. Doug is annoying and inappropriate, but Noah was...scary. I'd catch him watching me—at work. He'd check on a patient during one of my PT sessions, or be waiting in the hallway when I got out of a meeting. He parked outside my apartment, followed me to a restaurant. He isolated me from my coworkers and friends. He pulled rank on anyone who did stand up for me." Her gaze dropped to where their fingers were linked together. "After a while, no one stood up for me."

Gray released her hand to hug his arm around her bent

knees and pulled them farther across his thigh, tucking her closer to his side. He folded his right hand around both her hands, this time pulling them into his lap. "Not going to happen anymore. Not with Boggs. Not with Friesen."

It was a comforting, warm embrace. Allie rested her cheek against Gray's shoulder and snuggled in. "I only had a year until I either had to re-up or leave the Navy. I thought I could ignore him and put up with it—until his games impacted one of my patients. He switched medications to make it look like I'd made the mistake. The patient had an allergic reaction and went into anaphylactic shock and nearly died. No one believed me at first when I reported him. He was part of an old boy network—officers protecting officers, that kind of thing. I kept documenting each incident with my superiors. A patient nearly dying wasn't something anyone could overlook. He was finally arrested and put away, based mostly on my testimony."

"Sounds like you've had combat experience, after all," Gray whispered. "He's in prison for harassment? Malpractice?"

Allie was exhausted, her emotions spent. She wanted nothing more than to climb onto Grayson's lap and feel his arms wrap around her. Instead, she yawned against his sleeve and finished the story. "When I reported the incident with the patient, Noah received a reprimand in his file that cost him a promotion, and the JAG office set up a hearing about revocation of his commission. Noah was pretty pissed about his career imploding. Of course, he blamed me. And he…he tried to kill me."

Grayson's entire body tensed beneath her. Allie would have pulled away if she didn't feel the press of his lips against the crown of her hair.

"You aren't calling the prison at 0900." His words were husky. Terse. Her hair caught in the stubble of his beard. "I'll put Chelsea to work. She'll pull a complete profile for Boggs and give us a location on him. You won't have to talk to the prison again."

Although Allie felt as though a burden was being lifted from her shoulders, she was hesitant to surrender her independence. Standing up for herself was the one thing that had kept her safe, had kept her alive. "We're not in the military anymore, Gray. You can't tell me what to do."

"The hell I can't. Even if you do call Charleston, I'm getting the information through Chelsea. In the meantime, I'll be working the investigation from the scientific end of things. Solving problems is what we do. Let me help."

"I'm really tired. Tired of being on my own. Tired of fighting this. Just...tired."

"I know, babe." She felt his lips against her hair again. "If you trust me, close your eyes for a little while. I've got your six."

Grayson's scent surrounding her was the last thing Allie remembered as her eyelids drifted shut.

THE VISITOR SAT in the car parked in the shadows.

Interesting. Light glowed through the window shades of Grayson Malone's apartment. Even at this late hour, there was activity in his residence, while the lights in Allison Tate's apartment had never come back on once the police and CSI van had left the building.

The visit to the woman's apartment that afternoon had caused an even bigger stir than one could have hoped for. The wait had been worth it—gathering all the necessary intel, getting to know the right people, formulating a plan that would do the most damage, deliver the most pain, before justice was finally served. After losing so much, there would finally be vengeance.

Now that the plan was in action, things were moving more quickly than anticipated. And this twist—the veteran Marine and the Navy lieutenant spending the night together—was as unexpected as it was welcome.

The visitor snapped a photograph for the scrapbook before starting the engine. "I don't get it. I must have struck a real tender nerve for you to be turning to him."

And the Marine must be beside himself, trying to figure out how half a man like him was ever going to save the girl next door.

The driver in the car laughed before driving away into the night.

This was going to be so satisfying.

Chapter Five

Grayson looked up from the printout he'd been reading as his cell phone vibrated with an incoming text. He pulled the phone from the pocket of his lab coat and set it on the stainless-steel lab table where he was working. He smiled and shook his head. Who would have guessed that Allie Tate could be so chatty? Or that he was enjoying these messages they'd been sharing throughout the day? She must be texting him between patients. So far, they'd touched on everything from a reminder that she'd forgotten to leave his gray hoodie at his apartment before changing for work this morning to discussing favorite take-out places and what their best home-cooked specialties were—he was a simple steak-on-the-grill guy while she claimed to make some mean pasta dishes.

He was grinning with anticipation as he typed in the unlock code and pulled up her latest text.

Mind if we do another sleepover? Officer Cutler just called to let me know I have full access to my apartment again. But I'm not ready to face the mess yet. Maybe after this weekend. I'll have more time to clean/paint/burn it down so it feels like home again.

A second text quickly followed the first.

Or, there's a hotel close to the clinic. I can make a reservation there. I don't want to overstay my welcome.

Gray typed in his response. She wasn't staying by herself in a hotel. She wasn't staying by herself anywhere. She was keeping the damn hoodie if it kept her warm, and she was staying with him.

Allie claimed she didn't have many friends in Kansas City yet, and her parents were teachers in a small town more than two hours away in central Missouri. She'd severed ties with her former military friends and coworkers who'd let her down so royally after Noah Boggs had targeted her for retribution. She didn't have anyone to lean on—not that she was used to doing that. But she had him. And Gray wasn't about to let her down.

My sofa works just fine.

He spun his chair away from the equipment at his station and rolled over to the desk near his workstation. There was still work to do on the "Payback" case, as the crime lab's director, Mac Taylor, had dubbed the break-in at Allie's apartment at this morning's staff meeting. It had been a challenge for Gray to separate the blood samples he'd taken, simply because there were so many of them. Thus far, they'd all come from human donors. He'd already identified seven of the eight blood types, including those with positive and negative Rh factors. But it would take much longer to name the source of individual samples through DNA, if they were in the system, along with the trace substances he'd found in the blood. And that was if the trace substances hadn't contaminated the identifying elements in the samples.

His mind automatically went back to the Jamie Kleinschmidt case. Gray had identified the same embalming fluid that had preserved each jar of blood. But because of the toxic substance, several of the samples had degraded to the point that they couldn't build a conclusive DNA profile, and some of Kleinschmidt's victims remained unidentified to this day, as a result. If Gray didn't know his criminal history, he might think Kleinschmidt had something to do with this case. But Jamie Kleinschmidt hadn't fared well in prison, and he had hanged himself in his cell barely two years into his sentence. Another logical supposition was that they had a copycat serial killer on their hands. But why target Allie? She was relatively new to KC and civilian life. What could a blood collector be seeking payback for from her?

That took him back to her military connections. After listening to the details of the hell her last year in the Navy had been, Gray wanted to ram his fist through Noah Boggs's face for the pain he'd put Allie through. He'd never met the man, or even seen a picture of him yet, but he knew Boggs would be a pretty boy. Handsome. Entitled. Full of himself. He'd love to break the doctor's pretty nose and let him know in no uncertain terms that he'd have the wrath of the Marine Corps coming after him if he so much as looked sideways at Allie again.

Gray's nostrils flared as he inhaled a deep breath and exhaled that wildly emotional response to the man who'd hurt Allie. He was just now getting reacquainted with using his new legs again—he wasn't ready to put his fist through anybody's face. But he could still feel those protective urges pricking beneath his skin. Allie Tate was a strong, funny, beautiful woman—and Noah Boggs had tried to break her because she'd stood up to him and done the right thing when no one else would. She'd sacrificed her Navy career, her relationships and her ability to trust.

Now she was his…

His neighbor. His physical therapist. His friend, Gray amended.

He didn't know why Allie had turned to him for help, but she had. And he wasn't going to let her down. He didn't need to be the big, lean fighting machine he'd been in the Corps to help her. He needed to listen and be there for her. He needed to be the smart guy at the crime lab and figure this out so that she'd feel safe. Allie needed answers more than she needed a champion to stand between her and the enemy.

So, answers she would get.

Setting aside his turbulent thoughts, Grayson pulled up the screen on his laptop to jot his findings in his report and map out the follow-up tests he and others needed to make. He'd ask Lexi to put Khari Thomas to work on the DNA profiling while he continued identifying the number of blood donors. He'd give Chelsea O'Brien, the crime lab's resident computer geek and queen of all things online, the job of tracking potential sources of that much blood. If he couldn't identify the non-biological components of the blood paint, Gray would get one of the crime lab's chemists to concentrate on that. Finding out what the evidence was made of could lead to finding out where the evidence had come from, which, in turn, could lead them to a suspect who had access to that evidence—like Jamie Kleinschmidt who'd worked a part-time job at a funeral home, where he'd gotten the embalming chemicals he'd used with his victims' blood.

Noah Boggs was a doctor, albeit one who'd lost his license to practice medicine. But he probably had the knowledge and connections to put together yesterday's break-in and vandalism. If Gray's research couldn't tie the blood samples to Boggs, he hoped he could tie them to the man's accomplice.

Aka, answers.

Gray's phone vibrated on his desk. He pulled up Allie's response to his invitation to stay the night at his place.

Whew! One less thing to worry about today. Thanks! I promise not to fall asleep on you and drool on you this time.

Funny. He'd liked the way Allie had curled her body into his and gone slack against his side as mental exhaustion and the late hour had claimed her. Allison Tate was a toucher—her head on his shoulder, her thighs butting against his, her hands interlinked with his. Without hesitation. Without making him feel self-conscious about his legs. Last night, she'd burrowed into him, held on tight, relaxed against him enough to fall into a hard sleep—as if his body was better than any bed he could offer.

In fact, he'd sat there a good half hour after he heard the first soft snore because it felt so good to cuddle with a woman again. He felt more like a man with Allie sleeping beside him than he ever had making love to his ex-girlfriend.

Brittany had barely been able to look him in the eye when he'd come home from the hospital, and she hadn't been able to mask her shock and pity when she saw his legs, even though she'd tried valiantly a couple of times to help him change his dressings or massage in some therapeutic skin cream. He'd been able to feel the stiffness in her when he hugged or kissed her. She'd wanted to be with the old Grayson Malone—Marine Corps veteran, war hero. But the 2.0 version was a harder man to love, to be herself with, to love as freely as she once had. And it wasn't just the legs. Grayson had been in shock himself, getting acquainted with his new body, relearning his new normal. He'd been fighting not to let the grief and anger over all he had lost color his relationship with Brittany. But it had. He'd become a lot of work to love.

No wonder she'd left him.

Allie was made of stronger stuff. She'd seen more of the world—dealt with a hell of a lot more danger and conflict—than Brittany had ever had to. And Gray was in a better place mentally now. Not all charm and confidence anymore—but not full of rage and fear, either. A woman like Allie could handle him on his worst day. She challenged him. Called him on his excuses and self-doubts. And, apparently, she needed him in a way Brittany never had.

He typed in a reassuring response.

You had a tough night. Drool just means you finally relaxed. I know how to do a load of laundry.

He could almost hear Allie's laugh.

We really need to work on your sweet-talking skills, Malone. You do not agree when a woman admits to drooling.

So, I shouldn't tell you that you snore, either?

Just wait until you're asleep, Malone. I'm bringing in a whole film crew to record your embarrassing habits.

"Knock, knock." Gray hit Send on a laughing emoticon before he looked up from his phone to see Chelsea O'Brien walk into the lab with her arms hugged around her laptop and a stack of file folders. She set them all on the corner of his desk before handing him the top folder. "Hey, Grayson, I've got some intel for you."

He opened the folder and studied both the prison mug shots and last Navy dress uniform picture taken of Noah Boggs. He knew it. The man had a pretty face. Gray's fingers curled into a fist with the urge to wipe that smug look off his Allie-hating expression. *Answers, Malone.* His job was to collect all the facts and let Officer Cutler and KCPD do their job—not to inflict retribution. He forced his grip to relax. "Is this everything I wanted to know about my suspect?"

"And more." Chelsea frowned behind her glasses—decorated with daisies for spring, he supposed—perhaps reading the protective anger coursing through him. "I can confirm that Boggs is incarcerated and hasn't left the military prison in Charleston for any reason since his sentence began. He isn't even scheduled for a parole hearing for three years. That dossier includes his service record, as well as a link to transcripts of the trial. Or admiral's mast. Or whatever it's called."

Gray thumbed through the pages of medical school transcripts, military police reports and more. Allie had done her job, reporting both medical and military infractions. As grim as last night's account of Boggs's harassment campaign against her had been, he could see she'd glossed over some of the details that would have made him lose his mind—like Dr. Boggs's final effort to silence Allie by tampering with her car and forcing her off a bridge into an accident that was meant to kill her.

Gray quickly closed the file and concentrated on a logical, rather than emotional, response to Chelsea's report.

"You remember the Jamie Kleinschmidt case?"

"Not the question I thought you'd ask." Chelsea hugged her arms around her waist and shivered dramatically from head to toe. "The one with all the blood in the basement?"

Gray nodded. "Where does someone get a lot of different types of blood—unless he's a serial killer who collects it?"

"Is this a creepy rhetorical question, or are you asking me to do some research?"

"Research." Gray jotted a note on a sticky pad. "I'm going to pull some old case files, see if anything pops for me. But if you can track down thefts from blood banks, hospitals, clinics—even a series of insignificant losses—or tainted or expired blood that's been disposed of—"

"Okay. Enough grossing me out." Chelsea had her hands up now, waving aside any further suggestions. "I don't like it, but I get the picture. I'm looking for someone amassing a large enough quantity of blood to paint your girlfriend's apartment."

"Allie's not my girlfriend."

"If you say so." Chelsea nodded to the phone on the lab table. "But I've never seen you text a woman—well, anyone—as much as you've been on your phone today."

"You spying on me?" he teased, making light of the fact someone else could see his interest in Allie.

"It's tech. It draws me like a magnet. Besides, you smile when you see who the message is from. You were grinning from ear to ear when I came in." She flipped her long brown braid behind her back and smiled indulgently. "And you don't smile often."

"Allie said the same thing."

"She knows you well, then. I think I like her."

He did, too. Despite his better judgment about getting involved with anyone after his disastrous breakup with Brittany. Gray pictured Allie falling asleep on the sofa, curled up against his side. He could still remember her heat seeping into him through their clothes. He'd sat there with her for thirty minutes, trading warmth and inhaling her scent, before he laid her down and covered her with a blanket. Allie possessed a strong outer shell, which he admired. Yet he'd discovered she was achingly vulnerable when she let her guard down. The fact that she'd let him see that vulnerable side last night felt like sharing a secret. He was honored, humbled and more than protective to be on such intimate terms with her.

Yet he was scared that even if the attraction was mutual, which he was beginning to suspect was the case, that he'd let her down—that he might not be everything she needed. He hadn't been enough for Brittany, in the end.

"Why don't you make her your plus-one for Buck's and my wedding?" Chelsea's invitation snapped him from his thoughts, surprising him.

Her light, happy tone reminded him that other people found their happily-ever-afters, even if he couldn't. Gray was genuinely happy for his self-avowed geeky friend and the ex-cop who worked as a consultant for the crime lab. "You and the old man finally set a date?"

"One, Buck is not old. The man's got moves. He could dance circles around you."

He tapped his thigh. "Anyone could."

She made a face at his disparaging joke. But it got him to thinking about Allie and her insistence that dancing would be excellent therapy for his balance issues. Maybe dancing wouldn't be such a bad thing if Allie was the woman he was holding in his arms.

"You know what I mean."

"I know," he assured her.

"And two, yes, we set a date for the fall."

"Congratulations." Gray reached out and traded a light hug with his coworker. "You and Buck are the oddest couple I've ever known. But you bring out the best in each other. I'm happy for you."

"Thanks. I offered to elope to Vegas whenever Buck wanted to, but he insisted I have a ceremony and reception with all the bells and whistles since I never had any big family events growing up. I think he likes to spoil me." Buck was a veteran cop and security expert, as tough as a bulldog and as much of a man's man as Gray had ever met. But he was an overprotective marshmallow—Chelsea's words—when it came to the woman he loved. Gray was glad for the reprieve in discussing his feelings for Allie. Not that he could have stopped Chelsea, anyway. The woman did love to talk when she got on to a subject that interested her. "My dogs are going to be our ring bearers. Buck's son will be the best man, and I asked my friend Vinnie from the Sin City Bar to give me away since he's like a grandfather to me. Lexi is going to return the favor and be my matron of honor. I'm inviting all my friends here at the lab, of course. You guys are my family now." She adjusted her glasses on the bridge of her nose and tilted her gaze to his. "And I'd like you, pseudo big brother, to be one of our ushers."

"Sounds like you've got it all planned out." She caught her bottom lip between her teeth, as if she expected him to say no. Gray wasn't about to disappoint her. "I'm honored you included me. I wouldn't miss it for the world."

"Great!" Chelsea jabbed a finger in his shoulder to get his attention before pointing to his mouth. "You'd better be wearing that smile when you come to the wedding. And save a dance for me."

"Will do."

She gathered up her laptop and files and turned to make her next information delivery. Gray stopped her before she reached the door. "Hey, Chels?"

"Hmm?" She turned.

"When you had to testify against Dennis Hunt—after all the things he did to hurt you and intimidate you—how'd you do it?" He knew it was a difficult topic for her, but Gray also suspected Chelsea might have an insight to Allie's situation that he lacked. "How did you stand up on that witness stand and do the hard thing? I know it's a tough question."

"Wow. Um, actually, it's not." She hesitated for a moment before drumming up a tight, sympathetic smile. "I could do it because I had Buck in my corner. And my best friend, Lexi, who got Dennis arrested. Plus, I had all of you guys. My family. You were all there in the courtroom with me. I knew I had people who had my back." She inhaled a deep breath before crossing the lab and perching on the corner of Gray's desk. "Does this have something to do with Allie? You know how alone I used to be. All I had were my rescue pets. Until I met Buck, and all of you. If Allie is facing this break-in, and whoever is responsible for it, alone—don't let her. Be there for her. And not just as the guy who's working her case."

"I may not be the best man for her to depend—"

"That's bull."

Gray's eyes widened at her huffy protest. Then Chelsea blinked and her typical quizzical expression returned. "Look, I know I'm the flaky one around here. But I see things. I get vibes about people—good or bad. I knew Dennis was trouble—and I knew Buck was my safe place." She hugged her things in one arm and reached out to squeeze his hand. "I see how you've been today with all those texts. And Lexi told me Allie's staying with you. I get a really good vibe about her. You care about her. I've never met Allie, but I'm thinking she sees you as more than a crime lab chemist and blood spatter expert." She dropped her gaze to Gray's phone. "I get the feeling she likes you, too."

"Thanks." Gray nodded before releasing her. "Buck's a lucky man."

"And Allie's a lucky woman." Chelsea stood, waving off the personal conversation. "I sent everything I have on Noah Boggs to your inbox, including a list of visitors he's had in prison. He's a surprisingly popular guy. I'm still gathering the deets on who everyone is, and if they have any connection to Kansas City and Allison Tate." Interesting. A lot of visitors meant a lot of opportunities to get word out about a tall physical therapist with honey-blond hair, and to reignite a harassment campaign against her. "If you need anything else, let me know. In the meantime, I'll be on the trail of a blood collector. Ew." Chelsea's shiver shook from her shoulders to her feet before she exited the lab. "I can't believe I just said that out loud."

After the door closed behind her, Gray picked up his cell and texted Allie.

I've been thinking about what you said about dancing. You willing to work with me?

Nearly an hour passed before she responded, reminding him that they both had work they needed to get done. He had just finished reading Boggs's file in detail, and the email Chelsea had sent, when his phone dinged with an incoming text.

Anytime, Malone. Not much of a response. But he knew that toward the end of the day, when patients were getting off work and out of school, was her busiest time for appointments. That was why he was surprised when she texted again. Are you coming in today?

I'm not scheduled again until Friday when I'm driving. Remember?

I forgot. Gray frowned. The Allie Tate he knew didn't forget things. A few seconds later, she asked, Do you need a ride home?

Was she trying to create more time with him? Even if Chelsea's hypothesis was correct and Allie was interested in more than friendship, he'd expect her to be more direct than that. He reminded her of the schedule they'd discussed this morning.

Jackson is giving me a lift. I'll be there when you get in and get dinner started.

Could he drop you off at the clinic, instead? It's closer to your lab. Then I could drive us home.

These texts sounded almost cryptic compared to the teasing back and forth they'd shared earlier. But what was the underlying message here?

Is something wrong? Is Doug giving you grief? Need a boyfriend to warn him off? I can ask Jackson to come in with me. He can scare anybody.

Not funny. Jackson's not the one who made me feel safe last night.

The alarm finally went off in his head. The phantom pain in his legs urged him to stand and take action. He couldn't, of course. Grayson swore. You don't feel safe?

...

Hell. Why wasn't she answering him?

Allie?

Can you please come? There's something I need to show you. Besides, I'd like to see you sooner rather than later.

He'd like to see her, too. No, he *needed* to see her as soon as possible if something was wrong.

On my way.

Chapter Six

Stay busy. Don't think. Don't feel.

Hell. The chant wasn't working. The overly fragrant flowers were giving Allie a headache. Or maybe that was the tension of the past twenty-four hours throbbing at the base of her skull. Maybe it was the one-handed former Marine scowling in silence on the far side of the counter or the silver-haired socialite with the bad hip, heaving an overly dramatic sigh every couple of minutes despite her indulgent smile.

Or, it could be Douglas "Clueless" Friesen's inability to take a hint and stay out of her personal space that had finally pushed Allie's patience out the window and made her snap. "Back off, Doug."

Doug had led both Ben Hunter and Ivy Burroughs into the patient area, announcing their arrival for their appointments. At the same time. Then he'd followed her into the space between the two long storage and supply counters at the end of the open physical therapy floor. His brown eyes sparkled with humor, as if her burst of temper amused him. "All I asked is if you needed my help. You don't have to jump down my throat. Take a break. I can handle this for you."

"I don't need you to handle anything for me." Allie glanced at her phone before stuffing it into the pocket of her scrubs jacket. No new messages from Grayson. Did he get stuck at the lab? Was he really on his way? Why did it feel like she was barely hanging on until she could see or hear from him again? She wasn't sure exactly when her neighbor had become so important to her—maybe he had been all along, but she'd ignored her longings out of respect for his nonverbal cues to keep things casual between them, as well as not wanting to endanger the inherent trust between a physical therapist and her patient.

But all that denial and patience had gone out the window the moment she'd opened her door to Noah Boggs's threats, and she'd been terrified of facing the enemy again. She'd tapped into every bit of her mental, emotional and physical strength to survive Noah the first time in Florida. She wasn't sure she had the strength left to beat that threat again without knowing—without trusting with her very soul—that she had someone on her side this time. Someone who believed she wasn't making anything up. Someone who let her fight her battles without taking over or demanding something in return for his help.

Despite his words last night, she wasn't sure that Gray wanted the job of guarding her six. But he was the one her soul said she could trust.

Allie picked up the heavy, gilded porcelain vase that had been delivered to her at the clinic and moved the flowers to the back counter. But the stems and greenery were so tall that they didn't fit beneath the upper cabinets there. Dumping them in the trash would draw even more attention to the flowers she didn't want. With a huff of frustration, she carried the bouquet back to the end of the front counter. Looking at them made her a little queasy, but the patients would probably enjoy them. "I can do my job, Doug. I just need a few minutes to work the problem so I can fix this mix-up."

"Sometimes people make mistakes. Even you." Doug reached in front of her and dragged the appointment calendar in front of him. "I'll bail you out. Which patient do you want me to take off your hands?"

Allie looked down at the cell phone in her hand and wondered if her instinct to contact Gray had sounded panicked or desperate. She'd been trying to keep things fun and cool and casual so she wouldn't scare him off, when all she'd really wanted to type was, *Get your tight butt over here. I need you!*

Allie eyed the two patients who were waiting for her answer, then turned her back to the vase of flowers and gestured to the book. "I did not schedule Ivy and Ben to come in at the same time. These two need full-time supervision—her for safety and Ben to keep him on task."

Ben Hunter tugged on his long beard before scrubbing his hand over the top of his close-cropped, nearly shaved head. "Are we going to do this, or what?"

Ivy Burroughs wore a smile instead of a frown. The silver streaks in her dark hair were perfectly coiffed and sprayed into place to highlight the chin-length waves. She wore enough rings and bracelets that she clinked and clacked when she gestured with her hands. "Your flowers are beautiful, dear. I know you want to call your boyfriend and thank him, but I really do need to get my appointment started. I'm playing cards with my girlfriends tonight. That's why I requested the earlier time. I want to clean up and change before I go. You know, in case, I—" she pressed her fingers to her lips to mask an embarrassed giggle "—sweat."

"You didn't mention needing to come early yesterday, Ivy," Allie gently insisted. "I would have remembered."

"Oh, I'm sure I did, dear." She reached over to stroke her fingers along the gold lines of the vase. "Maybe you were a little distracted with your man problems. Did you two have a fight? Is that what the flowers are for? I know my flowers. These cost a pretty penny. My son is always so good about apologizing when he makes a mistake." One moment she was talking romance and caring, and the next, she was back to complaining through her practiced smile. "Cards are always the first and third Thursdays of the month."

"Yes, but you never needed the extra time…" Allie held up her phone and rested her palm on the appointment calendar on the countertop, pointing out both places where she recorded her schedule. "I write it down, so I don't overbook appointments." Yet there it was under her name at four o'clock. Benjamin Hunter *and* Ivy Burroughs. "I didn't write this. Look." She opened the calendar on her cell phone to show each of them. "I've got Ben at four, and Ivy at five."

"It's not a problem for me to switch," Ben offered. "I can wait in the lobby. I've got nowhere else to go."

"Stop that." Allie pointed a stern finger at him. "You are not a second-class patient here. We'll get this straightened out without you having to make a sacrifice."

"Time, dear." Ivy tapped the watch face on the engraved gold bangle she wore. "Let him make the sacrifice. I don't want to be late."

"Ivy, please. Every patient matters here." Allie's head was ready to explode when the door from the lobby swung open, and Gray rolled his chair into the PT room. His green eyes swept the room. The moment his gaze landed on her they were both moving.

The tension left her on a noisy breath, and she leaned in to hug him. But his hand was out, reaching for hers, and poked her in the stomach. Then he spread his arms open as she extended her hand. Allie curled her fingers into her palm, retreating from the awkward meeting. She didn't get far. Gray's hand shot out to capture hers and he tugged until her thighs hit the side of his chair. His other hand slipped beneath her scrub jacket and settled at the small of her back to rub soothing circles that warmed her through her scrub top and athletic shirt.

"Talk to me," he ordered.

Allie gripped his hand between both of hers. It wasn't the full-body contact she wanted, with his reassuring scent filling up her head. But Gray was here. She'd asked and he'd come. Reluctantly or not, no one had stood up for her in Jacksonville. She focused on those green eyes, and she could breathe normally again. He gave her the reprieve she needed to think clearly for a few precious moments. She remembered that she was strong and capable. Allie nodded to the bouquet on the counter beside her. "Are those from you, by any chance?"

"No."

"Then I'm officially freaked out."

"You don't know who sent them?"

She shook her head. "Even if the timing wasn't suspect, I'm not a big fan of surprises."

"Obviously. She's been snippy with everyone all day." Why did it sound as if Doug was tattling on her? Was he jealous that she'd dashed to Gray's side and clung to him when she'd shrugged off Doug's touch? "I would think getting flowers would make you happy. Don't all women love that?"

"White roses and gardenias? It looks like a funeral bouquet. No, I don't love that. Plus, the coward didn't have guts enough to sign the card." Allie reached into the vase to pull the card out, being careful to touch only the edges as she showed it to Gray. "There's no message." Just *Allie* written in a loopy, decorative script. "This guy's got a knack for making one word sound like a threat." She pointed out the two red spots below her name. "And…is that blood?"

"My guess is yes, judging by the irregular shape of the drops. I'd have to test it." Gray pulled a plastic evidence bag from his pocket and had her drop the card inside. "You think these are from Boggs?"

"From Noah, or someone doing it for him."

"Who's Boggs?" Doug asked from somewhere behind her.

Allie ignored him. "I can't prove it. It's not his handwriting—it probably belongs to the clerk at the floral shop who put the bouquet together. But it feels like they're from him. It feels like before."

"Boggs sent you flowers before?" Gray pressed.

"Who is Boggs?" Doug forced himself into the conversation. "You got another guy you're stringing along somewhere?"

Allie whirled around. "Get out of my personal space, Doug. Unless you sent those flowers, this has nothing to do with you."

"Lighten up, Al." Doug held his hands up to placate her. His charming smile was suddenly absent. "I didn't send you the stupid flowers. It could be a mistake by the florist, and they sent them to the wrong Allie."

"There's no mistake." Allie turned her attention back to Gray again. He understood the flowers were sent to terrorize her. "After I broke up with Noah, he sent a bouquet every day for a week, or delivered them himself. At home or at work. He apologized over and over and tried to win me back. Then he was pissed that I wasn't grateful, and he couldn't change my mind. And then..."

"And then the crazy stuff started happening."

She nodded, claiming his hand again. "I'm a daisies and sunflowers kind of woman—not all these fancy, stinky flowers. Honestly, they make my nose run. Bigger and more expensive was always better with Noah, no matter what I wanted. If he'd only listened. If the relationship wasn't always about him."

Gray nodded. "Daisies and sunflowers. I'll remember that."

"I'm just making a point. I don't need you to send me flowers."

The lobby door swung open again and Jackson strode into the therapy room. He must have let Gray out at the door before parking the car. He set Gray's bag and crutches on the floor beside his chair. "She okay?"

Several therapy sessions stopped as patients and staff alike noticed the overbuilt stranger with the prizefighter's face and unsmiling countenance. Allie immediately extended her hand to dispel some of the curious glances. "Hi, Jackson. Thanks for bringing Gray."

The big man's nod must be his code for *You're welcome* or *No problem* or *You're a pain in the butt, lady.* Who knew what he was thinking behind those ice-gray eyes that seemed to always be scanning his surroundings?

Gray held up the bagged card. Jackson took it and studied it front and back, the two men silently communicating some evidence-processing scenario. "Ask Chelsea to track down whoever put together the bouquet at Robin's Nest Floral. See if she can find out who ordered them. I'm guessing it was in cash, maybe even using a fake name. And ask the florist if he or she poked herself on one of the thorns, or if they can even tell us who filled out the card. I'll type the blood myself later."

Another nod. "You want me to see if I can get anything off the flowers?"

"Take them. Please." Allie picked up the vase and shoved it into Jackson's hands. "When you're done getting fingerprints or finding out who sent them, donate them to a hospital or retirement home. If they don't survive whatever tests you have to run, just toss them. I don't want them back. I don't want any of it back."

Doug leaned on the counter beside her. "You're throwing away the bouquet? You've got a secret admirer, Al. You should show a little appreciation."

They still had their audience. Ivy reached across the counter to pat Allie's hand. "Doug is right. You're being awfully rude to whoever sent those." She looked at Gray, as if she hadn't heard or didn't believe his denial about sending them. "You're hurting his feelings, I'm sure."

Ben Hunter swore under his breath. "Give it a rest, lady. She said she doesn't want them."

"I wasn't speaking to you, young man. My son would never talk to me like that, and he certainly wouldn't use that language."

Another voice entered the fray when Maeve Phillips joined them. "Hey. You guys need to lower your voices. Your arguing is upsetting the other patients." She shied away from Jackson, who stood head and shoulders above her. But when her gaze met Ben's perpetual scowl, she nervously tucked her short dark curls behind her ears. "Is there something wrong with the flowers?"

"They're evidence in an ongoing investigation," Gray explained.

"Oh." Maeve seemed reluctant to meet his gaze, as well. "Is everything okay?"

Allie reassured the younger woman. "It seems I might have an old boyfriend stalking me. I'm taking care of things right now. Sorry if I'm worrying anyone."

"Stalking?" Maeve reached across the counter to grasp Allie's arm. "You worry about staying safe. We can handle the gossip mill. Just keep it down if you want this conversation to stay private." Maeve whispered, "Every table and workstation has ears."

Allie squeezed Maeve's hand before she pulled away. "I'll make sure the drama stops. Thanks."

With a nod, Maeve returned to her patient at one of the tables. Ben watched her from the corner of his eye, then resolutely turned away. He plopped his arm with the hook on the counter and leaned in. "Can we get this show on the road?"

Jackson looked down at Gray, who simply nodded.

Allie had seen sailors on the same SEAL team communicate the way Gray and Jackson seemed to. Baffling as it was to her, something about their backgrounds and training put them on the same wavelength. Maybe it was a man thing. Or a crime lab thing. Accepting Gray's dismissal and assurance that he was no longer needed, Jackson tucked the vase under his arm and headed back to the lobby. "I'll keep you posted."

"I'd better see to my own patients," Doug announced. Now that his effort to swoop in and save the day for her had been usurped by Gray's arrival and the resurrection of her own backbone, he wasn't eager to hang around. "If you need me to bail you out, holler."

She wouldn't.

Ivy wasn't so easy to dismiss. Maybe it was her age or her social status as the widow of a high-ranking officer, but she expected to be catered to. She tapped her manicured nail on the countertop. "Allie. I won't be charged for this session if we miss it, will I?"

"You're not going to miss it, Ivy. And you won't be late for your card game."

With the reminder of the terror campaign she'd survived gone with Jackson's departure, and Gray parked at the end of the counter beside her, Allie felt her equilibrium returning. "Ben, you want to bike or do the treadmill today to warm up?"

"I prefer running."

"Good. Thank you." The military man seemed to handle the word of an officer—even though they were both civilians now—just fine. She'd need a softer approach for the older woman. "Ivy, why don't you put your purse and jewelry away in your locker. I'll get Ben started, then I'll be ready to work with you when you come back. I'll meet you at the recumbent bike."

"All right, dear." Appeased by the compromise, Ivy limped off to the changing room.

Allie pointed out the open treadmill to Ben. "Once Ivy is set with her warm-up, I'll be back to start the occupational therapy for your new hand. We'll practice household tasks again today. If I'm running long, I'll send someone else over to monitor your form and progress."

"Just don't send Sweetcheeks."

"Who?"

"Maeve." He rubbed his right hand over the hook on his left. "I scare her."

"I doubt that..." But she could see that Ben believed the younger woman was afraid to work with him. If so, she didn't believe it had anything to do with his disfigurement. They worked with several disabled veterans here. But the clock was ticking, and Allie didn't have time to point out how the grumpy personality Ben wore like a shield might be the thing that made shy Maeve uncomfortable around him. She opted for teasing, instead. "Fine. I'll send Doug over to help if I'm in the middle of something."

Ben snorted a laugh. "You don't want to be owing that guy any favors."

"No, I don't. So, get to it, Sergeant."

"Yes, ma'am." He eyed her hand resting on Gray's shoulder before leaving.

Allie squeezed Gray's shoulder as she circled around his chair to follow Ben. "You sure you don't mind hanging out?"

Gray caught her hand before she pulled away. "I won't be just sitting and watching the clock. My PT told me I needed to get in more practice walking on my new prostheses instead of relying on the chair."

"She sounds like a smart woman."

"I think so." He reached for her other hand and pulled her to the front of his chair where her knees bumped against the end of his thigh. Although he quickly shifted his leg away, he didn't let go. "It seems like you've got everything under control now. But are you really okay?"

"You think because I texted an SOS that I..." Gray wasn't smiling at her effort to make light of his concern. Good grief, the man was going to make her cry if he didn't stop looking straight into her soul with that piercing gaze. "I just… I have a raging headache, and I guess I had a panic attack when I saw the flowers. My blood pressure spiked. My patience vanished. Everything hit all at once. I didn't get enough sleep, I feel drained after rehashing my history with you last night, and—"

"And you needed someone to have your six, so you could catch your breath and think for a minute." Yeah, exactly that. "It's okay to send me an SOS when you need backup."

"Good to know. I'd better get going."

"Not yet." When she started to pull away, his grip on her hands tightened. "Breathe in through your nose." She did. "And out through your mouth. Again." Gray's presence, his command, calmed her. She did two more relaxing breaths with him before he smiled. "You got this, Lieutenant."

Allie nodded. Gray's strong hands, the understanding in his eyes, the fact that he was simply here because she needed him, meant more to her than the most expensive bouquet in the world. Obeying the impulse that surged through her, she cupped the stubbled side of his jaw and leaned down to kiss the corner of his mouth. The texture of his skin was sandpapery against her lips, the temperature was warm, and yeah, she caught a whiff of the crisp, icy scent that was all him before pulling away. "Thank you."

Gray reached up to cup her cheek and jaw the same way she'd held on to him. For a split second, Allie held her breath, expecting him to repeat the same action she had, hoping he would. He brushed the pad of his thumb across her bottom lip, and she felt the friction from the caress all the way down to the tips of her breasts and deeper inside. But there was no kiss.

Instead, his shoulders lifted with a deep breath, and he literally backed his chair away from her. "Go. I'll be around."

Was he dismissing her gratitude? Embarrassed by the public display of affection? Was he self-conscious about being in a wheelchair and unsure how to handle the physical intimacies of a kiss when she stood a foot taller than him? Or was Gray simply fighting harder than she was to deny the chemistry between them?

No matter the reason, Allie tried to remember how grateful she felt to have him in her corner, and not feel dismissed. They were friends, after all. Allies. And for the next hour, she needed to focus on the challenge of her job, not feel rejected by the man who was coming to mean more to her with every passing moment.

Chapter Seven

An hour later, Ivy Burroughs hugged Allie and thanked her for a rejuvenating workout with the feel-good recovery of an electrode and heating pad massage. The older woman waved to Gray, who was walking up and down the stair platform on his prosthetic legs. He was talking on his cell phone, deep in what looked to be a serious conversation with periodic nods and terse replies. He doffed Ivy a polite, two-fingered salute and continued his conversation. Allie started to smile at how he barely used his hand on the railing to steady himself. The man was distracted with work and not thinking about using his new limbs—he was simply doing it.

Then Ivy butted her shoulder and whispered a weird comment that Allie suspected was supposed to be a compliment. "He's a handsome man when he's standing up."

"He's handsome all the time," Allie argued, feeling weary and irritated by the unsettling events of the day. She did not need this woman spoiling the spark of a good mood with her insensitive ignorance. "Why would you say something like that?"

Ivy waved aside Allie's defense with a jangle of rings and

bracelets. "Oh, I didn't mean anything about Mr. Malone being a cripple, dear."

A cripple? Allie fumed. "Mrs. Burroughs, we have several disabled veterans who come to the clinic for PT. You really need to watch your words. They can be hurtful, and even undermine a patient's recovery."

The older woman continued on as if Allie hadn't spoken. "Your man came to your rescue today. And he's had his eyes on you nearly the entire time he's been here. You clearly mean the world to him. I was hoping I'd get a chance for you to meet my son. I'm sure he's here to pick me up by now. But I see where your heart lies. Hmm… I wonder if Maeve Phillips is seeing anyone." She tossed her purse over her shoulder and winked. "Don't let that Mr. Malone go."

How Ivy Burroughs managed to sashay out of the clinic with a cane and a limp, Allie didn't know. But she had the uncharitable thought that she was happy to see the demanding patient go.

She glanced over to see Ben Hunter back on the treadmill again, running off the stress of his session. The Army veteran had opened up a little bit, sharing how much he missed his K-9 partner who'd been killed by the same explosive device that had taken his hand. But the touchy-feely conversation, combined with his frustration at the precision training on his prosthesis, had clearly dredged up some unwanted emotions, and Allie had encouraged him to run to his heart's content, provided he didn't go past her fifteen-minute time limit or break the machine.

Allie looked up at the clock with a weary sigh. Ten minutes to go. Her gaze was instinctively drawn to Gray again, and her feet followed. She met him at the bottom of the three-step unit and tilted her face up, taking in just how tall

Grayson Malone was. She liked looking up at a man for a change—liked looking up at this man. She felt her cheeks burn as she recalled Ivy's tacky comments. Standing in his faded USMC sweats and T-shirt, it wasn't obvious that his lower pant legs were filled with steel rods. But even if he wore shorts or sat in his wheelchair, he was a whole man to her. And as much as she loved him holding her hand, she could admit to herself that she wanted a lot more. If he'd stretched out beside her and slept with her last night on the couch, she wouldn't have protested. And if that touch of his thumb to her lips earlier had been a real kiss…

"Thanks, Chelsea. Good job. As usual." He ended the call and tucked his cell into the pocket of his sweatpants.

"Work?" she asked, anxious to know if he had any answers for her.

"I've got some preliminary results from our investigation." His forehead creased with an apologetic frown. "I can confirm that Noah Boggs is still incarcerated. Chelsea talked to the Judge Advocate General's office in Charleston. He had the guards do a visual check to confirm that he's in his cell. She's combing through a copy of the visitors' log and phone records now to see who your ex has been in contact with recently."

It should have been comforting to learn that Noah wasn't here in Missouri. But that just meant he was working with someone, or that someone was copying his terror campaign—and that meant she had no clue who was tormenting her. "Has Chelsea found any connection to Kansas City yet?"

Gray shook his head. "Don't give up hope, Lieutenant. We're still going to find out who's doing this to you and put a stop to it." He released his grip on the railing and leaned toward her, as if to comfort her. But he wobbled a bit as his balance shifted, grabbed on to her shoulders to stop himself from falling and muttered a curse. "I'm such a smooth operator. I seem to grab you as much as Friesen does."

Allie reached up to wind her fingers around his wrists to maintain the connection. "You can hold on to me anytime, Malone. The difference is that you have my permission to touch."

"Yeah?"

"Yeah. I hope the permission is reciprocated, as well." With her thoughts already turned to needing and wanting, Allie moved one hand to the center of his chest and gently pushed his shoulders over his hips. "Remember to center yourself."

"This would be easier if I had at least one good leg to rely on." He quickly righted himself without really needing her help.

But Allie didn't move her hand from the warmth of his skin through his cotton T-shirt. "Forget the legs. Rely on this." She patted his firm belly and felt him suck in his breath. "You've got more muscles than just about anyone here, including the staff. Your prostheses are fitted properly to your larger thighs now. Use the muscles you've already got. You're not going to walk like you did before. But you're still going to walk."

"And dance." Allie chuckled as he slid his hands down her arms. "You said that was the best therapy for me." He tucked his left hand beneath her jacket at her waist and captured her right hand in his. "Let's keep it to a slow waltz, though, okay?"

"Okay." Allie let her fingers settle at the side of his neck. They swayed back and forth in a silent two-step and even managed a three-point turn that made Allie proud. "That's it. You've got this."

"What did Mrs. Burroughs say that upset you?"

Allie didn't bother denying her reaction. But she did fudge a bit on the details. "She thinks you're handsome."

"And you disagree? You're jealous? I swear I'm not into women who are old enough to be my mother. Oh…" He read the meaning in her gaze dropping from his. The dance stopped. "She said I was handsome for a handicapped guy."

"Something like that."

"You don't have to defend me against rude comments from small-minded old women. They can't hurt me."

Allie's chin came up. "Well, it hurt me. No, it ticked me off. You're important to me." He didn't believe how attracted she was to him, and she had a feeling that careless, ignorant comments like Ivy's had a great deal to do with his inability to trust a woman's feelings for him—to trust *her* feelings. His ex, Brittany, had probably said something similar, not meaning to hurt him, but making him feel different or less. Making him doubt himself. "I stand up for the people and things I care about."

"Easy, Tate." Gray's hand tightened at the nip of her waist, pulling her back into the swaying rhythm that in no way matched the soft background music being piped into the clinic. "You'll stand up and say or do what you think is right, no matter what it costs you."

She nodded, urging him to move in a circle around the stair unit, challenging him to take bigger steps and control his balance. "I had to stand up to Noah. I couldn't let him hurt anybody else. I couldn't let him win."

"Have you taken up a new cause since moving to Kansas City?"

Other than obsessing over the criminalist next door? Allie shook her head. "Settle into the new job. Find the best running paths. Adapt to civilian life."

"Nothing worrisome in any of that," Gray agreed. "So, what battle do you think he's trying to win this time?"

Allie shrugged. "'Payback?' I didn't provide the only evidence against him, but the JAG said my testimony is what got him convicted."

Gray's eyes narrowed with a deep thought. "He's still in prison. Trying to kill a patient, trying to kill you—he's going to be there for a while. Tormenting you doesn't change his situation."

"It probably gives him some emotional satisfaction." Allie had pondered Noah's motives, too. It all came down to his ego and punishing her for not worshipping the ground he walked on. "He's probably thinking, scare her. Give her an ulcer. Make it impossible for her to trust another man and move on with her life—maybe make it impossible to trust herself."

"I accept that hypothetical scenario. Hurting you makes him feel better. But what's his end game? Turn you into a recluse? Drive you crazy? Finally succeed in killing you?"

Allie stopped in her tracks. Although she was pleased to see that Gray maintained his upright posture at the abrupt halt, the dark turn of their conversation chilled her. "Well, you just took a perfectly nice dance and turned it into a trek down nightmare road. I thought you were flirting with me with the dancing and small talk, but you're working the case."

"Oh, I was definitely flirting with you. I'm just not very good at it. Totally out of practice."

Allie shoved her fingers into her hair, rubbing at the base

of her skull and tugging loose some of the strands from the top of her ponytail. But she couldn't seem to ease the tension there. "So, I can't read your signals, and you can't read mine. I guess we've both been hurt enough and share enough distrust that we'll have to come right out and say what we're feeling if we want to clue the other one in… And what are you getting at?"

"Noah Boggs is stuck in South Carolina. Who's doing the work for him in KC? It's not like his accomplice can call and give him a daily update. If no one is reporting to him regularly, then he doesn't benefit from terrorizing you. Who does?"

"I don't know. Maybe he's getting off on just imagining how scared I am. Does it have to make logical sense?"

"For me? Yeah." Gray reached out to capture one of the long strands of hair she'd pulled from its binding and brushed it back across her cheek to tuck it behind her ear. His fingertips dug into the knot of tension at the nape of her neck. Although she welcomed his touch, the topic didn't change. "We need to be looking at other people in your life. Who else in this world wants to hurt you? And is this going to culminate in someone else running you off the road and trying to kill you again? I don't even want to think about it. The perp has stolen a page out of Boggs's playbook because he knows those kinds of mind games will hurt you the most. I believe someone else is doing this."

Allie wanted to lean into the hand that cupped the side of her jaw and neck. No, she wanted to lean into that USMC logo over Gray's chest and really feel him hold her. She did neither. He was offering answers, not comfort. "It's not bad enough that one man wants to hurt me, ruin me, kill me? Now there's someone else out there I've really pissed off?"

She hugged her arms around her waist and shrugged, dislodging his hand. "I don't have any idea who else could be behind these weird happenings. Much less why."

She smelled the sweat a split second before she heard Ben Hunter's voice behind her. "I'm in."

Startled by his sudden appearance when she'd last seen him across the room, Allie jumped and fell against Gray. To his credit, her crush-worthy neighbor remained upright and shifted her to his side, leaving his hand at the small of her back. "You're in what?"

"Whatever's going on here with Allie." Ben glanced at her but focused his unhappy glare on Grayson. "I'm going stir-crazy with no job and all these physical and mental attitude adjustments. Clearly, someone is screwing with your woman. Gossip runs freely here. I know about the break-in at her apartment. The blood. That the flowers are probably from an ex—or someone who wants her to think they are. I want to help. Give me something to do."

Your woman?

Before she could explain the details of her relationship with Gray, the two men were exchanging phone numbers. Since Gray wasn't making any effort to correct Ben, she fell silent and let him take command of the formerly enlisted man. "I'd like to have eyes on Allie when she's here and I'm not. I'll be there when she's at home, but when I have to be at the lab…"

Ben pulled his towel from around his neck and wiped his face above his beard before nodding. "I can do that. Recon's about all I'm good for right now, anyway." His golden eyes shifted to her, and Allie drifted back into the warmth of Gray's palm. "Let me know your work schedule. Unless

I've got an appointment with one of my doctors or therapists, I'll be here."

Allie was torn between relief at knowing someone else would be watching her back, and concern that Gray had recruited her volatile patient to do the job. "You aren't going to hurt anyone, are you?"

A smile never cracked his face. Ben looked up at Gray, then over to the counter where Doug was writing on the calendar, then to her. "Do you need me to?"

"Um…"

"No." Gray chuckled despite her worry. "Right now, all I need is a point man to keep eyes on things here at the clinic. Report to me if anything looks hinky. More unwanted gifts arrive. Friesen not keeping his distance. Someone watching the building. Following Allie. That kind of thing."

"Yes, sir. I'll try not to let you down."

"Thank you, Sarge." Gray extended his right hand, holding it without any sign of retreating for the several seconds it took the bearded veteran to respond to the friendly gesture.

Finally, Ben slapped his palm against Gray's and traded a sharp nod. Panic flared in his eyes when he realized Allie wanted to express her gratitude, as well. He held up both his hand and his hook, shook his head and stalked away toward the bank of lockers where patients stored their jackets and other personal items.

Allie hugged her arms around her waist. "He scares me sometimes."

"He's where I was when I first hit stateside with no legs, no job, just lost the woman I thought I was going to marry, with no more connection to the Corps and my buddies there. If Ben surrounds himself with the right people, finds a purpose outside of the military, he'll come around."

Allie glanced up at the man beside her. "Do you think he'll be okay?"

Green eyes met hers. "Do you think I'm okay?"

Allie summoned a weary smile. "You're okay enough for me. Thank you for coming. You being here this evening is exactly what I needed."

"I'm glad you texted me." That strand of hair had fallen over her cheek again and Gray sifted it between his thumb and finger before tucking it behind her ear one more time. "How much longer do you have to stay?"

"Ben and Ivy were my last patients of the day. I need a few minutes to update my reports in their files."

"I'll pack my gear and grab my chair. Meet you out front."

Allie caught his arm when he turned toward the lockers. "Would you walk me out? I'll help with your chair, but I want to walk beside you." When she saw he was going to argue, she hastened to add, "I don't want the Mrs. Burroughses of the world to think that you're only my patient. Or neighbor. I want the world to know that I think you're hot, and that I'm laying claim to you. Maybe you're not ready for that. Maybe my timing sucks. I need the emotional support, a break from the endless stress. I want to hold your hand because I find comfort and strength in that. It's a mental thing—heaven knows I've had enough games played on me the past twenty-four hours—but—"

Gray shook his head. "As flattering as all that is, I'm not as mobile yet on foot. If something happens, my reaction time is slower than it is when I'm in the chair."

"If something happens, I'll take the guy out myself. At least stall him long enough until you can throw a punch or whack him over the head with a crutch."

He scrubbed his palm over his wheat-and-bronze stubble

and muttered a curse. "I haven't thought about how'd I'd do hand-to-hand combat with the new me." He pulled his cell phone from his pocket. "I'd better talk to Aiden Murphy to see if he can give me a few tips. Or Chelsea's fiancé, Buck, runs security ops—"

"You do it the same way you did before, Marine. You're already in fighting shape. Assess the situation, look at the options available to you, rely on your training." She curled her fingers around his wrist to keep him from making the call. "Please. If your back is really bothering you and you need to use the chair, I understand. But I'm having a rare girlie moment here. I want to hold your hand, and I can't do that if one of us has to push you in your chair."

His eyes narrowed as he processed everything she'd just spewed out—from confessing she liked him to feeling beaten down by the relentless stress of reliving Noah's tortuous mind games to Gray remembering his military training. Then he dropped his gaze to his wrist and pulled back until he could capture her hand in his. "FYI? You're always girlie in my book." He squeezed before releasing her and glancing over at the counter. "Finish your paperwork. And steer clear of Friesen. I'll walk you out."

Chapter Eight

By the time Allie got on to her computer tablet to update her patient files, Doug was thankfully gone. A quick scan of the PT room showed he must have left as soon as his shift ended. Maeve and a couple of the newer therapists had gotten stuck with the late shift and were busy with patients. But there was no sign of anyone who had caused her grief today.

There was no sign of Gray, either, but she assumed he'd be waiting for her in the lobby to walk her across the street to the staff parking garage. Thankfully, she'd found a spot on the ground floor, so he wouldn't have to negotiate the stairs or wrangle his chair onto the garage's small elevator. She figured she was already pushing him out of his comfort zone by insisting they walk. Add in her straightforward announcement that she thought he was hot, and she didn't want to press her luck and have him rebel and shut down on her the way he had last night at their building, before she'd discovered the break-in. She wanted that whole man-woman experience that she'd once hoped to have with Noah. After that relationship crashed and burned, no man had ever gotten under her skin and into her thoughts the way Grayson Malone did. She was ready to try being a couple again, ready to care, maybe even ready to give him her heart. She'd have to go slowly. The man was still working through some trust and self-esteem issues from the loss of his legs and his military career. But as long as he gave her a chance—gave them a chance—she would plant the seeds of a relationship and nurture it as much as he needed her to.

Or she'd go Navy lieutenant on his ass and shove him out of his comfort zone. She liked Gray. She wanted him. He challenged her intellectually and made her laugh. She trusted him enough to feel safe about lowering her guard. He wasn't put off by her strength, didn't try to diminish it the way Noah had. But he seemed to understand that just because she could handle almost anything on her own, she didn't always want to. She didn't have to wear herself out mentally and emotionally because when she needed a break, she believed Grayson Malone would have her six.

After double-checking tomorrow's schedule against her phone and the written calendar to ensure there were no more discrepancies, Allie closed down her computer. She waved good night to Maeve, then opened her locker in the back room and put the tablet away. She slipped the long strap of her envelope purse over her shoulder and pulled out her keys with the attached pepper spray canister, sliding them into the pocket of her scrub pants. She closed her locker, spun the combination lock, then hurried out through the lobby to meet Gray at the exit. He had his wheelchair folded beside him, his equipment bag slung over his right shoulder, and he was tall and handsome and perfect for her.

Well, almost perfect. She noticed he had one crutch cuffed around his right forearm. Better than two crutches, but she had to ask, "Do you really need that?"

He held the crutch up and swished it back and forth as

if he was wielding some sort of samurai sword. "In case I have to whack somebody over the head."

Allie laughed out loud. "You really did listen to that whole spiel I gave."

"I listen when you talk, Lieutenant. Then I process the words and the meaning behind them until I reach the logical conclusion."

She loved it when he talked all sciencey geek to her. "And what conclusion did you reach?"

"That I want to hold hands with you, too." Gray held his left hand out to her. "Shall we?" When she took it, he sealed her hand in his strong, gentle grip.

She pushed the automatic button to open the door and was greeted by the rumbling of thunder in the distance. Allie tipped her face to the dark gray clouds gathering overhead. The air already smelled like ozone ahead of the cold front. "Looks like rain. Do you want me to run and get the car and pick you up over here?"

"It's not raining yet. And you're not going into a shadowy parking garage on your own." He tugged on her hand, and she fell easily into step beside him. "You said we were walking. Let's walk."

The first drops hit before they reached the entrance to the garage. Allie dashed ahead, pushing the folded wheelchair out of the rain. When she turned back to help Gray, he was already moving at what looked like a three-legged trot. Although it was only a matter of seconds before they hurried beneath the protective overhang, the clouds skipped the sprinkling stage and opened up with a steady downpour. It was enough to soak the shoulders of her jacket and drip through her hair until it trickled along her scalp. Once they got inside, Gray released her to scrub his hand over the top of his short hair and shake off a palmful of water.

"Well, that was exciting." Allie plucked her scrubs away from her shoulders and breasts, then shook at the sudden drop in temperature against her wet skin. "I'm not far from here. Next aisle over, about halfway down."

"Wait." He propped his crutch against his thigh and shrugged out of his hoodie. He flung it around her shoulder and urged her to poke her arms into the sleeves. "You're shivering."

"You're wet, too." She half-heartedly protested the gallant gesture, already absorbing the lingering warmth from his body and dipping her nose to inhale his scent clinging to the cotton.

"My bag kept it pretty dry. And I like you wearing my jacket. The gray brings out the soft color of your eyes." Before she could savor the compliment, he zipped the hoodie all the way to the top, then pulled the neckline together beneath her chin before resting his forehead against hers. "Besides, you've got that freaky cold-natured thing going on and I need to warm you up. I'm not holding on to ice cube hands."

Allie burst out with a laugh and was rewarded with a smile. Gray swung his bag over the shoulder of his T-shirt, hooked the crutch over his forearm and reached for her hand. As they walked farther into the parking garage, the pungent fumes of gasoline and oil spills on the concrete gradually overpowered the fresh scent of the rain. And even though he was walking beside her as she'd requested, her hand folded snugly into his, she couldn't help but notice the hyper alertness of his gaze, scanning each and every car they passed. He walked with his typical uneven gait, but his broad shoulders were back, his balance squared exactly as she had taught him over his hips. The man was charming and considerate, and completely on guard against any unseen threat.

His watchfulness had Allie scanning up and down the long aisle of vehicles, too. "Are you sure we can trust Ben with a security detail?"

"I think he's looking for something to focus on. Keeping watch would have been drilled into him by the Army. The setting and the enemy might be different, but the job should feel familiar."

She wondered if being on guard like this was familiar to him, too. And if that was a good thing, or a job that made him doubt his current abilities even more. "You're sure you're not trusting him just because he's military? After all, Noah was military, too. The government wouldn't need a prison the size of NAVCONBRIG CHASN if every soldier and sailor was a saint."

Gray stopped and swung his gaze around as if he'd heard a noise she had missed. She saw nothing but rain falling in a dreary gray curtain beyond the entrance. That must have been all he could make out, too, because he tugged her into step beside him again. "You think Ben could be doing this to you?"

"He seems too hotheaded to do the research to recreate incidents that happened before. And I never met him until he came to the clinic as a patient a few weeks ago. But he does seem to have a pretty wide angry streak running through him."

"I'll keep him on my suspect list. One of the reasons I agreed to his help is so we can keep a closer eye on *him*. A lot of times, a perp will insert himself into an investigation to keep tabs on it and get an extra thrill of seeing the aftermath of his handiwork."

"Like me freaking out at work?"

"If that was you freaking out, I'm not worried. Once you had a chance to clear your head, you took charge of the situation. Everyone got what they needed, and you came out of it looking like a champ."

"Which would have totally pissed off Noah." Allie had to release Gray's hand to pull out her keys as they neared her car. "And you're convinced someone besides him is behind this?"

"I think it's a possibility. I don't want KCPD or the crime lab to focus solely on your ex and miss a threat that's closer to home. Someone like Ben, who seems a little unstable, or Friesen, who wants to get in your pants. Have you talked about what you went through in Jacksonville to anyone at work?"

Allie shrugged as she hit the remote and the trunk popped open. "Maeve, a little bit. I told her I had a bad breakup. I didn't tell her about him sabotaging my car and running me off the road. She said she's familiar with lousy exes—we commiserated."

"Friesen could have overheard, done a little research. Maybe he's punishing you for turning him down—or maybe he expects you to turn to him for comfort."

"That'll never happen." Allie frowned as another possible suspect sprang to mind. "Bubba hits on me when I run into him in the building. I try not to be home when he's doing repairs. He's been in my apartment twice in the past month. First to repair my garbage disposal, then to replace it."

"Bubba Summerfield? Our building super?" Gray shook his head. "I didn't get an upgrade. I'll make a note to double-check whose apartments he's been going into recently, and how often. If you've been singled out, I'll have Officer Cutler question him again."

"While Doug is annoying, Bubba feels harmless. To be honest, I can't see him having the brains or the patience to stalk me without revealing his identity. He'd brag on purpose or let something slip."

Allie reached for the wheelchair, but Gray was already lifting it and loading it into the trunk. "Unless someone is telling him what to do. We're still combing through the visitor log at NAVCONBRIG CHASN. Someone in your world here in KC may have a connection to Boggs."

She stepped back as he loaded the bag, as well. "This feels like before. Booking the two most vocal, least flexible patients who'll raise the biggest stink at the same time? I wouldn't give myself a headache like that. And the anonymous flowers are just like Jacksonville. Things seem normal on the surface. If you're outside looking in, nothing seems wrong." She hugged her arms around her waist, standing back as he retrieved the second metal crutch. "But I know things are off. There's someone out there, plotting against me—undermining me, isolating me, forcing me to relive the worst time of my life. It's all leading to whatever *Payback* means. I don't think I can go through this again."

Gray closed the trunk and turned to her. "Look at me. You're the strongest woman I've ever met. And I know a few."

"I don't feel strong. A little mix-up like double-booking patients shouldn't have rattled me like that. Then the flowers came, and Doug was being too *helpful*, and I lost it." She reached up and touched her fingertips to the corner of his mouth. "I'm sorry if I made you feel uncomfortable with that kiss. I know you're super conscious of how people perceive you when you're in your chair. The last thing I want to do is screw up anything between us. I mean, I want there to be something between us. But I know this is going to get worse before it gets better, and you're not going to want to be a part of that."

"Come here." Gray shifted both crutches to one hand and tunneled the fingers of his free hand into the base of her ponytail.

Not the reaction she'd been expecting. She thought he'd have a logical argument, a sympathetic word. Instead, he palmed the side of her neck and pulled her into his kiss.

Gray's mouth covered hers in a thorough stamp of possession. There was no hesitation, no getting acquainted, no apology. His lips moved against hers, stroking, taking, claiming. His tongue teased the seam of her lips and she willingly opened for him. Allie felt him rocking closer as he slid his tongue inside her mouth to dance with hers. Allie's hands fisted in the front of his T-shirt, then slid up around his neck to palm the prickly crispness of his damp hair. Moving her fingers across the fine shape of his head stirred up the scents of rain and man, until she was surrounded by it, consumed by the smells she craved so much.

It was as if they'd kissed a hundred times before. Gray's mouth felt familiar on hers. His stubble teased her sensitive skin and his firm lips and raspy tongue soothed. It was just his mouth on hers, his hand in her hair, the tips of her breasts pearling and rubbing against his chest. The kiss was commanding, seductive, a testament to his strength and control. Gray's lips claiming hers blotted out all thoughts except the rightness of the two of them together. Two wounded warriors. Two kindred spirits. Man. Woman. Comfort. Need.

And then Gray pulled his mouth from hers with a deep-pitched groan. His fingertips were still tangled in her hair, pulsing at the nape of her neck. He dropped his forehead to rest against hers, his breath gusting against her face. "Damn, woman. Shouldn't have kissed you like that."

Allie was feeling a little like she'd just pushed herself to run a six-minute mile, riding an endorphin high, gasping for air and equilibrium. She clung to Gray's shoulders because they were the most solid thing she could anchor herself to at the moment. She looked up into his turbulent green eyes. "Why did you?"

"I needed to distract you—break the downward spiral of those thoughts."

Her nostrils flared as she took in a deep breath and tried to hide her disappointment. She dropped her hands to the slightly more neutral location of his biceps and pulled her forehead from his. "You kissed me to distract me?" Her voice was still husky with passion, and she tried to tease. "Smooth, Malone. Your dating skills are a little rusty."

He tangled more of her ponytail between his fingers and tightened his grip on her neck, silently asking her not to retreat. "For the record, your kissing me at the clinic didn't make me uncomfortable. What made me uncomfortable was how badly I wanted to take you in my arms and turn that kiss into something more." His gaze dropped to her mouth. "I wanted to kiss you. I wanted visceral proof that we share a connection. That we're a team." His eyes found hers again. "I swear you will not be alone this time. I'm not going to abandon you to some superior officer who controls your fate. I'm not sure I can hold up my end of the deal, but

I want to try. My brain says help you, protect you, kiss you. My body doesn't always comply with what my instincts and training tell it to do. But I wanted to try. I wanted to comfort you. I wanted to find out what your lips tasted like." He pressed the pad of his thumb to her swollen bottom lip and nerve endings tingled in her breasts and between her thighs. "A perfect blend of sweetness and sass, by the way."

This man. How could he ever think he was anything less than a potent, virile male? "Wow. That's a much better explanation why you wanted to kiss me."

He chuckled deep in his throat, a gravelly, sexy sound. "I'm working on my flirting skills. My therapist said I needed to up my game."

"I'll make a note of the improvements in your file."

He replaced his thumb with a quick brush of his lips over hers. "Are we really doing this? Are we falling for each other?"

"I'm already halfway there. The heart and hormones are willing. Not too sure about the timing, though."

He nodded. "We're both practical people. We've both been burned pretty badly by past relationships. We both have complications in our lives."

She couldn't argue with any of that. She could do slow if that was what he needed. Or she could throw caution to the wind and jump in with both feet. She had a feeling Gray wasn't sure how he wanted to move forward yet. But they were moving forward. They were on the same page now about the possibility of a relationship, and that gave her hope. Allie hadn't felt hope for a very long time. "I'm glad to have the Marines on my side. The crime lab. You."

He finally pulled away entirely to slide the cuff of his crutch on to his left forearm. "Let my team do their job.

We'll find answers, confirm the who, and figure out the how and why. In the meantime, you're staying with me. You're wearing my hoodie. And you're never alone, not until we catch whoever is behind this."

"That was an awfully bossy set of rules, Malone. It chafes against my independent nature." He started to explain his reasoning, but she cut him off. "But it makes me feel better—it makes me feel safer—to share this psychological terror campaign with someone. However, I have a few rules I'm laying down, too. One, I want you to kiss me like that again. Maybe several times. And two..." She reached for his hand and laced their fingers together. "I want to sit on your lap and bury my nose against that sexy, manly scent that comes off your skin while you hold me in your arms. Tight. I want to cuddle."

His cheekbones turned rosy with a blush. "That's it? Those are your rules?"

"And I want to share expenses and help take care of your apartment. Also, I missed my run today, so I'll want to exercise tomorrow. It's the best stress reducer for me—plus, I want to stay in fighting shape in case I need to, you know, fight. And if you and your friends are coming over Saturday afternoon to help clean my apartment, I insist on buying beer or sodas and pizza for everyone."

"This is getting to be a long list. Anything else?"

"Maybe." She tilted her chin and leaned in to kiss the corner of his mouth. "But I don't want to scare you off."

"You haven't yet, Tate."

The rumblings of thunder and steady drumbeat of rain against the pavement must have masked the sound of an engine starting. But there was no mistaking the squeal of tires fighting for traction as a car rounded the end of the aisle and raced toward them. "Gray?"

For a split second she flashed back to the sounds of Noah's truck racing up in her rearview mirror, ramming her car and spinning her over the railing of the bridge. Her breath lodged in her chest, and she couldn't seem to move. The bright beam of headlights blinded her.

"Allie!"

A vise clamped around her waist and she was off her feet, flying backward, out of the path of the car bearing down on her. In a span of milliseconds, she realized the lights kept her from seeing the driver's face. She felt the breeze of the car rushing past. Gray lost his footing and they were falling until he caught her bumper with one strong arm and pushed them both upright.

A fist-sized projectile flew out the open, passenger-side window and Gray shouted a warning, even as she tried to push him out of the way. "Look out!"

A glass jar sailed through the air and shattered against the trunk of Allie's car. She felt a sharp nick on her cheek and something warm and viscous oozing down her face and neck. The car careened around the corner and left the garage with a cacophony of honking horns as it skidded into traffic.

Gray's arm was still anchored around her waist as he righted himself over his legs and pulled out his cell phone.

"Are you all right?" Allie asked, wondering at the breathless, distant sound of her voice. Spots of red dotted the sleeve of his T-shirt and bare arm. "What the hell?"

Gray dropped his crutches to free his hands. He put the

phone to his ear and touched his fingers to her jawline. "Is any of that yours?"

"Is any of what mine?"

"The blood." He studied her with unblinking intensity as his call picked up. "This is Grayson Malone. KCPD Crime Lab. Someone just tried to kill my girlfriend and me. Attempted hit-and-run. The car's gone. No license plate. Send units. Send a bus. Send Lexi Callahan-Murphy and her team from the lab." After giving their location, he hung up. "Talk to me."

Allie touched the cut on her cheek and dragged her fingers through the ooze, trying to shake off the shock and the memories and understand what had happened. Her hand came away covered with blood. The hoodie she loved so much had rivulets of scarlet goo running down the front. "I think it's just a little cut on my cheek. Where is this all coming from?" There was blood pooling on the trunk of her car, running over the edge and dripping off the bumper. Shards of glass littered the pavement at her feet. When she reached for a curved piece of glass on her trunk, Gray caught her wrist and pulled her away from the car. "He threw a jar of blood at us? What does that mean? Gray?"

"I'm right here with you, babe. Don't touch anything else." He brushed aside a lock of hair that clung to her cheek and tucked it behind her ear. "I want nothing more than to take you in my arms right now and hold you tight."

"Yes. That's what I want, too." She stepped toward him, but his grip on her wrist and cheek tightened, strong-arming her out of his personal space. The mix of anguish and anger on his face made her retreat another half a step. "What is it?"

The shock dissipated with a frightening realization.

"You can't hold me."

He shook his head. "I'm sorry, babe. You're the crime scene."

Chapter Nine

Gray opened his eyes to the golden-orange glow of sunrise bleeding into the apartment around the blinds at the living room window. His bed was hard, and so was he. His mind snapped awake at the unfamiliar sensations, and he quickly processed each one.

Not in his bed.

Not alone.

For a split second, the urge to escape to familiar territory jolted through him. But a long strand of honey-blond hair caught in the scruff of his beard and stirred up the scents of a faint flowery shampoo. Allie.

He breathed her in again and felt his body relax. He grinned. Well, most of his body. That seemed to be happening a lot when he spent time with Allie.

Waking up curled around a woman's body was an experience he'd forgotten—her back to his chest, her bottom nestled against his groin, his thighs tucked behind hers, and nothing more. After Brittany's teary-eyed freak-out about missing half his legs, he'd expected that every woman would be hesitant to be physically intimate with him.

But not Allie Tate. In fact, she seemed to seek him out—to hold his hand, to snuggle against his arm on the couch while they talked through the events of the afternoon and evening. Although the hoodie he'd given her yesterday had been bagged up and taken to the crime lab to process the blood sample on it, she had longingly eyed the one he'd put on—the gray-and-red one with *Marines* written on it. He'd happily handed it over for her to wear like a robe over the T-shirt and lounge pants she'd changed into after cleaning up. There was something possessively right about a special woman wearing *his* clothes—even if it was an oversize, well-worn sweatshirt with a faded logo on the chest. He felt protective, and more like a man than he had since that RPG had blown up his convoy.

Even when he'd been 100 percent before that last deployment, Brittany hadn't been this much of a toucher. Yeah, they'd had sex. They'd hugged and kissed. But it had never been like this—like something would sneak in and tear her apart if she didn't have contact with him. Even in sleep, Allie clung to the forearm he'd cinched around her waist.

Last night, it was clear she was too wired to sleep. So, he'd streamed a movie for them. But she wasn't really watching it. They'd discussed Noah Boggs and how the progression of events here in KC echoed the mind games he'd used to intimidate and isolate her back in Jacksonville. They were both exhausted, but rehashing the clues and possibilities wasn't helping her relax. So, Gray had put some soft music on and offered to hold her until she got sleepy, with the promise he'd tuck her in and let her sleep in as long as she needed in the morning.

The strain beside Allie's gray-blue eyes had softened. She'd tucked her hands beneath his left arm, curled her knees up over his thigh and rested her cheek against his shoulder. Then she'd made a sweet joke about how her feet were as cold as her hands, so, in a way, he was lucky he didn't have anything below his knees she could press them against. He felt her hold her breath for a few seconds, anxious to learn if she'd offended him or amused him with her practicality. Allie Tate talked to him as if he was a normal man—she prodded and teased, argued and laughed. She didn't make a big deal about his disability, but she never turned her head and shied away from it, either.

So, Gray had laughed at his good fortune, rolled her onto her back and proceeded to kiss her the way she said she liked, the way he liked, with grabby hands and dueling tongues and sexy moans, with those sweet, small breasts tightening up like buttons and rubbing against his chest—until she'd yawned against his mouth. Gray wasn't offended. Instead, he was pleased that he had a way to distract her from the thoughts that plagued her. Her day had been hellishly long and full of stress and she needed her rest. Besides, when he lay down behind her and she cuddled into him, Gray felt a sense of rightness, of hope, swelling inside his chest.

Maybe he'd been falling in love with his neighbor a little bit more each day over the past few months they'd lived side by side and worked together at the clinic. But he hadn't let himself act on those feelings. He'd been guarding his heart with an emotional flak vest, afraid of not being enough, of not being the man a woman needed.

But bloody messages, frightening mind games and someone with a devious, dangerous plan forcing himself into Allie's life had pierced that vest and forced the man inside him to shove aside the bad memories and self-doubts. That car racing toward them tonight could have shattered every bone in Allie's body. She'd been in shock, on the verge of some kind of flashback, and wasn't moving. If his reaction time had been any slower, she would have ended up with a lot worse than a cut on her cheek. He could have lost her before they ever had a real chance to begin. The woman sleeping so trustingly in his arms this morning was a gift he would protect with his life. He wanted her. He needed her to be safe.

But caring like this might get him hurt again. Allie was a strong woman with an independent spirit. Noah Boggs had tried to frighten that out of her, and he hadn't succeeded. She'd learned how to endure all on her own. Without a man. Without anyone. Maybe once he found answers and the man terrorizing her was behind bars, she wouldn't need him anymore. She'd see him for what he really was—a has-been not good for much beyond running scientific tests and keeping her warm—and go back to being alone. If he couldn't have a real relationship with Allie, Gray didn't want any. He could distance himself as her neighbor—be friendly and polite but limit the chances of running into her by changing his schedule. He'd probably have to find a new physical therapist, though. He wasn't sure he could deal with her touching him and it not meaning anything.

And if he failed to keep her alive and safe, Gray wasn't sure he could come back from that. It would be proof that he wasn't the man he used to be—that he'd never be that Marine again. If he felt guilty about surviving a war zone when his buddies had died, the guilt he'd feel at losing this good woman would break him.

Allie whimpered in her sleep and hugged herself more tightly around his forearm, clearly agitated by some subconscious thought. He kissed the back of her neck and shushed her back into a deeper slumber. She sighed in contentment and whispered his name in her sleep.

Ah, hell. He was in so much trouble. He was in love with her.

That flak vest he'd put up around his emotions was useless now. If he wanted Allie—if he wanted to earn her love, in return—he'd need to move past all his personal baggage and fight for her, show her he was the man she could love and depend on. He'd trained his body as a Marine. He'd trained his mind as a criminalist. He needed to train his heart to be the man Allie Tate could love.

Baby steps, Malone. He masked a chuckle at the irony of that statement.

First, he needed to extricate himself from Allie's grasp and dress and get ready for the day—a task he still wasn't sure he wanted the woman he needed to impress to witness. Pushing himself up, then pulling himself along the back of the couch until he could move freely, Gray spider-walked to the end of the sectional where he'd removed his prostheses and pads last night. There was no point in putting them on until he got through his shower. His wheelchair was still beside the front door where they'd left it to dry after getting rained on. There was no way to do this gracefully.

He glanced back at Allie, tucked the comforter around her sleeping form. Then, dragging his legs and crutches behind him, he scuttled into the bedroom and adjoining master bath.

ALLIE WASN'T SURE why Gray was so quiet this morning. Snugged up against the furnace of his body, she'd gotten the best night's sleep she'd had in months. She had a feeling the night could have ended with something more, based on her body's wicked reaction to his kisses and his obvious response to hers. Even though giving herself to Gray was on her future agenda, he'd been smart enough to see her fatigue and had ended the make-out session on the couch with the promise of holding her through the night.

Maybe he was disappointed they hadn't gone all the way? Maybe he was still hung up on her perception of his physical attractiveness and ultimate reliability, and he'd been relieved she'd been willing to stop. Maybe he wasn't a cuddler, and her clinginess had been a turn-off—although the man sure was a pro at it.

He was all ready for the day by the time she'd roused herself from sleep and gone into the guest bathroom to freshen up. He'd cooked them a healthy breakfast of veggie omelets and toast while she packed a bag of clothes she could change into at work. He'd encouraged her to go down to the building's gym and run on the treadmill for about twenty minutes until they had to leave for the clinic. While she insisted that getting back to her running schedule would be good for both her physical and mental health, Gray was adamant that she not run outside by herself. Either she needed a running buddy, or she was doing it here in the building. After the events of the past few days, Allie hadn't argued—she had no desire to be out there in the world alone with an enemy lurking in the unseen corners of her life.

She was pleased to see that he'd put on his prosthetic legs again after getting out of the shower. Legs or chair or neither, Grayson Malone was a hottie who had awakened both her heart and her hormones. But the therapist in her knew he needed to spend more time getting used to his new prostheses. He probably worried that they wouldn't fit properly and would start rubbing and causing lesions like the last pair. But that had been his own fault for working out to the extreme and negating the original fit. He needed to learn to be comfortable in any situation and feel confident that he was in control of his body—not that his chair or prostheses controlled him.

She was also glad they'd already made arrangements for him to drive them to work today. That way she didn't miss her car quite so much while it was impounded at the lab and then sent on to her dealer's repair center to get detailed and have the dent removed from where the blood-filled jar had hit.

Conversation over breakfast was polite, but nothing too deep or personal. They'd probably covered way too much of that the past two nights on his sofa. She wondered if he was thinking about the investigation, or if he was regretting that he'd gotten involved with her mess of a life, or if he was simply a quiet guy in the morning.

When she asked him about it, he tapped his watch and pointed out the time, reminding her that she needed to get going if she wanted any time in the gym downstairs, or they'd both be late for work.

Allie crossed to his side of the table and folded her arms in front of her. "Changing the subject is not an answer to my question, Malone."

He chuckled before pushing back his chair and standing up. A ripple of awareness shivered through her as he straightened above her. Mistaking her tremors for her susceptibility to cold temps, he cupped her shoulders and ran his hands up and down her arms. "Keep the jacket."

"Still not an answer to the question. But thank you." She was reassured that he was touching her again. She returned the favor and splayed her hand against his chest. "Do I need to be worried about anything?"

"No. Nothing new." He leaned in to press a quick kiss to her lips before pulling away. "I've got a lot on my mind this morning—some things I need to figure out. I don't like feeling that this guy is smarter than I am. I promised you answers. I haven't got any yet."

"You will." Allie gathered up their plates and rinsed them in the kitchen sink. "And last night? Are you okay with the way things turned out?"

"I haven't been in a relationship since Brittany, so I feel a little rusty. But I'm very okay. I figure if the time is right, it will feel right. For both of us." He brought the pan and spatula to the sink and stood beside her. "You?"

"I'm better now that you're talking to me again."

"I'll finish these." Gray nudged her aside with his shoulder. "Go. Run. I'll be down in twenty, twenty-five minutes. Do not go outside."

"Yes, sir." Allie saluted him, then tilted her lips up to kiss his stubbled jaw.

With the promise that he'd get her bag and purse loaded into his van, Allie grabbed her keys and hurried out the door.

Fifteen minutes later, Allie was rethinking her effort to clear her head.

Stretching her muscles, expanding her lungs and raising her heart rate felt good. But there was an unspoken rule that runners enjoyed their alone time. She was here to get her endorphins sparking and find that zen sense of peace in her mind.

But even the whirring of the treadmill and the rhythmic stamp of her feet couldn't drown out Bubba Summerfield's meaningless prattle. The short and stocky building super had spent the last ten minutes up on an aluminum ladder, changing the fluorescent lightbulbs in the ceiling. A friendly greeting and going about his business in the same room was one thing, but she'd already learned that Mrs. Wyatt who lived across the hall from her had complained about the noise from the crime lab team and curiosity seekers who'd been at her apartment the other night. And she'd been terrified to have Aiden Murphy's K-9 partner, Blue, in the building, even though the dog had been well-behaved and had only growled at Bubba himself for barging in. Bubba had laughed off that part of his story, saying he had never been very good with dogs, anyway, that he was more of a cat person.

Allie adjusted the incline of the treadmill and quickened her pace, mentally trying to outrun the man. She thought the rattle of him moving the ladder behind her was a sign he was leaving, but he set it up right next to the treadmill and climbed up. And kept talking. Allie tried to blank the tan coveralls from her peripheral vision, and picture images of Grayson Malone kissing her like she'd never been kissed before, popping the suction off his prosthetic legs last night and allowing her to massage some lotion into the scarred stumps of his thighs—which she suspected had been the epitome of trust for him, making the contact feel like a secret intimacy between lovers. She remembered how he had wrapped his body around hers in a way that chased away every troubling thought and potential nightmare and allowed her to sleep.

But Bubba's fingers wrapped around the handle of the treadmill for balance as he descended the ladder, and she nearly stumbled as she shied away from the almost touch. Why hadn't she thought to bring her earbuds and a podcast to listen to?

"...the family in 4B. Since they didn't pay the pet deposit

for that cat, replacing the carpet will be coming out of their pocketbook." He moved the ladder to the last ceiling light, thankfully beyond arm's reach. Apparently, he didn't need a comment to continue the conversation. "You know, that carpet won't be in for a couple of days. I've got time this afternoon and tomorrow to get into your apartment and start bleaching walls and repainting them. Not sure what I'm going to do about your cabinets, though. If I can't get them clean with some good elbow grease, I might have to replace them."

"No." Allie's ponytail caught in her mouth as she turned to Bubba. She pulled the strands from her lips and faced forward again. "I've got friends coming Saturday afternoon to help with the cleanup." At least, Gray had promised *his* friends from the crime lab would come. Her rhythm had gotten a little off, so she pushed the button to slow her pace. "I don't want anyone in my apartment." She wasn't about to explain the sense of violation she still felt about the break-in, the loss of control that she wasn't calling the shots in her own life anymore. The chatty super didn't need to know any of that. "Thanks, anyway, though," she added, hoping to end the conversation, and run that last couple of minutes in peace and quiet.

"What difference does it make?" Was that a snap of frustration in his tone? "You haven't been staying there, anyway. Isn't my work good enough?"

"You've been watching my apartment?" Allie dropped the incline of her run and slowed her pace to a cool-down speed.

"Hey, I'm part of the security around this building. It's my job to keep an eye on things."

"It's not your job to know my personal business."

"It's no secret around here that you and Mr. Malone are sweet on each other. You two doing the nasty yet?"

"What?" She tried to make eye contact with him, but Bubba was too far behind her, and she couldn't risk tripping and falling. "Who are you going to share that tidbit of gossip with?"

"I don't have to share it." He snickered as if he couldn't understand why she'd be offended by his question. "Everybody knows stuff in this building. I'm not the only one watching you guys."

"Who else is watching me?" Allie pulled the safety key from the treadmill keyboard, stopping it abruptly the same time she heard Grayson's voice from the doorway.

"Get your eyes off her ass, Summerfield." Now, *that* was the voice of a Marine.

With her equilibrium still spinning a bit after the abrupt stop to her run, she reached for Gray's hand where he clasped his crutch. He instantly released the handle and turned his hand to hold on to her, instead. "You don't speak to Lieutenant Tate like that, either. What goes on inside any apartment in this building is none of your business."

"Easy, Mr. Malone. I didn't mean nothing about the two of you hooking up." The super put his hands up in a gesture of placating surrender. "But it's true? The two of you are together? I didn't want to believe what folks were saying."

"What folks? Who's talking about us?" Allie demanded.

"I kind of fancied asking you out myself."

Allie glared into his beady brown eyes and wondered what he found so amusing about this conversation. But she spoke to Gray. "Bubba said he's not the only person who's been watching me."

"I need names, Summerfield. A description. Who have you seen?"

Grayson's glare must have been a little more intimidating because Bubba retreated half a step. His keys rattled as he rested his forearms against his tool belt. "Some guy. I've seen him in the garage or parked out front or across the street. Because, you know, your apartment is in the front of the building."

"Some guy?" Gray demanded clarification while Allie's spirit withered a little at the thought of spies all around her, and she'd been completely unaware. God, hadn't she learned anything from Noah? How had she gotten so complacent? "I need more."

Bubba shrugged. "I can't tell you much. It's not like I've seen his face. He's always hiding it. In the shadows or with a hat. But I know he doesn't live here."

"How do you know that?" Gray pushed.

"Doesn't have a building permit sticker on his windshield."

"Can you describe the car?" Allie asked, dredging up a vision of headlights racing toward her, and a blur of black flying past.

Bubba grinned, looking much happier to be talking to her than to Gray. "An older car. Four doors. Black. And no, I didn't get a license number."

Gray reached into his back pocket to pull out his wallet and a business card. He handed his contact information at the crime lab over to the super. "You see that guy or the car again, call me."

Bubba tucked the card into his coveralls. "Okay."

"I mean it. It's a matter of personal security for Lieutenant Tate."

Bubba frowned. "Allie? This guy wasn't watching her."

"You just said—"

"Mr. Malone. I think he's watching *you*."

Chapter Ten

Cutting the corner into the crime lab parking lot too close and bumping his tire over the curb was the least of Gray's problems today. True, he wouldn't be driving his van in the Indy 500 anytime soon, or running any races on his prosthetic legs, or winning any bachelor-of-the-month contests. But he damn well thought he'd been on the trail of the right stalker, at least. Now he wasn't so sure.

Somehow, a discussion of Chelsea O'Brien's wedding plans had led to the women of the KCPD crime lab meeting in Lexi Callahan-Murphy's office over lunch, while Gray and the men he worked with sat around a big table in the lab's memorial lounge, polishing off sandwiches and takeout, and drinking bottles of water and cups of coffee.

"Sorry you all got roped into Chelsea's plans for the wedding." Buck Buckner, Chelsea's fiancé, was a veteran cop with a bulldog face, salt-and-pepper hair, and an absolute soft spot for the lab's quirky computer guru. "But since she grew up without a family and never had so much as a birthday party, much less a fancy dress-up event like a wedding, I want her to have whatever she wants."

"We get that, man." Rufus King, Buck's former partner at KCPD, and now the uniformed ops sergeant who helped the director run the crime lab, rubbed his palm over his shaved head. "Chelsea's part of our family here at the lab now. We want to help the two of you celebrate. Besides, we are all behind her getting your grumpy butt married off and out of our hair." He tapped his mahogany scalp. "So to speak."

There was shared laughter among friends, some congratulatory comments about the marriage, teasing about the improvement in Buck's personality since meeting Chelsea, along with the absence of Rufus's hair. But they were guys, and that was about all the talk about weddings and romance they could manage. Conversations around the table quickly turned back to work, as these informal bull sessions in the lounge usually did.

Gray sat at one end of the long table, his crutches leaning against the table beside him as he swirled tepid coffee around in his travel mug. "It's not lost on me that I'm the lab's blood expert, and there's an unnatural amount of blood involved in Allie's case." Not for the first time that morning, he wondered why he hadn't made the connection sooner. Or maybe there was no connection, and he was trying to force the coincidences of bloody warnings into the answers he so desperately wanted. "If this perp is tailing me, maybe it's just a means to get to Allie. I'm not the one this guy is trying to gaslight. She's the one who's gotten hurt."

"The super could be an idiot," Shane suggested, taking a bite of a sprinkle-laden cookie that had probably been decorated by his toddler son. "You and Allie live next door to each other, so you're bound to run into each other a lot. Plus, you commute every day you have PT in the morning. Not to mention all the time you've spent at the clinic. If you guys are together, who can say if they're watching her or you?"

"You think there's a connection?" Mac Taylor, the director of the crime lab, sat at the opposite end of the table. If possible, his brain operated with even more pure logic than Gray's did. "Between Allie being stalked and the presence of so much blood?"

Gray leaned back in his chair. "Well, I don't believe in cosmic karma. Why not use paint in her apartment? Why not toss corrosive liquid that could do real damage to her or her car? Why real blood on that florist's card? Why throw a jar of it at her?"

Brian Stockman, the oldest uniformed officer in the room, who oversaw the CSIU, or Crime Scene Investigation Unit, and coordinated their crime scene assignments with the police department, said, "Technically, the driver targeted both of you, tried to run you both down."

Gray scrubbed at the stubble of his beard. "Maybe I've been looking at this all wrong. Focusing on Allie. Maybe this is about hurting *me*. We're not a couple, not until recent events threw us together. She might be collateral damage."

Aiden Murphy snorted a laugh. He leaned against the beverage counter where his K-9 partner, Blue, was dozing at his feet. "Are you kidding? You two have been shootin' sparks off each other for weeks now. She always makes a point of coming over to talk to you at the clinic, even when you're not assigned to her. You do that dancing thing."

"Dancing thing?"

"I've seen it, too," Shane pointed out.

"Yeah, I don't know what kind of therapy holding on to each other like that's supposed to be—" Aiden went on.

"It's to work on my balance—"

"—but every time I've given you a ride, you two always seem to be touching each other. Lexi's commented on it, too." As usual, Aiden smiled at the mention of his wife. "I can't tell you how many times she's asked me if you two are dating. I think she wanted to set you up with a friend if you were free."

Gray frowned. "She doesn't need to set me up with anybody. I'm not interested."

Except for a couple of snickers, the silence around the table told Gray that he had just made Aiden's point.

"Allie and I look like a couple?"

As usual, his buddy Jackson waited until he had something important to say before speaking. "Drop everything here and get you to the clinic when she sends you an SOS?"

While part of his brain was processing the idea that others had seen him and Allie together as a couple before he'd even considered the possibility, Gray was figuring out something quite different. "Anyone watching me would mistake us for a couple, too." Jackson's reminder of his response to Allie's text for help finally convinced him. "If they wanted to hurt me—not physically hurt me, but tear me up inside, distract me, get me off my game—they'd go after Allie."

Even though he ran his own security firm now, Buck still thought like a cop. "But why replay the scenario of all the things her ex did to her? Not wishing anyone to put his hands on her the way they did Chels, but why not just attack her? Why the mind games?"

Gray knew the answer to that. "Because that's how you hurt her the most. Allie's a tough, confident woman. Trained in the military. A strong runner." He thumped his chest, fully admitting his guilt. "Doesn't put up with guff from stubborn patients or creepy coworkers. She'd be hard to take down physically. But you get into her head, and it makes her question her surroundings and doubt herself. Takes her back to the scariest, loneliest time of her life."

Buck seemed to understand. "Whether it's physical or psychological, someone threatens the woman you love, and that's all you can think about."

Love? Yeah, these guys had read his feelings for Allie long before he'd admitted them to himself.

Aiden moved up to the table. "The need to watch over your woman makes a heck of a diversion, too. You got any big cases you've been neglecting?"

Rufus King was on the same train of thought. "What about an old case you've closed? Did any of the perps threaten you? Have a spouse or sibling swear retribution?"

Shane added his two cents. "Do you have any open cases where the victim or a family member has threatened you if we don't get answers soon enough for them?"

Brian Stockman pulled his notepad out to jot down some information. "It would be easy enough to check who's out of prison now. Or who's still in—and could be getting help from the outside. I'll have Chelsea do some research."

Didn't that scenario sound familiar?

"I've already asked Chelsea to go through Noah Boggs's phone call and visitor log in South Carolina," Gray said.

"Allie's ex?"

Gray nodded. Brian made a note. "Good. We'll extend that search to people you've helped put away here in Missouri."

Mac stood. Everyone else in the room closed ranks around him, sensing they were about to be given a mission to complete. "Priority one. Gray, I want you to scan through your cases and see if any suspects pop up. We still have other cases on the agenda but use anyone on your team who's available to help."

"And I want to run tests on that blood from the parking garage last night," Gray said. "The blood drops on that florist's card tested as human. I'm still stymied where our perp is getting that much blood to work with. The donors have to be identifiable. Either from a blood bank, a hospital or another crime."

"I can read your files," Jackson offered, "to free you up for the lab time."

"If we get a call to a crime scene, I'll pick up the slack with Lexi and Zoe," Shane added, "so you can stay on-site."

Mac ran the administrative end of the forensic department now, but he still knew how to work a crime scene. "Put my name on the call list, too, Brian, if their team needs the help. In the meantime, I'll look through the open cases, see if anyone looks particularly displeased with Malone."

Gray had lost his two best buddies to that RPG in the desert. He'd been sent home to heal and discharged from the Marines. With the military career he'd planned for his life no longer an option, he'd reinvented and reeducated himself as a criminalist. Although he understood about training himself to do a job, he'd missed the brotherhood, the certainty that whatever he had to do, he wouldn't be doing it alone. For the first time, he truly realized that he was still part of a team. The men around this table, and the women he worked with, too, were the people he wanted by his side in this fight. They might not wear combat gear and carry assault rifles. They weren't fighting a war against terrorism or helping political allies survive civil unrest. They were fighting a war on the home front. This team would help him uncover the truth. They would stop whoever was messing with Allie and bring the perp to justice.

They had his back on this mission to find the answers he needed.

They had Allie's, too.

GRAY SWORE AS he read the results of the printout. He should be happy that he'd finally found a match to the blood sample from the parking garage. But identifying the donor left him with more questions than answers. "Shaquina Carlyle? Who is that?"

Jackson pulled the laptop he was using closer and typed in a search, waiting far more patiently than Gray could for any results to show up. His eyes met Gray's above the equipment on the stainless-steel lab table separating them. "Missing person case."

Gray walked around the table to read the details over Jackson's shoulder. "Twenty-two-year-old female. Left work from a convenience store one night and never made it home."

"No viable leads. Looks like she got moved to Cold Case." Jackson rolled his stool to the side when Gray leaned forward to type in his own search parameters. "What are you thinking?" he asked in his deep, grumbly voice.

Gray adjusted himself back over his crutches, subconsciously remembering Allie's advice to use his core and balance over his legs. "I was going over the list of missing blood that Chelsea compiled for me."

"You said the only significant volume was from that hospital where the refrigeration unit went out and they had to dispose of the tainted blood supply. This missing person report was filed long before that incident." His arched brow asked Gray to explain what he was thinking.

Gray thought back to the basics of his scientific training. "None of the blood I've tested would be viable for a transfusion. The red blood cells lose their ability to produce oxygen after six weeks. But adding a disodium calcium complex and freezing it could make the supply last a lot longer, giving our perp time to accumulate it."

"Did you detect the preservation chemicals in your tests?"

Gray nodded. "Where else could our perp get his hands on that much blood in the first place? There had to be a gallon or more used at Allie's place. That's almost as much as in one human body."

Jackson's brain went to the same dark place where Gray's had gone. "Serial killer." The big man sorted through the stack of closed case folders he'd been reading and pulled one out. He laid it open over the keyboard. "Like Jamie Kleinschmidt."

Gray nodded. "He drained the blood from his victims' bodies and stored it in his basement. There was a freezer full of the stuff in baby food jars from multiple victims. Took me weeks to get through it all. I could conclusively match the three victims he was convicted of killing. The other samples were too degraded, or I couldn't match them to any donor. The samples that weren't destroyed are still in our evidence storage facility. Chelsea confirmed that those are all accounted for."

"You think he had another stash somewhere?"

"Him or someone like him. Though, I haven't seen any indication that there's another bloodletter in KC."

"Kleinschmidt's dead."

No need to point out the obvious. "There goes my suspect list."

"Friends? Family? Fanatic?"

Retribution was a definite possibility. Kleinschmidt had been a disturbed young man who'd claimed his murders were a cleansing ritual—that he only killed sinners and whores. Gray's cool, thorough, scientific testimony on the witness stand had negated the emotional fears and sensationalism of the deaths inside the courtroom. But other zealots outside the courtroom had claimed he was a man with a divine purpose who was purging the ills of society. Of course, there had been just as many opponents arguing the victimization of women. In the end, Kleinschmidt, not interested in being a symbol for any cause and unable to stand the pressures of prison life where he was serving three life terms, had hanged himself in his prison cell. "I don't remember him having family there in the courtroom. Without any healthy support system, it's no wonder he was so unstable. And if there is a copycat, he's not killing the women—at least, we haven't had any dead bodies that show that kind of controlled exsanguination. Kleinschmidt used the funeral home where he worked to drain his victims. Started off by using legitimate corpses being embalmed or cremated by the mortuary. Until that wasn't enough, and he started hunting for new victims in no-man's-land."

Jackson frowned. "Most funeral homes upgraded their security after Kleinschmidt's trial."

"I haven't seen any reports of break-ins at funeral homes, either." Gray turned his focus back to the laptop as the information he sought scrolled on to the screen. "No reported bloodletting deaths in the KC area or outstate Missouri." He studied the grim facts, hoping they would reveal a lead he could follow. Just like with his military training—when the enemy blocked one route of attack, the team sought out another option. "Maybe instead of looking where blood is missing, we look at where that much blood can be stored."

"I'm on it." Jackson scooted back in front of his laptop while Gray picked up Jamie Kleinschmidt's file and carried it across the room to his desk where he woke his own laptop.

"Kleinschmidt always claimed there was more to his stash than what we found in his basement. That's how his lawyer got the death penalty off the table—there was always the hope that his client would reveal the identity and location of more of his victims." Gray skipped the KCPD databases and logged in to the county clerk's public access site to type in Kleinschmidt's last address. "So where has that blood been all this time? Did someone find it? Did someone keep it for him and is using it now?" The image of an empty, overgrown lot filled the screen. "The house where Kleinschmidt lived and kept his trophies has been demolished. Lot's for sale."

Jackson grunted. Yeah, it probably was hard to resell a house where a serial murderer had lived and kept his trophies.

"I don't see any other properties owned by Kleinschmidt." He'd have to call the Realtor selling the lot to see who the owner was. Maybe that person had run across a more secret stash of the killer's souvenirs. "We're certain he worked alone, right?"

"Your testimony, not mine," Jackson reminded him as he jotted down some possibilities from his research. "Wholesale storage caves along the river. Refrigerators at closed restaurants. An old butcher shop."

Gray nodded at the list where a perp could store a large quantity of blood that wasn't on any medical registry. "We could check utilities and see if any of those businesses are still generating electric bills." Gray typed in one more search. "I wonder if there was any vandalism of Kleinschmidt's house after he was arrested, and we cleared the evidence. If one of his fanatics who thought he was doing good work discovered something we missed, he could be using that blood to target me by terrorizing Allie." Yet another dead end. "No break-ins. No more jars of blood unearthed when the construction crew razed the house."

Scrubbing his hand over his cheeks and jaw, Gray leaned back in his chair. "Kleinschmidt's blood is a dead end for now." He stretched his arms out, easing the tension in his shoulders. "How long have we been at this?"

Jackson grunted at the joke as Gray eyed the clock. It was after five. Time to wrap things up and get over to the clinic to pick up Allie. She'd be pleased that he'd worn his legs all day, but he was feeling the strain. He felt the beginnings of a smile relax the corners of his mouth. Maybe since he'd been a good boy and had listened to her advice, she would massage his back tonight. He'd be happy to return the favor. Or maybe he could convince her to rub the therapeutic lotion into his thighs again tonight.

Allie hadn't freaked out when she'd seen the scarred skin last night after he'd changed into a pair of shorts for sleeping. In fact, she'd been the one to ask permission if she could touch him. No one but medical professionals and his own hands had touched his legs since the last operation. Certainly not Brittany. And no other woman except the nurses when he was in the hospital. Allie's hands had been gentle, yet strong, easing the discomfort of ravaged skin and overtaxed muscles without hurting him.

His eyes drifted shut and he imagined her hands massaging other places. There was nothing broken or missing in his body's reaction to her touch. Nerve endings sparked to life just thinking about it. A hunger pooled in his belly. His fingers danced with the desire to bury themselves in her long, silky hair. His manhood twitched with the need to bury himself inside her. He'd be awkward as an untried teenager making love to Allie. And he had a feeling being with her would be just as memorable as that first time he'd made love. No, it would be even better, because it would be Allie's soft blue-gray eyes he'd be looking into. It would be her sweet, strong body clinging to his. He knew without a doubt that his Navy lieutenant would make him feel like a whole, desirable man, even as he did his damnedest to please her in whatever way he could.

Gray heard Jackson clearing his throat and he realized he'd taken a mental vacation for a few minutes. Jackson's gaze shifted to the cell phone sitting on the desk beside Gray's laptop, and he realized he'd been pinged with a text.

Gray eagerly picked up his phone and unlocked it. It was probably Allie joking about losing track of the time, begging him to rescue her from a recalcitrant patient, or even making simple small talk about what they'd have for dinner.

He frowned when he saw the number.

Not Allie. Something worse.

He was already dialing when he read Ben Hunter's message.

Call me.

The moment Ben picked up, Gray spoke. "Is Allie okay?"

"She's not hurt."

The unspoken message was that something else was terribly wrong. Gray should feel relieved that she was in one piece, but his racing pulse was pounding with alarm. He grabbed his crutches and pushed to his feet. "Another threat?"

"You need to get here. It's not good."

Anchoring the phone between his ear and shoulder,

Gray hooked his crutches on to each forearm. "I need details, Sergeant."

Gray was aware of Jackson closing his laptop and rising like a leviathan from his side of the table.

The Army sergeant who'd claimed he could do reconnaissance and watch over Allie at the clinic gave a concise, if worrisome, report. "She's locked the door to the staff locker room and won't come out. She won't talk to me. To anyone. I didn't think I should break down the door."

"I'm on my way."

Hiding was the last thing Gray expected his Allie to do. She was the one who armed herself with pepper spray and guarded his six when he checked out the break-in at her apartment. She was the one who ignored her fears and answered every question the police put to her. She was the one who pushed when he wanted to retreat, who shut down lecherous coworkers with a sharp word, and who faced off against a superior officer in a court of law to make sure the truth was heard. Allie Tate might need to hold his hand or walk by his side or share his kiss to bolster her courage, but she didn't lock herself in a room and shut herself away from the problem at hand. What could have happened?

Gray wished he could snap his fingers and be there for her instantly. He'd have to settle for putting the portable siren on top of his van and racing to the clinic as fast as traffic would allow. Ben was right. This wasn't good. "If the situation changes and you hear any signs of distress, break down the door."

"Understood."

Apparently, the one-handed Army sergeant wasn't into goodbyes and Gray didn't need one.

Jackson asked, "Need help?"

Gray strode to the door as quickly as his legs and crutches allowed. Style wasn't a consideration. "Text Allie. Text her until she answers. I can't walk and text at the same time. Tell her I'm coming. I'll drive."

Jackson took the phone and fell into step beside him. "I'll notify the team where we're headed."

Despite rush hour traffic, Gray made the drive to the PT clinic in ten minutes. He didn't care that he'd lurched to a stop with the front right wheel up on the curb. He didn't care that a small crowd was gathering in the lobby. He didn't care that the only response Jackson had gotten was an OK acknowledging the texts.

What he cared about was that Allie was in trouble. But was she too independent, or too terrified, to reach out to him for help?

With Jackson following behind him, Gray spotted Ben Hunter through the front door and hurried to meet him. "Report."

Ben fell into step with him. "No change. She cussed at me the last time I asked if she was all right. Something about it being safer for everyone and to go away."

"You're certain she wasn't hurt?"

"She wasn't the last time I saw her. She seemed happy. Joked a little about me being hairier than her regular shadow. She said she was done for the day, grabbing her stuff and heading out front to wait for you." Ben pushed open the lobby door into the clinic room. "Next thing I knew, she was bolting the door."

When they entered the clinic's treatment area, Doug Friesen stepped away from the hallway wall to greet them. He thumbed over his shoulder to the closed door of the staff's changing room. "She's gone all diva on us. Won't talk to anyone. Some of us would like to get in there and get our stuff so we can go home. If she makes me late for my date…"

With a lightning-swift move his combat training sergeant would have admired, Gray thrust his forearm across Friesen's clavicle and shoved him back up against the wall. "Did you say or do anything to her?"

"Lighten up, Loverboy." Friesen tugged at the arm braced across his chest. But with the full weight of Gray's body leaning into him, the other man couldn't escape. As usual, he let his big, annoying mouth do the talking. "You know, she's been nothing but trouble since she started working here."

"She's trouble because she hasn't fallen for your cheap lines and unwanted touches?"

"Like her last boyfriend? I heard she caused a stink there, too, after he dumped her. Got him into serious trouble."

"He tried to kill her." Gray enunciated the fact right in Friesen's face.

He felt a restraining hand fold over his shoulder and heard Jackson's voice in his ear. "Priorities."

Right. Friesen and his sneering misinformation didn't matter. Getting to Allie did.

Gray held both hands up as he released Friesen and backed away. The other man adjusted his wrinkled polo shirt and slid out of Gray's way. "I see you brought your whole posse with you. If it was just you and me, Malone, this conversation would have a different ending."

Ignoring the taunt, Gray followed the direction of Ben's hook, pointing to the closed door. "In there."

Gray nodded his thanks. The surly veteran had done exactly as he'd asked of him. "Sergeant, secure this back area.

No one else comes in until I say so. Jackson, have my kit ready." He looked beyond his friend's shoulder and eyed the crowd of staff and patients who had shifted into the end of the hallway. He spotted the worried frown on Maeve Phillips's face. "Ma'am, if there's anything you can do to divert attention away from whatever's happening with Allie, I'd appreciate it."

The curly-haired brunette nodded. "Of course, I'll get the rest of the staff to help me." She nudged the coworker still brooding beside her. "Move, Doug. You may be off the clock, but you still work here."

"Man, she's rubbing off on you, too. Not a compliment." When Ben and Jackson added their considerable glares to back up Maeve, Friesen snorted his protest before fixing a smile on his face and turning to a group of patients. "Come on, folks."

Maeve glanced back to meet Gray's gaze. "Tell her I'm worried about her. We'll take care of things out here."

He gave the young woman a curt nod, then turned his full attention on the locked door. He knocked. "Allie? It's Gray. I need you to let me in." When there wasn't any answer, he knocked again, a little more forcefully. "Lieutenant. I don't want you to be alone."

He couldn't detect any movement until he heard Allie's voice from the other side of the door. "Just you?"

Thank God she was responding to him. "Just me."

The lock turned and the door opened just wide enough for him to step in. He took a couple of steps past her as she relocked the door behind him. When he turned to face her, she walked into his chest. She cinched her arms around his waist and rested her forehead against the juncture of his neck and shoulder. She breathed in deeply, once, twice. Her chest expanded with a third deep breath, and she seemed to relax a bit as he closed his arms around her and dipped his nose to her hair to nuzzle her temple. She didn't seem to mind that his crutches were dangling against her backside. She simply aligned her body to his as if he was some kind of healing therapy she needed to concentrate on for a few minutes.

Still with no clue as to what had happened, Gray swept his gaze around the room. Typical locker room. Walls lined with lockers. Benches in front of the lockers. Two bathroom doors. A rolling basket filled with used towels. Her cheek felt chilled against him, but he couldn't detect her shivering. She wasn't crying. He hadn't spotted any blood on her clothes or marks on her face or hands. The only thing that looked out of place was the gray-and-red hoodie he'd loaned her lying in a heap on the floor in front of an open locker.

It was his nature to process the details around him, but he needed context for any of this to make sense. When he felt her posture shift slightly, some of her strength returning, he spoke. "Allie?"

"I know. Talk to you. I didn't want anyone in here in case you wanted to process it. And…" Her breath gusted with a weary sigh. "I'm just peopled out."

He hoped he'd picked up on the important information here. "Process what?"

He felt a quick kiss to the angle of his jaw before she stepped back and pointed to the open locker. "In there."

"Yours?" he asked.

She snorted a laugh that held no humor. "Who else?"

Gray automatically pulled his sterile gloves from the pocket of his jeans and moved around the bench to inspect the open locker more closely. *Please don't let there be more blood.* The woman had already been surrounded by far too much of it. He made a visual sweep of the standard metal locker. No graffiti. No obvious signs of tampering with the lock. Her skinny purse with the long strap hung from a hook. He saw the sweatpants, T-shirt and running shoes sticking out of a tote bag that sat on the bottom shelf. From this angle, he could see a blank white envelope on the floor beneath his jacket.

She moved in behind him, keeping the width of the bench between them. "On the top shelf. I haven't been in there since changing this morning. It wasn't there then."

Glad he had his legs on so he could easily see the top shelf, Gray noted that there were only two items—a pack of gum and a key. Shiny and new and recently made, he had a sick feeling he recognized that key. He needed to remain calm. She needed him to be a criminalist. "What am I looking at?"

"A key to my apartment. Possibly the one 'Payback' used to get inside. Who knows how many copies he made?" She hugged her arms around her waist. "I checked. The original is still on my keychain."

One small key. Clearly a taunt. Gray reached back to cup the side of Allie's face and neck. It felt wrong to have his sterile glove separating her soft skin from his touch, but she didn't seem to mind. "You're not going back to your apartment. You're staying with me. You don't even have to look inside your place until Aiden or Officer Cutler and I clear it for ourselves." With her understanding nod, he turned back and closed the locker door most of the way. "The perp could have slipped the envelope through the grates at the top of your locker. He wouldn't have to know the combination or force it open." He was working, thinking like a criminalist. It was the best way to help her right now. He glanced up to the corners of the room. "There are security cameras in the main room to monitor the patients' well-being. Are they back here, too?"

"No. Whoever stuck that in my locker wasn't caught on tape."

"That means a staff member put it there." Although his thoughts immediately went to Doug Friesen, who seemed like he would enjoy upsetting Allie, Gray was too well trained to rule out any possibility. "An outsider could have asked someone on staff to do them the favor of delivering it. Gave them some story about how you lost or forgot your key. The patient himself could sneak back here if the room was unlocked. Anyone who could get past the lobby could..." But when he saw how hard she was hugging herself and could clearly see her shivering as she stared into the locker, Gray got into her space. He rubbed some warmth into her upper arms, and ducked his head to look her in the eye. "Babe, you need to talk to me right now."

Her gaze didn't shy away from his. "Maybe this *is* about you. About *us*. I'm sorry I ever got you into this mess."

"I'm not." He would never regret meeting this woman, becoming friends, falling in love with her. He couldn't say what the future between them looked like, couldn't guarantee they had one, but he would never regret loving Allie. She'd reminded him he was a man. She'd taught him he had value beyond being a forensic chemist or a survivor. She challenged him to become whatever she needed him to be. He searched the locker again. "The key was in the envelope?"

"Read the note."

"The note?"

"I dropped it so I wouldn't contaminate any evidence you might find on it. And…" Whatever she'd seen had shut her down. "I just needed to get away from it."

"I'll find it." He found the folded note card behind the tote bag in the bottom of her locker where it had fallen. Irregular red dots decorated the outside. Recognizing blood spatter, Grayson cursed. Allie had taken a direct hit to any sense of security she had left. He read the blood-spotted note.

Noah sends his regards. He's not happy that you've gotten involved with another man. He wants me to send him a sample of YOUR blood when I'm finished with you. Give my regards to your boyfriend. He'll suffer as much as you when you're gone.

Payback will be complete.

Chapter Eleven

"You're sure you want to do this?" Allie asked, her gaze darting from Grayson's friend Aiden Murphy to Aiden's K-9 partner, Blue.

"Blue and I work out every day," Aiden assured her, tucking his KCPD T-shirt into his running pants and double-checking the small gun secured in a holster around his ankle. "Sometimes, it's agility work or patrol training, followed by play—and sometimes, it's a good old-fashioned run. As long as he's busy and gets his Kong to play with or a tummy rub at the end, he's a happy camper."

Happy indeed. The Belgian Malinois watched his partner's every move, possibly waiting for the signal to go, while his tail thumped with rapid excitement against Gray's front door. "I've been doing this for years," Allie felt compelled to point out. "Ran cross-country in high school and college. I take things at a pretty fast pace."

"We can keep up." It wasn't that she doubted the blue-eyed officer's fitness, or that of the muscular K-9 who was wagging his whole butt now.

But she couldn't help but remember how Bubba Summerfield had intruded on her run yesterday morning. She didn't do this for chitchat or introspection. She ran to get away from the mind games that were closing in all around her and suffocating her with fear. She hated being afraid. She wanted to clear her head enough so that she could seize the anger she felt inside her, as well. She'd been targeted once before because she was a strong woman who wouldn't back down from the wrong man. Now her world was spiraling out of control again—and she'd made Gray a target, too. The note in her locker yesterday had indicated that making Gray suffer was part of this creep's plan, as well.

She was getting too used to having a man she relied on to be there for her, too used to sharing meals and daily conversations, too used to sleeping on Gray's couch with his strong arms curled around her. If anything happened to him because of her, she'd never forgive herself.

Aiden stooped down to tighten the knot on his shoe and fended off Blue's eager tongue. He pushed the dog away and stood, apparently ready to go. "Besides, I don't think Malone is going to let you out of his sight unless Blue and me are with you."

"Malone doesn't want her to go at all." A third voice joined the conversation. It was early enough in the morning that Gray hadn't put on his prosthetic legs yet. He rolled his chair over to the entryway and reached for her hand and squeezed, silently telling her that despite his protective instincts, he understood that she needed to do this. Running was her therapy, the way she cleared her mind and got her heart pumping hard enough to reset her strength against the malaise her stalker created in her. It was probably killing him that he couldn't do this run with her. "I owe ya one, Murph."

"No, you don't." Aiden shrugged off the offer. "It's what friends do. You guys are the team Lexi always wanted to work with at the lab. She trusts you and values your respect in return. She feels safe to go to work again, with you and Dobbs and Chels and Shane, Buck and Rufus and Mac there to back her up. I don't take that lightly."

Gray nodded. "I don't take you having Allie's back this morning lightly, either. This is important to her."

When she felt his gaze drift up to her, Allie leaned down and kissed him. "We'll be back within the hour."

He caught her ponytail in his hand and let it sift through his fingers. "I'll have breakfast ready and drive you to the clinic when you're done."

Grayson Malone showed more understanding than she'd ever expected from a man. More caring than she probably deserved, because there'd been nothing but trouble in her life since they'd grown closer to each other. "Thank you." Those piercing green eyes caressed her very soul as she pulled away, keeping them connected in a way that filled every lonely spot inside her. "Gray, I…"

The words *I love you* danced on her tongue. She felt them in her heart. But with everything that had happened over the past few days, she couldn't quite wrap her brain around the idea Grayson Malone was the man she'd been hoping to find. How much of what she was feeling was gratitude or a craving for the emotional security he provided? He might be what she needed, but was she what *he* needed? Had circumstances forced them together and elicited feelings that had blossomed in the heat of the moment? Could the love she felt be real?

"I'll see you soon," she said instead, offering him a genuine smile.

He nodded and held the door as Aiden opened it and Blue

tugged him down the hallway. "Keep her safe, Murph," Gray called after his friend.

"Will do."

Gray caught her hand one more time before she exited after her running partners. "Keys? Pepper spray? Phone?"

Allie giggled. "Yes, Dad."

But Gray didn't laugh. "Come back to me."

Allie nearly stumbled over her own feet at the stark request. She cupped the side of his jaw and leaned down to kiss the corner of his mouth. "Always."

Admitting out loud how much she wanted to be with Gray was probably more of a surprise to her than it was to him. But Allie didn't stop to evaluate what they'd inadvertently admitted to each other. She needed a little time to process the depth of what was happening between them. They'd both been hurt so badly in the past that she didn't want to make a mistake and hurt either Gray or herself.

Besides, this was her running time. Not time for thinking. Not time for feeling. Not time for stress. Time simply to be free.

She jogged down the hall to join Aiden and Blue on the elevator. When she turned to watch the door close, she saw Gray in his wheelchair in the middle of the hallway, watching until she disappeared from sight.

MORNING RUSH HOUR traffic was getting thicker and the air was getting smoggy as Allie jogged at a fast clip along the sidewalks around the Western Auto building and headed back up the hill toward Crown Center and the World War I Memorial. Even with a streetcar system and overhead walkways installed to reduce commuter traffic and encourage walkers, cyclists and public transportation, there were plenty of delivery vans and carpools and drivers funneling into downtown KC off the highways that the relaxed feeling of the first thirty minutes of her run was quickly dissipating.

She kept her eyes peeled for the stream of pedestrians filtering out of parking garages and bus stops and tramcars onto the sidewalk ahead of her. She tried to keep to the left side near the curb to allow the slower walkers plenty of space so that she didn't mow anyone down or announce herself to the people who veered in front of her. As long as she could see the people ahead of her and avoid getting caught at the line of traffic waiting to pull into their reserved parking garages for the day, she wouldn't have to make conversation with anyone. She could concentrate on the rhythm of her feet hitting the pavement, check her watch and pulse periodically, and monitor her breathing. She was on the homebound leg of her run, and she was right on track to make it back to the apartment building in the forty to forty-five minutes she'd promised Gray.

She was aware of Aiden and Blue jogging the same path about half a block behind her. True to his word, the K-9 cop and his Belgian Malinois had no trouble keeping the pace Allie had set. And he'd been fine with her concept for solitude on the condition that she stay in visual range and do exactly as he ordered if he spotted anyone or anything that looked like a threat. Since Noah and his copycat associate seemed to thrive more on sneaking around the fringes of her life without showing themselves, she doubted Aiden would spot the mystery man who'd been tormenting her. But she understood rules and security protocols. She wasn't putting herself out there as bait. If Aiden said duck or run faster, she'd do exactly that.

In the meantime, she was going to exhaust her body and recharge her brain and hurry home to Gray.

Even as the thought struck her that there were more vehicles and pedestrians than she would have expected to see downtown on a Saturday morning, she nearly plowed into a door opening beside the curb. "Sorry!" she shouted, darting around the obstacle. When it registered that the woman getting out had had green sparkly hair, she remembered that there was a convention in town up at Bartle Hall. Suddenly, she focused in on the pedestrians who had been a blur in her peripheral vision. Men and women, children and even pets were in costumes reflecting various movie franchises and what she suspected were anime characters from graphic novels or video games.

Of course, she'd picked the weekend for one of the biggest conventions in the Midwest to assert her independence. *Not smart, Lieutenant.* If she had thought about the convention, she could at least have picked a less public route through the city. She'd mistakenly thought she'd be safer with more people around her and fewer places for the stranger stalking her to hide. But apparently, until the convention opened for its morning sessions, the streets and sidewalks would be packed with people waiting to go inside Bartle Hall.

When Allie reached the next traffic light she stopped at the crosswalk and turned, hoping to catch a glimpse of Aiden and discuss a different, less populous path they could take back to her apartment building. Still jogging in place to keep her heart rate up, and thankful she was taller than a lot of the people surrounding her, she scanned a horde of placards and costumes being steadily fed by the patrons of the convention gathering at the same intersection.

It took her a few seconds to spot Aiden, who had stopped

farther up the sidewalk to answer a question or give directions to a group of women dressed in sparkly fairy costumes. When she caught his eye, she waved and pointed across the street, hoping he'd get the message that she wanted to alter their course away from the crowd. She supposed she should shoot him a text to explain her concern and suggest an alternative. But when he gave her a thumbs-up, she pushed her phone back into the pocket of her sweats and changed course to cross the opposite direction.

Her timing sucked as the light chose that moment to change and the crowd that had gathered behind her surged forward. Allie uttered her fair share of *excuse me's* as she pushed her way to the side and found herself waiting at yet another traffic light.

As a woman, she tried to always be aware of her surroundings. Yes, she could defend herself if she had to. Chances were that she could outrun most people who tried to pursue her on foot. But that was when she was at 100 percent. As a woman being stalked, she didn't feel 100 percent. Her stalker's mind games were wearing her down in a way that being targeted by Noah hadn't. Maybe she wasn't fully recovered from surviving her ex, and she hadn't been ready to take on another subversive enemy so soon. Maybe knowing that "Payback" knew about Grayson, and had sent that convoluted message about making him suffer as well, had thrown her off her game. She was distracted. Missing the signs of danger and intrusion on her life. Second-guessing the observations and choices she did make.

Maybe that was why the black car that had pulled up to the stop light beside her didn't immediately register. And now that she was aware of how it had changed two lanes of traffic to claim a parking spot across the street shortly after she had signaled Aiden and changed directions, she questioned the vague memory that the car looked familiar. Was she just imprinting Bubba's description of a car that had been watching her and Gray on to the vehicle? She remembered the car that had nearly run them down in the parking garage across from the clinic had been black. But was every black car a threat?

She listened to her first instinct and studied the car while she waited. Black, four-door sedan. She couldn't see the license plate. She couldn't see a parking permit sticker on the windshield. But then, the absence of a sticker was hardly a help when it came to identifying a car, considering there were more cars without stickers in Kansas City than with. Its tinted windows meant she couldn't see the driver. Also no help. And no one was getting out of the car.

Her pulse rate slowed as she felt her body cooling down, and knew she needed to get moving soon, or she'd lose her momentum and have to build up speed and her breathing rate again. Did she go back to Aiden for help? Continue her run? Stand here in overthinking paranoia until the next troupe of conventioneers swarmed around her and carried her away in the flow of pedestrian traffic?

"It's just a black car," she whispered to herself. "You have Aiden and Blue with you. There are hundreds of witnesses around here if something does go wrong." When the crosswalk light hit zero and the light changed, Allie latched on to the confidence wavering inside her. With a quick wave to Aiden to make sure he saw where she was headed, she stepped into the street and jogged across, lengthening her stride into a run when her feet hit the opposite sidewalk.

Her nostrils flared as she took in a deep breath. Noah hadn't broken her. "Payback" wouldn't, either.

She was inhaling the fragrant aromas coming from the coffee shop on the corner when she heard a woman scream. Allie slowed her pace and glanced over her shoulder as tires squealed on pavement and horns honked. A dozen costumed people were yelling and pushing and pulling each other back from the crosswalk as the same black car careened around the corner. With the grid of one-way streets in downtown KC, the car pulled into the left lane right next to the sidewalk where she was running. The driver stomped on his brakes as he neared her. There was nothing between her and the driver behind the tinted windows besides the row of parked cars at the curb as he slowed to keep pace with her.

This time, Allie didn't ignore the alarm bells clanging inside her head. She pulled her cell phone from her pocket and punched in Aiden's number. When she increased her speed, the car kept pace with her. When she passed the void of an alley, the black car swerved slightly into the empty space, and she jumped back against the gray brick of the building behind her.

The car was going much too fast to make the turn and swerved back out, scraping the bumper of the car in front of it. As the vehicle raced on down the street, Allie shifted direction and sprinted back toward the convention center.

Aiden picked up. "What's up?"

"I'm being followed."

Her friendly fellow runner was all cop now. "Where are you? There are too many people. I've lost sight of you."

"I'm doubling back toward Wyandotte."

"You need to get out of sight."

"He's in a car heading the opposite direction now. He has to stay in the street, right? I'm hugging the buildings so he can't get to me."

Another chorus of horns blared behind her, and she turned to see the black car screeching around in a U-turn and weaving back up the street against oncoming traffic.

Not her imagination.

Allie swore like a sailor. "He turned around. He's going the wrong way."

She ran through a crowd of people and heard their comments.

"That guy's going to cause an accident."

"Is he drunk?"

"He's crazy."

Aiden was slightly breathless as he ran, or maybe that was the sound of Blue panting beside him. "Describe the car. License?"

"If there's a plate, I can't see it. It's black. Tinted windows."

"Like the one in the parking garage?"

"Possibly."

"KCPD! Police officer! Get out of my way!" She imagined he was shouting a warning to the people or drivers who were in his way. Then he was talking to her again. "We're coming to you. Get to the coffee shop on the corner. Go inside."

Wait. A crowd of people? Allie's pace stuttered. "But all these people—"

"Negative. Backup is on the way. Get to safety."

Metal crunched against metal behind her. The warning complaints of all the horns was nearly deafening. Rubber screeched against pavement. There were police sirens filling the air now. He just kept coming.

After her. He kept coming after her.

And she was in the middle of all these innocent people.

Allie waved her arms in the air. "Everybody needs to get away from the street!" She grabbed a woman's arm and pulled her away from the curb. "Get inside! Get out of his way!"

"Allie!"

The woman and her friends screamed and cursed, but they were moving.

"Stop!" she shouted, warning the group entering the crosswalk to retreat. "Get off the street!"

Then someone shouted, "Look out!"

Allie caught a glimpse of Aiden at the top of the street before she spun around and saw the black car jump the curb and barrel into the alley where she'd stopped. She swore she felt the heat of a dragon's breath singeing her back as she ran as fast as her long legs could go. She wove back and forth, trying to stay ahead of it. The black car exploded through a pile of trash bags and scraped the side of a loading dock before Allie figured out her escape.

Her heart pounding against her ribs and her lungs gasping for air, she ran up the steps of the next loading dock and threw herself against the metal door there. It didn't budge. "Damn it!" Of course, it was locked. With all these extra people in the neighborhood, the business couldn't risk an intruder sneaking in the back.

Before she could come up with a plan B, the black car swerved past the loading dock toward the far end of the alley. But the driver overcorrected the turn and bounced off the wall of the other building. The car scraped along the bricks, shooting up sparks until it plowed into the next concrete loading dock. The front end crumpled, and the air bags inflated as steam instantly clouded up from under the hood.

Although she could barely hear herself think over the

pulse hammering in her ears and the continuous blare of the car's horn, her training as a medical professional kicked in and she climbed back down to the pavement. The combination of off-the-charts adrenaline crashing through her body and her heavy breathing after that life-saving sprint made her a little light-headed. She swayed for a moment and had to lean against the stair railing for a few seconds to regain her equilibrium before she could check on the driver.

She heard someone shouting her name through her muffled hearing as she pushed away from the railing. Then the car door opened and a man fell out onto his hands and knees.

"Are you all right?" she called to him. "Who are you? Why are you doing this?"

Instead of answering, the man pulled the ball cap he wore low over his dark hair. He lurched to his feet and pulled the collar of his jacket up to his chin without ever looking back.

When she realized he was leaving the crash, Allie tried to run. "Stop! Why are you doing this to me?"

There were other voices behind her, shouting for the man to stop. He staggered a few steps, then found his bearings and sped into a jog, disappearing around the corner onto the street before she reached the car.

Realizing what she thought was steam was actually smoke and that the car was now a fire hazard, Allie leaned inside the open car door to turn off the ignition. As soon as she pulled her hand away from the tarnished silver key ring, she froze. Memories buffeted her like a punch to the gut and she instinctively retreated.

Into the hands of Aiden Murphy. "Don't touch anything!"

With a startled yelp, she spun around.

"You okay?" he asked, dipping his head to assess her eyes.

Allie put up her hands, telling him she knew who he was

and she was fine. "He didn't hit me. I climbed up on one of the loading docks…" Why hadn't he run her down? Was she really that fast a runner? Had something changed his mind at the last second?

"Smart thinking." Aiden squeezed her shoulder. He could barely contain Blue, who was straining against his leash. "Where's the driver?"

"He took off on foot. That way."

With a curt nod, Aiden pulled away. "All right. Blue can track him. Backup is on the way. You call Gray." When she didn't immediately respond, he squeezed her shoulder again. "You okay if I leave you?"

Get your head in the game, Lieutenant! Understanding speed was of the essence if Aiden had any chance of catching the driver, Allie nodded and pulled out her phone. "Calling Gray."

"Blue. *Such!*" Aiden gave the dog a sharp order in German, and then he and Blue jogged down the alley and turned right onto the sidewalk.

Still wondering how the impossible could be true, Allie ignored the concerned citizens and curiosity seekers making their way down the alley and coming out of shop doors and leaned back inside the car. She realized now there was blood on the steering wheel. The windshield was a spider web of cracks and there was an indistinct, bloody handprint on the dashboard.

But her gaze was focused on the keys again. Only two keys—the one in the ignition with a few drops of blood on it and another hanging from the metal ring. But it was the key ring itself that was speaking to her, haunting her. A round bangle of silver with the letter B carved into its matte finish.

B.

Boggs.

She snapped a picture of it with her phone and retreated to the far side of the alley to pull up Gray's number.

Noah had a keychain like that. She'd bought one exactly like it for a birthday present for him on their fifth and last date. A trinket from a souvenir stand at an amusement park. She thought it was fun. He thought it was cheap, said he'd spent a hell of a lot more on her just to get them into the park.

She squeezed her eyes shut and shook her head before opening them again. Maybe she was dreaming. Maybe something in her had finally snapped and she really was losing her mind. She was surrounded by a crowd of aliens and time lords and cartoon characters. She was looking at more blood.

And Noah Boggs's keychain.

THE DRIVER PULLED away from the curb into traffic almost before the passenger closed the door behind him. The passenger was breathing heavily and stinking up the car with his fetid breath.

"I'm bleeding." He pulled a tissue from his pocket, held it up to his nose and tipped his head back. "I didn't think it was going to hurt that much."

"Did you leave the souvenir as I instructed?"

"You know I did. I've done everything you told me to. I even told the lies you wanted me to almost word for word." He moaned like a toddler with a stubbed toe. Children in distress had always been something to be avoided. The sound was even more annoying in an adult. "Didn't you hear what I said? I controlled the crash, but I still got hurt.

And man, that was a sweet car. I wouldn't mind driving one like that for real. It was a shame to bust it up like that."

And now the complaints started.

"You said you wanted to be more than my eyes on the woman when I hired you. I'll let you have your time with her. But only on my terms. And that doesn't include giving you a new car." The passenger's help was vital to completing this plan, and he'd been a willing, even eager, participant thus far. But one could wish for someone who didn't question or complain about every little thing. The driver reached into a bag and handed a towel to the man across the seat. "Use this for that nosebleed." After being so careful with transporting the blood from the refrigerator to each of Allie Tate's gifts, it wouldn't do to have this man's blood leaving trace in the car. "I'll get you fixed up. Is it just your nose, or have you cut something?"

The passenger sounded like he had a head cold as he spoke through the muffling of the towel. "You don't understand. My blood is now at that crash site. They can trace it back to me. That's what Malone does at the crime lab."

The driver curbed impatience as they slowed with the rest of the traffic crawling through downtown. Two police officers on bicycles wove through the stalled traffic while a black-and-white unit wailed its siren as it passed by. "Is your DNA in the system?"

The passenger turned his head to the side and adjusted his ball cap to hide more of his face. Not that it was necessary with the car's tinted windows. Besides, it was highly doubtful the police would give either of them a second look when they were focused on responding to the scene of the crash and crowd control. "Yeah, it is. I was in the military.

They take samples from everyone in case they have to identify our remains."

The crime lab might have to put that particular piece of information to use when all this was said and done. But the driver told the passenger what he wanted to hear.

"Then we'll have to finish this before the boyfriend can trace that blood back to you." Moving up the timetable wasn't an issue. Allie Tate was primed for the final act. Then, retribution would be complete. "You'll be in the Cayman Islands or wherever you want to take your money before that happens."

"When do I get to hurt her?"

The driver laughed. "When I say so. And not a moment before. I need the stage set for everything to play out just as I planned. I won't be satisfied until then."

Chapter Twelve

Gray pulled his van into the alley and parked behind the CSIU van where Jackson and Shane were taping off the area around the wrecked car. Lexi was in a conversation with the driver of the tow truck parked at the opposite end of the alley, while Aiden was nearby, playing that silly re-ward game with the hard plastic toy his dog loved so much.

Although his training told him to head straight to the black car to start collecting the blood Lexi reported finding inside, Gray spotted Allie sitting on the steps of a concrete loading dock. Her long ponytail fell over her shoulder as she concentrated on whatever she was reading on her phone. After acknowledging Shane's and Jackson's greetings, Gray headed straight for the bowed head of honey-gold hair.

She heard his awkward steps crunching over the gravel and looked up. The moment their eyes met, she launched herself off the steps. Gray stopped, bracing himself. But Allie made it easy to keep his balance by slowing the last couple of strides, sliding her arms around his waist and snuggling against his neck. He released his grip on his crutches and held on to her, instead, dipping his nose to the crown of her hair and pressing his lips against her forehead. She felt good plastered against him, holding on as if his arrival was exactly what she needed. "Easy. You okay?"

He hadn't seen any blood on her. She wasn't limping or holding anything as if she was in pain, but he needed to know she wasn't hurt.

She nodded, clutching him tightly. "Better now. He was definitely following me. He did a U-ey and drove the wrong way up a one-way street when I changed directions. It could be the same car from the parking garage, but I'm not sure. You don't have to be mad or feel guilty about me running this morning. Aiden was right with me. No one got hurt." She glanced back toward the black car. "Well, except for the driver. There's blood inside the car, and Lexi says the trail of blood drops goes all the way out to the sidewalk."

"I'm not mad at you." He feathered his fingers into her hair and stroked it down against her back. "And I'm doing my damnedest not to feel guilty because I know there's no way I could have stopped you. You tend to have a stubborn streak."

Her giggle vibrated against the skin above the collar of his T-shirt. "And I really was feeling better until I realized I—and all the innocent bystanders he could have hit—were in danger." She wasn't smiling when she unwound herself from his body and pulled up a picture on her cell phone. "Look at this. I wonder if he crashed the car on purpose. Just so I could find it."

Gray dropped his gaze to the image from the interior of the car. The pattern of blood droplets on the steering wheel and column indicated a pooling injury with drips of blood, not the spray of an impact injury. Chances were the driver had broken his nose or split open his forehead. The pressure of his hand, or even his face against the steering wheel, had stanched the blood flow until he released the pressure. But Gray doubted that was what she wanted to show him. "What am I looking at?"

"The keys. B. Noah Boggs." She was adamant as she tapped her phone to enlarge the image carved into the silvery disk. "I know this is his key ring because I gave it to him."

Gray frowned because she'd been traumatized enough to believe the impossible. He was a scientist. He needed evidence to believe what she was telling him. "Boggs is in prison, Allie. Chelsea and the NAVCONBRIG CHASN commandant confirmed it."

"Who else do I know whose name starts with B? Ben Hunter? Bubba Summerfield?" Did she really think this was the clue that would break the case wide open? That her stalker must be someone with B in their name because of the key ring?

"Brittany Carter."

Her eyes widened like saucers, then narrowed with a frown. "Your ex? I've never met her. Why would she want to hurt me?"

"If you're grasping at straws, then so am I." Gray snapped his fingers, pointing out how unfounded her suspicions were in an effort to help her think clearly again. "Mrs. Burroughs at the clinic."

"A self-important old woman with a limp is not lurking in the shadows terrorizing me." Allie swiped the image off her phone before tucking her cell into the pocket of her hoodie. "Maybe Noah sent the key ring to someone, and the driver left it behind with the intention that I'd see it."

"Maybe Doug Friesen changed his name."

"Did he?"

"I have no idea. And neither do you. Take a breath, Allie." She paused for a moment before doing just that. "And another." He saw that the moment the irrational panic left her eyes they softened to their beautiful color. "Stay in the here and now with me." His crutches dangled from the crook of his elbows as he gently framed her face between his hands. "This guy is not making you crazy. He's making you mad. Understand? He's not scaring you. He's forcing you to be smarter and stronger than he could ever hope to be."

Allie nodded, getting the point of his pep talk. She latched on to his wrists and held his gaze. "He's not isolating me. He's driving me closer to a man I care a great deal about, a man who I believe will fight by my side any day of the week."

"He will," Gray promised before leaning in and pressing a brief kiss to her lips. She kept hold of his hand when he stepped back and glanced at his friends from the crime lab and KCPD who had gathered around them. "You've got more allies and friends in your camp now than you ever had before. Plus, Maeve at work. Ben." Aiden released his dog and the Belgian Malinois ran between the two of them to nuzzle where their hands were joined. "Blue."

"I know you're not Mr. B." Allie scratched Blue around the ears and Gray patted his warm flanks. Content that he'd been suitably rewarded for his friendly overture, Blue trotted back to Aiden's side.

Aiden ordered his partner into a sit. "Blue tracked the driver's scent until it went cold. Not too far from the end of the alley. Witnesses say he got into another car. Passenger seat. They drove away."

"He has an accomplice?" Gray asked.

Aiden nodded. "That's probably how he's getting everything done without getting caught. One can drive while the other throws the blood out the window. Two people could get your apartment painted in a lot less time with less chance of being noticed."

"One could create a diversion while the other sneaks into the locker room." Allie realized another probability. "There was no way for anyone to know I was running this morning." She looked up at Gray. "You and I didn't discuss it until last night. One of them must be watching the building, like Bubba said. Saw me leave with Aiden, then either followed us or called his accomplice to toy with me."

Gray agreed that the possible scenarios were more easily explained by a team of stalkers. That was already a departure from the story Allie had told him about how Boggs had thought he was such hot spit that he didn't need anyone's help, and gave credence to Bubba's claim that this might be about him as much as it was Allie. "Did you get a description of either driver?"

Aiden snorted at the question. "Nothing usable. Black. White. Latino. Skinny. Stocky. Ball cap. Team logo. No logo. No ball cap. The only thing they agreed on was that the driver of the wrecked car was a man. You would think with all the costumes around here, a regular Joe would stand out."

"Where eyewitnesses fail, forensic evidence steps in and tells us the truth." Lexi came up beside Aiden and rested her hand on Blue's head. "Go. Let us work the scene, see what answers we can find here." Then she reached for Allie's hand and grinned. "Are we still on for an afternoon of cleaning and painting?"

Gray was thinking more along the lines of taking Allie home and locking her up in his apartment with an armed guard outside.

But Allie *did* have that stubborn streak. "You guys still want to help me?"

"You're important to Malone, so that means you're important to us." Lexi winked. "Besides, Chelsea found this miracle cleaning solution online that she's brewing on her stove. Guaranteed to get bloodstains out. She's anxious to try it."

"Brewing on her stove? Is it going to disintegrate my walls?"

Everyone but Gray and Jackson laughed as Shane explained the way Chelsea's mind and big heart worked. "That's our Chelsea. Smartest one in the room, but she marches to the beat of her own drum. If she's determined to help someone, you can't stop her."

"Well, I wouldn't want to hurt her feelings," Allie teased, understanding their appreciation for the most unique member of their team. "All right. Yes. Thank you. You all come on over whenever you're ready. I'll have food and drinks for everyone." After each of them said their goodbyes and moved on to get their crime scene kits and start gathering evidence, Allie turned to Gray. "I need to get to the clinic. I told Maeve I'd work for her this morning. The clinic is busy on Saturdays, and they'll be short-staffed if I don't show up. I'll need to stop at the store on the way home."

"Someone just tried to kill you." The locked apartment and armed guard were sounding better and better to Gray.

"I don't think so. I'm following your lead and trying to stick to rational thinking. If he wanted me dead, why not shoot me? Why not run me down when I was crossing the street? Why play that cat and mouse game?" She held up the picture on her phone again. "Why leave me this?"

Gray settled his hand at her back and turned toward his van. "I'll take you back to my place to relax."

Allie quickly stepped in front of him, stopping him. "I won't sleep. I need to stay busy. Plus, I gave Maeve my word."

"All right. I'll go with you."

She splayed her fingers at the center of his chest, and he automatically pulled his shoulders back the way he did when they were working together at the clinic. "No, you won't. You're needed here. Find the answer, Gray. Make this stop. I want to have a regular date with you that doesn't involve me freaking out or either one of us looking over our shoulder."

"A real date, huh?" He leaned into the heat of her hand.

"Yeah, stud. So, get to work. I'll have Aiden ask one of the traffic officers to drive me to the clinic. I've got a spare set of scrubs I can change into there. Then you can pick me up when you're done here. You must be feeling more confident with your driving if you got through convention traffic okay."

"I'll be there." When she started to leave, he caught her hand and curled his fingers around her waist, the way he did when they were dancing for therapy. But he kept right on pulling until her hips butted against his and he could lean in and capture her lips in a kiss. Her mouth softened under his and clung, long enough for him to remember they had an audience. But he didn't care. He didn't think he would ever get his fill of kissing Allie. And he couldn't stand the thought of anyone taking that opportunity away from him. The old Gray reared up in him, making a promise. "This guy doesn't get to win. Be safe, babe. I want that date, too."

ALLIE'S APARTMENT WAS a whole new shade of beige by the time Gray stretched out in bed and stared up at the ceiling. He'd put on a favorite old boot camp T-shirt and his sleep shorts. A hot shower had eased the ache in his muscles. And a quick massage of therapeutic lotion into his thighs had eased the chafing of wearing his prosthetic legs for several hours longer than he was accustomed to. He'd been well compensated for all the painting he'd done, with several slices of pizza, a cold beer, and the relief of watching Allie's trepidation about being back in her apartment, surrounded by that hateful word, turn into smiles and joking with his friends.

Chelsea's miracle cleaner had done the trick and removed the blood, although it had also ruined the finish on the cabinets above Allie's kitchen peninsula. Allie figured Bubba Summerfield should be called in to do at least some of the work he was paid to do. And Gray figured he'd make sure he was on hand and Allie was out with friends or at work while the super who kept eyeballing her and making her uncomfortable was in her apartment making the repairs. Maybe he'd ask Aiden if he could borrow Blue for a visit that day, too. Since Bubba had claimed to be intimidated by the K-9, Blue's presence might make him work faster.

If he had the energy, Gray would have grinned into the darkness at the idea.

He'd been up early to make sure Allie got off safely for her run. Then Aiden had called with the news of Allie being pursued and the subsequent crash. Gray didn't think driving the modified van was going to be an issue for him anymore since he'd proved on two occasions now that he could drive it fast and get to Allie when she needed him. Or maybe a truer statement was when he needed to see her.

After that, he'd worked the crime scene with his team and then gone back to the lab to type the blood samples he'd taken from the car, and to spend some time on the phone with the commandant at NAVCONBRIG CHASN. The commandant had been especially interested in the idea that one of his prisoners could send a personal item to someone in Kansas City or give it to a visitor there. Although there was no evidence of outgoing mail from Boggs, they couldn't rule out that he'd arranged something with one of his visitors. Gray had requested photographs of all of Boggs's visitors over the past few months, and the commandant had agreed to pull shots from the video in the visitation room and email them to Gray Monday morning. Then he'd picked up Allie at the clinic—thankfully with no drama there, with Friesen off duty and no unwanted gifts showing up. Gray had then spent the afternoon priming and the evening painting.

His body was exhausted, but his brain couldn't seem to shut down. He felt cold in his apartment tonight. The bed was too soft. It was too quiet, lying here by himself. It was surprising how quickly he'd become addicted to having Allie beside him. But she insisted she needed to stay at her own place tonight. If she didn't face her demons on her own, she might not ever be able to. Gray thought that was a load of manure—Allie Tate could face down any enemy and come out on top as long as she believed she could. So, with an invitation to come over for breakfast, he'd come back to his own apartment. Let independent Allie have her space. Let her solidify her strength in the way she needed to. Let her go.

Even for one night, it was the hardest thing Gray had ever had to do.

He missed her. The jolt of her cold hands in his. The soft sounds of her breathing as she slept. The uninhibited way she coiled her body around his.

Although they'd shared as many deep, sometimes troubling, discussions, they'd shared just as many light and trivial conversations. Her parents lived in the small town of Fulton, Missouri. Her favorite color was pink. And she couldn't stand to watch horror movies. She'd trained as a medic and had served aboard an aircraft carrier before specializing in physical therapy and getting reassigned to Jacksonville. She'd survived Noah Boggs's campaign to terrorize and discredit her, testifying in front of an Admiral's Mast, and an attempt on her life.

And she made Gray feel more like a man than he'd felt since that last minute before the RPG had hit. She made him feel strong, necessary, normal.

But if her need for him was just about this case, just about keeping her grounded and warm until this guy was identified...

He heard the soft knock in the hallway outside the apartment. Gray shut down his thoughts and tuned in to the sound. The noise was so quiet that it could have been someone knocking at another apartment door. Allie's? Gray sat up, as alert as he'd been on a nighttime patrol over in the Middle East. As underhanded as this stalker had been, would he really knock on her door in the middle of the night and announce himself? This guy was about stealth and surprise, not, "Hey, I'm here. Let me in."

When someone knocked again, he realized it was his own door. Gray could think of only one person who'd be paying him a visit. He pulled his chair to the edge of the bed and swung himself onto the seat. He heard Allie's voice calling to him as he wheeled his way through the apartment.

"Gray?"

He unlatched the dead bolt and turned the knob before

she could knock again. She startled when the door swung open, and she retreated half a step.

"Were you asleep?" she asked, hugging her arms around her waist.

"No."

"I can't sleep, either." Gray held out his hand and she followed him into the apartment, keeping hold of him while he shut and bolted the door. Then she did the damnedest, most beautiful thing and sat on his lap. She turned sideways across his thighs and hugged her legs up toward her chest. "It's amazing how fast I've gotten used to you holding me in your arms. Besides…paint fumes."

If he was meant to laugh, he didn't. Instead, he wound his arms around her and pulled her to him. He buried his nose in the honey-colored waterfall of her unbound hair and inhaled its freshly washed scent. "Such beautiful hair," he murmured before kissing her temple. "So beautiful," he whispered against her mouth before claiming her lips and worshipping them.

Her lips parted and their tongues battled for supremacy as they stroked and tasted each other. She tasted of minty toothpaste and smelled like flowers. Gray closed his teeth gently around the swollen curve of her bottom lip and she moaned. He felt the vibrations of that sexy sound humming through his blood and feeding that most male part of his anatomy.

"Are you safe?" he managed to ask when he came up for air. "Has anything happened? Are you hurt?"

"I'm fine. The demons…" Her breathing sounded as ragged as his. "I want to stay with you, Gray. Please let me stay. I need you."

"All of me?" he asked. His body was desperate to have hers, but his brain needed to hear her say the words.

"Yes."

Thrilling to the surge of power her demand gave him, Gray anchored Allie's arms behind his neck and freed his hands to push them into the bedroom. This felt right, inevitable, maybe, to have her here in his space again—to feel her hip pressed against his groin, to absorb her heat and scent, to hold her, to love her, to be with her.

When he reached the bed, he lifted her in his arms and tossed her on top of the covers. He pushed himself up and spider-walked to the center of the bed where she was kicking off her slippers and unzipping the hoodie he'd lent her. He crawled over her, stretching out until her breasts were pillowed beneath his chest, her sharp nipples goading him to taste them through the thin cotton of her T-shirt. She gasped as he closed his mouth over a turgid peak and swirled his tongue around the sensitive nub. With the material wet and clinging to the dimple of her areola, he plumped the taut, responsive mound and sucked her into his mouth.

"Gray!" She bucked beneath him, calling his name on a strangled gasp of pleasure.

When he turned his attention to the other breast, she clasped the back of his head and held his mouth to her, even as she writhed beneath him, letting his hard body get intimately acquainted with every soft curve of hers. She ran her hands down along his flanks and swept them back up beneath his shirt.

"I want to touch you," she begged, pressing a kiss to his pectoral muscle, then groaning in frustration when the shirt caught beneath his arms.

Chuckling against her tender breast, Gray did a push-up

to give her the space she needed to whisk the shirt off over his head. But the angle pushed his hips into hers and his thigh jammed against the damp heat of her pajama pants. Allie whimpered and Gray immediately rocked back onto his stumps on either side of her thighs. "I'm sorry." His face burned as his body cooled. "Did I hurt you?"

"What? No, I—"

"I don't know exactly how to do this." Damn. Now he looked like a giant spider hovering over her. He swung his leg over her and sat beside her on the bed. Frustrated and embarrassed and angry at himself for forgetting his limitations, Gray raked his fingers through his short hair. "I've haven't done this since…"

She sat up facing him, her eyes narrowed in concern, her hair falling in wild disarray around her shoulders. "Gray, tell me exactly what's wrong. You didn't hurt me. You hit the money spot with your leg, and your weight plus the pressure building inside me shocked me with a zing of pleasure."

"A zing?" He shook his head. "Then that was a lucky shot. I don't know how to balance myself so I don't crush you. There's no sensation in the ends on my legs so I can't tell if I'm zinging or hurting you. I used to do this without thinking. I want you so much, but I'm not sure I can make this good for you."

"Not good?" He shouldn't have been surprised when Allie tugged on his thigh, turning him slightly before she crawled onto his lap. She curled her legs around his hips, settling herself right against his swollen member. His legs might not be working, but that part of his body was all too aware of her heat nestling against him. "Oh, I don't know. You kissed me senseless, then you carried me to the bedroom." While she talked, she shrugged out of the hoodie and pulled the damp T-shirt over her head so that they were both topless as she guided his hands to her waist.

"How romantic," he scoffed. "I was in the damn chair—"

"I did not walk." She wound her arms around his neck and pulled herself closer until those button-tipped breasts branded his chest. She rubbed them against him, as if she enjoyed the sensation of friction as much as he did. "I'm not a petite, delicate flower of femininity, Gray. But you hauled me into your lap like I was a delicate little thing. You tossed me onto the bed and were on me before I even stopped bouncing. All impulsive, needy, Neanderthalic turn-ons for me." She dragged her fingers down his chest and teased the flat of his stomach where it met the waistband of his shorts. Gray sucked in a breath and his fingers clenched at her waist. Oh, he was so far gone with this strong, beautiful woman. "And you want me, Gray. Hopefully, half as much as I want you right now."

"But I want it to be good for you."

She hooked her fingers into the material of his shorts and tugged them down. "Is that for me?" Gray leaned his forehead against hers and groaned as she wrapped her hand around him. "Then it'll be good. Do you have a condom?"

Gray growled and nodded before reaching past her into the nightstand. He pulled out an unopened box and handed it to her.

Her eyes widened. "Well, that's a lot of pressure to go through all of these in one night."

He snorted a laugh at her wry comment. Bless this woman. She was putting him at ease and turning him on at the same time. She'd coached and prodded and laughed with him and stood her ground to get him to walk again—to teach him to dance on his new legs. She was doing the same now and he loved her for it. He tunneled his fingers into her hair and showed her how grateful he was with his kiss.

Her skin was flushed from her cheeks to her breasts, and they were both breathing hard by the time he pulled away.

"Let's start with one." Allie's fingers shook as she opened the box and ripped open a package. "Okay, now I'm a little nervous."

Gray chuckled and took the condom from her. "Big man, big business."

She laughed as he rolled it on. "Totally Neanderthalic turn-on."

"Is Neanderthalic even a word?" he teased. He could do this for her, for them.

"Gray, I haven't been with a man since before Noah. And, obviously, I don't have good memories there."

"Then we'll make new ones. Good ones."

She wound her arms around his neck and kissed the corner of his mouth. "I'd like that. I'd really, really like that."

"I've noticed that you still have clothes on," he pointed out. With a flurry of bumping hands and stolen kisses and shared laughter, he helped her to her feet so she could shed her pajama pants. "I want you more than my next breath, Allison Tate. But I still need to figure out how all this is going to work. Will you be patient with me?"

Holding his hand for balance, she climbed back onto the bed and straddled his lap, fitting her slick heat against him. "No."

She pressed her finger to his lips, silencing his protest and helping him understand her answer meant she wanted him as badly as he wanted her.

"We have desire. We have trust. Everything else will fall into place."

Later, when they were sated with each other's bodies and Allie was sleeping securely in his arms, Gray felt as if everything he'd ever wanted for his new civilian life had indeed fallen into place.

And he wasn't going to let some cowardly, obsessed stalker and his mind games take it from him.

Chapter Thirteen

"Anything new?" Mac Taylor asked, catching Gray skimming through the information packet that had just been delivered from Colonel Martin Wilcox in Charleston, South Carolina.

The Monday morning staff meeting was one of the few times during the week that the entire team of criminalists and lab techs got together to discuss progress on ongoing investigations, reassess case assignments, check where help might be needed and map out priorities for the team. Gray had jotted down a note on a shooting where he needed to analyze the blood spatter and determine if the wound had been accidentally self-inflicted or was the result of a drunken brawl that had gotten out of hand. But beyond that, he had spent most of the meeting with his mind on the weekend he'd spent with Allie and reading the colonel's report on Noah Boggs's recent activities.

They'd spent a good portion of Saturday night and Sunday morning in his bed, making love and discussing future plans, including the decision that she would be moving in with him for the time being. Yesterday afternoon, they'd gone next door to her apartment and packed some clothes that were now hanging in his closet and folded up in his drawers, along with the flower-scented shampoo and shower gel that were sitting in his shower. The plan was to live together until "Payback" was identified and put away—both for Allie's sense of mental and emotional security and his own. And after that? He was still working up the courage to lay his heart on the line again. Gray had no doubt that he was in love with Allie Tate, and would get down on whatever legs he had left and propose to her. But the idea that history might repeat itself made him cautious about giving any more of himself. The man he was now hadn't been enough for Brittany in the long run. What if it turned out that he was the man Allie needed now, while they weathered this crisis together—but when she was free and able to cope on her own again, she'd be thanking him for the good times and moving on.

But great sex and Allie moving into his place probably wasn't the *new* that Mac wanted him to report on.

Gray included everyone seated around the conference table and leaning against the wall behind the table in his report. "Colonel Wilcox has isolated Boggs in the brig until he can determine if and how the prisoner smuggled his keychain out. There is a picture here from Boggs's personal effects that confirms that the keys Allie found in the black car were his." He held up the envelope and another file folder that he wanted to compare to the visitors' log the colonel had sent. "Other than his attorney and a distant cousin of some kind, all of Boggs's visitors have been women. Wilcox thinks he might have some kind of pen pal fan club going on."

"Ew," Chelsea piped up from her laptop and the far end of the table. "I never understood how that was a thing. I've known several guys who have gone to prison. And nothing about them makes me want to marry them or even write them."

There were chuckles around the room before Mac spoke again. "What about the blood in the black car Saturday morning. You'll be processing that today?"

"Yes, sir." Gray shared an affinity for the crime lab boss and a great deal of respect. Mac was also a disabled criminalist, having been blinded in one eye in an explosion several years ago. Despite his handicap, he'd worked his way up through the ranks of the KCPD Crime Lab, from its old location to this new facility. He'd married and had a family. Gray hoped to be running his own lab and raising his own family one day. "I can already tell you that the blood I processed came from the perp hitting his head when the vehicle crashed. The airbag created a serious head injury, but KCPD should be looking for a guy with a couple of black eyes from a broken nose, or one who has stitches in his forehead."

Aiden Murphy added his two cents to the report. "The car had stolen plates, and the VIN number had been etched off, probably with acid. I'm guessing it came from a chop shop, so nobody's going to be reporting it stolen."

Mac made a note. "So, that's a dead end." He gave out some secondary assignments related to Allie's case. "Jackson, you follow up on Boggs's cousin, see if there's any way he could be our guy. Chelsea, I want to ID all those pen pals who've been to see him."

"Yes, sir."

Mac had one more question for Gray. "What about any leads from the Kleinschmidt case? Do you think Allie is being used as a means to target you?"

Gray shrugged. "A couple of things are pointing that way.

But I've got no hard facts to confirm it yet. Just a creepy building super and a bloodstained note."

"Stay on it. I liked Allie when I met her Saturday at her apartment. I think she's good for you. Let's keep her safe."

"Thank you, sir. That's the plan."

Mac moved on to the next agenda item, and Gray returned to his lab after the meeting was dismissed a short time later.

He was on his third mug of coffee, gleaning through the file of names Chelsea had dropped off a few minutes earlier. Noah Boggs's pen pals were a varied lot of five women— blonde, brunette, turquoise hair; two of them young with drugs and prostitution on their record; one a spinsterly, lonely heart who was looking for a connection wherever she could get it; and one older woman with snow-white hair. The grainy image from the camera didn't offer a straight look at her face, but the woman looked old enough to be his mother.

Gray shook his head as his disgust for Noah Boggs grew. That man was a player who was used to getting what he wanted, and who wasn't above using anyone who could help him reach his goal—or hurting anyone who tried to keep him from it.

He spread the files from NAVCONBRIG CHASN out across his desk and pulled up the Jamie Kleinschmidt file on his computer. He'd pored over every bit of information available to him from Charleston, South Carolina, and here in Kansas City, Missouri. He wished the answer he needed was as easy to analyze as a drop of blood under a microscope. But it was proving to be as difficult as losing his legs and his buddies and learning how to walk and trust again.

Since blood was his field of expertise, maybe he should

go back to comparing the samples he'd taken from Allie's apartment to the victim samples Kleinschmidt had stored in his basement. Hell, maybe he should cross-match blood types and see if any of them were B-positive or B-negative. Maybe that explained the connection to Allie's key ring.

Wait. B-positive?

Gray sat up straight in his chair as the germ of an answer toyed with the fringes of his memory. He shuffled some papers and scrolled through the file on his screen until he had nothing but biographical data on display.

Jamie Kleinschmidt had B-positive blood.

The man listed as his father did not.

His mother was B-positive.

"His mother…"

Gray scanned the images from the courtroom from Kleinschmidt's trial. In all the days he'd reported to the witness stand, he'd never seen a father or mother. It had always been Kleinschmidt alone with his attorneys on one side of the courtroom, and the DA and the parents and families and friends of Kleinschmidt's victims on the other. Kleinschmidt had a sister, but apparently, she'd disowned him when he was arrested. She'd never showed up in the courtroom, either.

"B-positive…" *Think, Malone.*

He looked back at the pictures of the women who'd visited Boggs in prison. One of them could be Kleinschmidt's sister. Could the cousin be the accomplice?

"B…"

Gray swore.

The answer had been staring at him the whole time. Part

of it, anyway. And it had never even registered. Well, it registered now.

Hurting Allie was all about hurting *him*. *He* was the *Payback* Allie's stalker and accomplice wanted. Yes, they were using the same tactics Noah Boggs had used against her to keep her from testifying against him. But this wasn't about Boggs at all. He was the tool, but her stalker was the one wielding the information he must have provided.

Boggs wasn't playing those women. One of them was playing him.

There it was in black-and-white at the very top of the file.

Payback for a disturbed young man who'd killed himself after Gray's testimony had sent him to prison.

Jamie *Burroughs* Kleinschmidt.

Nothing was more dangerous than a mother protecting her young.

Unless it was a mother taking vengeance on the man she blamed for her child's death.

GRAY STUMBLED OUT of the lab, catching his right crutch and dropping his phone. He'd only gotten off one text to Allie before his legs started itching with the need to move. To take action. To get to her before it was too late.

Where are you?

By the time he picked up his phone, she'd answered.

At work.

What patient are you working with?

He'd picked up an audience by the time he'd typed in the next message. Jackson and Mac were strolling out of the lounge with fresh mugs of coffee in their hands. Their posture changed from relaxed to intense in a heartbeat when they saw how Gray was trotting down the hall in his uneven gait. Damn it. He should have looked into those running blade prostheses Allie had told him about. How was he supposed to get to her fast enough when her life could be in danger this very minute?

Jackson handed his mug off to Mac and cupped Gray's elbow to balance him. All three men moved at a faster pace. "Figure it out?" Jackson asked.

Gray nodded as he read Allie's reply.

What's going on? Is something wrong? Did you match the blood to someone? Is that Noah's key ring?

He handed his crutches off to Jackson and leaned on his friend's strength to free his hands to type.

Get into the locker room and lock yourself in. Tell Hunter I'm sending the police and he needs to guard that door with his life.

"Don't have the accomplice yet, but it's related to the Kleinschmidt case."

Okay, now you're just pissing me off. You're scaring me, and I don't need that. What is going on? You obviously think I'm in danger. I'm not going to save myself and leave my patients and coworkers to face whatever is happening.

Ivy Burroughs.

Gray said the name out loud as he typed.

"Snooty old lady at the clinic?" Jackson confirmed.

Mac shook his head. "An old lady is behind this?"

"Maybe not so old," Gray explained. "And maybe that's why she has the accomplice."

What about her?

Is she there?

Yes. She's working with Maeve.

"Damn it. The perp is with her right now." Gray tried to run.

A minute passed before the next message hit.

GRAYSON MALONE, TALK TO ME!

Ivy is Jamie Kleinschmidt's mother. I didn't remember her because she was never at the trial. I didn't meet her until PT.

Mrs. B is the widow of an Army colonel.

"Am I driving, or are you?" Jackson asked as they neared the exit.

"Take the CSIU van," Mac ordered, meaning Jackson was at the wheel. "It'll get you through morning traffic faster. If that woman is there, you can process her from head to toe. I'll notify Brian Stockman. You want police backup?"

"Yes."

"In the meantime, I'll get a search warrant and send Lexi

and the rest of the team to Ivy Burroughs's address. See if we can find links to the blood, the gifts or either of you two."

Jackson set Gray's crutches inside the cab of the crime scene van and offered his shoulder for Gray to boost himself up into the passenger seat. "Thank you, sir." He kept typing, knowing Allie wouldn't answer a phone if she was with a patient.

Her husband was a grunt who was killed in Desert Storm. She reinvented her history before coming to the clinic. Hell, she probably doesn't even limp. She could have gone to a doctor and faked the symptoms to get prescribed PT just to get closer to me. To find out what I care about. How to hurt me.

Yeah. Hurting Allie definitely cut him deep with guilt and pain.

Why wouldn't she be at the trial supporting her son? Unless she disowned him for killing those women? But then why seek vengeance for his death?

Jackson swung the van out of the parking lot and turned on the siren as Gray recalled the information Chelsea had compiled for him.

She was in the hospital during the trial. Are you locked inside the room yet?

She feels guilty for not supporting him when he needed her. Then he kills himself and she thinks this is how to redeem her motherhood badge. By taking care of her son's needs after his death. Better late than never?

Now she wanted to play psychologist? The why's didn't matter. Ivy's note had promised that payback would be coming soon. He needed Allie to get to safety.

She was in a mental hospital.

OMG.

Now she understood the urgency of the situation.

Yeah. Just lock yourself in.

I don't see Ben. Or Doug.

Still have no clue who's helping Ivy. But it has to be someone with access to you. Watch your six.

Several seconds passed without any reply.

Allie?

Lieutenant?

Talk to me.

The next message came from someone else.

Go home, Mr. Malone. She's mine now.

Chapter Fourteen

The power was out at physical therapy and chaos reigned supreme when Gray and Jackson pulled up.

Traffic had been barricaded off at the end of the block in either direction. There were two fire engines from Station 13 and an ambulance parked in front of the building. Although he didn't see any hoses leading into the building, or any ladders extended, there were plenty of firefighters moving in and out of the place. Gray got a sick feeling in the pit of his stomach when he saw a woman wrapped in a blanket, sitting on the bumper of the ambulance. "Son of a bitch." The van was still rocking to a stop as he pushed open the door. "Allie?"

He recognized some of the patients and staff gathered across the street at the entrance to the parking garage. But he didn't stop to check on any of them. He made a beeline for the ambulance when Ben Hunter stepped away from the police officer he'd been talking to and put up his good hand to stop him. "It's not her."

Gray exhaled a sigh of relief and took a moment to survey their surroundings. Jackson showed up beside him with his crutches, enabling him to move more securely on his own. He recognized the officer Ben had been talking to, Gina Cutler.

"Officer." Gray acknowledged her, but kept searching the crowd for a tall woman with a honey-blond ponytail.

"Mr. Malone."

"When I called it in, they said Cutler was already working the case," Ben explained.

Gray's gaze went back to Ben. "Then where is Allie?"

"Not here."

Gray leaned toward the shorter man. "What do you mean she's not here? You're supposed to be keeping an eye on her."

"I know, man. I dropped the ball. I was sitting in the lobby, reading a book, when the lights went out. I immediately went back to try and find her, but folks were panicking. I pulled the fire alarm to get everyone moving toward the exit and I waited for her to come out." Ben tugged on his beard. "But she never did. I went in to look once things were clear, but the firefighters arrived and ordered me out, too."

"You told them she was unaccounted for? They searched for her, too?"

Ben nodded. "They said a circuit breaker had been thrown. It was no power outage."

Ben looked appropriately contrite, but Gray wasn't ready to give up his anger yet. "Anyone else unaccounted for?"

"I don't know. I was only paying attention to your woman. I saw her when she started her latest therapy session. Then she was having a texting conversation—"

"That was me."

"—Then the lights went out and she was gone."

And Gray had no idea where Ivy and her accomplice had taken her.

"Where's Ivy Burroughs?" He swiveled his gaze from

Ben to Gina Cutler and back, demanding answers. "She's Jamie Kleinschmidt's mother. Possibly mentally unstable. She's got an ax to grind with me."

"Kleinschmidt the serial killer?" Gina's dark eyes widened, and she pulled out her notebook.

"Yeah."

"She blames you for her son's death in prison?"

Gray nodded. "The messages? Following Allie? She got that info from Allie's ex—probably the only way you can knock that woman down is to put her through the mind games he played on her again. But the blood is about me. My blood evidence is what got Kleinschmidt convicted." He fisted his hand and tapped the top of Gina's notebook, willing her to understand how desperate he was. "She's going to hurt Allie. She's going to drain her blood or something equally horrible to get to me. To punish me. I have to find her before that happens."

"You don't think Allie could take down that little old biddy?" Ben apologized to Gina or whoever he thought he'd offended. "There's no way that witch could have dragged Allie out of here. Even if Allie was drugged or knocked out, she couldn't move the body."

Jackson explained in his shorthand way. "Accomplice."

"Who?" Gina Cutler asked, taking down notes.

"Some guy with a broken nose or fresh cut on his head." Gray turned to Ben, checking for bruising on his face and on every other man who walked past them. "You haven't seen anybody like that around here, have you?"

Ben shook his head. "I've lost my edge. I've been out of the game too long."

Officer Cutler closed her notebook. "I'll put a BOLO

out for Allie and Mrs. Burroughs. I'll send someone to her home address right now."

"A CSI team is already en route," Jackson reported.

Home?

Go home, Mr. Malone. She's mine now.

Jackson knew how to read his friend. "Something just popped into that head of yours." Gray nodded, backing toward the van. "Where you going?"

"Keys in the ignition?"

"Malone? You can't drive that van."

"Then you're driving."

"Where?"

Gray pointed back to Ben. "As soon as KCFD clears the scene, I want you to go back inside and search again. Open every locker, every storage cabinet. Look under every bed and table. If it can help us find Allie or convict Ivy, I want it in our lab."

"Mr. Hunter is not a member of KCPD or the crime lab," Gina pointed out.

"Then you stay with him and make sure anything he does is legit."

"Where are you going, Malone?" Gina demanded. "What aren't you telling me?" She grabbed Gray's arm to stop him climbing into the van. "These people may be killers. You need backup."

Gray pulled his shoulders back and centered his balance over his hips. "I'm a United States Marine, Officer. I *am* the backup."

ALLIE'S CHIN BOBBED against her chest and she snapped it back, fighting to stay awake despite the headache pounding through the fog in her brain. Her arms and legs felt like they were trapped in a vat of gelatin. She squeezed her fingers into fists, trying to regain the feeling there, and she wondered why she couldn't raise her arms to pull free the strands of hair that were caught in the corner of her mouth.

She blinked her eyes open, struggling to bring the world into focus, sensing that it was utterly important that she know where she was. She heard the jangling of metal clinking together before she saw a woman's head with dark hair with the striking white stripe of a birthmark running through the perfectly coiffed style.

And then a burning hot poker pierced the back of her right calf and Allie screamed. Only, the sound seemed to reverberate in her ears and stuff up her nose.

"Like that?" a man's voice asked from behind her. "There's not much blood. Can't I go higher?"

"No." A woman's sharp voice answered from the direction of the white stripe. "That and the arms are enough for now. Much higher and you'll nick the femoral artery and she'll bleed out before the show's over."

The red-hot poker stabbed into her left calf and Allie whimpered. She realized now that the man was cutting her. Nothing like inflicting some of the worst pain of her life to jolt her senses awake and rouse her from the stupor of whatever drug they'd given her.

Allie had been in an alarming conversation with Gray, hurrying toward the safety of the one door in the clinic she could lock, scanning every table and treatment room for Ivy Burroughs. She'd pushed open the door to the staff locker room and quickly checked the bathrooms and run her hand along all the locker doors to make sure they were empty. She'd turned back to the door to see Ivy standing there.

Faking a smile, Allie greeted her. "Hey, Mrs. Burroughs. This is a restricted area. Did you lose track of Maeve?"

The older woman smiled. That was when she realized Ivy Burroughs wasn't as old as she pretended to be. She wasn't limping, either.

Then the lights had gone out, she'd felt a sharp prick in her neck, and she was waking up here.

Ivy Burroughs was stalking her, copying the nightmare of her relationship with Noah. But why? What had she ever done to this woman beyond trying to help her heal from her hip injury, which apparently wasn't a real injury, at all? And who the hell was the man behind her who seemed to be taking such pleasure in swiping his fingers through the blood trickling down the back of her leg, then smearing it up to her bottom, then all the way back down her leg.

Alarmed for a moment that she was completely vulnerable to these people, Allie looked down and inhaled a breath of relief through her clogged-up nose to see that she was wearing her bra and panties. Sad to say, she wore nothing else. And even as she thought of how cold it was here, a sea of goose bumps erupted across her skin, and she shivered violently. Shaking herself awake.

Stay busy. Don't think. Don't feel. Just get through tonight. Don't let him get into your head and take anything else from you. You can fight again tomorrow.

The mantra gave her some comfort simply because it reminded her that she was a survivor. Although she had a very scary feeling that if she didn't get busy and figure out how to get away from this couple right now, she might not have a tomorrow.

With her head still downcast, she opened her eyes and saw her toes dangling above a spotted tarp on the floor beneath her. Red spots. Blood drops. Her blood. She raised her gaze to the kitchen cabinets. Her kitchen cabinets that had been defaced by these two, and thoroughly cleaned by true friends just this past week. There was a row of empty glass baby jars lined across the counter.

She was hanging from the ceiling fan in her kitchen, hanging by her arms. Bubba had made a point of bragging about his handiwork, how that fan could hold a side of beef because he'd double-anchored it to the crossbeam that ran across the ceiling. She'd thought it a weird, uncomfortable conversation at the time. Now she was the side of beef! Still weird. Still uncomfortable.

Still bleeding.

Oh, my God. Gray! They were doing this to hurt Gray.

Not that she was feeling real whippy at the moment herself. This was all related to that serial murder case Gray had talked about. They were going to fill those jars with her blood. Then what? Throw them at him? Ruin one of his investigations? Torture him with them somehow? Were they going to drain his blood, too?

Gray! Where are you? You said you had my six. Come find me, Marine.

No. Don't come. They want to hurt you. Stay away!

Her man had known such pain already. Too much pain for him to bear alone.

She wanted to be his helpmate. His partner. His friend. His lover. His wife.

When he was ready.

Oh, she was so ready to take on the grumpy Marine.

To teach him his value. To show him her need.

I love you, Grayson Malone.

Believe that you are loved.

That you are whole. That you are perfect.
That you are mine.

Allie felt something take root inside her, something warm and powerful that seeped into every frightened neuron and spread through her veins, clearing her fuzzy brain and giving her a fire these two pretenders could never take from her.

"She's awake." Ivy Burroughs sounded pleased, as if whatever sick game she was playing could now continue.

Somehow, the feral scream Allie roared inside her head had been heard. Or her posture had changed with her new-found resolve. Or she was just putting off that don't-mess-with-me vibe that she'd learned in her Navy self-defense classes.

And if Bubba Summerfield put his hand on her butt one more time…

Allie twisted her body around, glaring down at Bubba's matching black eyes. He must have broken his nose in the car crash in the alleyway. Her accusatory words came out as a growl, and he laughed at her inability to communicate. "Can I stick her now?" He grabbed her hips and spun her back around, the sudden centrifugal motion tearing through her arms and making her dizzy. He drew the dull edge of the knife across the back of her thighs. It wasn't sharp enough to cut, but she felt the cold metal burn her skin as if he had drawn blood. "I'm going to stick you for every time you smacked my hand away. Every time you told me off with one of those clever lines you thought were so funny. Every time I told you I was interested, and you shot me down."

"She loves the cripple, James," Ivy explained, her bracelets jangling as she held her hand out for the knife. It was odd to hear Bubba called by his given name. But then,

Allie couldn't imagine the haughty older woman even uttering the word *Bubba*. "That's the only way this could work. I needed to find out what Mr. Malone loved so that I could take it from him. The same way he took my son from me."

She rested the blade against Allie's sternum and pushed until Allie felt the skin split open. She whimpered at the pain, but refused to look away from the madness in Ivy's eyes. She'd thought the woman was pushy, eccentric, self-entitled. Instead, she'd been pushing her and Gray together, prepping her like a lamb to slaughter. She must have talked to Noah, discovered what scared her most and proceeded to carry those acts out to make her turn to Gray for help and comfort, and trigger his protective instincts.

"He's going to figure out that message you sent him, Ivy," Bubba whined. "Let's finish the job, get my money and satisfaction, and get out of here."

Ivy set the knife on the counter and made herself at home in a chair that was going straight to the dumpster when all this was done—if Allie survived. "Not yet. I want to be here to watch Mr. Malone break the same way he broke my son when he sent him to prison. Jamie was too fragile for incarceration." A serial killer? Fragile? Really? Oh, if this gag was gone and her snark could come out. "I couldn't be there for him during the trial to hire a better lawyer and keep him out of prison. But I'm here for him now. I'm making things right." She tilted her scarily calm eyes up to Allie. "You know, dear, this was never personal. I believe I might have liked you under different circumstances. But I could see you had caught Malone's eye. That made you expendable." She crossed her arms in a jangle of bracelets. "I really did like those electric heat pulse treatments you put on my hip. I'll miss those."

Big. Fat. Whup.

"Come on, Ivy," Bubba whined. "I don't intend to be here when the cops come." He picked up the knife. "You can stay and watch the show if that gives you the satisfaction you need. But I'm cutting her and getting out now."

"You'll do no such thing." Ivy leaped from the chair, older maybe, but certainly not infirm. She wrapped her hand around Bubba's on the knife and a struggle ensued. Allie was fairly certain this wasn't a good development for her. Their grip on the knife loosened and the knife flew past her stomach. Allie sucked in her breath to avoid the blade.

"What is this, some kind of suicide mission for you, lady? I'm not going to prison."

"You work for me, young man. My son would never disobey me like this."

Bubba stumbled against Allie, knocking her into motion like a pendulum. "I'm not your son, you stupid old woman."

Allie bumped into Bubba and started spinning. She heard the slap of Ivy's palm across the man's cheek. "How dare you speak to me like that!"

Feeling nauseous, Allie tried to spot anything she could latch on to so she could stop her spinning. When she swung into Bubba again, she knew.

"Allie!"

Gray!

She screamed his name behind her gag as a heavy, metal ramrod splintered through her door and knocked it open.

The crash was enough of a distraction for Allie to pull her long, strong runner's legs up and wrap them around Bubba's neck. He clawed at her legs and she squeezed even tighter.

Her arms felt like they were coming out of their sockets as he sputtered for breath and started to go limp.

"No!" Bubba's knife clattered to the floor and Ivy scooped it up as police officers swarmed into her apartment. "This isn't how it's supposed to happen. You have to watch her die!"

"Nobody's killing the woman I love!" Gray stumbled into the kitchen in his beautiful rolling gait. In a graceful maneuver any man would have been jealous of, Gray flipped his crutch in his hand, jammed the handle between Ivy's ankles and yanked, flipping her flat on her back.

The knife flew across the kitchen. Stunned by the hard fall, but determined to have her vengeance, Ivy rolled onto her stomach and crawled toward the weapon. "She dies... she destroys you..." Ivy gasped. "Jamie..."

But Gray beat her to the knife and set his immovable prosthetic foot on the blade. "Your son was guilty. And so are you."

As Gina Cutler moved in to handcuff Ivy, Gray turned his attention to Allie.

"I've got this." Two other officers had braced themselves beneath Allie to hold her up and keep her from dislocating both arms or suffocating herself. He wedged his shoulder beneath her bottom to keep her aloft himself. "It's okay, babe, you can let go now. He can't hurt you."

Jim "Bubba" Summerfield was dead weight in the vise of her legs, but she couldn't seem to give up the fight. Allie shook her head. Tears burned her eyes and spilled over as the adrenaline that had given her the strength to survive began to ebb.

"Oh, babe. I'm so sorry. I'm so sorry." His hands were gentle as they swept the length of her legs, urging her to relax. She couldn't feel the cuts anymore. Oh, hell. She was probably going into shock. Gray noticed. There was rarely any detail about her he missed. "Somebody get that gag off her so she can breathe."

She was vaguely aware of Jackson Dobbs sliding a chair over and climbing up to peel away the tape with a surprising gentleness for his big hands. Her mouth was too dry to spit out the dishcloth stuffed in behind it, so he reached in and pulled it out, dumping both items into an evidence bag that Lexi Callahan-Murphy held out. Lexi quickly sealed the bag and set in on the counter where she labeled it, along with the knife and jars Shane Duvall was packing into his kit.

Allie loved her nerd friends. Supportive and silly and smart. She wasn't alone anymore. Noah hadn't ruined her life.

A tear rolled down her cheek and dripped onto Gray's. She tried to dredge up enough saliva to speak, but her words still came out in a crackly whisper. "I love you, Grayson Malone."

He smiled up at her, the strength of his shoulder never wavering. "I know. I love you, too."

"I know."

His piercing green eyes never left hers as he relayed orders to the people around him. "I want the blanket off the couch, some bolt cutters for that chain up there and this scumbag away from my woman." After a flurry of voices responded with *yes, sir* and *on it*, Gray patted her thigh. "Let go, Lieutenant. I've got your six."

Feeling weak as cooked noodles, Allie allowed her legs to drop away and Bubba sank with a plop to the floor. Her arms screamed with pain as the chain was cut loose and she could lower them into their normal position again. She was surrounded by warmth, shielded by police officers and snug in the sure grip of Gray's arms.

With Jackson at his elbow to steady him, Gray carried her to the gurney waiting out in the hallway. He leaned in to kiss her, and she wished she was strong enough to wrap her arms around him and thoroughly kiss him back. It was over. They were alive.

As the medics stanched a couple of the worst cuts, Allie did find the strength to rub her fingers over his ticklish beard stubble. "You know, one good thing came out of this, Mr. Marine."

"Only one?" He pulled her hand down to warm it between both of his. "What's that?"

"Ivy could see that we meant something to each other even before we admitted it."

"We would have figured it out eventually."

"Yeah, we would have. I'm in love with a very smart man."

"And I'm in love with a very strong woman." He leaned in to kiss the corner of her mouth again. "Thank you for teaching me to dance. And everything else that goes with it."

"Thank you for having my six."

"Always."

When the paramedic scooted Gray aside to inspect another cut, Allie cried out at losing the treasured touch of his hand. "Gray?"

"Yeah, babe." He reappeared above her head, stroking his fingers through her hair, and she smiled.

"How did you know where to find me today? Those two could have taken me anywhere."

"That's easy, Lieutenant. Ivy said I needed to go home.

This is the first place that's felt like a home to me for a very long time. And that's because I fell in love with the girl next door."

* * * * *

COMING SOON!

We really hope you enjoyed reading this book. If you're looking for more romance be sure to head to the shops when new books are available on

Thursday 6th July

To see which titles are coming soon, please visit
millsandboon.co.uk/nextmonth

LET'S TALK
Romance

For exclusive extracts, competitions and special offers, find us online:

f MillsandBoon

🐦 @MillsandBoon

📷 @MillsandBoonUK

♪ @MillsandBoonUK

Get in touch on 01413 063 232

MILLS & BOON

THE HEART OF ROMANCE

A ROMANCE FOR EVERY READER

MODERN
Prepare to be swept off your feet by sophisticated, sexy and seductive heroes, in some of the world's most glamourous and romantic locations, where power and passion collide.

HISTORICAL
Escape with historical heroes from time gone by. Whether your passion is for wicked Regency Rakes, muscled Vikings or rugged Highlanders, awaken the romance of the past.

MEDICAL
Set your pulse racing with dedicated, delectable doctors in the high-pressure world of medicine, where emotions run high and passion, comfort and love are the best medicine.

True Love
Celebrate true love with tender stories of heartfelt romance, from the rush of falling in love to the joy a new baby can bring, and a focus on the emotional heart of a relationship.

Desire
Indulge in secrets and scandal, intense drama and sizzling hot action with heroes who have it all: wealth, status, good looks…everything but the right woman.

HEROES
The excitement of a gripping thriller, with intense romance at its heart. Resourceful, true-to-life women and strong, fearless men face danger and desire - a killer combination!

To see which titles are coming soon, please visit

millsandboon.co.uk/nextmonth